ALSO BY ANNE RENWICK

ICY

THE ELEMENTAL WEB CHRONICLES

BOOK 5

BETRAYALS

ANNE RENWICK

Icy Betrayals/ Anne Renwick. — 1st ed.

ISBN 978-1-948359-63-4

Cover design by James T. Egan of Bookfly Design.

Edited by Sandra Sookoo.

To Iceland's stark winter beauty, its many geothermal wonders, and the ferns that grow beside its waters

THANK YOU TO...

My husband who drove the ring road of Iceland while I stared out the window. Without putting feet on black gravel —walking between continents and behind waterfalls, shivering in windy snowstorms and soaking in hot springs—this book would be an entirely different story.

Karl Ágúst Úlfsson for generously fixing my Icelandic—fictional and factual—and carefully pronouncing each word and sentence.

My mom and dad who made reading, travel, history and science priorities.

Sandra Sookoo, my brilliant editor who mercilessly ferrets out weaknesses and sets my work on a better course.

Mr. Fox and his red pen.

CHAPTER ONE

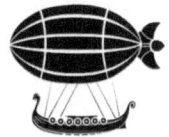

London
January 1885

"I don't like this," Val muttered under his breath. A rat scurried past his ankles headed in the opposite direction. Never a good sign.

The low brick arches of the pub's basement turned his height into a weakness, forcing him to bend and crouch as they followed a crooked, mazelike path beneath The Three-Eyed Bat in Hatton Garden. Tiny needles of apprehension pricked at his spine. Never one to ignore instinct, he flicked loose the button of his left cuff, folding it back for swift access. The sheathed knife strapped to his forearm was sharp and deadly. It had saved his life more than once.

"If you did, I'd resign effective immediately," Hildur hissed back.

He heard a familiar soft snick, the sound of her gauntlet's wrist blade sliding into position. The one she usually reserved for trolls. Not that he expected to run into any in such an urban environment.

Second in command, his partner was even more lethal than he was. Those who appealed to her feminine side for mercy often found the bite of her blade at their throats swiftly disabused them of any illusion presented by the golden twists of braids in her hair, by the swell of hips encased in fitted trousers.

Smuggling, profitable though it might be, was rife with risk. He and his crew had chalked this job up as "done" and had been ready to set sail when the mechanical raven had landed on his ship's bulwark with an unwelcome message bound to its ankle. Hence their unplanned evening excursion into the bowels of London. Though they'd yet to meet anyone in this maze of tunnels, from time to time, the sensation of being watched skittered down his spine.

They ought to turn back now. Rescuing Katla Dagsdóttir wasn't worth his life, not after what she'd done. But Val had questions and she would have answers. Not to mention a bottle of absinthe.

Not just any bottle of absinthe, mind, but Tyrian Absinthe.

A highly alcoholic drink flavored by the leaves and flowers of the wormwood plant, *Artemisia absinthium*, as well as anise and fennel, absinthe was a popular bohemian drink with a reputation for causing hallucinations. Which, naturally, only served to enhance its appeal. Absinthe itself was a clear spirit. If one wanted to add a bit of flair, absinthe verte—green—was traditional, a color achieved by adding macerated herbs before bottling. A process that left the chlorophyll chemically active and added a complexity of taste to the drink.

So what made this particular new brand so very special? Its purple color and its rarity.

The color was the exact shade of a dye secreted by a predatory sea snail in the Mediterranean, a tint that was once so expensive and difficult to produce that it became known as royal purple. Tyrian purple.

A color that denoted royalty, and no one had been able to locate the distillery that produced this particular unlicensed alcoholic spirit. Bottles of the drink had been delivered to the royal courts of the Nordic countries—Finland. Sweden. Denmark. But not Norway, subject as it was to Sweden's rule. Which made Jarl Haukr all that more desirous of sampling the drink. As the future king of Iceland, the indignity of not being included festered.

All of which inflated the value of this Tyrian Absinthe to absurd levels.

Nobles and minor royalty had minions scouring the black market, to no avail. No more bottles of the drink could be found. Securing one for trade would refill Val's coffers.

Which made the bottle in Katla's possession priceless.

He'd offer it first, of course, to the future king of Iceland. His mother would love attending the royal wedding. He'd make it a condition of the sale. Which was why he kept walking, regardless of an uncomfortable and growing sense of foreboding. Risking their lives in tunnels that even rodents found anxiety-provoking, all to keep his airship afloat.

Denmark, home of the jarl's betrothed, Princess Margrit, had constructed a floating castle, a modern marvel of engineering and architecture, to mark the historic occasion of his marriage and subsequent succession to the throne of Iceland. Currently en route to the North Sea, the palace was as yet empty of important guests. A skeleton staff of engineers oversaw its progress while servants bustled about preparing for the onslaught of high-ranking individuals from Europe and beyond.

Once vows were spoken—and the bride bedded—Iceland would finally be independent, its own country, a nation, separate from Denmark.

Iceland and Denmark had spared no expense in their efforts to mark the event, issuing a finite number of invitations. Such scarcity meant those in possession of an invitation were flocked by flatterers and sycophants, all working to convince the owner to include him or her in their retinue. Even as protests spilled into the streets. Norwegians, subject to Swedish rule since 1814, when Denmark grudgingly ceded their country to another monarch, were offended. After all, theirs was the land from where the original kings of Iceland hailed. They, too, demanded sovereignty.

If negotiations succeeded, Val thought it likely a new king of Norway would also demand his own bottle of Tyrian Absinthe to mark the beginning of a new era.

"Why would anyone," he muttered under his breath, "want to drink alcohol tinted with snail mucus?"

Behind him, Hildur snorted. "Over-inflated nonsense. A few purple grape skins, some red cabbage..."

"It's the label," he repeated for the fiftieth time. "And—"

"The shape of the bottle," she grumbled. "Easier to track down an empty one and set about refilling it."

A smirk tugged at Val's lips. The idea held appeal.

The guide they'd hired led them down a set of crooked stairs, deeper into London clay and gravel. The ground beneath his feet became uneven and the mortar—a generous term—between the flagstones grew damp. An unpleasant, musty smell snaked through the stale air in tendrils, a reminder that many of the city's former rivers now ran underground in the form of sewers.

"We'd best be close," Hildur bit out. "Didn't think to bring a ball of yarn to unwind behind us."

"Almost there." The man in front of them called himself Digger. His less than reassuring words echoed around them, losing strength as they bounced off the nooks and crannies along with the glow of his bioluminescent lantern.

A sickly yellow glow illuminated a distant section of the underground maze accompanied by the foul odor of rancid meat with the acidic, vinegary note of fermenting apples. Val pocketed his light, freeing both hands for a fight.

He didn't want anything going wrong. Not when tomorrow they lifted off and headed home. Many awaited the foreign goods tucked into his hold. Did he look forward to being paid? Of course. But mostly he anticipated a few weeks tethered down where he could work openly upon the airship's wings. Where his crew could rest, visit family.

One last stop remained. A glassworks factory in Scotland.

They turned a corner and stepped into a vaulted room illuminated by a single oil lamp. An all-but-abandoned storage room lined by wooden casks. Broken chairs were piled at the far end beside a table or two. A pile of rags. A stack of old newspapers. Disarticulated bits of broken machinery. All items salvaged in hope they might one day be useful.

"Katla?" She'd recognize his voice, given how close they'd once been.

No answer.

Hildur swept the light of her lamp across the wreckage, searching the shadows while Val kept his hand wrapped about the hilt of his knife and his eyes trained on the man.

"Empty." She frowned, shoulders stiff.

That easy? No trap? That didn't sit right. Not with either of them. He'd not expected to pass through the tunnels unchallenged. The Three-Eyed Bat was known for harboring henchmen, villains and other assorted criminals. Perhaps it was the unholy odor wafting through the dank air?

Hildur grimaced and nearly gagged.

The fetid scent that clogged his nose threatened to choke the life out of them both if they lingered much longer. How close were the sewers? A dozen dead rats rotting in the corner, serving as hosts for a deadly mold, might explain the repulsive miasma.

Might.

Did Digger purposefully toss their corpses here, a crude form of repellant to discourage anyone from investigating the contents of this room? Could be. An effective, if unsanitary, approach.

"Where is she?" Val wanted this over and done.

"Gone." Unconcerned, Digger lifted a dirty bundle of rags and unwrapped a bottle containing a purple-tinted fluid and presented it for their inspection even as he kept a strangle hold about its neck.

Not the main purpose of their underground visit.

Val raised his eyebrows. "I came for the woman." Much as he'd like to bargain for the bottle and leave, Katla was the daughter of a dignitary and finding her would resolve a lot of outstanding problems.

"Katla wouldn't come here." Hildur shifted her stance. "Not voluntarily."

The man shrugged. "Lotta people go underground when things fall apart."

Was that it? Distressed and fearful, the fae woman had sought the closest thing to the tunnels and chambers of the Huldu mountain? These city tunnels were filthy and uninhabited, save by vermin. What could have scared her enough to seek out such a hiding spot?

Five years had passed since she'd run away with Eirik Rømer, disappearing without a trace. Val had set the past aside. Built a new life for himself. And now this. A rope around his neck, yanking him back to a past he'd rather forget.

"I want to speak with her." The bottle was the bonus, not the goal. "And will pay for the privilege."

A mercenary light gleamed in Digger's eyes, then faded. "Can't help you with that. The bottle is mine now. If you're not interested..." He started to turn away.

"Fine," Val conceded. No point in wasting this opportunity to acquire a bottle. They'd stay one more day in London, see if they couldn't pick up Katla's trail. "How much?"

"This libation is restricted to the anointed." Digger puffed his chest as he spouted unfamiliar fancy words. "Procuring it comes at a price. Especially when you'll be selling it to a jarl who is not yet a king." The man grinned. "Twenty pounds is not beyond him."

It might be.

Ever since the *Grænndreki* tethered down in Wapping, a steady stream of the jarl's liveried footmen had delivered newly purchased luxury household goods fit for a princess— furniture, carpets, lamps, books, to name a few—to Val's dirigible for transport home. Enough so that Jarl Haukr might well bankrupt Iceland should he fail to secure the princess's dowry.

But it was not his place to comment. So long as the jarl paid his bills.

Purple color. Gold-embossed label. "It *appears* to be the real thing." Val reached for the bottle, but the man snatched it back.

"Appears?" Digger huffed. "Changed my mind. Fifty pounds."

Val opened his mouth to barter, then snapped it shut

again when Hildur shot him a gimlet-eyed glare. The sooner they left, the happier she'd be. And the price might well go up again. From an inner coat pocket, he pulled out a bundle of five-pound notes and counted. "I've only forty-five." He held them in the air, watched temptation flair in the man's eyes.

"Fine."

The merchant's grimy hands wrapped about the money and the bottle was shoved against Val's chest. Their guide snatched up his lantern and turned.

"Hold." With suspicion in her eyes, Hildur moved deeper into the shadows to investigate a cloth-covered lump. "What's this?"

Val shot out his free hand and fisted his fingers about the man's collar, stopping his flight. Dread curled in his gut as his gaze followed the beam of light. Boots in that position were usually attached to legs.

She bent and tossed back the sooty sheet. Then let out a string of curses that could curl paint. "We have a problem."

They did indeed, for they'd found Katla. She wore nothing but a coarse gown, torn stockings and worn boots. If she'd entered the tunnels possessed of a winter cloak, it had been stolen from her. The holes in her stockings revealed pale white skin where green vines had once twisted.

"Is she alive?" A wave of guilt swept over him, one quickly followed by a flush of anger. Once again, he cursed himself for allowing his father to coax him into the social circles of the upper echelon. Working in the laboratories was vastly preferable to council drama, but funding for research projects had to come from somewhere.

As such, he'd dressed appropriately and conversed politely with the other gentlemen of his father's circle. A promising evening until he'd made the mistake of glancing at a beautiful young woman.

His father had leapt on the opportunity and Val soon found himself engaged. An event that had grown tendrils, growing and spreading like an invasive vine until he was entwined in drama. A tangled mess that he still struggled to escape.

And now this.

Hildur pressed two fingers to a pulse point. "Barely."

"It wasn't me who hurt her, I swear." Digger was visibly sweating. "She was sick when I found her, when I offered her a place to hide. Wild-eyed and keen to guard that bottle, she begged me to send you a note via that strange bird of hers."

He shoved the man into a corner. "Sit. Stay." Then knelt beside Katla, uncapping his flask of green absinthe. Lifting her shoulders—she was skin and bone under her dull wool gown—he tipped a measure of the spirit into her mouth.

Katla sputtered. Her eyes flickered open. "Valtýr?"

"It's me. Who did this to you?"

"Eldskrift," she whispered. Not a name but an old legend.

A stale guilt roiled in his gut. He bit back a string of curses. "Eirik Rømer?"

"Eirik." Katla clawed at the neckline of her dress, at the

rough cloth, exposing a few inches of pale skin marked by thick, raised scars in the shape of runes. "He found a way. Save her. Save them."

"Save who?" He tipped more absinthe between her lips, but the green liquid ran down the side of her cheek. Her eyes were fixed. Her chest no longer rose and fell. "Katla?"

Hildur shook her head. "No pulse. She's gone."

He turned to Digger with malice in his heart. "You knew she was alive and did nothing to rescue her? Left her here in this dark, dank hole in the ground?"

"Saw an opportunity to profit," Hildur concluded. "Took it."

"No!" The man objected, jumping up. "I tried to help her. Fed her and everything." He gestured at a slanted table where an empty jug and a dry crust of bread sat. "But she just kept getting harder."

"Harder?" Val frowned. Not rigor, for she'd just died in his arms. But when he flexed her arm there was a strange resistance.

"She's been like that for days!" A protest that ascended in a crescendo. "She could barely move. Touch her face. It's unnatural, I tell you!"

Val pressed his fingers against Katla's cheek. "*Helvíti.*" Pushed harder. "Her skin feels wrong, as if someone filled her with sand."

"I told you!" Digger's aborted attempt to run had him twisting at the end of Hildur's arm.

"You'll come with us back to the airship," he decided.

Where no criminal elements skulked about unseen. "We'll sort this out there."

"No!"

They ignored him.

Hildur cleared her throat. "Isn't the ambassador in town?"

Frigg and Hel. Katla's father.

Val closed his eyes a moment. "He is." And attending the ball tonight alongside the jarl and his retinue. He gave a sharp nod, his responsibilities clear—clean himself up, draw the ambassador aside. With that duty behind him, he'd find one of the jarl's men to pass along news of the opportunity to purchase a bottle of Tyrian Absinthe. Because damned if he'd do all the work of tracking one down then hand it over without recompense. "I'll carry her."

Katla would go home in a pine coffin, but her family would finally know what had become of her. He scooped the dead woman into his arms. Every sensation defied explanation. It was as if he'd hefted a bag filled with coarse wet sand and broken shells.

Hildur slipped the bottle into the bag slung across her chest, then pointed her knife tip at Digger, releasing him. "If you want to keep the money, you'll cooperate and lead us out of this rat warren."

Muttering, Digger stepped out into the tunnels.

The dull glow from the stairwell leading upward into the pub was just visible when Val's skin prickled. They were being watched.

"Who's there?" Hildur demanded as the shadows shifted.

Digger yelped and ran for the crowded taproom full of notorious criminals.

"Give me the bag," a voice growled. "Set the woman down." A glint of light flashed off the muzzle of a pistol.

A lazy, opportunistic criminal he could understand. Let someone else risk a trip into the tunnels, steal the prize bottle as they returned. But claiming the dead body of his former fiancée? Not happening.

"Run!" Hildur yelled, toppling a pile of rickety chairs to slow their pursuer.

Struggling with Katla's weight, Val ran up the steps with her hot on his heels.

Bang!

A bullet whizzed past his head. Missed.

Hell-bent on escape, they tore through The Three-Eyed Bat to shouts of annoyance. The door slammed open, rattling on its hinges, releasing them into a narrow alleyway. Ahead lay the main thoroughfare with the clattering wheels of carriages, the rhythmic stomp of iron hooves and the promise of streetlamps, a chance to lose their pursuer in the evening throng of traffic.

They ran.

"Stop!" A cry of desperation, for there was no chance they could be caught now.

Bang!

A dull thud struck the bag Hildur carried.

"I'm fine," she yelled, not slowing her steps.

But as they whipped around the corner, purple fluid trailed in their wake, cascading to the ground and pooling between the cobblestones. So much for the Tyrian Absinthe.

Frigg and Hel.

Breathless, they threw themselves—and a corpse—into a crank hack and ordered the driver to hurry.

So much for profit. Instead, he'd dragged his past back into the light.

CHAPTER TWO

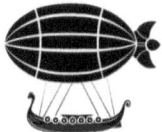

"How dare he!" Angela hissed. "Treating me like chattel to be bartered away." She didn't dare yell. Not when the ball they hosted for the Icelandic delegation was in full swing outside the library doors. Instead, she took out her ire upon the innocent globe squatting atop the low table, spinning it hard upon its axis, watching Iceland fly past over and over. "This is not medieval times when a gentleman might marry off his sister for his own personal financial gain."

Grim, Olivia nodded. "Not without your consent."

"He stole my dowry," she spat. "Sold the land beneath my feet. Now this?" She slapped her hand down on the Atlantic Ocean. If only travel was as easy as climbing aboard a boat. "You have to help me. I need to find an Icelandic husband. Tonight."

Olivia was her closest friend. The only one she trusted.

Marcus's lavish indulgences now threatened her work.

Her other brother Jack was abroad doing who-knew-what and returning who-knew-when, leaving him unaware how dire the situation had grown. Worse, he couldn't be contacted.

Her family's finances skated on thin ice. Creditors knocked at their door. All while Mother continued to cater to her son's every whim. And their only plan to cover immediate, unavoidable debt was to sell Angela off to the highest bidder?

Ever since Grandmother's death, her world had turned upside down. Her family no longer needed her to look after a half-mad relative hidden in the countryside, a woman who was only calm inside a greenhouse filled with ferns. Which meant Angela was now a liability instead of an asset. Hence the estate's sale and her incarceration in London.

With the mandatory period of mourning at an end, she'd been ordered into the ballroom. Spinsterhood was, of course, an option, but if she refused to comply with her brother's demands, he might well lock her in the attic and throw away the key.

Not that she was completely opposed to marriage. All she required were discretionary funds to continue her studies. A greenhouse. And Icelandic citizenship.

Time to trade one island for another.

With the royal wedding set for late spring, she'd thought to have months to select a husband from among the throngs of ranking Icelandic men in temporary residence as they worked to establish diplomatic relations with Britain.

But Marcus, desperate for funds, had announced an auction.

A growl rattled deep in her chest. Her ears grew hot. Short of murdering her brother while he slept, tonight's ball might be her last opportunity to make an escape with her reputation intact.

Relatively intact. Either way, she was certain to become the *ton's* latest scandal.

"A bold move." Olivia tipped her head. "Do you propose to force Mr. Black's hand?"

More than ready to escape her family by serving her country, Angela had met with a mysterious man in the back of a bookstore last week, showcasing her language skills, ones which qualified her to eavesdrop upon members of the future royal court. And Mr. Black had been interested, listing the expectations. A brief marriage to a man the British government suspected of misdeeds, followed by a swift termination of the legal bond, leaving her a free woman with access to significant funds under her sole control.

Until he'd learned her family's name and abruptly ended their meeting, citing an unfair and ridiculous unwritten rule.

"Exactly that." She grinned back. "The 'one spy per family' rule strikes me as a convenient lie. One that hides an unspoken gentleman's code, preventing him from offering a fellow agent's sister as a liaison." As if she ought not be allowed to determine her own future. "If the deed is done, will Mr. Black swoop in to salvage the wreckage by turning the situation to the Crown's advantage?"

Olivia laughed. "He will indeed. But must it be

Iceland?" She gave a dramatic shudder. "Icy cold winters with no sun? Subsisting on dried fish, yogurt and other unspeakable fermented foods? Why not British Honduras, where the warm, humid climes support an abundance of moss and ferns?"

Iceland. A land of snow and ice, one where volcanoes might erupt at any moment and send rivers of molten lava pouring over the countryside. A land without a university, cutting her off from educated society and scientific dialogue until or unless she braved a rough ocean crossing back to civilization.

A year ago, she would have agreed with her friend. But then Grandmother was murdered.

Which led to her present situation. "I'm afraid it's non-negotiable. It must be Iceland. Will you work your magic on my behalf, help me trap a husband tonight?"

An impish light flickered in her friend's eyes. "I know several gentlemen who fit the bill. And tonight is the ideal opportunity." A catlike smile stretched her lips. "If you snag one, you'll attend the wedding of the century on his arm." She exhaled a long sigh of personal regret. "I've all but lost my chance to dance in the ballroom of a floating castle. Promise you'll describe it all to me in a letter?"

A grand event, the approaching wedding of a Danish princess and the Icelandic jarl who would be crowned king that same day. Fights over the invitations had reportedly broken out in the parlors of even the most esteemed. Her own mother was prune-faced about her son's lack of one.

"I promise." She'd enjoy that. Cinderella off to the ball while her mother was forced to stay home.

Tonight's ball was intended to shore up British support for Iceland's position in the face of Norwegian protests. A population that—rightfully so—resented Sweden's continued rule over their country when a small frozen island would become a new kingdom by doing little more than celebrating a marriage with ostentatious pomp and circumstance.

"Then paste on your brightest smile." Olivia grabbed Angela's hand and dragged her out of the library to the edge of the ballroom. There, hiding behind a stand of giant ostrich ferns, her friend pointed out a number of promising options. "Pick one. Lead him into the garden. I'll search out a few friends. After ten minutes..."

THE TRAIN of her ice-blue gown swept behind her as she permitted Jarl Einar to lead her onto the shallow balcony overlooking the snow-dusted garden. Though lamplight illuminated its winding pathways with a soft inviting glow, tonight's weather carried a sharp bite with a hint of snow. Guests inclined toward dalliances were conducting them in warmer climes beneath the lemon and lime trees of the conservatory.

A cold breeze ruffled the white fur that edged her low-cut bodice, a feature designed to draw male attention. Shivering, however, was not an option. A bride suited to long, dark winters would find such an English winter's night mild.

"Beautiful, is it not?" He pressed a glass of champagne into her hand.

"It is." Angela allowed her escort to stand closer than propriety dictated as she sipped from her glass. Gulping the bubbly drink seemed ill advised, no matter how much she needed the false courage.

Of all the men she'd conversed with, Jarl Einar was the only one to return any interest. Well, save for a particularly forward Norwegian who'd fixed her with an unsettling and possessive stare before hinting that his bid for her hand would win.

A comment that made her that much more determined that he would face bitter disappointment come morning.

The jarl waved a hand toward broad steps. "Would you care to—"

No. But at least this man had straight teeth and no gray hair. That he was friends with the future king would entice Mr. Black's assistance. She could do worse. "Certainly." She smiled and slid a gloved hand through his proffered arm.

But before they could turn, a gentleman hastened across the flagstones. "Mr. Einarsson! Jarl Haukr would like a word with you."

Angela froze, then hissed under her breath at her companion. "All of London is convinced you hold the rank of jarl."

His answering chuckle made her back teeth grind together. "We all play our games." He tweaked one of the tiny buttons at her waist. "A shame, Lady Angela. We would have had fun." With that, he waltzed away, uncaring that he left her standing in the cold with a man to whom she had not been introduced.

"Wonderful," she muttered. In this scenario, he was the cat and she the mouse. Rife with pitfalls and promise, there was a reason chaperones usually accompanied young ladies as they navigated the marriage mart.

"There's no excuse for my countryman's behavior." The newcomer grimaced. "He's one of the jarl's entourage and prone to taking advantage of his position, leaving a trail of disappointed ladies across Europe in his wake."

Ruined, he meant. And she would have been next. Mortified frustration clogged her throat. How could Olivia have made such a horrible mistake? Such a man was difficult, if not impossible, to force into matrimony. And likely resentful if such was accomplished.

Was this the reason a societal liaison was promised a brief marriage, one that could be forcibly terminated if necessary? Better to hold one's spouse in mild disdain, thereby erasing the moral conundrum of eavesdropping and reporting their every secret to the Crown?

Her—admittedly impulsive—scheme was *not* proceeding according to plan. Unless her friend had hastily sent this new gentleman on a mission not only to rescue Angela, but to rectify her error? He did possess the necessary accent.

She glanced over his shoulder at Olivia, who unhelpfully shrugged a single shoulder and gave a small shake of her head. The man before her was an unknown. But the hour was late, and she was out of options.

Why not this man who towered over her like a Viking

warrior pulled from the ancient sagas? His face was handsome and rough-hewn, like he'd been sculpted from unforgiving granite. There was raw strength in his broad shoulders, tempered by a quiet calm in his steel-blue eyes that made her pulse quicken. Heat rose in her cheeks as his mouth curved into a half-smile, hinting at a warmth beneath his rugged exterior, at a secret only she might discover.

With raised eyebrows, she addressed the tall, blond newcomer, lacing each word with doubt and suspicion to mask her interest. "And are you a jarl?"

He snorted. "No, Lady Angela. Not even remotely. I'm captain of *Loftskipið Grænndreki*."

An airship? Even better than a boat. A marriage offering travel abroad. The Crown might prefer high rank, but Olivia held sway and Mr. Black would reconsider his stance when his agent's sister found herself in hot water.

And this Viking knew her name.

That last part was most promising. Full steam ahead. "Have we met?"

"Not many ladies attended yesterday's scientific lecture at the Rankine Institute." One open to the public touting the possibility that, one day, humans might replace the use of coal by harnessing the photosynthetic energy of green algae. A hint of mischief entered his smile. "I made inquiries."

"Did you?" Her grin was genuine. A handsome man of science in command of an escape vehicle? Yes, please.

"Valtýr Árnason at your service." He bowed. "I found your question about subnivean photosynthesis thought provoking."

"You did?" Not a single man had ever praised her scholarship.

A nearby stone urn held an arrangement of dry, brown stems ending in the spiked cones of long-dead flowers. He took the champagne glass from her hand, dumped its contents over the railing and tucked the stemware among its many branches. Safe until someone retrieved the crystal. He crooked an elbow. "Care to discuss the topic further in the solitude of a midnight winter garden?"

Even if her mission failed, why not enjoy the moment? "I would."

Which was how she found herself perched on an iron bench beneath an arbor of bare twigs, deep in a conversation about Icelandic moss.

"So, while it may well be able to live and grow under snow, *Cetraria islandica* is not a moss, it's a lichen," she insisted, enjoying every moment of their playful academic dispute. "There's nothing plantlike about it. It's a symbiotic relationship between algae and fungus."

He shrugged, slid her a teasing grin. "I only know that my mother forces the horrid tea upon anyone with a sore throat."

She laughed and one long evening glove lost its grip upon the frozen skin of her upper arm and slid to her elbow, exposing one of her secrets. Before she could yank the satin back into place, he brushed the rough pad of his thumb across the tiny fiddlehead fern tattooed on her inner elbow.

"Pretty."

A shiver ran down her spine. Mother considered the

small embellishment an embarrassment as young ladies of the *ton* ought not decorate their bodies in such a manner. Angela disagreed in principle but hid her tattoo from inquisitive eyes because she did not wish for anyone to examine them closely, lest they ask about the unusual "ink".

But he said nothing more.

She slid her companion an appraising glance, shivering as the chill seeped through the thin blue silk of her gown. His kindness and decency had her rethinking her plans. "Should you be out here with me?"

"No." He shrugged off his coat, unbothered by the chill, and wrapped it about her shoulders. The large woolen garment engulfed her, bringing with it the addictive male scents of peat smoke, leather and pine trees.

A Viking who casually offered comfort to a woman. A point in his favor. Yet his coat was now a weapon that presented her with opportunity. Was she still open to the drastic solution to obtain a husband? Were there any acceptable alternatives when her brother busied himself negotiating her market value?

Ought she offer Valtýr a chance to escape, warn him that Lady Olivia would soon arrive with friends? Friends instructed to overwhelm the scene, to cause a commotion, to spring a parson's trap in a manner that would ensure there would be no escape.

"Beautiful gowns, dancing and champagne." Words she spoke on a sigh. "After long days of attempting to extract the phytochemicals of lichens, moss and ferns using electroporation without altering the molecular structure, I ought to welcome such evenings as a respite. But my presence is forced by the need to acquire a husband."

Her final words were a warning.

"It's the restrictive clothing, my lady." He flicked a finger against the coiled steel boning of her corset, then loosened his cravat with a sharp yank. "Accompanied by political maneuvering, where everyone presents a gilded façade to conceal the selfish moral decay that motivates their every decision."

Guilt crystalized in her stomach like shards of broken glass. "You're not mistaken," she agreed. "Were you compelled to attend?"

"You could say that." He tipped his head back to study the sky, like a caged bird longing for escape. She knew the feeling well. "I need to deliver distressing news, and the garden offered a temporary respite with a beautiful woman."

He was very, very wrong.

Above the silhouette of London's skyline, smoke billowed upward from thousands upon thousands of chimneys, all of them burning coal. If only they could install photovoltaic power cells on every roof, the smog might lift.

A lonely snowflake drifted through the air, then another and another. Flurries. She drew the two halves of his coat together and shifted on the cold iron bench. "You must be cold. We should go in."

"I wouldn't say I'm warm but watching stray snowflakes catch on the long lashes of a beautiful woman is worth enduring the chill." He scooted closer, pulling her up against his side. Heat radiated outward, but she was hard put to

ANNE RENWICK

notice anything beyond the strong muscles of his leg shifting against her own. "Hot springs do, however, much improve the experience."

Was she really doing this? Yes. With a man like this in her bed, could Iceland be so awful? "In the Land of Fire and Ice?" She tipped up her face, inviting familiarity. "I would imagine so."

"Back home, we strip naked and slip into the steaming pools, soaking in the heat until we can bear it no longer— then leap from the water and fling ourselves into the snow."

Was he flirting? A flush rose to her cheeks. Other parts warmed. "For men." She huffed in annoyance. "No doubt the women are denied such activities."

"You'd be surprised." He tweaked her nose. "I could make private arrangements."

Was that an invitation? "Promise?"

"Promise."

The sounds of hushed voices met her ear. Olivia and friends, ready to fracture their moment with a sharp snap. Did he not hear them? Why did he not run? "Naked?" She whispered the word, ignoring the panic that clawed at her stomach. No need to summon a blush to her cheeks. Her face was already flaming.

"Of course." His words sparked fires in places she'd not known could burn. "I'd not have it any other way." His fingers threaded into the twist of hair at the base of her skull, pulling her face gently toward his. Did he think to kiss her?

Perhaps, but she was out of time.

Feet crunched on garden gravel. She grabbed his cravat

and hauled him even closer, smashing her lips into his. A counterfeit moment of passion intended to set tongues wagging.

"Valtýr Árnason!"

"Lady Angela!"

Valtýr yanked himself from her grip and sprang to his feet, standing between her and the intruders.

Angela leaned around his side. A man wearing a diplomatic uniform bearing the gyrfalcon crest of Iceland gaped at his countryman. Accompanying him were the Duchess of Avesbury, Angela's own prune-faced mother, and Olivia.

Hardly the gaggle of giggling debutants she'd been promised.

Her friend offered her a faint smile of apology.

"How wonderful," the duchess deadpanned. "How lovely. Our very own international wedding to arrange."

CHAPTER THREE

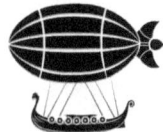

"THIS IS A BAD IDEA." HILDUR FROWNED as she peered through the brass spyglass, scanning the busy streets below the airship, watching for her wife's return. "I strongly advise you against it. She'll divorce you as soon as she finds out."

His first mate was correct, of course. But with spies breathing down his neck, marriage was the fastest and easiest way to legally extricate Lady Angela from London. And failing to rescue her, to leave her behind in London with her horrid brother, would be no better than shoving her off the rim of a volcanic crater directly into molten lava.

After last night's incident, Dagur Sveinsson had sent Val back to his loftskip along with a handful of his guards. Val was released on his own recognizance in exchange for his pilot, Lauf, spending some quality time with the Icelandic ambassador as his "special guest".

Lauf had readily agreed, looking forward to having

"staff" for a day. A comfortable hostage experience with throw pillows and catering.

"I will endeavor to ensure the situation is resolved in the lady's best interest." As much as one could expect a duchess to promise. "But can exert only so much influence over a fellow peer. Mr. Black will be in touch."

He'd been instructed to write to Lord Aubrey, Lady Angela's brother. Hours upon hours had passed with no news. He grew tired of waiting.

"Because I'm an airship captain of dubious social rank conducting clandestine research on behalf of the Huldu?"

"Though such are among the *many* reasons you should not marry her, those are the least egregious lies of omission. She is a *lady*, sister to an *earl*. Her brother possesses multiple properties, one of which is a *palace*. I don't care what her dowry is, when she finds out you married her under false pretenses..." She slid him a narrow-eyed glance. "Kidnapping her would be much simpler."

She wasn't wrong.

Still, he shrugged. "The ambassador disagrees with your assessment." Outwardly calm, Val's jaw was tight with a swirl of emotions. Ones that defied logic and whispered only of need. "The ambassador ordered me to offer for her hand. Besides, I'm not the villain here. *She* kissed *me*."

If you could call it that. They'd embraced. Lips had touched. If one were rating kisses, this particular meeting of mouths would require a negative number. Yet somehow that wasn't off-putting. As soon as possible, he wished to repeat the experience that he might demonstrate how much better it could be.

"Alone. At night. In a dark garden. During an important social event." She collapsed the spyglass and lifted her eyebrows. "You knew exactly what you were doing."

An accurate assessment.

Guilt pressed on his lungs. Not that it was able to smother the inexplicable blaze of want twisting hot and insistent inside his chest. Research costs meant finances always cut close to the bone. Most would accuse him of social climbing. A lesson he ought to have learned years ago.

Though he certainly wasn't unhappy to learn of Lady Angela's considerable social status, he wasn't marrying for money.

From the moment she'd slid her arm through his and pulled him into a moonlit winter garden, he could imagine no other woman beside him. That mere physical contact could trigger such possessive instincts left him at a loss. And the reason he'd ignored her warnings, her not-so-subtle hints that he ought run fast and far.

With the help of powerful friends, she'd planned and executed a husband hunt, inviting him to take a risky leap into marriage.

Smart. Beautiful. Calculating. Fae.

Without a thought to her motives, he'd accepted without hesitation. And felt no regret. How was it his fault she'd succeeded?

He'd arrived at the ball intending to speak briefly with the ambassador before making a hasty exit. Until his gaze caught upon a dark figure, upon a man too focused upon one particular young lady. A woman surrounded by men who would soon comprise the King of Iceland's court.

Frigg and Hel.

As if his nemesis felt the heat of Val's stare from across the room, he'd turned. Rømer's cold, almost cutting stare was as clear as any spoken threat. Then, a faint smirk tugged at his lips and he stalked away, as if daring Val to follow him.

Tempting. Much as he wished to stick a knife in the man's kidney, Val found himself smiling. It was her, the woman from the lecture. Not only intelligent, but an enticing beauty that made him think of frosted windows and warm fires, of soft blankets and silken skin. He'd meant to introduce himself, but the crowd had swept her away. Then fate had handed him a second chance.

"You think I ought to have chased after Eirik Rømer? Abandoned her to Rolf Einarsson? When she's likely the woman Katla spoke of with her dying breath?"

"No. Her tattoo marks her as one of us." Hildur heaved a sigh. "If anyone can discover why she's living in London, it will be my wife." She hesitated. "As to the people Katla wanted us to save, she was dying, possibly hallucinating. Eldskrift is a fairy tale for fae children to keep them from wandering out into dark winter nights alone, nothing more."

Perhaps. Not that it had stopped Rømer.

"And how do you propose to explain the condition of her body?"

"That her tattoos were erased?" Hildur shrugged. "You believe Rømer lured her away under false pretenses and, given her condition, that seems likely. But her sister maintains Katla left with him voluntarily. Perhaps, during the early days of her infatuation, she voluntarily severed her connection to our people."

Photosynthetic tattoos were a point of pride among the Icelandic huldufólk. Had she hidden in the dark, allowing them to fade, to die?

"Or she was poisoned." Rømer wasn't a man to let ethics stand in his way. Forcibly extinguishing them by applying an herbicide wasn't beyond him. But that alone did not explain the state in which they'd found Katla. "And her granulated skin?"

"Eitr," Hildur whispered.

Another myth that haunted their kind, the existence of a deadly substance that could kill, one that was paradoxically also the source of all life.

He dragged his hand over his face. "Nothing fascinated Rømer more than the possibility of biological transformation."

"You think alchemy is behind this?" A question she hissed through her teeth.

He did. But he only offered her a casual shrug. "Formally, he studied chemistry. Privately, he studied ancient manuscripts that promised many unsettling things and postulated as to how one might go about testing such notions."

His former friend had enjoyed the idea of holding life and death in his hands. A fact Val had not discovered until after he'd shared too much. And now Katla was dead, her corpse little more than a bag of wet sand covered with strange runic markings.

Hildur nodded. "The condition of her body is most suspicious."

In many ways, he was relieved the ambassador did not wish to view his daughter's corpse. The man would demand an explanation when all Val had were suspicions, secrets, and wild conjecture.

A descendent of former nobility, Rømer possessed exorbitant wealth, an impressive home and extensive lands. He and Katla had lived a reclusive life in the wilds of Norway. Public records contained no documentation of marriage or offspring. Sightings were rare, but they were known to associate with aristocrats who championed independence from Sweden.

Not once had she reached out to her family or answered the many missives sent her way. Though Val's sources reported Rømer received regular deliveries of laboratory equipment and supplies, he published nothing. Katla's death had Val wondering if her time with the man had been entirely voluntary.

Especially now that the alchemist was in London looking for a bride. Rømer's reappearance in society accompanied a string of coincidences too suspicious to ignore. The misshapen corpse of his former paramour. A shattered bottle of mysterious absinthe. And a looming royal wedding.

"Coffin is stowed." Dýri sauntered onto the deck. "Think we should order an extra, Captain? You know, in case one of us slips and mentions the extra fiancée you have waiting back home."

Dry-eyed, the ambassador had ordered Val to take care of the situation. Dagur Sveinsson wanted this chapter of his life closed. His daughter had long been dead to him. A second funeral would not be held and there was no room for a coffin aboard his first class, coal-powered airship. A blatant lie.

When Val turned up in the arms of an innocent young lady not an hour later, the ambassador had been apoplectic. The thorny reminder of the past had him ordering Val to speak whatever vows absolved Iceland of his embarrassing behavior.

Which suited Val to perfection.

"They say the third time's the charm." Val flashed Dýri a sharp-toothed grin. "Not that a stray fiancée would be a problem." He clamped a hand down on the man's shoulder and squeezed, digging fingers into muscle. He shot Dýri a razor-edged glare. "If certain people would speak up."

Dýri growled and curled his fingers into a fist.

"Don't punch the captain," Lisbet said, flouncing onto the deck. She dropped a kiss on her wife's cheek, whispered in her ear, then turned to face Val. "You have a problem. Or perhaps it's a solution?" She tipped her head and fluttered her eyelashes at him. Never a good sign.

The petite woman had undergone a complete transformation. An aristocrat by birth, his engineer usually wore grease-stained coveralls. But hidden deep inside all the trunks she'd hauled aboard were silk gowns and all the other trappings to which the upper-class ladies subjected themselves. Gowns she only donned when she inserted herself among high society in order to gather intel.

Which, from the looks of an overburdened steamboat, she'd done by way of a shopping spree on Bond Street, accumulating a towering stack of paper-wrapped packages, several proposals of marriage, and all the gossip burning the ears of London's peers.

"It had better not be a bill," he warned.

"Tell him," Hildur said, nudging her wife. Val didn't care for the broad grins stretching across their faces.

"Lord Aubrey, the would-be-bride's brother, has declined your suit. Instead, he demands restitution, citing damage to his reputation." Lisbet brushed a stray seagull feather from her skirts. "He went so far as to insist you sell the loftskip, if necessary, to raise sufficient funds."

"What!" Val shouted. "Impossible!"

Dýri guffawed.

"And isn't that backward, a bride price?" Val protested. "It was my understanding English brides came with a dowry."

"Her brother squandered that," Lisbet replied. "Not that it signifies, given he has denied your suit."

"And what does Lady Angela have to say about this?"

"Word is that she is in her room under lock and key. Lord Aubrey has a staggering amount of outstanding debt due to assorted depraved habits that will eventually bring about his demise. Many gentlemen, upon learning you were discovered in the sole company of the young lady, withdrew their original bid—"

"Bid?" Val raised an eyebrow.

"For Lady Angela's virtue," she answered.

"For her virginity?"

"If you must be crass," Lisbet confirmed with a sniff, fully committed to her patrician role.

If the news hadn't sliced through him like a cruel joke, he'd laugh at the sharp contrast between the aristocrat who stood before him now and the engineer who kept his dirigible in working order. The woman he was most familiar with ruled the engine room and, when cogs and gears broke, Danish profanities poured forth that, when translated, were shocking enough to peel the skin off a man.

"As I understand it," she continued, "any who still wish to marry Lady Angela must submit their offer by midnight. Lord Aubrey intends to see her married by the week's end."

"Is her consent not required?" Such a brazen attempt to force a woman into an unwanted marriage was likely to end with a dagger in the groom's heart.

"He has warned all potential grooms that his sister may not be in her right mind." The disapproval in Lisbet's voice dripped acid. "Which, rather than an accurate description of his sister's mental state, is generally considered a coercive threat to commit her to an insane asylum should she refuse to comply."

He pinched the bridge of his nose and closed his eyes.

"You'll like this next part even less," Hildur said. "Tell him."

"How can there possibly be more bad news?" he asked.

"Eirik Rømer submitted an offer for Lady Angela's hand."

And not twenty-four hours after his former paramour died. *Frigg and Hel.* His eyes snapped open. Val dragged his palm down his face. "Did you inquire about her ancestry?" He hoped Lisbet could shine light upon Lady Angela's lineage—or lack thereof.

"I did." His engineer nodded. "The dowager countess's given name was Eyrún."

He stopped breathing. "Eyrún Guðjónsdóttir? Sólættir?"

Sólættir were the equivalent of the British *ton*, perhaps more so. Taking Lady Angela as his wife would mean he married above himself twice over.

Lisbet shrugged, but a speculative light danced in her eyes.

Hildur frowned. "If Lady Angela's lineage is as suspected, a hasty marriage would be a mistake. I say we grab her, untether and make a run for it. Lauf will understand."

"Do any of us have experience flying an airship of this size?" Lisbet countered. Her question was met with a moment of uncomfortable silence. "I didn't think so."

"Or I could shoot Lord Aubrey between the eyes and put an end to all this nonsense," Dýri suggested. "Let the younger brother take over as head of the family."

"All reports indicate society would prefer that," Lisbet agreed. For all her appearance conveyed sweetness and light, she possessed a ruthless edge when injustices presented themselves.

"That might cause an international incident, much as it holds a certain appeal," Hildur said.

"And does nothing to address the unwelcome involvement of the Queen's agents," Val reminded them.

Like it or not, his crew recognized the need to cooperate with the British spies. Which suited him.

Last night in his bunk, endless erotic fantasies had disturbed his sleep. A hot spring, its water at the perfect bathing temperature. He'd tossed his bride in the water, fully dressed. Peeled soft, wet silk from her smooth skin...

Half hard at the very thought, he dragged in a deep breath and slowly exhaled.

Not that he would force himself upon a woman whose idea of kissing was to grind her mouth against his. But they would share a berth in his cabin and, provided the attraction was mutual, there would be no reason they couldn't enjoy each other's company. Intimately.

Except there was a fiancée back in Iceland. And he was not an oath-breaker. Presuming she was agreeable to the arrangement, he *would* marry Lady Angela, but there could be no consummation until after he spoke with Sóllilja to formally end their agreement.

She would forgive him for the short notice. Or so he hoped.

Lisbet sighed. "Much as Lord Aubrey might deserve such an end, my wife is right. Bloodshed is not the answer. While I was admiring a particularly large, feathered hat, a Lady Olivia—daughter of the Duchess of Avesbury— joined me."

That had Val's attention. "Daughter of the duchess who 'stumbled' upon us in the garden?"

"The very one." Lisbet nodded. "In light of Earl Aubrey's unconscionable behavior, the duchess has provided a Mr. Black with a bank draft and a blank marriage certificate. He'll be arriving with a minister at eight in the morning. All we need do is fetch the bride."

"A bank draft?"

Hildur groaned. "This is a bad idea."

Lisbet grinned. "Bearing your name and a number with a significant number of zeros."

The duchess would pay him to marry Lady Angela? Why?

Not that it mattered.

"Stow your negative opinions." He'd had enough. "My bride is one of us, whether she knows it or not. Tonight we free her from the tyranny of her brother. Plan for a wedding ceremony tomorrow morning, though no one will be forced to speak vows. If all goes as planned, we then take flight and quit London. I assure you all that Angela Eyrúnsdóttir will arrive at the mountain with her virtue intact. There, she will have the option to dissolve our union without penalty. I will not take her free will. Satisfied?"

Dýri cast him a thunderous look but said not a word.

Lisbet clapped her hands together. "Nothing like raiding foreign lands for a wife." She slid her own wife a dewy-eyed look. "I remember my own abduction fondly..."

His first mate cast her eyes toward the heavens. "Grappling hook it is."

CHAPTER FOUR

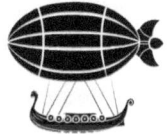

ER BROTHER HAD SET A GUARD OUTSIDE her doorway. And another beneath her window. The man in the hallway was quite comfortable but, as the hour grew late and snow swirled through the air, the man in the garden began to stomp back and forth in a futile attempt to warm himself. At some point, odds were high that he'd slip away for a few minutes to thaw, perhaps by stopping in the kitchen for a hot drink.

Which might be her only opportunity.

Working by firelight to avoid suspicion, Angela tiptoed in stocking feet about her room. The vasculum, a cylindrical case designed to protect the delicate feathery fronds of ferns, and a small valise were all she could hope to carry. Every item packed needed to be essential.

Shortly after midnight, she'd been escorted by the hall guard to her brother's study. Pleased as a kraken sinking an ironclad battleship, he'd reclined in his chair. His finger tapped the surface of Father's desk, where the shredded remnants of her petticoats lay beside a towering stack of gold coins.

How had he known? Every last bottle and jar had been hand-carried to the apothecary to maintain the utmost privacy—ladies did not engage in commerce. Wildly popular, her line of skin care products, compounded from the extracted phytochemicals of endophytic plants, had provided a steady stream of income. One she'd hidden from her brother by converting her profits into gold sovereigns and sewing them into the hems of petticoats. Not that the returns had been sufficient to allow for an independent existence.

Not yet.

Mother stood at the elbow of her favorite son, glaring at her daughter for daring to bring scandal into her house. As if Marcus wasn't the root cause of all their problems.

Angela felt a growl building deep in her chest. "How dare you!" she hissed at her brother. "I earned that."

"From your little pharmaceutical enterprise, yes." He'd smirked. "But your products were grown on Aubrey land with Aubrey supplies *without* Aubrey permission."

She glowered.

"Not that your behavior will be my issue going forward. You may discuss any future horticultural efforts with your husband." Barely concealed greed smoldered in his eyes. "You're to be married in the morning."

"And not to that social-climbing airship captain who ruined your reputation by daring to overstep." Mother's lips stretched into a tight smile. "While every British gentlemen worth having withdrew their offer, another recognized your mistake as opportunity."

Her heart stopped beating. Valtýr Árnason had been ordered by the Icelandic ambassador to offer for her hand. The Duchess of Avesbury herself all but declared them engaged on the spot. Stupid of her to allow herself to relax. She swallowed. "Did he not offer?"

"He most certainly did." Her brother threw a letter across the desk with a snort. "One inquiring about your dowry instead of offering restitution. See for yourself."

Worry cut into her stomach like shards of glass. Her plan had failed? With a shaking hand, she scanned the missive. Polite and formal, he'd requested permission to marry her, providing the name of a solicitor that they might draw up a marriage contract. She found nothing about the language amiss. The problem was her brother, not Valtýr Árnason.

She took an unsteady step backward. Her options were rapidly narrowing. Arguing with Marcus might worsen her already precarious situation. Though some token resistance on her part would be expected. "And the winning bid fell to?" An inquiry she edged with spikes of crystalized sugar.

"Eirik Rømer."

Bile rose to her throat. The Norwegian who had attempted to draw her attention at the ball? No. Impossible. She'd thought him handsome enough, contemplated him as a desperate last possibility given he mingled with the Icelandic contingent.

Until he'd spoken.

She would have recognized that voice anywhere. And

that moment had provided her a name. Fear wrapped icy fingers about her spine and squeezed. This couldn't be happening. Did they know? Had they been complicit? She forced herself to ask. "Grandmother's acquaintance?"

"Certainly not." Marcus frowned. "Eirik Rømer is of noble heritage and possesses significant political clout in the Norwegian court. More importantly, he's willing to overlook your indiscretion and the vulgar markings pricked into your skin."

The man had killed her grandmother and now wished to *pay* for her? A young woman with a strange tattoo? How much did he know?

She didn't want to find out.

A clink sounded as her brother placed a ring on his desk. The many facets of its diamond gleamed with a cold and cruel brilliance. "Your engagement ring. Wear it."

She obeyed, accepting she need lose this battle in an effort to win the war. Perhaps the ring would serve a purpose. Diamonds were, after all, known to cut glass. Her heart pounded. Time was running out, her options rapidly narrowing. She needed to leave. Tonight.

A few coins remained in her purse, enough to hire a crank hack. If she could reach Valtýr Árnason's airship before she was discovered missing, would he honor his proposal? If not, would he at least offer her a ride to Iceland?

Marcus offered a few more wedding details—unnecessary, as she wouldn't be present—then her guard had marched her back to her room. Where the only possible exit was her window. And for that, she needed a rope.

The sounds of tearing bedsheets would have raised the alarm. Hence her use of embroidery scissors. Though the process took twice as long, it was silent. As was knotting the long strips and braiding them into a rope that stood a chance of bearing her weight.

Were she inclined to calculate the risk, however, a larger concern might be the strength of her arms. Pharmaceutical botany, as a profession, did not provide much in the way of physical challenges. And, informed by the childhood memory of swinging on a rope, she wouldn't be able to hold on for long.

Falling was a decided possibility. A likelihood, even. If she broke her ankle, or worse, would Marcus delay this farce of a wedding? She very much doubted it.

She packed a silk gown suitable for a wedding and the corset capable of cinching her waist small enough to wear it. Added matching slippers and silk stockings. Valuable space wasted on extravagances, but ones an airship captain interested in a dowry might balk at supplying. Or sell along with the diamond ring.

Tucked in the remaining space were her powdered greens, glass vials containing dormant dinocysts and fern spores, a few of her favorite skin tonics, creams and soaps, and her grandmother's identification book of moss and ferns. One she'd inscribed with strange runic writing during fits of insanity.

Angela's most recent experiment—a small fern hiding in plain sight beside the window—was developing a reddish tinge. Yesterday, she'd inoculated the plant's roots with single-celled organisms and was waiting for them to spread throughout the fern, to burrow through cell walls in an attempt to establish endosymbiosis.

If trends held, her experiment would fail.

Still, she refused to leave it behind. One never knew when a breakthrough might occur. Whispering an apology, she wrapped the plant in tissue paper and carefully tucked it inside her vasculum. Closing the canister, she slipped her arm through the carry strap.

With her most precious cargo safely stowed, she sat on a low stool and wrestled on a pair of serviceable boots. Not an easy feat, no matter how loosely she'd laced her corset.

Angela glared at the engagement ring on her finger. Much as she wished to leave it behind, if the airship captain refused to let her aboard and she required funds, she would need to visit a pawn shop. She stuffed it down her bodice, stood and crossed to the window.

Watching, she waited for her chance, drawing deep breaths in an attempt to remain calm. The household servants would soon begin preparations for a morning wedding. As the presumed bride, her absence would be quickly discovered, and an alarm raised.

Still, she waited. And waited.

The outside guard finally abandoned his patrol. Time to leave. She opened the window sash and threw out the knotted sheets. Tiny sharp daggers of ice whipped into her bedroom, stabbing the skin of her face. Snowflakes at their most evil. Of all the nights for a storm.

Wool. She ought to have worn a warm and simple dress.

Instead, she'd convinced herself that fashion mattered above personal comfort when she intended to beg a man to marry her.

Nothing to do now. She was out of time.

Muttering, she tossed out her bag of bridal finery followed by her fur-lined cape. Hiking skirts to her hips, she threw a leg over the windowsill and, gripping the knotted sheets with tight fists, climbed out onto the stone ledge to lean back.

The first step was easy.

After that, her escape turned into a farce. The frigid wind bit through her silk stockings, yanked away the hat pinned to her hair, then howled with laughter at her plans to descend by spinning her about and twisting her skirts about her legs to deny her feet purchase before slamming her into the side of the house. Again and again.

There would be bruises.

Yet there was no returning to her prison. How to manage this? A hand over hand descent? Out of the question. Even holding on was proving a challenge. Maybe a controlled slip? That seemed her best bet, even if the concentration and effort it took to release her fingers, however slightly, brought tears to her eyes. But the only other choice was to plummet to the ground.

Muscles strained and burned and cried for relief. Her palms wept as they informed her that, with enough force, even the passage of the finest linen might strip the skin from her hands. Why had she not thought to wear leather gloves? No hope remained that she might "walk" down the building's side, a method she'd once watched her brother apply. Nor could she manage to wrap her legs around the braided rope or clasp one of the many knots between her feet.

As suspected, Jack's use of the technique was far superior and plaster casts—plural—lay in his reckless sister's near future.

Her upper body strength simply wasn't up to the task. A cold sweat broke out across her skin. This was going to hurt. A lot. But she couldn't hold on much longer. Squeezing her eyes shut, she offered up prayers to any of the old gods and goddess who might offer her aid.

She inched down the rope. Kicked off the wall in an attempt to protect the fern case. Adding insult to injury, snow began to fall.

"Let go!" a voice called. One pitched loud enough to rise above the gusting wind, soft enough to not raise the alarm.

She glanced down. Valtýr waited below, arms outstretched. She'd sprung a trap. Yet he'd come for her? An honorable Viking conducting a raid in the dead of night. Romantic or mercenary? Would he dump her back on the doorstep if he learned there was no dowry?

"I'll catch you! On the count of three!"

Let go? Was he mad?

"One!"

Nor more than she.

"Two!"

What choice did she have?

"Three!"

"Odin, protect us," Angela whispered. Closing her eyes, she let go.

Woosh! Her stomach swooped upward, lodging her heart in her throat. She knew a moment's weightlessness, a moment of an uncertain end, then solid arms wrapped about her, slowing—if not entirely stopping—her fall.

Momentum, along with other immutable laws of physics, tumbled them into the boxwood, cushioning their landing with the crunch of bent and broken stems. A sound followed by an awkward silence in which she found her face pressed to his chest and her legs wrapped about his, skirts akimbo.

"Do you always careen headlong into uncharted danger?" The deep rumble of his voice held a note of laughter. "Flinging yourself with unmitigated hope into the arms of a rescuer?"

"Only when invited to do so." She pushed herself upright and met his gaze, daring him to deny her words.

Valtýr's blue eyes danced, amused. By the gods, he was unnaturally handsome. A strong jaw outlined by golden-blond stubble. How was it that a single day's growth of beard could make a man even more handsome? It drew attention to his lips. Ones she'd smashed her own against in that awful farce of a kiss.

"Your technique needs work."

Heat flamed her face. It had been her first kiss, and she'd overplayed for an audience. Ought she be embarrassed? Or perhaps he was offering her another chance? Now, here in the snow?

Save he might be referencing her rappelling skills, in

which case she ought not let romantic notions overtake her thoughts. She drew in a breath but was too embarrassed and uncertain to ask.

Slow claps sounded above them. "A solid attempt, your descent. Points for bravery, if not execution."

Angela looked up into the face of a Valkyrie. Towering over them was a woman with long, chaotic twists of blonde braids. Beneath a sweeping cape, she wore boots, fitted pants and a body-hugging tunic that laced up the front. Add a sword and the woman would be ready to take on the gods. Odin himself, from the fierce look upon her face. But instead of a sword, she held a grappling hook attached to a length of rope.

Had they meant to rescue her? Abduct her like the Vikings of old?

Did she care? Not at all.

Strong fingers dug into her hips and thick shoulder muscles moved beneath her palms as Valtýr shifted her onto her rump, setting her down among the snow-dusted stems of last summer's plants.

"Hildur." He tipped his head. "We have a small problem."

Her brother's guard had rounded the corner and stood, mouth agape. He turned and ran.

"On it." The Valkyrie took off at a run, easily overtaking the man.

Angela gasped. "She won't hurt him, will she?"

"Not at all," Valtýr reassured her, holding out a hand. "Hildur will gag him, bind his hands and feet, then tuck him beside the kitchen door where the servants will soon find him."

She accepted, much impressed when he lifted her effortlessly onto her feet. Was she really doing this? Concern bubbled in her chest. Was she making a horrible mistake? "I have no dowry," she blurted, needing honesty between them. She stiffened her back and faced the consequences of her actions. "My family will disown me."

"So I was informed." He lifted her fur cloak, shook away the snow and wrapped it about her shoulders. "And before you state that you've little to offer beyond your scientific expertise, which is of considerable value, remember that marrying an airship captain comes with its own drawbacks."

"Such as no access to a greenhouse?"

"Let me allay such worries." He unbuttoned his shirt cuff and shoved his sleeve past his elbow, exposing a tattoo. From intertwined roots that wrapped around his wrist, a twisting vine grew. One with *green* leaves. "We share a common heritage. Access to sunlight is a guarantee."

Heart pounding, she touched a finger to the marks upon —*in*—his skin. A different design but, like hers, the ink was alive. "Grandmother always told me there were others."

"Your grandmother was Eyrún Guðjónsdóttir?"

She blinked. "You knew her?"

"Of her." He hooked a finger under the clasp of her cloak and pulled her against his body, enveloping her in comforting warmth. Time slowed as a steady fall of snow swirled about them, cocooning them in silence. "You do know the huldufólk are real?"

His seriousness curved her lips upward. "So she claimed. I'll allow that fairy tales are often spun from a tendril of truth. Once the underlying facts are uncovered, however, what passes for magic is readily explained by science. You, a gentleman who attends engineering lectures, ought not offer up such silliness."

"How generous of you to deny our existence so graciously."

She'd been so very lonely for so very long and his presence whispered of a home she'd never known, no matter the nonsense he spouted. "It's not that I don't want to believe Icelandic elves are real..."

He cupped her chin with his hand, dropped his gaze to her lips. Was he about to kiss her? If so, it was an effective distraction from his absurd claim. What was it about this man that made her body ache, made her skin beg for his touch? Every nerve ending begged for the soft press of his mouth. But he only gave a quiet shake of his head. "Did she warn you of our tendency to cling like vines to the traditions of our ancestors who, upon occasion, were known to kidnap women, to whisk them away to their mountain home?"

"Viking romanticism that is pure fiction." Her haughty reply did nothing to dim the bright humor dancing in his eyes. "Intended to discourage young women from wandering about on their own."

"Is that so?" An eyebrow lifted. "Alas, modern practices do require paperwork and a handful of witnesses. To that end, Mr. Black and the duchess have been most helpful. Yet

I find your casual dismissal of long-held traditions disheartening."

"Ready, sir?" The Valkyrie had returned, looking quite pleased with herself. She snatched up Angela's valise. "We ought to make haste."

"Almost." A wink was her only warning. Valtýr bent over, caught her behind her knees and stood, throwing her over his shoulder before striding toward the garden gate.

"Put me down!" Her lungs held barely enough air to protest. "What are you doing?"

"Adhering to traditions, my lady." He laughed at the words. "Any further revelations wait until after we speak vows."

CHAPTER FIVE

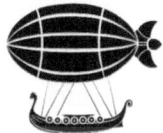

As the sun rose above the horizon, the wedding party assembled on his airship's deck. Well, all but his bride. A fierce winter wind snapped and plucked at the tethers that kept them anchored, urging them to hurry. An ominous warning that past sins nipped at his heels.

Lady Olivia and Mr. Black served as British witnesses for the minister who traveled in their company while his rough-looking crew represented Val's family. They *were* family. Much as his mother might regret missing this moment, she'd foretold of his impromptu shipboard wedding long ago while pointing to a golden thread in her weavings. Only rarely did she misinterpret a sign.

Though his mother *had* missed the part about being hounded by spies. Lady Olivia's agenda was clear. Not so much Mr. Black's. Which left one Dr. Quinn McCullough as the only unexpected guest.

Val had pulled the spy—for he could only be that—aside and lifted his eyebrows in question.

"Think of him as a temporary wedding gift," Mr. Black began. "The body you retrieved possesses characteristics that indicate the cause of the woman's death was rather curious."

"How did you find out—" Val frowned. The man had eyes everywhere. "The crank hack driver? The ambassador?"

Mr. Black pressed his lips together. "It worries me that one of the huldufólk came to such a bad end on British soil." He nodded at Val's sharp intake of breath. "Yes, we know of the hidden folk. An Icelandic subpopulation of Nordic people with a long history and unique traditions. Rest assured, Dr. McCullough reports only to me and will keep his lips sealed. With your approval, he'll remain aboard, examine the body with the assistance of your soon-to-be wife, then disembark when you reach Glasgow."

That the British knew of his people ought not come as a surprise. That they knew of his underground London adventure worried him more.

He'd resigned himself to never knowing the specifics of Katla's death. Her father wouldn't request a postmortem. Nor would Val, for the council would demand an explanation. One he was not prepared to give.

Allowing Dr. McCullough to gather data was risky. Val might learn the extent of Rømer's efforts to revive Eldskrift, but so too would British intelligence—not that he or his crew would offer a spy's physician any clarity. On the other hand, without a proper autopsy, the information Val could gather on his own would be superficial.

He frowned. "Lady Angela's work means she possesses an extensive knowledge of dermatology. A few skin biopsies are not beyond her skill set."

One of her many attractions.

Mr. Black drew a deep breath. "Katla's past complicates things. Daughter of an Icelandic ambassador. But also the paramour of Eirik Rømer, an advocate for Norwegian independence as well as the man officially engaged to your bride."

Katla dead under mysterious conditions, with nothing besides a single bottle of Tyrian Absinthe in her possession, her dying words mentioning an ancient huldufólk tradition, the mad alchemist, and a warning that more people—fae?—were at risk.

"Given the protests, you understand my concern," Mr. Black continued. "We only wish to ensure the royal wedding takes place with as few complications as possible."

Val resisted an urge to shove his fingers into his hair. He bore a certain responsibility to assist, to help flip over slimy rocks. Rømer would be hiding beneath one of them, toying with things best left alone. He let go of the breath he was holding. There was little choice. Protecting his people came first and if that meant working with a British spy, so be it. "He can stay."

"Thank you," Mr. Black said. "I'd prefer to keep this quiet, between us. Unless a specific threat to international relations becomes clear."

Thank Odin. "Agreed."

"On to happier topics. As the bride's family refuses to

provide for her..." A slip of paper appeared from the spy's inner coat pocket. One gifting Val with enough British pounds to purchase freedom. A second sealed envelope followed. "Don't disappoint me."

"I protect my own." He'd not be swearing any kind of allegiance to a foreigner.

"Good enough."

With that, they'd returned to the group.

"I hate to point this out." On tiptoes, Lady Olivia leaned over the bulwark, focused on the city streets below. "But a small commotion is brewing. One that draws closer."

Hildur lifted her spyglass. "A steam coach with Lord Aubrey's crest approaches. I'm willing to bet Rømer rides inside." She cast her gaze across the gathering. "Any takers?"

Dýri cleared his throat. "I'll take the long odds if it wins me a night with you and—"

"No." Hildur smacked the backside of his head. "Never happening."

"Save your coin." Lisbet rolled her eyes. "Polish it bright and a pair of trolls might oblige."

"Nah. They're not flexible enough for what I'm imagining." Dýri waggled his eyebrows. "Ow!"

This time Val smacked him. "Shut it and show some respect. This is a wedding."

His wedding. One preferably concluded before trouble arrived. Better if the ink was dry on the paperwork and vows spoken before Lady Angela's family interrupted the proceedings.

Was he really doing this? Binding himself to a woman

he'd just met, one who might possess divided loyalties? Absolutely. She was the missing variable in his life that made him rework every equation.

Not that he would force her. Both parties married voluntarily. Or not at all.

To give her time to change her mind, Val had left her in the hands of Lisbet. Thrilled, his engineer had whisked Lady Angela away to help her dress the part of a fae bride. So far, she'd not asked to disembark.

Even after the wedding, if they found they did not suit, she could choose divorce. Perhaps she might refuse to stand by him when she learned of his youthful mistakes. He glanced over the edge of the loftskip. But he'd not abandon her to the likes of Rømer.

"Sir," Hildur drew his attention, pointing.

"Is that—" *Frigg and Hel.* A second conveyance followed Lord Aubrey's carriage. One that bore Jarl Haukr's blue crest, one edged with red and emblazoned with a white gyrfalcon. The colors of ice, fire and sky. Likely Lauf was inside—the hostage returned too soon. If Aubrey thought to snatch up the airship pilot, it would put Val in an uncomfortable position. "We need to hurry."

"Agreed," Mr. Black said.

Val considered casting off sandbags, lifting them into the sky. But airspace mattered, and this wedding needed to be legal and binding. According to two cultures. Better to keep things short and simple. "Hildur." He tipped his head at the cabin door. "If you could speak with your wife and the bride, inform them we've run out of time?"

Enough primping. What they needed was speed. A brief ceremony reminiscent of an elopement followed by a race across the skies home. There was no avoiding the stop in Glasgow—to load supplies, to cash a check—but they could make it a short one.

His first mate nodded but managed only two steps before the door opened and his bride, transformed into Angela Eyrúnsdóttir, stepped onto the deck.

The air in his lungs froze. Gone was the rumpled, disheveled woman who'd dropped from a window. In her place, a lady dressed for presentation at court. A tight bodice accentuated an impossibly slim waist, generous hips and a full bosom. Folds of purple satin fell from her waist. Lace and tassels and ruffles danced in the wind. But the surprise didn't end there. Long, intricate twists of braids were drawn into an upsweep of glorious blonde hair crowned with a circlet of flowers, vines and sparkling crystals. As befitting a proper fae bride.

An amalgamation of British and Icelandic. Human and fae. Past and present.

As she walked across the deck to place her hand in his, desire stirred. A flicker of heat stirred in her eyes, uncertain yet edged with unguarded anticipation. He was in so much trouble.

The reverend spoke first and, within a few short minutes, Hildur stepped forward to hold out his sword. The minister blinked in shock, but wisely said nothing as Val lifted one of the two simple silver bands resting upon the sword's hilt and slid it onto his bride's finger. She returned the favor, and the minister pronounced them man and wife.

But Val didn't kiss his wife. Not yet. Instead, he nodded at Hildur, who would serve as priestess.

Stepping forward, his first mate held out an oath ring inscribed with runes. "Both of you, grab hold."

Angela's gaze flicked to the ring. "A second ceremony?" A question, but her fingers closed about the ring without hesitation.

"Necessary if you wish to be bound in the eyes of our people."

By virtue of the tattoo that lived in her skin, she was already one of them. Though her position in his society remained to be confirmed. What she wasn't was married. Not yet. And until then, the protection he could offer her was limited. And, given the risks he was about to take, he wanted every legal stipulation signed and sealed.

He wrapped his own fingers around the iron ring, feeling its weight as something shifted in the air. An invisible current seemed to pulse between them, pulling them closer. He was both impressed and horrified by her efforts to escape her family. Calculating enough to husband hunt during a state affair. Impulsive enough to trap him in her web, to climb out her window when events did not unfold as she'd expected.

Ought he have asked if she was running away? Or if she'd intended to seek out his airship beside the docks? Did it matter? She had friends in high places. Ones who'd rescued her from her recklessness. Was she a knowing participant in espionage? Either way Mr. Black executed the most obvious infiltration by supporting their union.

Did he care?

Not today.

Speaking in Old Norse, Hildur called upon the gods and goddesses of the Aesir and Vanir to bless their marriage. Val and his bride spoke a second round of vows—ones she managed to pronounce with relative ease—proclaiming that they joined together of their own free will.

Then Hildur declared them bound, always and forever.

With these last words, his gaze caught that of his bride. The coy smile on her lips touched a flame to every molecule of testosterone that coursed through his veins and sent a wave of heat rushing across his skin. Primitive male instinct seized him. He wanted what he shouldn't touch.

Let her decide, Loki whispered in his ear. *You've done nothing wrong. Why not enjoy?*

Hooking a finger beneath the delicate point of her chin, he tilted her face upward and lowered his mouth to hers. A kiss to explore the shape of her lips, not technically their first, but the first that truly mattered. For it marked her as his. Gentle, yet firm, he dragged his thumb along her lower lip, then tugged, soft but deliberate. A claim. But also an invitation for her to stake her own.

Her breath hitched, and she rose onto her toes, fingers splaying across his chest, chasing more. Not one to waste opportunity, he parted her lips and slid his tongue over hers. She tasted of fresh berries, winter moss and a gentle breeze all wrapped in a cloud of gauzy silk. Delicate and fragile things carefully hidden beneath the brave exterior of an impulsive woman, determined to control her fate.

Utterly captivating.

And she'd chosen to trust him. Him. Of all people. The thought tightened in his chest. Once she knew about his past mistakes, would she judge him harshly, turn from him? He hoped not. For now, he'd do his best to protect her, to fold her into his world and hope that, later, she'd still want him by her side.

Cheers went up and he pulled away. Slowly. With great reluctance. And all too aware of their audience.

Dýri produced a drinking horn filled with mead and shoved the vessel against his captain's lips. Gripping the man's wrist, Val took a deep drink, then handed the mead to his wife.

She too drank from the horn before Dýri snatched it away. Refilling the horn cup, he passed it to all in attendance. Yes, even his British guests, not that they were given much choice.

Had he married a spy? Possibly.

He snorted. Nothing to do about it now. The runes had been tossed, and the reading was unclear. Would their lives mesh? Or would they go their separate ways? There were many facets of his wife's beauty, ones he looked forward to exploring in great detail, beginning tonight, as he attempted to convince her a life by his side was desirable.

Hildur grabbed his arm and dragged him away. "My

wife informs me that yours is an innocent." She narrowed her eyes. "There's to be no risk of a child until she understands the full consequences of her vows, until she understands her place in our society. Until your fiancée has time to extricate herself honorably from your prior agreement." She jabbed him in the chest. "Give me your word you'll not take advantage or I'll speak with her myself."

His teeth clenched, biting back hostile words. His second overstepped, yes, but she was also in the right. Promiscuity might be tolerated by their people and pregnancies rare, but women were expected to marry the father of their child. Or suffer the consequences. He ought to know. He'd lived them.

"Fine." He growled. "You have my word." Not that it meant he'd keep his hands to himself. Such was not a vow of chastity. He was no London-bred gentleman. There were many ways to achieve satisfaction without risking pregnancy.

Turning, he found Lady Olivia had wrapped her arms about her friend to hug her tight. He watched as she leaned back with a wide grin and pressed a fancy paper box tied with a bow into his wife's hands. The words she spoke were snatched away by the wind but made Angela glance in his direction and bite her lip.

Some risqué scrap of silk that Lisbet hadn't managed to acquire on Bond Street? Or a fine gossamer white lace gown showcasing virginal innocence? His groin stirred to life. Either would please him. He'd enjoy watching the play of light and shadow across her skin as he slid such a fabric upward, over thighs that trembled beneath the brush of his beard as he inhaled her scent.

The sound of a gun cocking snapped him out of his reverie.

CHAPTER SIX

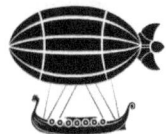

"**D**O YOU A WANT A CHILD STRAIGHT away?" Olivia pitched her voice loud enough for Angela to hear, soft enough that the wind would carry away the words before anyone else heard the question. She waggled a beribboned box in her hand. "From the way that Viking kissed you, there's very little time left to decide."

She glanced at Valtýr. From the heat in his gaze, she wasn't certain he'd wait for a wedding *night*. She hoped he wouldn't, not after a kiss that sent stars shooting through her veins, leaving her weak in the knees and desperate for more. She quite looked forward to being ravished by a Viking.

No, by *her* Viking.

At last, she'd have answers. Not that she was ignorant of the mechanics, not with brothers like hers, just inexperienced. Young ladies were wise to avoid such pitfalls before marriage.

She'd found the thin, well-thumbed book her brothers

had not-so-cleverly hidden inside a hollowed-out Latin text-book. Their mistake, thinking she wouldn't touch such a dry tome. But applicants to medical school were expected to pass a number of written tests, including Latin and Greek. Instead of grinding her teeth over declensions, she'd discovered herself blushing over the "naughty" pictures of an entirely different instruction manual.

Red-faced, Jack had plucked the book from her fingers while she was buried nose deep. "If anyone asks, you did not read this." She drew breath to object, for she had indeed. Twice. But he'd thrown the book on the fire and said, "No. Please. I'm begging you not to ask me any questions."

She'd had so, so many.

"A delay would be welcome." Angela swallowed. The aid of a spy inevitably came with strings. "Is that what's in the box?"

"Precisely that." Olivia pulled at the ribbon and slid a small mechanical device into her palm. "I'm no fan of needles, but a quick injection will provide you with a year of no consequences."

"After that?" Children would be welcome someday.

"All the usual risks of bed sport return."

Time to sort out her future would be welcome. She nodded. "Proceed."

"Hold still." Olivia tugged down Angela's sleeve to expose her upper arm. "This will pinch."

Something snapped, and she felt a sharp sting.

Olivia winked. "It's done. Enjoy yourself." She yanked the fabric back in place and tucked the device behind her corset. "Now, about your mission. In exchange for the special license, your assignment is to assist Dr. McCullough with an autopsy by analyzing the dermatological condition of Katla Dagsdóttir's skin. Mr. Black caught word of an irregularity, something about glass and sand."

"Autopsy?" An icy finger trailed down her back as fate laughed, reminding her that she'd agreed to this. Such was the work of spies. "Am I in danger?"

Her friend frowned. "Not anymore?"

"Why are you uncertain?" Words squeaked out of a tight throat. "And who is Katla Dagsdóttir?"

Olivia sighed. "The man whose suit your brother accepted, Eirik Rømer, is a known troublemaker who opposes Swedish rule of Norway. Which interested Mother because of the impending royal wedding—Britain wants no trouble with revolutionaries. However," she drew out the word, "given Katla was last seen in Rømer's company and the strange circumstances that surrounded her death, Mr. Black and I argued against her plan."

"She wanted me to marry *him*?" Angela shuddered. Something about Rømer's demeanor hinted at a life of pain and misery. Better an airship captain who sailed the skies. Even if they didn't suit, she'd find contentment in her research, tucked away inside a greenhouse, lost among her plants, traveling with him to collect ferns from distant lands, presenting her work at symposiums.

"As you are untrained, Mr. Black argued against your unorthodox inclusion in the program at all. I argued in favor of middle ground. Stick with your Viking and you should be safe."

Angela felt a weight lift off her shoulders, glad she'd snagged an airship captain instead of a statesman. Ingratiating herself among the elite in an attempt to gather gossip of interest to the British Crown held no appeal. "It *is* a grand airship." Words spoken on a relieved exhale.

"Lucky you." Her friend shot her a teasing smile. "Think of all the glorious places you might visit. All with a handsome man warming your bed and no need to plot his eventual demise. I almost envy you."

Never quite certain if Olivia teased or not when she mentioned casual manslaughter, Angela forced a laugh and diverted her attention to surveying her new home, a marvel of wood and steel.

The loftskip was built to resemble a Viking merchant ship of old, the bow and stern curving upward with the prow carved into the shape of a dragon's head and the stern into its tail. Of course, unlike its distant predecessors, a dirigible possessed no need of oars. Nor did it have a large central sail. Instead, an enormous oblong balloon floated overhead.

As promised, a greenhouse rose from an upper deck. Access to all the sunlight she desired—and perhaps laboratory space? A thoughtful smile curved her lips. A happy husband might be coaxed into dedicating a corner to her botanical pursuits.

Where they stood at present, little free room remained. Long rolls of thick canvas secured with ropes were tucked along the ship's starboard and portside, behind various crates and barrels. Valtýr had mentioned a stop for building supplies. Few trees survived on the island. Perhaps these were struts or beams of some sort?

A fitting vessel upon which to depart London. Save she'd had no time to prepare. She possessed no funds, no clothing beyond an extra gown and a pair of silk slippers—not so much as a hairbrush or a box of tooth powder. She knew her husband's name, that he was in trade, and that he claimed their living tattoos marked them as fae.

A claim she was inclined to dispute, even though Grandmother vowed it true.

As a child she'd enjoyed the fanciful game of pretending to be an elf living in exile, but she'd been fourteen when her grandmother tattooed the fiddlehead into the crook of her arm, warning Angela that "humans" could not hope to bear such an unusual mark and that she must not reveal the source of the green ink.

Struggling to reconcile science with myth, she'd shown the living fern in her skin to Jack, informing him that he too might be in possession of a unique biological talent. After all, he was family. Telling him wasn't a betrayal of Grandmother's confidence, was it?

Intrigued by the prospect, he'd offered up his own arm for experimentation. As a control, she'd used purified cells from the same plant used to prick the pattern into her skin. Much to both their disappointments, the "ink" failed to take.

Until now, she'd not met anyone else capable of hosting living plant cells within their skin.

Would that she could walk about the deck, sliding up the

ANNE RENWICK

sleeves of Valtýr's crew to confirm his claim. But that would be improper. On the other hand—she smiled to herself—she'd soon be able to examine every square inch of her husband's bare skin for more markings. A thought that flooded her body with molten desire. Finally, a chance to investigate the possibilities suggested in that "naughty" book Jack had ripped from her hands.

A shout rang out. One originating directly beneath them. "I demand her return! At once!"

Aubrey.

"Your brother found us with surprising ease." Frowning, Olivia slid her arm through Angela's and tugged her toward the airship's side. "Apologies in advance for the lack of practical clothing in your trousseau. Lisbet and I wanted to ensure you had an array of luxuries not easily obtainable on a frozen island in the depths of winter."

"You packed a trunk for me?" Angela brightened.

Her friend laughed. "You might curse me when you examine the impractical contents, but Lisbet assured me there was no shortage of wool in Iceland."

They joined Mr. Black, Dr. McCullough and Valtýr. At some moment during the pagan ceremony, the minister had made a hasty escape. She leaned over the gunwale to stare down at the commotion below. Her brother and Eirik Rømer abandoned their steam carriage to point at the pulley system that lifted both people and cargo aboard the airship, demanding to be allowed aboard.

But the dockworkers shook their heads, refusing to lower the platform.

"Is Aubrey likely to be a problem?" her husband asked.

"Not once you're airborne. His time will be spent appeasing his creditors." Mr. Black paused. "Rømer's interest, on the other hand, is an unknown variable."

"Not to me," Valtýr replied. He didn't elaborate.

Free from her brother, she could finally breathe. Impulse had won her a strong, intelligent and handsome husband. Adventure awaited. She'd miss Olivia. The Kew Gardens. But not the increasing restrictions and pressures placed upon a young, unmarried lady of the *ton* with a disreputable family.

Aubrey had stolen much. First, her ability to attend medical school. Then, when she'd turned to botanical pursuits, he'd banned any visits to Kew Gardens or the rooftop greenhouse of the Lister Institute, lest someone in London accuse her of botanical witchery. Slowly, he'd tightened the noose, relegating her to the countryside with their increasingly insane grandmother.

At least there she'd still had access to a full range of moss, liverworts and ferns. Here, in the city, she'd been forced to hide her experimental ferns by tucking them among more decorative plants in the townhouse conservatory. She'd managed. Until he'd announced her auction.

Much as it was a relief to leave England, she was also bitter. And angry. So very angry.

Her fingers curled into the railing, tightening. She'd like to wrap them around her brother's neck and squeeze. Furious heat flushed through her body at the memory of how he'd stolen all her hard-earned money, how her mother had stood there, complicit. For years she'd bitten her tongue and refrained from shouting at her brother, biding her time until she could wrest herself free from his authority as head of the family. And that time was now.

Heady with defiance, she rose up onto her toes and held her hand up that he might glimpse the simple silver band encircling her ring finger. "You're too late!"

Eirik Rømer glowered. A rich man furious that a coveted plaything was beyond his grasp.

Her brother spun on his heel and lifted his face. "Disembark now, Angela!"

Olivia dropped a hand onto her arm. "Ladies do not shout."

Angela ignored her. She'd married an Icelandic airship captain. A foreigner. A Viking. She could no longer claim a title. The moment she'd spoken vows, she'd left the gentry behind. What did it matter if she no longer acted the role? She reached into her bodice and fished out the engagement ring forced upon her. "Or what?" she yelled back. "You'll deny me my non-existent dowry?"

With that, she lobbed the ring into the air, grinning vindictively as the Norwegian dove to catch the expensive and ostentatious diamond.

Sprawled on the ground, Eirik Rømer glared, fist wrapped about his rejected favor.

"Making enemies already?" Olivia chided. "You ought to know better." A gentle reprimand, but one nonetheless.

"Unwise, wife." Valtýr glowered, his face hard and unforgiving. "While many despise the man, he holds much influence among the Norwegian elite who oppose the royal wedding. By marrying me, you've tied your fortune to that of Iceland. Next time, think before you act."

Mr. Black frowned. "You've made a powerful man drop to his knees. He won't forget. Don't make me regret helping you."

None of them knew that Angela suspected the Norwegian had murdered her grandmother. Without proof, there was little to be done save to avoid him at all costs. Still, she'd made a mistake by allowing her temper to flare. A bad one. Her gut twisted. Ought she apologize to her new husband? At the very least, she would need to explain her reaction to Rømer.

The only person who seemed to approve of her gesture was an Icelandic man below who threw his head back and laughed.

He'd arrived in the second conveyance. One that bore the crest of a gyrfalcon—the fierce predator of the Arctic—set against a blue field, imagery used by Iceland's independence movement. The newcomer had climbed out, but hung back, observing the contingent demanding her return with raised eyebrows and a laughing grin.

Aubrey stalked through a group of dockworkers. A cry went up when he yanked a pyrotechnic flare gun from a crate. But her brother's attire marked him as an earl and stayed their hands. "I'll not stand for it!" Aubrey cried, pointing the gun aloft, taking aim at the dirigible.

Which was when the man representing Iceland's interests sobered and rushed forward.

Valtýr's expression hardened and his hand moved to his hip, as if searching for a cutlass to sever the tethers and drop the sandbags that anchored them. Instead, he turned and walked away, barking orders as his crew scrambled into action, casting off ropes and raising sails.

Bang! Woosh!

Flames shot into the air.

She stepped back, palm pressed to her heart as she watched the Icelandic man leap on Aubrey, dropping him to the ground and yanking the flare gun from his hand.

"Your brother is an idiot of the first order," Mr. Black observed.

"A determined one," Angela agreed. "I'll not miss him. You'll let my brother Jack know I departed under duress?"

Mr. Black's lips flattened into a thin line. "If he lets me live long enough to offer an explanation."

Dockworkers hollered, pointing.

Olivia sniffed. "Is that smoke?"

Eyes wide, Angela leaned over the bulwark. A roll of canvas lashed to the side of the airship had caught fire and, for a moment, her heart stopped, half-expecting the balloon above her to ignite, for flames to crawl across its surface. Hydrogen? Helium? Aether? Would there be an explosion?

But no one seemed unduly alarmed.

Cursing, the man named Dýri snatched up a water bucket and doused the flames. *Crack!* Cold water following heat, a sharp change in temperatures had broken whatever the canvas protected. He pulled a pistol from a holster strapped to his hip. Gone was the jovial man with a drinking horn. As this one leaned over the gunwale and aimed at a British lord, his expression took on a lethal cast.

"Dýri!" Valtýr shouted. "Desist. Make yourself useful and throw our pilot a line." He spun on his heel. "Lisbet, start the engines. Hildur and I will lose the tethers."

Everyone scattered.

Grumbling about not permanently removing a clear threat, Dýri tucked away his weapon and grabbed a coil of rope. Tying off one end to a nearby post, he tossed the rope over the edge. With hands cupped around his mouth, he shouted. "Grab hold, hostage, or I'm taking control of the helm."

"Don't you dare!" the man yelled back before wrapping the rough hemp line about his arm and ankle.

Hostage?

Hand over hand, Dýri hauled him aboard.

Boots dropped onto the deck. "Val's new wife, I presume?"

"I am. Thank you very much for your assistance with my brother." Angela curtsied. "And you are?"

"Your pilot, Lauf." He swept her a bow. "Sorry to have missed the wedding, but I was detained by the ambassador to ensure the event occurred. And preventing Lord Aubrey from torching my loftskip seemed a final task in that regard. If you'll excuse me, I believe your husband wishes to depart with all due speed." He ran off.

Many people, it seemed, had colluded to make certain she married Valtýr Árnason. She was grateful to her friends, of course—this marriage was exactly what she'd wanted. But

Val's ready compliance made her wonder what, exactly, he stood to gain.

She watched her husband's crew as they worked to ready the dirigible for flight. *Her* crew? What responsibilities belonged to the captain's wife? She'd been trained to run a manor house, but this didn't remotely resemble one. Did the crew constitute her household? Questions she'd have never thought to ask before ambushing a handsome man attending an event for foreign royalty and dignitaries.

Worse, she'd caused all this... commotion. Not the best of new beginnings.

"That, Lady Olivia, is our cue to depart." Mr. Black offered his elbow as he tipped his head toward the lift. A glint stole into his eyes. "We will officially inform Lord Aubrey that the Crown rectified his sister's misstep by ensuring Valtýr Árnason upheld his duty."

"Wait!" Angela cried as they stepped away. Were those all the particulars she was to be given about her mission? Cut adrift. Left to manage on her own. "Is there no way for me to contact you?"

Mr. Black sighed. He reached into his pocket and pressed a single skeet pigeon card into her hand. "A long shot, but you might try sending a message by raven to a British ship in Reykjavik. They will forward your missive to me, but it could take months."

Her jaw dropped.

"He's teasing," Lady Olivia said as Mr. Black tugged at her elbow. "More likely only a few weeks."

The spy turned and threw Angela a wry smile over his

shoulder. "Your reputation is about to burn to a cinder, Angela Eyrúnsdóttir. Make good use of the flames."

Left alone on deck, she gathered her fur cloak tight about her and leaned into the wind, staring out over London for a long—and perhaps last—look. Beneath her silk, slipper-clad feet, floorboards shuddered and thrummed as an engine roared to life. Ropes fell away, and the dirigible bobbed gently in the wind, ready to raise them aloft.

Tempting as it was to stand there cultivating an air of melancholy while the loftskip rose into the air, Dr. McCullough had disappeared below decks. To conduct an autopsy. One at which she was expected to assist.

A fretful curiosity stole over her.

Her husband willingly cooperated with British spies. Did he believe his wife to be one as well? If so, why marry her? As a favor to gain Mr. Black's assistance in the form of a physician? What could be so disturbing about this woman's death that would inspire Valtýr to go to such lengths?

Much to do. Tend to her beleaguered fern. Investigate a strange death. Seduce her husband. She could scream. Or she could make herself useful.

For now, she chose movement over madness.

CHAPTER SEVEN

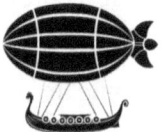

"NINE HOURS OF FLIGHT TIME," his pilot commented. A statement of the obvious laced with wry amusement. "You shouldn't waste them standing here when you've a willing woman and a room. With a bed. Four walls. And a floor."

"Here we go." Hildur groaned. "My ears need bleach."

"Not to mention the door," Lauf continued. "With hinges that open inward. Because brass nails aren't up to the task. Screws, maybe." He snorted. "But as you've banned all but crew members from—"

"Stop," Val interrupted him, but it was too late. The image of Lauf and his woman-of-the-afternoon sprawled on the floor atop a broken door, oblivious to onlookers as their mutual efforts crested with a climax. The loud crash had brought the entire crew running, weapons drawn, in time to witness Lauf's bare—

"Don't." Hildur snapped her fingers in front of his face.

"The more you turn an image over in your mind, the deeper the memory is engraved." Her lips pursed. "But he's not wrong. You chose this path. Walk it. Go work on convincing your bride not to divorce your sorry arse."

Snow-dusted fields stretched to the horizon. Not another airship in sight. They'd long since cleared London's airspace and Lauf had locked in the coordinates for their Glasgow destination—St. Roblox Glassworks. One unavoidable stop remained before flying home to Iceland with fully laden cargo bays. His crew members were more than capable of handling the loftskip. There was no reason for him to remain on the bridge. Yet his feet refused to move.

The easy part of his marriage was over.

He had two days to prove himself to Angela before she would learn the truth. Of his fiancée. Of her—potential—high-ranking fae relative. And if Sigríður Guðjónsdóttir, councilwoman, was indeed Angela's great aunt, divorce might be the least of his worries, as Hel herself would be summoned to claw Val into her underworld realm.

Keeping secrets from his wife was a slippery slope. Inform her outright and risk being barred from her bed? Hide certain truths in hopes of strengthening the fragile bond between them? Such were his choices. Both prospects equally terrifying, if for different reasons.

And that was before he began peeling back the layers of secrets he kept hidden carefully away.

Rømer's eyes had glowed with malevolence, his stare fixed upon Val with a promise of vengeance. It wasn't like the man—or hadn't been—to pursue a lost cause. Did he chase after Angela? Did he wish to reclaim Katla's body from the airship's hold? Both? What factors might be in play that Val had yet to consider?

Answering those questions meant he needed to learn all there was to know about his wife. A much more pleasant prospect than the problem of Katla's remains.

A hollow ache spread inside his chest. He'd never intended to build foundations atop lies. Val cleared his throat. "We'll need to replace at least one of the photobioreactors. Or contract for a tether." What were the odds of contracting a tow ship leaving Glasgow in the next few days?

That damned flare gun. Dýri had dowsed the fire, but the crackle of glass shattering beneath the folds of canvas might mean the cancellation of his experiment. He'd counted on extending the wings for additional power during the voyage home. Without solar power, they couldn't complete the journey on coal alone.

Hildur traced a *ýr*—a rune that offered protection and strength but also reminded one of the necessity of destruction before creation—upon on his forehead, then gave the mark a shove. "Off with you. Your project needs to wait. We can't repair anything with *two* spies on board."

One of whom was in his cabin and the other in the airship's hold, setting up a makeshift autopsy suite.

"What's wrong?" Lauf tossed him a curious look. "Did I miss something? Is your wife not a fan of the male form?"

That gave Val pause. Insecurity raised its ugly head and Loki laughed. He'd made assumptions. *Was* she attracted to him? He'd not imagined Angela softening beneath his touch, but what if it was an act, this entire arrangement a ploy?

"He's stalling because he's realized the error of his sneaky ways." Hildur crossed her arms and lifted an eyebrow. "She's *alone* in your cabin. A spy or two arranged your wedding. You might have spoken vows to a third. There's nothing at all in there that the British might like to know about?"

Val shrugged, glanced out at the horizon. "All the notebooks are locked away in my trunk."

She snorted. "Because no spy is ever in possession of a lock pick."

He opened his mouth, about to point out that she wouldn't be able to understand the complex mathematical model describing the interrelationships between key parameters of microalgae growth—temperature, pH, carbon dioxide and oxygen availability, availability of light and the precise nutrients required in the growth media. But he snapped his jaw shut.

He had recognized Lady Angela in the garden because they'd attended the same lecture at the Rankine Institute on capillary electromigration as a technique to separate and analyze the chemical components of *Camellia sinensis*, a plant more commonly known as tea.

A shared interest in plants. Ink-less green tattoos. Engineering knowledge.

She might well be capable of combing through his data and extracting hard won and key data points from various experimental projects that were in process. If she could manage all that, tucking a set of lock picks inside that crushing cage of a corset she wore wasn't beyond her.

"Freyja wept." He turned on his heel and strode away as Hildur laughed.

Until now, he'd managed to compartmentalize his life. But rescuing Lady Angela was a choice that trapped him between two granite rocks and applied seismic pressure. Metamorphosis was inevitable, but his destiny and the man he would become all hinged on Angela's reaction once they reached the mountain.

Regardless, he could no longer avoid his bride-of-the-moment.

Not that he had immediate plans to demonstrate the benefits of a sturdy airship captain's bed. Nor—and he cursed Lauf for planting the image in his head—ought he be contemplating how easy it would be to lift her small frame, to press her against the wall, spread her legs and tease her to a breathless peak.

He pushed open the door to his cabin and, while he certainly found the scene before him appealing, it wasn't at all what he'd expected. Half-dressed, Angela sat on the floor in a heap of billowing silk petticoats and skirts, hands clenched and lips pinched into a tight line.

The various frills and fripperies Lisbet had transported on board at the behest of Lady Olivia were scattered about, flung haphazardly. Kid leather gloves. Glass-beaded slippers. Delicate stockings embellished with intricate embroidery. Wisp-thin, gauzy undergarments. Silk corsets edged with ruffles. Bodices trimmed with ribbon and beads. A cloudlike confection of fabric that filled the lower half of his cabin.

He would regret asking. "What's wrong?"

"I've nothing to wear."

He waved a hand. "This is nothing?"

She stared back at him, her expression flat. "Not a single *practical* garment." Her voice was tight. Controlled. Angry. Despairing. "I'm on an airship with rough accommodations, married to a Viking of a man who has agreed to let a British physician autopsy a corpse he has stashed in his hold. An autopsy at which I've been ordered to assist." Each word rose in volume until her tirade approached that of a howling wind. "And I'm expected to dress the role of—" She swept a hand outward. "Of a pampered princess?"

He almost laughed. Almost. But mirth would paint him in a bad light. Nor did he wish to speculate about the chaotic eruption her surname might trigger among the council. If her grandmother was indeed Eyrún Guðjónsdóttir, there would be time enough to inform his wife of her high rank within the huldufólk, after which he would explain the squabble over Eldskrift and the reason Angela's grandmother left the mountain for England. Not before.

Irritation prickled at the back of his neck. He rubbed at it and growled as he told a half truth. "All gossip is focused on the royal wedding. Iceland is not known for luxuries, nor airship captains for providing them. Lady Olivia and Lisbet thought to do you a favor." Not that he expected to be among the honored guests. But there was a chance his wife might stand at another man's side during the ceremony if Val failed

86

to convince her otherwise. "For today, you can wear something of mine. Practical enough?"

"Will that work?" She scanned his form, then met his gaze. "You're rather large."

Heat flooded his body. Innuendo? Was she teasing him? No. Such was wishful thinking. He must be misreading the speculative look on her face. They were discussing proper autopsy attire, not him. Not that his groin cared. Was he doomed to spend the day half-erect, his balls perpetually blue?

Likely.

She was his wife now. Legally bound in two countries. And yet...

He exhaled slowly, contemplating all the truths not yet spoken. What would she think of him when she learned the whole? Of his lie of omission? Yet he couldn't bring himself to speak to her of Sóllilja, of their temporary arrangement. Not until his head cleared, until he was more sure of his new bride. Until Angela knew more of her heritage, until he was certain she wasn't a British spy, he'd do better to keep her at an arm's length, no matter his baser instincts.

"My clothing will have to do." Skirting the edge of the garment explosion, Val lifted his wife from the floor and deposited her on the bed which was, mostly, fabric free. He sat beside her. "Are you in a rush to join the doctor?"

Pressed upward and squeezed tight against the thin linen of her chemise, her breasts were in danger of spilling over the top of her corset. He ached to aid in their escape. She smelled like a summer's night when the angelica flowers were in full bloom—fresh, green and spicy—and he was struck by an impulse to tumble her backward onto the mattress, to peel away the remaining layers of her clothes, to—

A virgin, he reminded himself. And off limits until he severed ties with his fiancée.

He snapped his gaze upward and found a thoughtful—and not at all innocent—smile tugging at her lips.

"Yours? This shirt would do nicely," she purred, leaning forward to free the top button. A fingertip landed at the notch of his neck and trailed downward across his skin until it hooked upon the next button. "Should I take it off?"

Nor was there any reason to take things slowly. Perhaps he'd been overly hasty, dismissing the advice of his crew. If she was a spy for the British, keeping her close—on his airship and in his bed—would do more to keep her from listening at doors and poking her nose into political affairs.

"Help yourself." His offer slipped out, his voice low and gravel-edged.

Though his heart pounded, he held perfectly still, letting her take her time. Button by button, she worked her way down, her fingers a slow and tentative tease. Every movement calculated, every touch deliberate. She smoothed her palms over the crisp hairs of his chest, then slid them up to his shoulders, her fingertips trembling slightly as she pushed the fabric free. A quiet dare wrapped in vulnerability while she played at stealing his shirt.

He waited.

Leaning forward, she kissed the corner of his lips. Then

her palm swept along the edge of his jaw, turning his mouth to hers.

And he was lost.

What started soft and sweet quickly deepened, growing hungry. A kiss charged with everything their first had lacked. Together they fell—this time with him on top—landing on a far more forgiving surface than a leafless shrub. Her fingers threaded into his hair as he parted her lips and slid his tongue into the warm, waiting heat of her mouth. Sweet became desperate. Caution melted into claim.

Never before had he brought a woman to his cabin, led them to this particular bed, lest they form expectations. But wasn't that exactly what a marriage certificate provided? Possessive instincts dug in and screamed. *Mine. His. Hers. Theirs.* No one would stop him. *Her. Them.*

Her fingers fisted in the loose fabric of his shirt. She wrenched her mouth away. "Skin." Her word was a plea. "More skin."

Only a few buttons, a few laces. Perhaps a buckle or two. Then he would toss every single scrap of clothing on the floor and spread her bare beneath him on his sheets. Explore her at his pleasure. Find what made her cry out. Finally, at long last, he'd sink into her wet heat, chasing ecstasy and world-changing satisfaction.

They'd spoken vows. Made promises. One final step remained to seal their marriage, and every cell in his body screamed at him to stake a claim. But doing so would not irrevocably bind her to him. Not within the huldufólk tradition. Nor was he about to prey on her belief that the physical act would. He wanted partnership in their relationship, not subservience. And above all, trust. And that required time.

She arched her back and her tempting breasts rose. Her pelvis pushed against the painfully hard length of his cock, and the soft moan that escaped her throat was nearly his undoing.

Did she truly desire him, or was seduction a part of her assignment? Could he trust her? He didn't know. This needed to stop. *He* needed to stop.

Swallowing back a growl of frustration, he flipped his bride onto her stomach and began working at the tight knots of her corset strings, ones tied so very tightly she could not possibly untie herself. Which only presented him with new fantasies of hiking up her hips, of propping her on her knees, of taking her from behind.

At last, the knot gave way. With her free of her bindings, he slid from the mattress and took a step away. Distance. A few minutes beyond her reach, beyond her touch, would help.

Nothing shut down his libido faster than recalling why Katla occupied a pine box in his ship's hold. Dead from unusual causes, ones that had attracted the attention of the British. That Rømer was behind it all. That all of this was his own fault.

That he'd dragged Angela into the mess.

A shard of ice stabbed into his gut. Val regretted showing Rømer his green tattoos, regretted answering questions about the huldufólk, regretted showing his former friend the loose pages of an ancient book he'd "borrowed" from a locked drawer in his uncle's desk.

Vibrating with excitement, the alchemist had taken copious notes and tucked himself in a corner of a laboratory to conduct experiments he refused to explain or allow Val to examine.

"Soon," Rømer had promised. "A few more trials to confirm my findings, then I'll show you what I've discovered."

He never had.

Annoyed, Val had nonetheless left Rømer to his work, only to return a few days later to find the man missing, to be told the alchemist had returned home. Without warning. Without taking a degree. But with all of his notes.

No matter how many clockwork ravens Val sent winging Rømer's way, none had ever been seen again. Nor had a visit to the man's home, deserted from the looks of it, yielded better results. Rust-flaked wrought-iron gates. Tall windows covered with grime, a few broken. Moss spreading across roof tiles. He'd stood before the immense oak door and knocked. But not so much as a disgruntled servant cracked the door to investigate the noise.

At the end of the academic term, Val had returned to Iceland where he found his Uncle Aron pacing the laboratory, frustrated. Guilt-ridden, Val quietly slipped the "borrowed" vellum pages back into his uncle's desk drawer and applied his engineering skills to solve his uncle's research difficulties.

He had kept his silence, almost convincing himself that he'd done nothing wrong.

Until Rømer lured Katla away from Reykjavik, disappearing with her to his home in the distant Norwegian forest.

Until she sent a message from beneath London.

Now she was dead. Dull brown crystalline runes marred her skin. A bottle of Tyrian Absinthe found in her possession, spirits she wished to gift him in exchange for what? Safety? Information? Both? What stories of the past years—and of Rømer—might she have told?

A shimmer of frost coated his skin. Did her strange tattoos have anything to do with the runes written on the pages Val had shown the alchemist? He rather thought they did. Which meant this was his responsibility to set right.

Angela rolled onto her side, pressing a hand to her now-gaping corset as she looked up at him, confused. "Valtýr? Is something wrong?"

"No." He shoved his fingers into his hair. "Only that our marriage was rushed. We shouldn't—" The words threatened to choke him. "We should wait."

Her mouth fell open. "For what?" Words formed by full lips that could even now be on him. Around him.

This was self-inflicted torture.

In her world, men took and woman gave. It wasn't much different in his. But he didn't want a hasty coupling, didn't want a marriage devoid of affection and companionship. He wanted her body and soul.

And it was too soon for that.

He fell back on a convenient excuse. "For a time when we won't be interrupted."

But she wouldn't let go. "Is bedding the bride not one of your traditions?"

His laugh was rueful. "It is. Non-consummation is grounds for dissolving a marriage. Adultery and violence are reasons for a divorce. Yet, though there is nothing in the law about trust and honesty, I would have that first. Can we promise each other that this very moment?"

Wounded, her mouth snapped shut.

But he refused to apologize. "No. We can't. And so we'll wait."

Buttoning his shirt, he turned away, needing his blood in his brain, not heavy between his thighs, and unlocked his trunk. Flipping up the lid, he snatched out his notebook. Innocent or spy? Hard to say. Her commitment to escaping England seemed real, but he found her passionate kisses suspect. Were they laced with desire? Yes. But for him? Or merely to secure her position as his wife? How could he possibly judge when he knew so very little about her? At best, she'd chosen him for his nationality. At worst, she would spy upon him and turn any secrets over to the British.

Not that he could claim the higher ground. He'd wanted her, yes. For herself, but also because she might be the lost granddaughter of the legendary Eyrún Guðjónsdóttir. He wasn't above establishing social ties by the most old-fashioned of means, even if it soured some of his crew against his marriage.

Would his decision blow up in his face? Possibly. But it

was done. If he was going to carry, push and pull the huldufólk—and all of Iceland—into a future capable of tapping into the island's geothermal forces, he couldn't afford to be distracted by an emotion as base as lust. Especially not when it might turn the whole of the council against him. Which was why he needed to do more than bed his bride.

"Take whatever you'd feel most comfortable wearing aboard the ship," he said. "Female members of my crew often wear trousers for ease of movement. You'll be safe around them. Dýri is crude, but mostly harmless. When you're done with the autopsy, a tour of the airship can be arranged. We've a brief stop in Glasgow this evening to pick up supplies and to drop off Dr. McCullough before heading home to Iceland."

He turned and fled. Before he was tempted to say—or do —anything more.

CHAPTER EIGHT

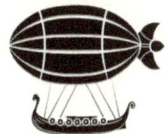

ANGELA GAVE HERSELF A MENTAL SLAP. Throwing a fit over a pile of expensive clothing? Pointless. Failing to seduce a handsome new husband? Utterly embarrassing.

All those glorious tattoos beneath her palms and barely a moment to study them before his kiss overwhelmed her, melting her bones with raw heat as he tumbled her onto his mattress. She'd felt the hard evidence of his interest. He'd admitted as much. But a need for trust and honesty had stopped him? Did he think her a spy? He might. Mr. Black and Olivia had not been hiding anything.

Still, there was an element of guilt written across his face. Did he hold some deep secret close, one he thought might turn her against him if she knew? Possibly, though she couldn't begin to guess at what. Her new husband seemed to possess a strong moral compass. A relief, given the family she'd abandoned in London. Though the loftskip was packed with crates and barrels. Was he involved in smuggling items he did not wish the British to know about? Possibly.

A shiver ran through her. What had she been thinking, attempting to seduce an airship pirate? She was in over her head. She was no societal liaison. Not when the duchess had argued in favor of Eirik Rømer. Did that make her a Queen's agent? Were Mr. Black's orders binding? He'd arranged and attended her wedding. But had done so out of a responsibility to Olivia, his employer's daughter. Did his orders to report on the autopsy place her under obligation?

Perhaps. But it was a questionable loyalty.

She'd not been issued a TTX pistol. Not that there'd been time. Still, she'd thought somewhere, buried in all the fripperies Olivia purchased, there'd be small practical items matching her instructions and befitting the wife of an airship captain. Instead of weapons or lock picks or so much as a wool day dress, she'd found nothing but fancy clothing useful only for presenting oneself to royalty.

Everything smacked of a hasty outfitting effort given little forethought. Which it was. Her fault for foisting her impulsive plans upon her friend. Olivia had done her best.

Too many conflicting emotions burned in her chest and roiled in her stomach. Logic dictated this marriage. Or so she'd told herself. Anything to escape her brother's clutches.

Where did that leave her? Not a societal liaison. Not a Queen's agent. Where was she to place her allegiance?

An excellent question.

All the energy she'd expended—escaping, marrying, seducing—left her hollow and confused. Her frustration and confusion, she decided, was nothing more than a severe identity crisis. Without a clear and coherent mandate, her loyalty was first and foremost to herself.

Still, she'd accepted help from a societal liaison and a spymaster. Which made her a British asset. A spy of sorts, if one with dubious loyalty. And spies did not indulge in emotions. Certainly not without putting them to good, manipulative value. The role was new to her and she was improvising on the fly after not sleeping for days. But, if stories were to be believed, seducing a willing man ought not be so difficult.

Had she been too forward, seeking his attention in broad daylight? Perhaps he'd found her enthusiastic reaction to his touch an unattractive trait in a new bride?

No. She'd felt him, hard and hot against her thigh when suddenly he'd changed his mind, snatched up a notebook and hurried from the cabin. He'd mentioned experiments the other evening. Perhaps he had work that required attention.

She sighed. No point in turning herself inside out when she barely knew the man. Instead, her time would be better spent in motion assessing the situation aboard this Vikingesque aircraft while fulfilling her various assigned and assumed roles. She'd decide what to do with the collected information later.

She took a deep breath. Exhaled slowly. And thought past the muddle she'd let her mind become. Regroup and redirect. She was a trained scientist and answering questions required a plan to gather appropriate data. Chin lifted, jaw set, she sprang from the bed. Her first sequence of tasks was an easy one: settle in her fern, sort through a selection of shirts and trousers that were at least two sizes too large, dress, then find Dr. McCullough.

The captain's quarters possessed two windows. Stretching beneath was a wide bench with cushions. A private place to sit half undressed and bask in the sun. To feed tattoos. Provided the airship pointed in the right direction, of course. Much as the sun's rays called to her, such indolence needed to wait. For now, her fern would serve as her placeholder.

Tugging the poor, much-abused plant from her vasculum, she pulled away the tissue paper and set her experiment upon the bench. Then frowned at its beleaguered appearance. Its once-lush fronds had turned a sickly yellow-green and drooped in surrender. The tips had browned and curled like burnt paper, brittle and crumbling. The fern was a ghost of its former self—and not at all red.

Another failure. She expected the plant would be dead by morning. Disappointing, if not surprising.

Which meant her test tubes filled with dinocysts were all that much more important. In a day or two, the airship would tether in Iceland. She glanced at a map of Iceland pinned to the wall above a desk. Hot spring by hot spring, she would explore them all. If the fire fern existed, she would find it.

Time to dress for an autopsy.

She dug deep into her husband's trunk, bypassing all the finer fabrics to yank out an old, plain and wrinkled shirt from the bottom. No point in ruining his best. Next, she hauled out dark blue breeches with brass buttons. She tugged the linen shirt over her head and fastened the cuffs. The sleeves ballooned outward and swallowed her hands. A problem easily fixed with a pair of tooled leather arm bracers. The wool trousers she kept from falling from her hips to her knees by hoisting them into place and securing them with suspenders. This in turn revealed another issue—the breeches gaped at her waist in a most unalluring manner. Not acceptable when her groom still needed seducing.

She frowned. This wouldn't do. Not for a woman married to the ship's captain. Heaving another sigh, she scanned the heap of silk and satin at her feet. And plucked a bodice with over-the shoulder straps. A bodice that laced up the front. A silk sash tied about her waist completed the look —and hid the fabric bunched at her hips. With that, there was nothing left but to button her boots and throw a cloak over her shoulders.

The Viking and his pirate bride. Or was that the Viking pirate and his bride?

Both worked.

She opened the door, stiffened her spine and stepped into the hallway. Avoidance was no longer an option, much as the oozy feeling that welled up in her stomach urged her to find a way to shirk her duty.

The physician would disembark when they reached Glasgow. But what if there were *more* autopsies yet to come? The floor heaved, then dropped from beneath. Her skin grew clammy. Skin. Her particular anatomical expertise was superficial and stopped at dermatology. Valtýr and Mr. Black couldn't possibly expect *her* to go... deeper. Would they?

Freyja help her.

On the cold, windy deck, she found Dýri perched on a barrel trimming his nails with a ten-inch knife. He surveyed her attire with sharp interest and an upturned twist to his lips.

Angela was not amused. She narrowed her eyes. "Can you lead me to the dead body?" A question that ought wipe the grin spreading across his face.

It worked. With a sober expression, he jerked his chin at a hatch in the decking, sliding his knife into a sheath at his hip as she walked past. "Fastest fuck ever."

Face carefully bland, she ignored him. Certain members of the male species possessed no ability to filter the lewd comments that flitted through their tiny brains. This wasn't the first harassment she'd endured, nor likely the last. It did, however, stand out as the most vulgar.

"I told him marrying you was a bad idea." A taunt spoken on a long, disgusted exhale.

Her efforts at indifference failed and her glance flickered. But she kept walking.

"There's only ever trouble when the upper crust marries with haste," he continued, unsolicited. "Whatever it is they're after, they rarely achieve it." His expression grew calculating. "But it's done. And should make things around here more interesting." He snorted and shook off his dire prediction. "Try not to hold your deflowering against the captain. He's not had a woman in his bunk in ages, let alone a princess. I expect he'll do better next time. If he doesn't," Dýri waggled his eyebrows, "I'll give him some pointers."

That brought her up short. This couldn't stand. Shoring up the validity of their marriage took priority. "Don't bother." She slid him a coy smile. "My husband exceeded all expectations." And she climbed down the ladder.

"Wait." He leaned over the hatch. "You're telling me..."

Ignoring him, she scanned the hold, letting her eyes adjust to the near darkness. Blue-white orbs of bioluminescent lamps swayed in nets overhead, illuminating a narrow pathway that led between bales of hay, sacks of oats, and other assorted items.

Thunk. Dýri's feet hit the planks. Hard. "Val with a wife. Never thought I'd see the day. Looking to survey his wealth?"

"Why not?" She struck out into the belly of the airship. "What's his is mine."

"Princess, if it's a life of luxury you're after, you ought to have skipped the wedding and just begged a ride home instead."

"Stop calling me princess."

He trailed along behind her. "When you could stand beside Sigríður Guðjónsdóttir in the inner circle and make eyes at future jarls?"

Guðjónsdóttir? The same surname as Grandmother. Before she'd married, of course. Did that mean she had family in Iceland? A distant relative, perhaps a great aunt? One who ranked. Her heart swelled as excitement grew. Save for her brother Jack, her family had been nothing but a thorn-filled thicket to be navigated with extreme caution.

Might still be. After all, Grandmother had fled her rela-

ANNE RENWICK

tives. And a woman known to Dýri would be known to Valtýr. Known to the rest of the crew. Yet all failed to mention this not-so-insignificant fact until after she'd spoken vows?

"You didn't know." He snorted. "Are you reconsidering your tale of Val's talents?"

Frigg. The smallest hitch in her step had given her away. Dýri was a pain in the arse, but an observant one. She'd have to be more careful. Slamming her lips together to hold back any ill-considered retorts, she forced her feet to keep moving. Where was Dr. McCullough?

"No. You don't. You have no idea." Dýri laughed. "This'll be fun."

The pungent smell of decay reached out and invaded her nostrils. Reluctantly, she sought out the source of the foul odor.

This time, Dýri didn't follow.

The doctor, who bore a suspiciously familial resemblance to Mr. Black, had tucked himself into a storage bay, repurposing crates, barrels and boards to construct a makeshift autopsy space. Bright lights hung from overhead hooks. As did a scale for weighing—she squinted—abdominal organs. A liver at present. Her stomach roiled. Nearby, a bloodstained cloth covered a deep bowl, the likely contents of which made her glad she'd not yet eaten.

"About time you arrived," Dr. McCullough grumbled, barely glancing in her direction as he placed a powered, toothed saw at the base of the woman's exposed skull.

Wouldn't it be easier to extract the brain from the top?

Cancel that thought, she wasn't asking. At least the corpse was, mercifully, face-down upon a length of waxed sailcloth stretched atop a long board.

Instead she opened by setting a clear boundary. "My expertise is dermatology." Any help she could offer would be skin deep. Literally. "There are histopathological changes to her skin?"

"Many." He threw back the cloth covering the woman's nakedness, exposing her from the waist up. "Her shoulders and arms are marked with long twisting strings of runes. At first, I believed them to be ink-based tattoos, but the marks appear crystalline."

Runes.

Of late it had become fashionable among those romanticizing the Viking age to tattoo themselves with various runes, claiming magical significance. These particular runes were of the older variety, Elder Futhark. Or Fuþark, if one replaced the modern "th" approximation with the more appropriate "thorn" letter of Þ or þ used in Old Norse.

She touched a fingertip to the reddish-brown marks. They were smooth and hard to the touch, unlike any tattoos she'd encountered before. "Unusual." A neutral comment the doctor would take to be based on traditional ink tattoos, not her own.

"Very. If you'll take a few skin biopsies? I've a few more samples—neurological ones—to collect, then we can focus our attention on microscopic analysis. Help yourself to the necessary supplies." He jerked his head to the right, then flicked a switch, powering up the bone saw and ending all conversation.

She turned her back on his gruesome task. But even as a horrifying sound assaulted her ears and a new terrible stench filled her nostrils, she gaped at the treasure casually resting atop a wine casket. A cutting edge ZEISS microscope. Her fingers itched to reach for the controls.

A good thing, given her first impulse was to flee the scene.

The other supplies Dr. McCullough had brought with him included a heated paraffin wax bath, cassettes for embedding tissue samples, and a microtome to slice them into paper thin sections. Glass slides and coverslips along with an array of bottles filled with colorful dyes to stain the specimens completed the impressively complete histopathology laboratory setup.

As the first step of making microscope slides was tissue fixation, she filled a number of small jars with formaldehyde and placed them onto a metal tray together with a scalpel and a grease pen.

The noise stopped, but before she could move away, bone snapped and a wet sucking sound followed. A sound so awful that her stomach clenched and sent wedding mead upward to claw at the back of her throat. She closed her eyes and swallowed, waiting.

"All yours, Lady Angela."

Back stiff, she turned. Carefully fixing her gaze upon the woman's thin arm, she selected a rune. ᛒ. *Berkanan.* Representing new life after death, the letter was sufficiently complex as to offer a larger surface area of tattoo to study.

Tattoo.

Katla Dagsdóttir. The Icelandic ambassador's daughter, but the markings weren't anything like Angela's own. Had the woman been capable of hosting chlorophyll containing cells? She didn't dare ask Dr. McCullough. The possibility left open the involvement of biological plant substances. But, if so, they weren't obvious ones. When had the tattoo glazed over? In life? Only after death?

Angela's living tattoo was soft and pliant and—to the touch—no different from the rest of her skin. This tattoo was rigid and, when she pressed the stainless steel biopsy punch against the runic mark, the surface of Katla's skin gave way, cracking like a thin skim of ice.

At the funeral, Angela had stroked her grandmother's tattoo, the one that curved along the side of her face, in a final goodbye. Her final wish, that the thick makeup she normally applied to her skin not accompany her to the grave, had been honored. Though the green had faded to a faint yellow, the mark remained pliant.

Treating skin conditions with her endophytic herbal concoctions meant Angela had seen her share of inked tattoos drawn with bone char, hoof gelatin, beetle shellac, beeswax, cinnabar... the list was long. But never had she come across anyone else hosting non-human yet still-living tissue.

Katla's tattoos were, to her knowledge, unique.

Breathing through her mouth, Angela pushed through

both the epidermis and dermis down to the subcutaneous tissue. At least death meant no blood oozed. She transferred the biopsy to a specimen jar. Then she randomly selected a few more runes, until a number of samples were suspended in several tiny jars of preservative.

With that misery behind her, she settled into the routine of slide preparation, working companionably alongside the largely silent Dr. McCullough as they processed samples.

Fixed tissue was embedded into wax and cooled. Thin slices cut from the microtome were caught atop glass slides. All heated, stained and topped with cover slips. Ready at last for inspection.

She placed a slide on the microscope's stage. Looking down the viewing tube, she dialed in the focus, adjusted the illumination and stared in shock and horror at the image that resolved before her eyes. Dinoflagellates. Several of them. Though they were mostly dead, one of the tiny creatures flashed a faint red. She watched as the color faded away.

Fine hairs on the back of her neck rose as ice skittered down her spine. Someone else was attempting to revive the Eldskrift traditions? By using whole live free-living dinofla-gellates? The ensuing infection would overwhelm the immune system and swiftly kill any victim of such a horribly unethical experiment. She glanced at the sickly thin corpse, amazed the woman managed to survive long enough for the inscribed tattoos to heal.

Who would do such a thing?

Eirik Rømer. A man who did not find murder to be an impediment. Was her marriage not the escape she'd hoped?

CHAPTER NINE

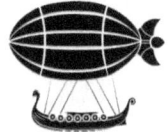

"A NYTHING?" VAL ASKED HIS SECURITY officer.

"Dull as grave dirt." Dýri snorted. "Expected better from a pair of spies. Neither of them has so much as peeked around the corner. They're in there, slicing and dicing. Barely talking except to cough out a handful of big words that probably fell out of a medical textbook and lodged in their throats."

Dýri had perched himself atop a nearby crate, the one in which they'd stored a vial of Tyrian Absinthe. Hildur and Lisbet had worked hard to squeeze the spirit-soaked canvas and, drop by drop, they'd managed to collect a little over nine milliliters of fluid. Not much, but enough to hope one of their chemists might be able to analyze the contents upon their return via liquid chromatography.

But Val was here to see if there was any progress in understanding the meaning behind the strange runic tattoos that covered Katla's body. Why had she died with a bottle of the purple absinthe in her possession? Why had Rømer been so desperate to claim Angela for himself? And what, if anything, might the alchemist's reappearance have to do with the royal wedding?

He couldn't shake the feeling that a distant clock was ticking, counting down the months, days, hours. Whose bright idea had it been to hold a grand event in such a vulnerable location? A floating castle holding Europe's most prominent royal bloodlines. The North Sea was an excellent moat, many argued. Val—and other engineers—disagreed. As did Mr. Black.

Which brought him back to his wife and the physician. He dreaded what they might discover. "The British have no reason to be against us."

Dýri scoffed. "Nor *with* us." The corner of his mouth kicked up. "Can't decide if she's a brilliant actress or not, your *wife*. I'd swear she knows nothing about her heritage." His grin widened. "Or how long a bridal bedding ought to last. Would'a been a wasted opportunity, I suppose, not swiftly laying claim to such a pretty prize. Told Hildur you'd not be able to resist. What man could?"

Wonderful. Dýri believed him a debased debaucher, incapable of resisting a willing female in his bed? Heat gathered beneath his collar as shame mixed with anger. It had been a near thing. "Not your concern."

"No worries. The princess gave you full marks for performing your marital duties. Lucky man." He hopped from the crate and punched Val in the arm. "A lusty wench with low expectations."

Val caught the man's wrist. Squeezed. "Drop the act. You know I'm not an oath-breaker. Sóllilja and I made a pact, yes. An engagement that would dissolve when one of us chose to marry." Words that wiped the smirk from his man's face. "You know as well as I who my fiancée wishes to marry, though I've warned her time and again you're too cowardly to ask."

Dýri yanked his arm away. "She wants to fight trolls."

Val cast his gaze toward the heavens. "Then let her. She's more than capable."

"She'd be ruining her life, marrying the likes of me."

"You think she'd be happy as a lady-in-waiting, dressed in silk and surrounded by frivolous gossip?"

"No."

"Then decide. And soon." Val narrowed his eyes. "But either way, I'll not have my wife—or our presumptive activities—spoken about in such terms." As captain, his was the last word. "Or you'll be finding your own way home from Glasgow."

"Noted." A grumbling agreement, after which Dýri slunk off to a dark corner to resume his watch and presumably contemplate his love life.

Braced for the unpleasantness of viewing mangled human remains, Val advanced with silent steps. Angela had helped herself to the older, rougher items buried at the bottom of his trunk. Oversized, his shirt hung from her narrow shoulders, his breeches from the flare of her hips. But an embroidered bodice wrapped around it all, nipping in her waist and pulling trousers snuggly across her backside.

Impossible not to stare, bent as she was over a microscope. A welcome distraction from the purpose of his visit, if not from the temptations this journey home would force him to confront tonight.

They'd turned the storage bay into a well-organized laboratory. Impressive, the technology arriving with Dr. McCullough. Technology that Mr. Black informed Val was his to keep. A wedding gift. He frowned. Working for a spymaster came with its perks. Though the presence of a dead and dissected body was a decided minus.

Bracing himself, he turned his attention to the autopsy. An oil cloth had been pulled over Katla's prone form, a small dignity.

Last night, before they'd set out to liberate Angela, he'd slipped off into the hold to painstakingly record the ribbons of glasslike scarified runes that twisted across Katla's skin. Anything to escape an ongoing argument between the two wives whether or not their captain ought to marry.

As a writing system, runes had been abandoned over a thousand years ago, placing those alive today at a disadvantage when confronted with such an alphabet. It didn't help that one rune followed the next without any notable spacing. He could, with effort, sound out the occasional word or phrase, but the language used was archaic and full of poetic kennings. None of it made any sense.

Once they'd made their way behind the waterfall, Val would confess his part in this mess to his mother, a practicing völva, to request assistance. Yes, his mother fancied herself a witch. No, he didn't quite believe all her prophecies. But she was right more often than not. More importantly, she easily read ancient runes and there was no better source on the history of the huldufólk in the entire mountain. With Rømer attempting to revive an old tradition best forgotten, she was the only person he trusted to advise him. So far, the Norwegian's attempts had ended in failure, but for how long?

Wiping his face clear of any expression, he stepped into the storage space. "What have you found?"

The pair of spies spun about to face him with matching expressions of confused fascination.

"Much that is strange, unique and largely inexplicable," Dr. McCullough replied. "Ladies first?"

Angela cleared her throat. "Incisions in the shape of runes were carved into her skin using a sharp blade. The reddish brown color of the runes originates from the presence of inserted biological material. Unidentifiable, unfortunately, due to its degraded state. The ink for many tattoos derives from botanical sources, which may explain a faint detectable red fluorescence." She tapped the crook of her elbow and shook her head, letting him know the tattoos weren't like their own. He knew that, but her loyalty to the huldufólk—when she might have revealed much to the British physician—filled his heart with hope, even if her words did not.

"A glow?" That worried him.

"Plant material often possesses an intrinsic fluorescence." Her explanation came with a shrug. "A natural dissipation of light absorbed by excited chlorophyll. Likely insignificant." Her words and actions were a casual dismissal, but her gaze shifted sideways.

He rethought his assessment. What if it wasn't fae loyalty? What if she was keeping secrets of her own? Something to investigate later.

"Stranger still," his wife continued, "is how the epidermal surface of her skin hardened into a thin, glasslike substance. Deeper in the dermis, I found small granular crystals, likely introduced along with the ink." She waved her hand at the physician, indicating he should speak. "But I am not qualified to speculate on the origin of such material."

The doctor took up the narrative. "Until today, such a possibility was nothing but a vague hypothesis." He all but vibrated with the excitement of discovery. "I believe this is the first example of a laboratory-created bioactive glass successfully incorporated into living tissue."

"Successfully?" Val's eyebrows rose. "She's dead." Which meant that, even after five years, the runes describing the creation of a fire guardian, an Eldvörður, had not provided Rømer with enough information, thank Odin. Not that it had stopped him from tampering with human—or rather fae—biology. "But tell me about this unusual glass. Silicon dioxide?"

Silicon dioxide was the simplest and most basic of glass formulas. Sand, essentially, if one heated the grains to their melting point, a temperature well over three-thousand degrees Fahrenheit.

Not that such was the only formula for glass. Other chemicals could be incorporated. Sodium. Calcium. Phosphorus. The industrial level glass tubes he and his crew were due to collect from the factory were made of borosilicate glass, a kind of glass capable of withstanding much thermal stress before fracturing. After all, the bioreactors he and his uncle built needed to survive the turbulence of circulating plant material. Currents, fermentation, heat, cold. And, inside the huldufólk mountain, a constant barrage of low-level earthquakes. Such was the cost of pursuing geothermal energy in a fault zone.

The doctor shrugged. "Hypothetically, the lab-created substance would be formulated to chemically bind to bone where it would form a kind of scaffold that would allow for tissue repair and hardening. Silicone, yes. But other minerals found in bone as well." He waved a hand in the air. "Impossible to know exactly until a laboratory conducts a full analysis."

Val would make certain that did not happen. "What can you tell us here and now?"

"I can tell you that this woman's existence generates more questions than answers." He whisked away a rag to reveal a bowl holding a human heart. Bloody and dark red, it glistened. Large and thick veins and arteries protruded from the crown, brutally severed. Smaller vessels branched from them, wrapping down and around the organ, splitting right and left.

Val fought a wave of nausea. A glance at Angela informed him she was likewise affected. She paled, her complexion turning a yellowish green, reminding him of a plant kept too long in the dark, deprived of sunlight. Placing an arm about her shoulders, he drew her close, steadying her. For a moment, she leaned against him. Then stiffened and pulled away. His fault. His earlier behavior had sent mixed messages. They needed to talk. Privately.

"Notice anything wrong?" the doctor prompted.

So much wrong. Beginning with the lack of a verbal warning. "I'm an engineer." Anything biological came to him second hand. "Gear ratios. Fluid mechanics. Axial load calculations..."

The doctor nodded. "But you understand the heart muscle should be pliant, capable of contracting and relaxing over and over to pump blood through the body." With a blunt-nosed steel probe, he tapped on the surface of the organ in question. There was a sharp crack, and a fissure opened. "Her heart was crystalizing. Imagine millions of tiny fractures with every heartbeat, all of them needing near instant repair to sustain life."

"Impossible," Angela whispered.

"Just so." The doctor agreed. "And yet here it is. At first, I suspected a few other diseases, but none of them are capable of coating an organ with a thin glass glaze. Nor are any known to accomplish this impossibility." He lifted a metal bowl and shook it, rattling the contents. "I collected these from her abdominal cavity."

Val looked down into a dish of clear quartz crystals. Hexagonal. With smooth faces and sharp edges. "How?" he asked. "Crystals such as this form when silicon dioxide precipitates from hydrothermal fluids. In places like steam vents when magma cools."

Dr. McCullough raised his eyebrows, offering no explanation.

How could he, when such temperatures would kill a living human. But would they kill elves, specifically the huldufólk?

What had Rømer unleashed from Hel?

With a grimace, Angela plucked a crystal from the bowl. "You believe the bioactive glass dissolved into her blood, traveled throughout her body, then fell out of solution, crystalizing in various locations?"

"If the bioactive glass was only present in hard tissues—bone, teeth, nails—she might have survived longer. But it's present in her skeletal and smooth muscle. Eating must have been torture and walking near impossible." He nodded at Val's horrified stare. "Every step, every breath, every beat of her heart would have brought her unimaginable pain."

Yet Katla managed to travel to London clutching a bottle of Tyrian Absinthe, hid herself beneath The Three-Eyed Bat, then sent multiple missives, begging Val to rescue her. Alas, the only one to reach him had arrived too late.

"Is—was—there any way to reverse her condition?" He needed to know.

The physician shook his head. "With no understanding of the substance, it's impossible to even speculate."

"What was the bioactive glass *supposed* to do?" Angela's face scrunched in deep thought. "And why? Those are the questions we ought to be asking."

Val nodded, agreeing. Not that he would speculate

aloud. Nor, it appeared, would his wife. They both kept their secrets close.

So deeply enamored with his discovery, the doctor turned back to his laboratory setup, intent upon preparing more samples, and failed to notice the charged silence.

Val could not recall references to any kind of glass—or recognizable modern chemical elements—in the ancient manuscript. Then again, his ability to read runes was rudimentary at best. Not so Rømer's.

Until Val's arrival at the Royal Frederick University in Norway, the alchemist had been delving deep into the academic library combing through old manuscripts in search of secrets and lost knowledge, convinced that the mythology preserved in the skaldic and eddic poems hid nuggets of truth. That once upon a time, the gods and goddesses of the Æsir and Vanir had lived among his ancestors. That today's descendants, no matter how removed in time, could reclaim some measure of their powers through a process of transmutation that unlocked their hereditary biological potential.

Rømer's official course of study was chemistry and Val's was engineering. Academic paths that would never have crossed, save for one fateful night in a pub. A mistake, arguing over the transformative nature of wormwood inside a bottle of absinthe.

Val cursed the day.

The dead woman's skin screamed of Rømer's direct involvement. Had he lost control of his lab rat? Had Katla, fearing for her life, scurried away, carrying with her a unique gift in hopes of winning Val's mercy?

"Why runes?" Angela asked.

"My guess?" Dr. McCullough grumbled. "A revived British interest in Norse mythology. Tattoos gone horribly wrong. The writing might provide a clue as to the identity of the perpetrator but probably isn't biologically relevant."

Val snorted. The man wasn't mistaken. But neither was he right. In Katla's case, it was a Norwegian attempting to wield ancient magic.

The alliance with Mr. Black and his minions was proving fruitful, even if it raised new concerns. Bioactive glass. Was Rømer the inventor? Possibly. Were his intentions honorable? Given a Huldu woman was dead? Doubtful.

His need to return home, to speak with his mother, grew by the moment. The chemical components of both the bioactive glass and the Tyrian Absinthe needed to be analyzed. In Iceland. By huldufólk.

"Thank you, Dr. McCullough," he said. "Is there anything more?"

The man shook his head even though, beside him, Angela's lips pressed into a thin line. She knew something. He'd learn it soon enough. After they left the good doctor behind in Scotland.

He turned on his heel and strode through the airship's hull. Dýri emerged from the shadows. Val kept his voice low. "The doctor will take samples. Be certain they are 'lost'." He hated to speak the next order aloud, but caution was warranted. "Ensure my wife continues on with us. She is not to disembark in Glasgow."

CHAPTER TEN

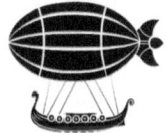

T HEY PASSED OVER GLASGOW AS THE sun dipped
below the horizon, not stopping until they'd
reached the shipyards and factories relegated to a
distant edge of the city. Below them, sparks and flames flared
as boats and steamers were built, repaired or ripped apart. A
vast junkyard stretched along the water, sorting piles of
various scrap metal by mechanical steambots and their
human overseers.

After the autopsy, Angela had returned to the captain's
quarters and washed. Sighing, she folded silk and satin and
lace, haphazardly tucking the garments into various boxes,
hesitating only briefly when her fingers wrapped around a
translucent, gossamer negligee so fine that the fabric might
have been spun by fairies.

Then she snorted. Fae.

Val couldn't seriously believe he—they—were huldufólk.

Stories of the hidden people were for children. Warnings and instruction in the form of entertainment. Nothing more.

She folded the garment and tucked it away with the others for "a time when we won't be interrupted."

Whenever that might be.

Instead of dwelling on the precariousness of her marriage, she ought to sit down at the desk with her grandmother's book of moss and ferns, see if anything in that tome might hint at an explanation for Katla's strange markings and resultant death. For years she and her grandmother had worked with the unusual dinoflagellates, trying again and again to find a fern that would welcome the single celled beings into their cells as if they were long-lost missing relatives. Then live, happily, as one organism in a symbiotic relationship. Each benefiting the other.

But, while their search turned up a handful of ferns that did—initially—take in the dinoflagellates, all sickened and died as a result. Despite the best care, her most recent plant also appeared deathly ill and not long for this life. Whispering words of apology to the poor fern, she tipped a little water over its roots, flicked some water across its fronds, and adjusted its position beside the window.

Once upon a time, or so Grandmother's story went, a red fern colony grew wild in Iceland beside a hot spring. Such were the plants harvested when new members were initiated into the Eldskrift tradition. When and why had the original plant become extinct? No one knew. But her grandmother had dreamed of re-establishing a colony of red ferns in Iceland. Angela had childhood memories of her pouring over ancient documents from Nordic countries. Of undertaking voyages to distant lands. Until the estate's greenhouse nearly burst at the welds with an enormous number of ferns growing within its glass-plate walls.

Raised on all things botany, Angela had been drawn in, intrigued by the strange challenge and keen to help. Now the task fell to her alone.

Conditions here, inside the cabin, were far from ideal. There was little humidity, and the temperature was too cool. What she needed was to run her experiments from start to finish inside a warm, humid greenhouse. Or inside a sealed Wardian glass case.

She turned to her grandmother's scribbles in the margins of her book. With the help of an Old Norse dictionary she found on Val's bookshelf, she applied herself to the runic scribblings in the margins. A difficult task at best, given how runes from three different fuþark alphabets were used—sometimes all at once—and how many runes could represent several sounds with no distinction between short and long vowels. Nor did it help that she often inked several runes atop each other, leaving her to guess at what word she might have intended. The process took an inordinate amount of time and left her doubting her choices—something Grandmother had done on purpose?

Her head was pounding when her eyes caught on Grandmother's usual assertions that the runic tattoos would glow a faint red if the procedure was successful, but none of the runes—according to Angela's translations—made mention of using glass or mineral granules. And there was no hope of her translating a word—if one even existed—for silica or quartz.

If Grandmother had scribbled anything that might connect the bioactive glass in Katla's body to the tradition of Eldskrift, Angela hadn't found it. After an hour of translation efforts, she felt her eyes cross and decided to abandon the task for the day. Time for some fresh air, no matter how cold. She was done waiting for Valtýr to come to her.

Pulling her fur cloak tight about her shoulders, she stepped out onto the deck, welcoming the icy wind that plucked at her clothing and whipped loose strands of hair about her face. She found her husband supervising dock-workers as they hoisted crate after crate aboard the airship.

Carefully. As if he had been charged with transporting all the cut crystal stemware for the royal wedding. She imagined the possibilities. The airship's hold might be filled with luxury items fit for a king and queen. Bolts of silk. Tins of tropical fruit. French wines. Alas, given the land of ice and fire was notoriously dependent upon imports—save for that of wool and fish—there were likely much more practical supplies aboard.

Save the scenario before her checked neither box. Not frivolous. Nor essential.

Instead, they were accepting delivery from an industrial glassworks factory situated at the mouth of the River Clyde. A number of boxes were some twenty-five feet in length. What could be so very long and so very fragile?

But she stood silently, so as not to disrupt proceedings,

pondering many questions and a variety of conflicting answers.

Val glanced at her, nodded a polite—if distant—greeting. "When we're done here, we depart for Iceland."

"Tonight?" She hesitated, dragging her mind from thoughts of strange tattoos. "Without any other stops?" Impossible to keep the incredulity from her voice.

"Correct."

She blinked. "Without tethering to a steam ship?"

A hint of a smile danced across her husband's lips. A confident one. He wasn't lying.

No airship could carry enough coal to travel that distance. Not even if the entirety of the hold was filled to overflowing. A woman married to an airship captain ought to understand the logistics of her new home, his loftskip— assuming he didn't intend to abandon her in some sod-roofed house and fly away.

"How?" she demanded.

"Nothing we want the Scots to learn about."

"*More* secrets?" Why not. The air was rife with them.

"There'll be no hiding them once we clear British airspace." His eyes danced with anticipation even as his voice held a note of warning. "And I intend to treasure the moment of reveal."

Valtýr Árnason confused her. He managed to appear warm and welcoming and open... all while revealing nothing. A tightly throttled Viking.

Which annoyed her. In the short time since they'd met and married, she'd seen flashes of a kind and generous man.

One willing to risk his reputation to rescue a woman from social ruin. To discuss scientific discoveries with her, treating her as an intellectual equal. To marry in haste and depart at great speed, all with the support of a loyal crew.

But save for a few promising kisses, he'd been gruff and dry today, much like the men of the crusty *ton* she'd happily left behind. What would it take to pry loose those iron bands of self-control? Not, it seemed, her half-dressed form atop his bed.

She frowned. Though he had let down his guard long enough to deliver a searing kiss, the likes of which she'd only read of in novels. Perhaps she ought to consider that a positive? Her own impatience might be the problem. She decided it was time to take a few steps backward. Perhaps a return to a scientific discussion? "Though I've barely glimpsed your tattoo," she began, "the markings on Katla's skin bear no resemblance to mine."

"Is that a request?" The corner of Val's mouth twitched. "A hint that you require more data points to study?"

Heat suffused her cheeks.

He threw back the corner of his fur-lined cape. With one hand, he unbuttoned the cuff of his shirt, turning back the fabric. Once. Twice. Three times. Movements that left her mouth dry even before he held out his arm for her inspection. A dark tangle of roots encircled his wrist, coalesced into a trunk, then branched outward, bursting into a scattering of dark green leaves across his forearm as the imagery disappeared beneath the crisp white folds of his shirt.

"Not all green?" She traced the bifurcating patterns,

allowing her fingertip to slip beneath the fabric, to caress the inner bend of his elbow. Then lifted her gaze to his.

"No reason not to incorporate artistry." He twisted his arm and threaded her fingers through his. Lifting her hand, he brushed a soft kiss across her knuckles. "Not everything needs to be functional."

A frisson of heat shot through her body, straight to her core. Where it smoldered, a fire banked low. There was hope for them, if they could find the right path."Functional?" she prodded.

A crinkle formed between his eyebrows. "Did Eyrún Guðjónsdóttir tell you so very little?"

"She held back much. Refused to speak about her life in Iceland until it was time for her to return. Death stole her away too soon."

"I'm sorry for your loss." He fell silent for a moment. The wind whipped and snapped, charged with anticipation. "I propose we trade knowledge. You'll reveal whatever it is you're hiding about Katla's death and I'll answer questions about the huldufólk."

"The hidden people again?" She smiled, indulging his teasing. "Icelandic elves. Supernatural creatures about which stories were invented to explain phenomena such as the shifting shadow cast by the strange shape of a volcanic rock."

"Not fictional. Not supernatural. Quite real." He drew her near, bending to speak in her ear. "I am one. As are you. We are Huldu."

The warmth of his breath across the side of her neck

distracted her for a moment, fogging her brain. Then she laughed. "You're not playing fair. There's no such thing as elves. Or dwarves or trolls. If such creatures existed, they'd be known. Studied and catalogued."

"Which is why we keep our secrets close." His reply held no amusement. "Even those who leave the community don't speak freely."

Her grandmother, a secret elf? Absurd. "You're serious?"

"Very." He nodded. "You're a scientist, a botanist, yes, but also a self-taught dermatologist. Explain the uniqueness of your tattoo. How many humans can you count upon this single hand," he squeezed her fingers, "who are currently in possession of a living tattoo?"

"If I include us both?" She lifted two fingers of their joined hands. "Though the color lingered in my brother Jack's skin for a few days."

"Jack?" he asked.

"The nice brother." No need to detail her many connections to the Queen's agents when her husband was finally thawing. "Who is abroad and unable to protect me from the horrid brother."

"Evidence of Jack's Huldu ancestry. But with a generation removed, it proved to be not enough." He lifted each of her fingers in turn, ending with the thumb, as he recited more names. "Hildur. Dýri. Lauf. An entire handful."

She stared at her fingers. Five people aboard this airship bore living tattoos. She glanced at Hildur, to where she stood with her wife. "Not Lisbet?"

He shook his head. "She is a Danish Hulder."

Angela squinted. "Hulder?"

"Also fae, but a distant cousin of our kind, several centuries removed. Born with tails, though many have them surgically removed, they are incapable of sustaining living green tattoos." He tapped the crook of her arm. "But you, *ástin mín*, are one of us. Huldu. Huldufólk. Elf. There are not many who manage a return."

Tails? She squinted at him, waiting for him to wink, to laugh, to... something. But he remained sober. "Fairies. Are. Not. Real."

"Believe what you will." He shrugged, releasing her hand. "Let's try a different approach. Your turn. What about Katla's tattoos left you so unsettled?"

"Beyond being composed, at least in part, of glass?" she asked. "Such a thing should not be possible."

"Yet you scoff at the idea of being Huldu?" His eyebrows rose. "Isn't all science magic until it's explained?"

He had a point. And would, she suspected, continue to maintain that she was not fully human.

As a child, she'd adored her grandmother's many stories, believing with all her heart. As an adult, she understood that the Icelandic tales of elves and trolls served a very real purpose: to discourage children from wandering alone across a harsh landscape. Nonetheless, they remained fiction.

At the age her skirts dropped to her ankles, she'd questioned Grandmother's obsession with creating a fire fern, labeling it "mythological nonsense". Which was when her grandmother dragged Angela into the greenhouse laboratory, instructing her to peer through the microscope at wonders invisible to the naked eye. Tiny creatures had flickered and flashed, swimming about by whipping tiny hairs behind them.

If tiny single-celled creatures could emit red light, was the possibility of a fire fern so outrageous?

Soon after, she'd received her first and only living tattoo. A thing of beauty that defied explanation—and her first step into botanical studies.

Moments of wonder were how scientists were forged. Just because something couldn't be explained—yet—didn't make it imaginary. But asking hard questions and insisting upon proof was a critical part of the scientific process.

"Fine." She would listen to his arguments with as open a mind as she could muster. For now, she would present him with tangible evidence. Perhaps he might offer insight. "Beneath a layer of the strange glass, in and among the crystals, were a number of dinoflagellates of a reddish-brown color."

"Dinoflagellates?" His brow furrowed. "What are those?"

"Tiny one-celled creatures in possession of two flagella, taillike structures used for motility. Botanists like to claim they are algae. Zoologists insist they are protozoa. Some possess chloroplasts, others do not. Plant or animal, the question is unsettled."

"Were the ones you found photosynthetic?" Tension

stiffened his shoulders, as if he braced for unwelcome, yet anticipated, news.

"Possibly?" She lifted a shoulder. A half-lie. For the creatures might be the same as those living inside her fern. Or of those stored in suspended animation, as dinocysts, inside her glass vials. Not that she could be certain without a proper laboratory. "The material was degraded, but their color could be attributed to a pigment similar to that found in red seaweed. I'd need a live, healthy sample to be certain."

"Which circles us back to the possibility that the runic incisions, into which glass and dinoflagellates were inserted, were meant to mimic our living, green tattoos."

"It would seem so," she agreed, then tried speaking myth as truth. "I assume Katla is—was—one of the huldufólk?"

He nodded. "Daughter of the Icelandic ambassador your friend's mother dragged along with her into the garden. He too is Huldu."

"Oh." That explained why the government official had been so very out of sorts. And perhaps why Mr. Black had insisted his physician be allowed to conduct the woman's autopsy. Her eyes swept the scene before her, locating Dr. McCullough as he climbed aboard the loading platform, about to descend to Glasgow without formally taking his leave.

Val's nod to Dýri was barely noticeable. She only caught the movement because she stood at his side. A signal of sorts to his muscled guard, who kept a close eye on the freight lift, wearing a smirk suggesting he was up to no good.

Which meant she was watching when Dýri *accidentally* let slip a single rope while lowering Dr. McCullough, tipping a corner of the platform ever so slightly, allowing the man's black bag to slide off the edge and fall into the deep brackish water of the River Clyde.

CHAPTER ELEVEN

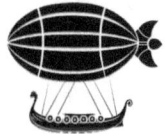

ER HAND TIGHTENED ABOUT VAL'S wrist. "Did you see that?" His jaw tensed and, in that moment, she knew the two men had arranged to prevent the British from analyzing any biopsies taken during the autopsy in their own laboratory. "You ordered Dýri to destroy those samples!" Her cape snapped in the wind, underscoring her accusation.

"Necessary, I'm afraid." His words confirmed her suspicion. "For the same reason you chose to withhold information about the tattoos from him. We are not a backward people. If the cause of Katla's death holds particular meaning for the Huldu, our own laboratory will inform us."

In other words, no secrets would be betrayed to the British Crown.

Val's stare challenged her to disagree.

She looked away.

On the ground, the doctor waved and pointed and

argued with ground crew, but Dýri shook his head, refusing to permit him back aboard the airship. Mr. Black would not be pleased. Likely he would look upon the "accident" as suspicious and demand Angela provide further insight as to the cause of Katla's death.

What would she say?

Something to meditate upon. For now, Val's move provided a measure of relief. Besides, she had never officially agreed to work for the British Crown. She had no weapon, no training. As far as she was concerned, Olivia and Mr. Black had acted in an unofficial capacity. As friends. Thereby reducing her obligation. If not erasing it.

"I thought you promised to cooperate with the British?" she pressed.

A large crate was shoved from the loading platform onto the deck. One that made Dýri frown as he flipped through pages attached to his clipboard. "This one's not ours!" he called to the dockworkers.

"Cooperation only extends so far between two nations." Val's focus fell upon this newest crate. "Something's not right."

"There's a lot that's not right," Angela agreed. "Runes carved into skin and embedded with an experimental material and bioluminescent creatures makes Katla's death especially worrisome. It spawns a lengthy list of questions, chief among them is 'who did this to her?' and 'how many more will be discovered?' and, above all 'why?'." She crossed her arms. "I suspect the answers involve Eirik Rømer and whatever it is you don't wish to share with me."

His shoulders stiffened. "Did you say 'bioluminescent'?"

Loki laughed. In her annoyance, she'd unwittingly tipped her hand. "What if I did?"

"Explain." An airship captain's hardness crept back into his expression. "This situation might have vast implications for my—our—people."

She rolled her eyes. "For the hidden elves of Iceland."

His eyes narrowed. "Yes."

Cold, hungry and tired, her frustration snapped. "Not that you've any intention of telling me why."

Her chin jutted. She refused to back down. She'd *married* this man. Tied her future to his with vows, speaking some of them in Old Norse during a ceremony that was older than time. Words she barely understood. *Freyja.* What exactly had she agreed to? A ball of ice dropped into her stomach. What if he *did* possess supernatural abilities and the words were binding in non-human ways? No. That was a ridiculous thought. She dragged in a deep breath. Wasn't it? Absolutely. Living tattoos weren't *magical.* They simply reflected the nature of a person's biological heritage. A unique variation of human biology, like skin, hair and eye color.

Dýri called Hildur to his side, pointing at the oversized crate. He waved at the hook and tackle overhead, crooking his fingers at the dockworkers, demanding they remove the box.

Voices rose as a heated argument over the removal of the disputed crate broke out.

Val shifted, as if to walk away from her without the courtesy of an explanation.

"What threat could supernatural beings possibly worry about?" she demanded. "Aren't all elves more beautiful, more handsome than mere mortals? Stronger and faster? Tell me, what magic do you possess? Able to summon fire with the mere snap of your fingers?" Rising onto the tips of her toes, she tugged at his earlobe. "Doubtful. Your ears aren't even the slightest bit pointed."

Val shifted his focus back to her. "Handsome?" With lightning speed, he spun her about and pressed her against a wall. Out of sight, protected from the wind. Somehow, he'd managed to plant himself between her knees. His fingers dug into the soft flare of her hips. "I'm glad you think so, for it's the first time I've felt like more than a convenient exit plan. Much as flames seem to spark whenever we're in close proximity, you've yet to convince me it wasn't feigned."

"You doubt our compatibility." She nodded. "A fair—"

He dipped his head and caught her lips in a slow, gentle kiss. Was it a test? Yes. One meant to fan desire, to tease, to hint at what might—finally—come next. He pulled away, leaving them both breathless. And unsatisfied.

Disconcerting how quickly he was able to tip her off balance, to leave her mind fogged with desire.

Thump. Thud. Thump, thump, thump.

"What the Hel?" Dýri cried, snatching up a crowbar.

"Everyone stand back!" Hildur instructed.

Val retrieved a knife from his boot, then left her with a simple, "Stay here."

Not likely. The crate rocked and banged. Whatever was in that crate, it wasn't industrial glass.

Curious, she followed.

"Angela." He spoke her name, an impatient warning. Then turned, snagging his wide-eyed pilot who stood, gawking at the commotion. "Lauf, take her to the bridge and bar the door. Guard her."

Lauf nodded and Val strode off without a backward glance. But she was not some delicate female who needed to be protected from viewing unpleasant things. She wanted— needed—to know what was in the box, especially as he seemed so determined to keep her from it.

She edged closer.

"Don't." Lauf caught her sleeve before she could take another step. His mouth was carved into a downturn. "Watch from here, if you must." He made no move to drag her away. Smart of him.

Crash! Wood splintered outward. A gray-skinned arm reached through the shattered crate, prying at the nailed planks that held it shut with—she squinted and her jaw fell open—three inch long claws!

"Troll!" Dýri swung at the monster's arm with the iron bar.

Crack! The sound that met Angela's ears sounded like a stoneware planter shattering on the gravel-strewn floor of a greenhouse. Jagged lines of fissures radiated outward across the troll's arm but appeared not to affect the creature a single bit. Disbelief left her gaping. How was this possible?

Dýri raised the crowbar high, twisting to bring it down

again with every ounce of strength he possessed. But this time, the troll screamed and caught the iron in its rocky fist. Electricity crackled in the air, surged from the troll's body, arched down its arm and leapt onto the crowbar, then coursed straight into Dýri with a searing jolt.

His body convulsed, muscles locking tight as the current ripped through him. The crowbar dropped with a clang. His legs buckled a heartbeat later. Dýri hit the deck hard, chest heaving, eyes wide with shock.

Hildur dragged him away from the crate, spoke low words. Yanked long wood-handle pike poles from a barrel, then jogged back to Val's side. "He's fine, sir."

"The troll electrocuted him." Val stared at the crate. "At will." He slid the blade of his knife back into its sheath.

Nodding, his first mate shoved a pike into his hand. "Seems so."

"If you choose to fight," he raised his voice at the staring dockworkers. "Use wood-shafted weapons only. Do *not* complete a circuit!" He hefted the pole, pointed it at the troll's elbow and jabbed. The cut sliced through gray skin and the creature let out a blood-curdling howl as a purplish fluid oozed from the gash. But the wound failed to slow the troll at all. If anything, the injury inspired further exertion.

A second arm reached upward and, with a giant wrenching sound, the troll pried off the side of the crate and stomped onto the deck with an ear-splitting roar. Val and Hildur fell back, crouching in anticipation of an attack.

Impossible. This couldn't be happening. Was today one long nightmare? A fitful sleep brought on by an overconsumption of wedding mead? The cold sweat that broke out across her skin suggested otherwise.

A low growl built in the creature's throat as its dark gaze scanned the enemies before it. With only mud-stained trousers to conceal its form, graveyard gray skin was on full display, including a single glittering rune carved into its chest. Though no taller than a man, the creature's bulk made it twice as wide and his form brought to mind boulders, tree trunks and roots. She gaped, staring at the troll's bulbous nose. At the pair of pointed and gnarly ears sprouting from its skull. At the riot of scraggy grasslike hair that fell from its face and sprouted from its shoulders.

She gasped as the creature turned. Glassy runes—ones that seemed to glow a faint purple—were carved into the ashy skin of the troll's back. Long strings of runes that ran in haphazard directions, forming a cross-hatched network of shimmering scar tissue atop the knobs and protrusions of the creature's spinous processes and flaring ribs. Did the marks reflect the airship's lamplight? Or was the flickering intrinsic light generated inside the troll's stoney skin?

"Bjarki?" Lauf uttered the name under his breath.

She glanced at him. "You know this... troll?"

He glanced at her but offered no explanation. She, however, needed to rethink her stance on the existence of trolls, fairies and elves.

Standing on the cabin's roof, Lisbet held a long spear aloft. "Hildur! Catch!"

Her wife turned, reaching an arm and an open hand, catching a long wooden shaft with a silver tip that glistened with an oily sheen. "Nobody move!" In a deep crouch, Hildur circled the troll, spear in two hands. The troll snarled, revealing broken and rotting teeth, and flexed its long, talonlike claws. Each of them sized up the other, looking for weaknesses, ready to attack, while everyone aboard fell silent and still, a collective holding of breaths.

Then a dockworker broke free and ran for the loading platform. Others followed, yanking at ropes and began a descent far, far too fast. The platform tipped and, this time, a man fell screaming into the water below.

The troll lunged and Hildur attacked, jabbing at the creature's knee. But the tip of the spear slid down near-impenetrable gray skin to lodge in the troll's ankle.

There was a brief sizzle, then *bang!* The spearhead exploded in a shower of sparks and smoke—taking the troll's foot with it.

Arms flailing, the creature threw his head back and howled in agony. But it didn't lose balance. Didn't so much as stagger. Instead, it stood there, lungs heaving. Waiting.

Hildur's gaze remained focused on its foot. "Val! What the Hel? Are you seeing this?"

Purplish blood congealed, then crystalized into a glistening rock-hard scab.

Was that—Angela squinted—amethyst?

The creature tapped the stump of its foot on the footboards of the deck. *Thump. Thump. Thump.* Testing the repair. Slowly, cautiously, it stepped forward. *Tap. Thunk. Tap, thunk.*

"Lisbet." Val's voice managed to be both calm and loud.

"The tröllabanar bow and arrows as well. The entire quiver, if you please."

The troll's head snapped up and its gaze met hers. An unholy light filled the creature's eyes. Its nostrils flared, catching her scent. Val was right—she ought to have hidden behind four safe walls. She'd do that now. Angela took a step backward. Then another. A few more steps and she would reach the door, slam it behind her and pray that one of Val's arrows found its neck.

But the monster anticipated her plan. With a roar, the troll galloped forward on one foot and a stump, the lop-sided gait not slowing it one bit.

She turned and dove for the door a moment too late. Before she crossed the threshold, a meaty fist wrapped around her ankle and pulled her backward, screaming—until a rock-hard arm crushed her ribs and cut off her air. She kicked, clawed. But to no avail. The troll's skin was made of tempered glass.

"Angela!" Val caught at her arm, but the troll backhanded him, tossing him easily aside.

The creature scooped her under its arm, crushing her to its body as it loped to the airship's side. "Mine," it growled. "Ours. His."

Then it leapt from the airship.

Her heart lodged in her throat as the ground raced upward, bringing with it certain death.

CHAPTER TWELVE

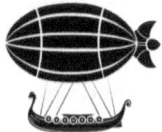

Horrified, Val watched as—at the last possible moment—the troll caught a rope in its giant fist. Not a complete free-fall, thank Odin. But there she was, hanging from a rope. Twice in as many days.

Her grandmother had done her no favors by withholding the full truth of the huldufólk. Running from a troll was the worst thing a person could do. Many would call him a fool, repeatedly rescuing a damsel in distress. Yet he'd sworn his life to hers, lifting a ring from the hilt of his sword and slipping it onto her finger. Did that explain the burning need to protect her? No. This went beyond personal responsibility. It felt like *inn mátki munr*, a mighty passion. Romantic love.

Was it? Did it matter? Their fates were entwined, and he wished to keep it so.

With a bone-deep longing, he wanted to walk with her behind the waterfall as his acknowledged wife. Greedy? Yes.

But after years of self-denial, this was the first woman that made him care about anything other than his airship and his crew. Angela was his.

She would not die in the clutches of a rogue troll.

"Arrows!" What was taking so long? "Where are the tröllabanar!" Without the right weapon, killing a troll was near to impossible. He held out his hand, afraid to take his eyes off the fleeing troll in the gathering gloom.

A leather cylinder slapped against his palm and he slung the quiver strap across his chest.

"Other side," Hildur yelled, then threw the strap of a crossbow over his head. "Go. I'll follow."

He couldn't afford to lose Angela. Sólættir. Spy. Wife. Was she valuable? Beyond compare. But so were the lives of his crew. "No." He yanked his leather belt free and threw the strap over an angled tether line, one that would drop him in close pursuit. "Not with Dýri injured. A troll makes for an excellent diversion. Who knows what might be next? Stay. Guard the airship."

Hands wrapped tight about the ends of the strap, he jumped. A fast, rough slide down the thick twisted rope as freezing wind clawed through his hair and yanked at his clothing. Then his boots hit the hard-packed ground of the junkyard, jarring every bone from his ankles to his skull in rapid succession. Shaking off the jolt, he ran, grateful for the sparks thrown by the arc welders disassembling all manner of items into scrap, if not for the miasma of burning metal and smoldering coal.

Occasional shouts rang out as the troll galumphed at

great speed past rusty turbines, oil drums and propellors. Val followed, setting his path according to the hollers of workmen and the sounds of crashing metal. Trolls weren't known for subtle movements and this one lacked a foot. Occasionally, he caught glimpses of the amethyst troll with his wife's limp body tucked under one arm.

What did trolls love above all else? Caves. And this one was no different. Injured, it instinctively sought out the closest structure that resembled one. The burnt out hull of a wrecked steamer ship that had been driven onto Port Glasgow's rocky beach. The front half of the ship had already been scrapped for iron exposing the vessel's innards and leaving a gaping wound that would allow the troll easy access.

Val needed to take a shot before they disappeared into its cavernous darkness.

He sprinted, darting up a stack of old drums secured by fishing nets. At the summit, he planted his feet, swung the crossbow into position and drew an oil-coated potassium arrow from the quiver. Notoriously hard to kill, his people had long-ago discovered a solution. When the element came into contact with troll body fluids, there was an explosive chemical reaction. Coating swords and arrows and spears had become the Huldus' approach to stopping the jötunn.

Traditionally, a lightning strike would be best. But the creature appeared to possess the power of Thor itself. A new never-before-seen feature in a basalt troll.

Gray, gravely skin was normal. As was blood that bled purple and scarified into glassy amethyst expected, if not its incredible healing speed. A feature perhaps linked to the bolt of electricity the troll had directed at Dýri? And that was before they addressed the glowing runes carved into the creature's back, marks that his gut knew, with a deep-seated twist, were chiseled into the troll's back by Rømer's own hands. Or that of his minions. A terrifying thought, that the alchemist might have recruited others to his experiments.

For now, he needed to focus on stopping this voltaic troll without hurting Angela.

Good that she was limp, draped over the troll's arm, allowing him to aim for the troll's head.

Quickly, he notched the arrow, raised the crossbow, placed the creature's skull in the cross hairs and pulled the trigger a moment before the creature disappeared into the ship's hull.

Woosh!

He ran down the mountain of oil drums as a satisfying bellow of pain echoed from inside the steamer's hull. He'd hit the troll. But the creature still lived.

Not that Val had counted on a single arrow stopping that muscular pile of moving rocks. Without breaking his stride, he ripped a headlamp from a roving steambot and pointed the beam of light into the ship, swinging it wide, searching as he stepped into the wrecked vessel.

Wires hung like cobwebs. Broken and bent pipes dripped unidentifiable fluid. An anchor lay beside a coil of chain. A flash shimmered in the dim light—Angela's golden hair, a beacon.

The troll turned its head, glowering. The arrow had

delivered more than a glancing blow, but not enough to incapacitate. A dull glimmer of purple coated an entire side of the creature's face, one that was rapidly solidifying into crystalline stone and obscuring the troll's vision.

Not that such slowed the determined jötunn.

The troll was climbing a leaning metal staircase, using one leg and an arm to balance as it limped upward, moving with surprising speed toward a lifeboat that hung from the rope of its davit, already half-suspended above the water.

Hel. Proximity to potassium and water could induce a deadly combination. Nothing had gone right since they'd tethered in London. Not one damn—

No, he'd found Angela. And he'd not be losing her again so very soon.

He'd expected the creature to hide, to barricade itself inside the engine room. But this jötunn was fixated upon escape, rather than exhibiting more common, if dull-witted, oriented troll behaviors. This task-focused behavior in the face of a threat was unusual. Was it under orders? Trolls weren't known for responding to authority of any kind, short of a direct threat.

Anger washed over him. Rømer had to be behind this. Who else would deliberately crate a troll and deliver it to his airship? Patience was not a troll trait, but the creature had waited, quietly, until the wooden box landed on his deck. Then it had burst forth, searching for its prey. This was an abduction. Someone had known of Val's glassworks order, of Angela, and plotted against him.

Why pursue her so intensely? Val suspected Rømer had

learned of her heritage, that the alchemist had plans for her. Specifically, ones involving red glowing runes. He very much doubted there would be a ransom demand. Angela would simply... disappear.

The troll had to be stopped.

Val followed, climbing the canted stairs like a ladder. The soles of his boots thudded softly on the treads, but the sound was enough to catch the creature's attention.

The troll glanced over its shoulder, growled, then tossed Angela—still unconscious—in the lifeboat and clambered in beside her. A callous move that made Val fear for her very life. A head injury. A broken neck.

And that was before he accounted for the electricity the creature had used to zap Dýri.

As the small watercraft swung unsteadily, the troll pulled a lever with a fat fist and the lifeboat's crane dropped them into the water with a loud splash. Without the slightest of hesitations, the creature grabbed a paddle and set to work. Not far from the shore, the gas light of a lighthouse beacon flickered from a small rocky island, warning ships that they entered the Firth of Clyde.

Above, a small dirigible hovered. A rope dangled from its side. Waiting to haul his wife aboard.

Rage filled Val's chest. He notched a potassium arrow into his crossbow. Stopping the troll's progress before it reached the small island was the only solution.

Launching one of the other lifeboats in pursuit was an option, but there was no matching the strength of the jötunn. Val might be fast, but no Huldu could hope to equal a troll's craggy strength. Even if he could catch it, hand-to-hand combat with a troll was ill-advised, especially without solid ground beneath his feet. A single blow from that gravelly fist could knock a man—an elf—unconscious. He'd be left to drown.

The first arrow flew astray, missing the troll and the boat. It pierced the water's surface and exploded. The troll roared and paddled faster.

Angela stirred and lifted her head, blinking. Not dead. Not gravely injured. Yet.

Val cursed as he drew another arrow. No time to hesitate, not with a widening gap. His second arrow lodged in the troll's shoulder. A shower of sparks, a column of smoke, a howl. And when it cleared, he confirmed the creature had lost a limb.

With only one arm, the troll paddled onward, ignoring the sparks that kindled a small but growing flame. The old, dry wood of the lifeboat had caught fire, one that was growing by the minute.

Frigg and Hel.

Hands gripping the side of the boat, Angela hauled herself halfway over its edge. He notched another arrow, praying to all the gods that this one would lodge in the troll's spine.

But the opportunity to fire again was stolen away when the troll reached out and grabbed her by the scruff of her neck, yanking her back to its side. But with only one arm, the creature lost its oar to the waves.

The boat would burn and, knowing trolls, the monster

would refuse to let go. Built of crystals, pebbles and boulders, they would both sink to the bottom of the estuary and drown. Not that Angela would go easily. She thrashed and kicked and clawed.

To no avail. The rock-hard creature didn't even flinch as it stared into the sky, bellowing its confusion at the moon.

No, at the airship. Which even now, slowly turned against the wind, pointing its nose in the lifeboat's direction. A basket ratcheted down the rope, ready to snatch his wife away.

He clenched his teeth. She needed to hold still. To drop. To provide him with a clean shot. "Angela!" His yell was all but swallowed by the wind, lost in the clank and hiss of ship-yard wrecking steambots behind him. He drew in as deep a breath as possible and yelled louder. "Angela!"

She looked up. He raised the crossbow in one hand, pointed down with the other.

Distracted by the approaching dirigible and confident Val wasn't a true threat, the basalt troll stood, reaching for the swinging basket.

Angela flopped like a rag doll and Val raised the cross-bow, aimed and sent another arrow streaking through the air.

The silver-tipped point lodged between the troll's shoulder blades. For a moment, nothing happened. The troll stood motionless. Petrified. Then the potassium broke through the outer coating of oil and began to smoke.

Not smoke, really.

The tröllabanar meeting blood was a beautiful example of a violent exothermic reaction, producing potassium hydroxide gas, hydrogen and heat. The potassium melted and ignited a violet flame a moment before the hydrogen gas caught fire with a shower of sparks, illuminating Angela as she dove overboard into the brackish water.

Val leapt into a spare lifeboat and pulled the rope that dropped the vessel into the water. Swimming in the Firth of Clyde was not an activity for January—or any other month. He needed to haul her out of the water before the cold sucked the life from her. Frantic, he grabbed an oar and paddled toward the smoldering wreckage.

The troll's arm fell, swinging downward, its momentum tipping the jötunn forward. Slowly at first, then all at once, careening into the dark water.

There! He spotted her blonde head. But a moment later, she sank back under.

Worse, his feet were wet and his trousers clung to his ankles. His lifeboat was taking on water.

Brilliant light poured down from above. A searchlight.

The water lapped at his knees now, and Val swore he could hear Loki laughing. Events conspired to force him into frigid waters. Accepting fate, he abandoned his capsizing boat, diving into the icy water to swim to where he'd last spotted her. Diving under the salty waves, over and over. Until his fingers wrapped around water-logged fabric.

He hauled her to the surface.

Coughing and sputtering, wide-eyed and panicked, she gasped for air. Struggling to keep her head above waves so cold they cut like thousands of razor blades into the skin.

Soon, they would lose their battle and succumb to hypothermia.

Which left no time for false reassurances.

"They're searching for us. You. We need to disappear." Bobbing beside her, he squeezed her hand. "Can you hold your breath? Kick. I'll pull."

"Yes." She sucked in a lungful of air. As did he. Then they sank into the freezing, brackish water. Kicking. Tugging. Hauling themselves up to breathe, then back down. The chill faded and numbness began to spread. Fingers and toes first. Then it crept into his limbs.

With each minute, it took more effort to kick, to pull, to surface for air.

Then the toe of his boot hit something. And another something. Rounded rocks embedded in rough sand were beneath his feet. They'd reached the shoreline.

With Angela pressed to his side, her arm draped across his shoulder, they stumbled over the uneven surface until they reached a relatively smooth stretch of the seaweed-strewn shore. Without letting her go, he dropped to the wet sand, cushioning her fall with his body.

Exhausted, he wrapped his arms around her. They'd move. Soon. They must. In a moment or two. "Angela? Are you hurt?"

A dozen tiny cuts and burns marred her face. Nothing that wouldn't heal. Thank Odin she'd been wearing, for the most part, his clothing. Wet skirts would have clung to her legs, twisting and binding and tugging her into the deep.

"Cold. So cold." Her face was blue, her lips purple, and

her body overcome with shivers. "The salt stings." Small cuts bled at her jawline. "But I don't think anything's broken."

They'd made it. Alive and intact. And the small airship had killed its lights, turned tail and was disappearing into the night.

Cupping her face with numb fingers, he touched his lips to hers. Softly, offering her what little warmth he had left. A gentle celebration giving thanks to the gods for sparing their lives. "Answer one question." He hoped she'd forgive him for taking advantage of the situation. "The runes upon the troll's back. Were they bioluminescent?"

"Stone should be solid and inert. Not alive. But, as Loki laughs," she uttered the god's name on a cold breath of air, "we might as well entertain the improbable and impossible."

CHAPTER THIRTEEN

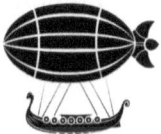

ANGELA AWOKE WITH A GASP. A SOLITARY Lucifer lamp rocked on a bedside table, throwing unfamiliar shadows across the room.

She was hot, so very, very hot. Feverish. Sick. Lying abed. Which explained the strange dreams of trolls. Of glowing runes. Of a wind-whipped marriage that ended with a handful of kisses. Save her arm was bandaged and a heavy weight wrapped around her waist held her tight against a man's form.

Not a nightmare.

Memories rushed back.

An electrified troll with purple blood. A terrifying fall that stole her consciousness. Waking in a boat as fiery arrows fell. A plunge into icy salt water. A rescue that ended with a soft, cold kiss and a promise to discuss the improbable.

She shifted, rousing various aches and pains that promised a variety of purple bruises. A touch to the side of her face confirmed a scattering of burn marks where sparks had landed on skin, later soothed with some kind of salve. Someone had peeled away her clothing, cleaned and bandaged her wounds. Her husband? A handsome man who —at great personal risk—had rescued her from a creature that ought not exist. Who had brought her home and tucked her in his bed, safe and sound. A unique experience, when most of the men in her life habitually tossed her aside at the slightest inconvenience.

So. Not a dream. But if trolls were real, could the same be said of the huldufólk? Was she married to an elf? Was *she* an elf?

An escape to the land of her ancestors had rapidly turned into something worthy of its own saga. Which begged the question of what came next. A tragedy that told a tale of malevolent creatures that separated her from Val? Or a romance in which husband and wife forged a steadfast bond and...

She hoped for the latter. Though, given recent events, there were bound to be many plot twists.

A soft hum filled the air. Every so often the room swayed. The loftskip was underway. Next stop Iceland. A journey of a day and a half, no more, to convince this man to keep her close, at his side. For, as he'd taken pains to remind her, consummation was a marital requirement. Such was also a critical task for a societal liaison.

Until then, their union could still be dissolved. Did she want that? No.

Knowing the duchess had entertained marrying her off

to a murderous Norwegian alchemist cast the entire affair into a dark light. No wonder Olivia resisted her mother's choices. But Freyja had smiled upon Angela that cold, icy night and sent her an honorable man who sailed the skies, one who wouldn't condemn her to a life of political machinations. For purely selfish reasons, she wanted him for herself.

All this begged the question of Rømer's involvement. A troll with glowing runes had attempted to kidnap her. There'd been a dirigible floating over the boat, a rope dangling from its side, ready to carry her away to... Norway? Had Rømer—or his minions—carved those runes into troll skin? Into Katla's skin? Did he intend for Angela to be the dead woman's replacement?

She rather thought he did. That her husband suspected the same. Was that why he'd married her, to prevent an enemy from staking a claim?

Val wanted trust and honesty? Fine. She would tell him everything, fill his ears to overflowing with the possibilities of the fire fern. But she would expect the same in return. He would explain what he knew of these runes, of the man who went to great lengths to kidnap her.

With a fingertip, she followed the sinuous path of a tattooed vine that wound its way across his muscular forearm, stretching for his elbow and beyond. He wore no shirt. And only a thin cotton nightgown separated their skin. Would he wake, turn her to him and kiss her with all the carnal passion of a man who desired his bride?

Her fingers found a button buried in a froth of lace beneath her chin. She set it free. Then the next and the next.

Baring herself to her waist. Unwrapping the package in hopes that her husband would find the contents irresistible. A sleepy seduction.

She slid his arm upward, across her ribcage, filling his rough palm with her soft breast.

"Mmm." He pulled her closer and nuzzled her neck, a movement that set her blood on fire.

A backward nudge of her hips provided further encouragement and growing evidence of his approval.

Teeth nipped at the edge of her jaw. A thumb brushed over her tight nipple. Reaching behind, she smoothed her hand over the stubble of his beard. Angular features where she had only rounded ones. A contrast designed to inflame the passions.

His palm left her breast, and she froze, heart thudding against her rib cage. Had he awakened and thought better of touching her intimately? Disappointment welled, and she opened lips to... What, exactly?

But it seemed he was no more interested in conversation than she. Beneath the covers, his hand smoothed over her curves, down a stretch of her thigh, then fisted in the soft cotton, dragging the material upward to bare more skin to his explorations. His teeth scraped across the back of her neck. Rough fingertips explored the hollow of her hip, then flexed on her pelvis and stilled.

"So tempting, Angela." The words whispered behind her ear held a note of annoyance. "But there are complications we've yet to address."

Now? Freyja wept.

"There will be no children, not for a year." It pained her to confess, but he deserved to know. If knowing their hasty marriage wouldn't require a cradle in nine months, might he let his hands resume their explorations? "Olivia offered a contraceptive. I accepted."

If anything, her words darkened his eyes. Desire flickered there, barely leashed. "Wise. I approve. But I'm more concerned with your loyalty."

"I'm not a spy," she breathed. "Only the two of us know about the tiny creatures—and I've no intention of sharing that information with the British or anyone else." A promise she made, uncaring if she betrayed the country of her birth.

"Why not?" His hand moved, palm brushing over damp curls. A finger toyed at her slit, a teasing incentive to spill her secrets.

"Because the answers belong to those who can host a living tattoo." The reason she'd kept the family secret all these years.

"Host?" Fingertips pressed, then began a slow circle. Delving deeper with each pass, dipping into a growing wetness before circling around the bundle of nerves at her center. Methodical torture that made her squirm.

"Now? You want a lecture *now*?"

His laugh rasped in her ear. "A few words, carefully chosen as a gesture of goodwill." He thrust against her buttocks. "I'll make it worth your effort."

The words rushed forth. "Revival of the Eldskrift tradition."

A sudden stillness underscored the significance of her

revelation. But he didn't contradict her, didn't ask her to explain. No, he'd expected her answer. How much did he already know?

He rolled onto his back, hauling her with him, her back to his front. Unbuttoned cotton and lace parted, baring her breasts to cold air and the heat of his breath. Roughly, he pulled at her knee, spreading her legs such that one rested between his own woolen-clad thighs. An unfair advantage, but who was she to complain at the erotic feel of coarse fabric against her soft skin. "You know far more than you've been telling, more than I suspected." His voice rumbled.

"As do you." An accusation, but one without any bite. She was about to demand he also share a secret when the rough pads of fingers pinched her pebbled nipple. Hard enough to jolt her against his chest. Pleasure stopping just short of pain. A moan was all that passed her lips, for his other hand was back at the juncture of her thighs, tracing one sensuous circle after another until her hips flexed of their own accord, begging for more.

"Like that, *ástin mín*." A single broad finger slid into her. "So wet and ready. So very tight."

In and out. A second finger joined the first and she knew a moment's burn before the stretch was pure pleasure. This. *This* explained all the fuss. Why so many chased such sensations against all reason. "Val." His name emerged as a soft, strangled gasp. She tried to turn, but his arm banded about her waist, locking her in place. She threw her arms overhead instead, grabbing at his neck and shoulders, feeling hard muscle move beneath her palms as his hand moved between her legs, relentless as he drove her ache to new heights. "More."

His thumb joined in, pressing down upon her throbbing pearl while, under her, his cock thrust against her backside, rock hard and insistent. But he didn't stop, didn't reach for his waistband or make the slightest effort to free himself.

She ought to help him, but it was difficult to think, to plan anything beneath his bone-melting touch. Desire sparked and raced along her nerve endings, short circuiting all rational thought save to cry out a craving for more.

"You're untried?" His teeth scraped at her throat. "You've not known a man?"

"There's been no one before you." She'd eyed a stable hand, considered a footman. All in the name of scientific inquiry, of course. But the consequences of an error were too high a price to pay. Now the repercussions of not bedding a man, her husband, were far more dire. There was duty, but there was also desire. A longing for this man, for Val, to possess her fully and completely. "Please. I need…"

For him to roll her, flip her. Anything he wanted so long as he buried himself deep between her legs, joining them as man and woman. According to the book, whatever pain was involved would fade soon enough, leaving behind only pleasure. And she was shockingly eager to explore the many possibilities.

When he bit down on her neck and shoved his fingers deeper, she cried out. The sting was nothing compared to the breathtaking ecstasy of being stretched even wider. A moment's annoyance washed over her—this was not a man bedding his wife—but her hips flexed against his hand, her body uncaring of how it reached for more.

"Like that." His palm swept upward across her rib cage, cupped her breast, found her nipple. Teasing, tugging, rolling. All while his other hand kept pushing, plunging, thrusting. It was almost too much. Rough stubble scraped over her neck and shoulder as his voice growled. "Come for me."

The base of his hand shoved against her center and her world fell apart, shattered and melted. Fizzing and sparking, pleasure raced through her limbs with a shocking, electric vitality that stole the breath from her lungs.

Slowly, the bliss faded, leaving trails of warmth and energy beneath her skin, and the awareness that he remained stiff under her buttocks grew. Their union was incomplete in the eyes of the gods, the law, until there was the chance of a child. Not that legalities were at the forefront of her mind. She rolled onto the mattress, then pressed herself along his side, dragging her fingers over his rough trousers to measure his hard length.

But when her grip tightened, he caught at her wrist. "Stop."

"Why? We're married. Attracted to each other." An icy trickle of doubt flowed down her spine, chilling her. She shot him a narrow-eyed glare. "Or are you about to tell me you only tucked me in bed because no other crew member would agree to the task?"

"As if I'd trust one of the men." A snort. "As we're en route to Iceland, Lisbet is needed in the engine room and

Hildur has her own duties. Besides, her wife is the jealous sort. Your injuries are, thankfully, of a minor variety. More concerning was hypothermia."

Her stomach dropped. Would he not have crawled in bed with her at all had her health not been in jeopardy? "I am reduced to an impulse you now regret?" She flopped on her back to stare at the ceiling. Her chest felt hollow, as if someone had scooped out her heart and left it aching.

"No." He slid from the bed, stealing away his heat. Bare feet planted on the floor, he reached for his shirt and shrugged linen over twisting vines she longed to trace. In the shadowed room, it was hard to make out the details of his tattoos. "But we've yet to establish mutual trust."

"I thought we'd moved past that."

His only answer was a soft, rueful laugh which served only to inflame her anger.

She re-buttoned her nightgown, shoving each tiny mother-of-pearl through its hole with enough force to strain the fine fabric. "Any impediments to our union ought to have been addressed before we spoke vows."

"Trust takes time and you've yet to learn my story." He caught her hand, rubbing his thumb over the ring he'd placed upon her finger. "Everything between us happened in a great rush. If, *after* you meet your Huldu family, you still want this." He ran her palm down his linen-clad chest, over the flat of his stomach, stopping when the fabric disappeared beneath his waistband. "We'll pick up where we left off."

Warm thoughts of such activities distracted her for a moment, then she blinked. "Family?"

"There's a possibility that Sigríður Guðjónsdóttir is your great aunt."

"You knew! Knew I had family? And you're just now informing me?" She narrowed her eyes, suspicious. Why withhold such information until now? "Who is she?"

"You know nothing of her?" His eyebrows lifted. "Of the sólættir?"

She shook her head, frowning. "Grandmother stopped telling me fairy tales once I scoffed at them. Instead, we spent our time in the greenhouse laboratory."

Most of them involving ferns and dinoflagellates, but Angela had branched out, ill-content to keep repeating the same failed experiment over and over. Building upon their many efforts to create a fern-dinoflagellate symbiont, she'd studied endophytic organisms—entirely new species that formed when microorganisms colonized plants. A handful of carefully designed flora had produced completely novel bioactive chemicals that had, in turn, inspired her to compound extremely effective skin care lotions, ointments and salves.

"High-ranking individuals." His lips pursed, as if he remained unconvinced of—and slightly annoyed by—her ignorance. "Much like your *ton*. Sigríður is a woman of considerable importance. But given your grandmother lived in exile, there is no knowing if she'll claim you until we arrive at the mountain."

"Mountain?" So many questions, but where did one begin? She held up a hand. "No. Don't answer that." Her eyes closed, unable to believe the words she was about to utter. "Instead, explain the troll to me? I find I must retract my earlier statements of disbelief concerning the..." She trailed off, searching her memory for the word her grandmother had used long ago. "*Álfar?*"

Was that the collective term for Nordic creatures that ought to not really exist?

Val's head snapped up, distracted from the process of pulling on his boots. A faint smile tugged at his lips. "Trolls we lump with the jötunn. We, the huldufólk, fall among the elves. Álfar."

"And the reason the troll was rock hard?"

"They all are."

"All?" She sat up. "How many of these creatures are roaming about?"

"No one has an exact count. They largely confine themselves to caves and rocky hillsides in the north. From the glowing runes carved into its skin, however, it would appear Rømer found and captured at least one for his experiments. Then sent the basalt troll to kidnap you."

There was a lot to unpack in that statement. Where to start? "Basalt?"

"Iceland is often called the land of fire and ice." He bent to lace his boots. "But at its most basic, it's a giant heap of volcanic black basalt rock."

"An environment suited to trolls?"

"Exactly." He nodded. "The bulk of troll anatomy forms from silicon dioxide."

"Silica." They'd discussed this with the doctor. "Like the

quartz crystals found in Katla's stomach. And the bioactive glass in her runes."

"A telling consideration." He shrugged on a waistcoat. "In this case, trace amounts of iron colored the blood of the troll that attacked you. It's why its wounds solidified into amethyst."

"Amethyst," she repeated, uncertain of the significance. "Its purple blood is amethyst."

He nodded. "Most trolls bleed a dark brown or black color—smokey quartz with activated aluminum impurities—due to their origination from the Lake Mývatn area. But all trolls keep to the dark hours, roam more in the winter months as their skin burns easily in sunlight and, when healing, tends to harden."

"Into stone."

"And you thought your grandmother's tales were pure fiction." He flashed her an encouraging smile.

She blinked. Scientific explanations for trolls? Not twenty-four hours ago, she'd have laughed at such nonsense. No more. By marrying Val, she'd stepped into a new—and dangerous—world. One in which an unknown creature might appear without warning and spirit her away. "And the reason you need to shoot flaming arrows at them?"

"Not flaming." He grabbed his jacket. "Potassium arrowheads. If you can pierce a joint, connect with the liquid portion of their blood, an explosive chemical reaction takes place. It's virtually the only way to kill one."

Wonderful. It did, however, explain the chemical burns on

her face. She crawled across the bed and peered into the looking glass above the washstand. Tiny blood-crusted spots mottled one side of her cheek. Unattractive, to say the least, but better than being at the mercy of a madman. "Thank you," she said. "That was quite the rescue you executed. Which brings us back to the topic of unusual runes carved into the creature's back. And why was only one rune, othola, inscribed on the troll's chest?"

Scab? Scar? Tattoo seemed the wrong word. What did one call the blood of an amethyst troll once it hardened on the skin's surface? All of it impossible, but as her reality no longer existed, why belabor the point?

"Othola?" His gaze caught hers, confused. "There was a single rune on its chest? You're certain?"

"Very." She threw aside the covers and crossed to his sea chest, snagged his best linen shirt. "And all the runes had a purple shine that seemed to flash or flicker or glow. Reflection or bioluminescence, I couldn't say. But given its blood turned to amethyst, the presence of living creatures seems unlikely." If they bled liquid gemstone, why not? She threw off her nightgown.

"Angela." A groan edged with warning as he turned away.

Deliberately provocative? Yes. But before a single flirtatious word could pass her lips, she caught sight of the dark bruises that marred her hips and knees. A stark reminder of how close she'd come to death or captivity.

"Othola." Val thumbed through the pages of a book. "An old rune eliminated from Scandinavian runes in the eighth century. Representing homeland. Ancestral property. Inheritance."

"A hint at Rømer's motive?" She dropped his shirt over her head, then pulled on her skirts. Instead of a corset, she chose a vested bodice with an attached ruffled waterfall bustle. Practical and feminine. A feat difficult to accomplish considering present circumstances. Sufficient until she could find a modiste. A complete wardrobe overhaul was in order.

"Given the man is obsessed with his country winning independence from Sweden? Jealous that Iceland is about to become an independent kingdom with something as simple as a royal wedding? Yes, I think it likely." He snapped the book closed. "A common trend has presented itself."

"So it has. Runes. Ones that flash with light or at least present the illusion of such." She struggled with the absurdity of the words that fell from her lips. "As the creature now rests on the sea floor, what more can you tell me about troll anatomy?" She flipped his sea chest closed and sat, hiking her skirts to pull on warm woolen stockings, keeping the motion simple and no-nonsense, yet enjoying how his eyes were drawn to her ankles. As her boots rested drying before a stove, wet from their evening plunge, she pulled on a pair of silk slippers.

"Virtually nothing." He threw his hands in the air. "Trolls keep to themselves and are rarely encountered. They know better than to tangle with huldufólk. On the rare occasion that they cause enough trouble to warrant killing, their bodies are left where they fall. No one hauls home a pile of rocks to autopsy—their skin is ridiculously tough to pierce.

And I've never heard of a troll carving runes into skin to purposefully induce ossification."

"Which brings us to yesterday's autopsy." She crossed her arms and fixed him with a long stare. Time to light a fire. "We promised each other honesty. Make a gesture of good faith. You and Rømer were once friends. How? When? Why?"

CHAPTER FOURTEEN

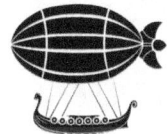

"How did you—" The second the words left his mouth, Val *knew*. He'd just told her himself.

Her eyebrows rose. His wife was intelligent and crafty and beautiful. The attire she'd cobbled together by pilfering items from his trunk to mix and match with things from her own wardrobe ought not flatter anyone. Yet there she sat, damp golden hair tumbling over her shoulders, stealing tiny pieces of his heart with every word she spoke.

Dragging in a deep breath, he began his confession. "We attended university together, met at a pub and fell into conversation." Snatching up a hairbrush, he moved behind her and started untangling knots that still held a lingering hint of sea salt.

She sighed. "That feels wonderful."

As did the silk of her hair sliding through his fingers. "Officially a chemist, Rømer fancied himself a modern-day alchemist. The notion of evolution and its relationship to transmutation intrigued him. He believed—believes—the skaldic and eddic poems hold truths, that those of us descended from Vikings possess unrealized magic potential that could be unlocked if only he could find the right key. Biochemical transmutation, he called it."

"Evolution? The process by which a new species develops, in this case by acquiring new physiological abilities?"

"Something like that." The tangles of her hair began to fall free. "One late night, he started pondering the existence of elves and dwarves and their relationship to the Nordic gods. I made some comment about the transformative nature of wormwood found in a bottle of absinthe, *la fée verte*."

"The green fairy," she translated. "Colored with the chlorophyll of various herbs that sustain our kind. Preferred alcoholic drink of the huldufólk as it helps maintain the vibrance of our tattoos." Her voice hardened. "Tell me you did not make the mistake of telling him about your green tattoos."

If only he could. "I believed us friends. Trusted him." His hands stilled. "When he shoved up my sleeve, stared at the vines and began asking questions—"

She gasped, turning to gape at him over her shoulder, incredulous. "You answered?"

"I thought we might work together." He drew a deep breath. She would meet his uncle soon enough. "Before I left to study in Norway, I stumbled upon pages from an ancient manuscript that told an unusual tale about the Fire Script Guardians, the Eldvörður." He'd stared for hours at the faded inscriptions inked in runes on yellowed vellum. "In our stories, Eldskrift, fire script, is always said to burn bright, but the pages made no mention of fire, only of 'red'. I started to wonder, what if the tales were wrong?"

"You began to doubt that Eldskrift actually glowed."

"Exactly that." He'd studied the old words, pondering the stilted and archaic language.

Red. Rauðr.

"Perhaps the word referred to dulse or Irish moss or another of the red-tinted seaweeds? Even better, I thought, as all such 'plants' grow in low light conditions. Conditions our people face living inside a mountain. I started to wonder if it was possible that such an ocean plant might offer clues as to how we could improve our efforts to build functional biore-actors to grow algae."

Believing so, Val had liberated the loose pages from his uncle's laboratory and hauled it with him to university with plans to use any knowledge gleaned to advance fae technol-ogy. His mistake was sharing his hopes and dreams with Rømer, letting his former friend read the ancient writing. Now Katla was dead. Dull brown crystalline runes marred her skin.

A shimmer of frost coated his flesh. Her strange tattoos had something to do with the runes inscribed in the old manuscript, only he wasn't certain how. Regardless, it was his responsibility to set right the events his actions had set in motion.

Angela pivoted, frowning. "What is this mountain home you keep mentioning?"

"Home of the huldufólk? Our destination?" His turn to stare in disbelief. She knew so much and yet so little. "I'll tell you more—as soon as you tell me what you know of Rømer."

For a long moment, she fell silent.

"My grandmother never spoke of her life in Iceland. All she shared were the stories. Magical sea cows. Giant worms that fed on gold. Grýla and the thirteen Yule Lads."

"The Yule Lads are trolls. Troublemakers and quite real." He grimaced. "They've an irritating habit of skulking about on winter nights causing trouble."

She blinked. "As my mother favored London and my brothers were, for the most part, away at school, my grandmother raised me on our family's country estate. A life she preferred, claiming the rejuvenating properties of her photosynthetic tattoos made too many women her age jealous of her apparent youth. In the countryside, we spent our daylight hours surrounded by plants, either outside or in the greenhouse or its laboratory. To secure my future, she arranged for me to marry the neighboring gentleman."

"Joining two estates."

"All was well and good until, about a year ago, Aubrey sold the grounds from beneath our feet. To my fiancé. Who quickly broke off our engagement."

Val smiled. "You cannot expect me to express regret."

She laughed, but a rueful smile stole across her lips. "I mourned the loss of that greenhouse more than a man I barely knew. We'd been told to pack in anticipation of a move into the city when a letter arrived. One she tossed in the fire and refused to speak about. She took to working long hours behind locked doors, convinced she was being watched and spoke of returning to Iceland, of taking me 'home' where we would be safe."

"Did anyone come to visit her?" Val's hand stilled. "Rømer?"

"Visit?" Pain flickered in her eyes. "Not exactly. One night I woke to the sounds of a loud argument. I pulled on my robe and crept down the stairs. A man was inside the study with my grandmother, demanding she hand over her notebooks."

Eavesdropping, as any good spy would. But he said nothing.

"Not the raw data supporting her published works, but her findings with regard to fire script."

His hand tightened on the brush. "Eldskrift."

"She, of course, denied knowing anything." Angela twisted a button on her bodice. "The conversation grew heated. I could hear the scrape of drawers being opened, the thuds of books being thrown on the floor. I tried the door, but it was locked. Grandmother began to babble in Icelandic and he yelled at her to speak English. I banged on the door, begged him to stop." She shuddered. "There was a sickening crunch followed by silence. By the time I woke the servants, forced the study doors open, it was too late."

"I'm so sorry." Guilt swept over him. However indirectly, Val was responsible for the old woman's death. And the danger Angela now faced. Such was what came from the arrogance of a young man who thought nothing of ignoring

ANNE RENWICK

the wisdom of the elders in a quest for glory couched as a search for knowledge.

"A fire iron to the side of her head. He left via a window. What, if anything, he stole, I've no idea. I never saw him. Never heard his voice again." Her expression hardened. "Until the ball."

"When he returned for you."

"Perhaps?" She withdrew a book from her bag on the natural history of ferns. "Or was it for this?" He reached for the book, but she clutched it to her chest. "Your turn." She closed her eyes. "Fae. Trolls. Eldvörður. I suppose you're about to tell me the red glowing runes of fire script do, in fact, grant the host exceptional abilities."

"So go the tales." She knew so little of her own history. "While our ancestors arrived in Iceland alongside the first Vikings, we soon parted ways with humans. Over time, we became a new kind of fae."

"The huldufólk."

He nodded. "But whereas our Nordic fae ancestors—the Hulder—hid themselves away in forests, wood was a precious commodity on the island and not a safe place they could live openly. They chose, instead, to build a hidden city away from the humans inside a mountain."

"*Inside?*"

"Hard work, digging tunnels into volcanic basalt. Especially during the long dark winters. All that activity attracted unwanted—and deadly—attention from trolls."

"They're rumored to like caves..." She sighed. "Not a rumor."

"Not even remotely. Sunlight harms their skin. To guard our people as they worked, a few huldufólk volunteered to become fire script guardians, the Eldvörður. Marked with red glowing bindrunes, they roamed the mountainside, fighting off encroaching trolls. Once the city was established —and fortified—the trolls retreated and the Eldskrift tradition faded away."

"Bindrunes?"

"Symbols created by stacking the runes that spell out a word, one atop another."

"Is that what's scribbled in here?" She pushed the book into his hands.

He flipped through the pages. The book seemed nothing special or out of the ordinary. Until he found the inked runes that filled the margins and sprawled across illustrations. At first glance, it was madness. But when he bent close and forced himself to decipher some of the runic writing, bits and pieces—but not the whole—fell into place.

Her grandmother's notes echoed parts of the manuscript pages he'd stolen from his uncle's library. But added an entirely new level of understanding. This was modern work, data carefully collected in the confines of a laboratory, complete with controls and variables.

"This is amazing," he breathed. "She wrote in Elder and Younger and Icelandic Fuþark runes—all three at once." He stabbed a finger atop a symbol. "And, yes, she also mixed in bindrunes. No one writes with runes anymore, not beyond using them as small decorative poetic phrases. Untangling this mishmash will take time. With effort, I can sound out short stretches." He looked up, his eyes sparkling with excitement. "What is this about introducing pyros to ferns?"

"A few times we've come close." She stared at him, expectant. Then her eyebrows rose. "Is it possible I know something of our history you don't? You've not heard of the fire fern?"

"Fire fern?" He glanced at her dead plant. Desiccated bits of its fronds were scattered across the window bench. "Is that what you were trying to... create?"

"It is. Was." She sighed. "Grandmother was convinced we only needed to find the right host species, a fern that would incorporate the pyros into its cells to produce a red bioluminescent plant. And red light preserves night vision..." She tapped her chin. "That fits the stories she told of the Eldvörður with their ability to see in the dark. Along with extreme cold tolerance and swift healing. If Rømer wants to create a new kind of human—or fae—such would explain his interest in fire script tattoos. But it seems he knows about the pyros, the red bioluminescent dinoflagellates, but nothing else."

"Which is why he developed bioactive glass, laying down strands of the material in Katla's skin before implanting these pyro creatures?"

She nodded. "A process doomed to failure, though it may have succeeded on a temporary basis, given the glass had time to break down and move into her circulatory system before crystalizing at random locations in her body. Perhaps tattooing trolls with pyros worked because their skin contains large amounts of silicon dioxide, but our kind—"

"Huldufólk." Why did he need to hear her say it aloud?

"Fine. Why not? Elves." Her lips pursed for a moment, as if the word soured on her tongue. "Given only the huldufólk can host photosynthetic tattoos, there is every reason to believe fire script tattoos must also derive from living plants, in particular the fire fern."

"My ancient pages only provided him with hints at what might be possible." He tapped her grandmother's book. "This, however, is modern work." He stabbed his fingers into his hair. "Capturing you is his goal. Not only are you Huldu, you possess the knowledge—living and written—that Rømer wants."

"You think he'll follow us?"

Frigg and Hel. Val pinched the bridge of his nose. "Yes."

A knock sounded at the door. "Breakfast," Lisbet called.

Angela pressed a hand to her growling stomach and offered him a faint smile. "It seems surviving a troll kidnapping has made me hungry."

Val opened the cabin door. "Shouldn't you be flushing out the wings?"

"Done." Lisbet pushed a laden tea tray into his hands. "I thought after a long night..." She frowned at him, then rose up on her toes to peer over his shoulder. "You've already dressed?"

He raised an eyebrow. "Do I hear disappointment?"

"Perhaps." She laughed. "But we do need to take flight soon."

"Yes. Wait for us." Clear of British shores, no reason remained to hide his—their—people's technological secrets.

And if they were to have a future, it was time to trust his wife. He shut the door on his grinning mechanic and placed the fancy tea tray on the desk. Lisbet enjoyed the delicate things in life. Such as teacups of wafer-thin porcelain, silver forks, and white linen napkins. Even better, two plates held an assortment of flakey pastries topped with fruit and sweetened cream.

"She baked?" His wife lifted a tart. "On a dirigible?"

"The engine room is hers." He shrugged, let a smile tug at his lips. "If she installed a small oven, who are we to complain?"

Angela took a bite. Her eyes fluttered shut as she savored the taste. "Mmm. This is heavenly."

Tendrils of want and need twisted around his heart. Every moment spent in her company deepened his attachment. But was it love? Had the adrenaline rush of recent events merely conspired along with hormones, resulting in a natural biological urge to—

He tore his eyes from her mouth and swallowed a groan. A known side-effect of danger and excitement suppressing all rational thought in favor of a primitive instinct that had yet to dissipate.

The sooner they were on deck, the better.

Angela sipped her wormwood tea. "What is this about wings?"

He cleared his throat. "This loftskip is more than a merchant vessel. It's a flying research laboratory." If one that ran on a deficit. The reason he'd hoped for a dowry, to snag a bottle of Tyrian Absinthe. Anything to generate funds, though legitimate business was preferred to smuggling.

Her eyes grew round. "You have actual laboratory space?"

The faint light of dawn crept through the plate glass of the porthole.

"We do." He smiled. He was, after all, married to a botanist. And was rapidly forming a strong attachment. "You can take inventory. Let me know what equipment we lack." There was little he wouldn't endeavor to provide. Anything to entice her to remain married. "But let's begin the tour outside. My crew and I need to make the most of the winter sun so as not to waste coal." He lifted his fur-lined cloak from a peg and held it open for her. "It'll be all hands on deck to deploy the airship's wings."

Her mouth dropped. "This airship truly has wings?"

CHAPTER FIFTEEN

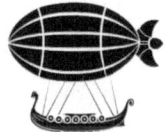

THE BRIGHT SUN OFFERED NO WARMTH on an airborne dirigible soaring above a wind-whipped winter sea. Light and air were, however, the perfect antidote to the dark meanderings of their conversation. Angela was grateful for the fur-lined cloak as Val tugged her out onto the deck.

Val flashed her an excited grin. "Notice anything unusual?"

Like most airships, the *Grænndreki* hung suspended beneath a silver aether-filled balloon and a large coal-powered propeller spun at the rear, hurtling them forward while smoke billowed from a stack overhead.

Slowly, she turned about. "We're headed directly to Iceland?"

"We are."

No shoreline was visible. No tether linked them to a steamer ship below. This was open ocean. Panic would be a reasonable response. Save, were Val and his crew in the habit of floating adrift, they would have been long since lost at sea. The pride in his voice and his engineering degree had her contemplating what mechanical wonder he'd constructed.

"Any airship carrying enough coal to travel nearly two days without stopping to refuel would have no room left in the hold to transport anything else."

"Unless..."

"You possess an alternate source of power?" She lifted an eyebrow in challenge. "You mentioned wings. Do you intend to engage some kind of mechanical, flapping device? One using a windup clockwork mechanism? I'm no engineer, but that seems more likely to snap the hull in half and send us plunging into the waves below."

"So it would." He laughed. "No, no flapping. That would break the glass panels."

"Glass as an engine?" Her frown deepened. The wind snatched at her clothing. "That makes no sense. None at all."

But, sure enough, Dýri and Hildur were prying open one of the crates from the factory. Her mistake, assuming the large flat boxes loaded aboard contained only sheets of glass for mere windows—greenhouses, for example.

"Easier to show you. Come." He crossed the deck to aid Lisbet in her wrestling match with oilskin tarps, tugging them away to reveal stacks of shimmering green metallic windows.

Save they weren't square, but triangular. Various hinges and pins, struts and braces connected them, folding them neatly alongside the dirigible's edges. Steel girders ran the length of the wing, all pinned together, one after the other, with a single massive bolt affixed to the shoulder—

She glanced at the airship's carved figurehead. A dragon. *Loftskipið Grænndreki.* This dirigible really was a flying green dragon. "These are the dragon's wings?"

He beamed. "Powered by the sun. The only dirigible in existence that is, at least in part, alive."

"Alive?" More magic? She thought of the electrified basalt troll with liquid crystal for blood and looked down, half expecting to see the deck beneath her feet heave as the airship drew breath.

"In a sense. But not sentient." He laughed, tugging her over to the wing and pointing. "Inside these insulated cords run wires that conduct the electricity generated from the biophotosynthetic solar panels to the airship's engine." A frown tugged at his lips. "Extremely expensive panels that are all but impossible to replace."

Lisbet, her petite form an asset, scrambled across the folded wing. She was small and light enough to crawl over glass without cracking it. Wrench in hand, the airship's engineer worked to disconnect the thick cables from a cracked panel.

"Is that what my brother broke in an attempt to stop our wedding?" Her lips pursed, recalling the fire of the flare gun followed by a cold bucket of water.

"It is."

"Did you learn anything at the Rankine Institute about harnessing the photosynthetic energy of green algae?" She laughed as the wind whipped her long hair. "When you might have been delivering the lecture?"

Of late, the scientific community often exhorted the advantages of electricity, a cleaner power source for lighting than the burning of coal gas. Capturing power from plants was, at best, a distant hope, no more than a hypothesis. But before her was more than theory. The dragon's wings integrated biology and mechanics, somehow managing to capture the electricity created by photosynthesis before the plant turned the sun's power into sugar. A marvel of engineering decades ahead of anything under discussion.

"Not a single thing," he admitted. "Save for the existence of a beautiful woman and the thoughtful insight my bride provided about subnivean photosynthesis. The idea that some plants are able to thrive beneath a thin layer of snow, to continue growing, gives me hope that we can adapt these solar panels to work on stationary buildings in remote areas of Iceland. Once the technology is perfected, of course."

She blushed. Maybe there was hope for them. "How does one grow plants inside a glass panel?" The wind gusted, and she crossed her arms, tucking away cold fingers, wishing the cloak came with a hood.

"Are they plants?" He rocked his hand, reflecting conflicting scientific viewpoints. "I'm rather in agreement with those who argue filamentous green algae aren't true plants, lacking roots, stems or leaves, but they do possess the advantage of growing in seawater."

"Algae?" She reached out and pressed her palm gently but firmly against the smooth glass, watching as the green globules of living organisms shifted beneath its surface. "But how?"

"Copper and titanium coated glass panels with a layer of green algae in-between create a kind of battery. When exposed to light, the algae generate a flow of electrons."

"Harvested by the cables and delivered to the engines?"

"Just so." His face lit up. "Though everything is still in the experimental phase, we've had moderate success." He waved a hand. "*Loftskipið Grænndreki* is a floating laboratory disguised as a trading vessel while we iron out the details."

His work, once perfected, would bring about far-reaching changes in industry. That she could not deny. But she needed four walls, a roof and a door. Access to soil and fresh water. And that was before she listed out the equipment she required. Could he truly provide her with all that aboard this airship?

"Ready to replace the broken panel, Captain," Lisbet said, joining them. "Angela! You're shivering. Where is your hat? Have you no mittens? Take mine, I'm not using them." She pulled a pair from her pocket and held them out.

Grateful, Angela accepted. "Are these nålbound?"

Lisbet grinned. "A hobby that helps pass the dull parts of dirigible life and keeps me warm. I could teach you?"

"I'd love that!"

Val produced a hat of similar stitching and tugged it over her head. "Apologies for not providing hats or mittens."

Beneath the thick wool her fingertips and ears began to thaw.

"A hand, Captain?" Dýri called. He and Hildur crab-walked across the deck, struggling under the weight of a triangular panel. A replacement for the broken one.

Val dropped a quick kiss atop her lips, setting her heart aflutter, before joining his crew. Viking. Airship captain. Engineer. Her husband was a man with many facets. Thoughtful, she watched as they set about prying the broken panel from its frame.

"Ready?" Val called. Each person grabbed an angle and bent at the knees. "Three. Two. One!"

As one they heaved the broken panel over the side. Tumbling. Falling. Consigned to an informal burial at sea. As the old triangle disappeared from view, Val, Dýri and Hildur slid a new one into place and Lisbet set about reconnecting the cables.

Val pried open a barrel and hauled out a jug of green sludge—the filamentous algae. He slotted one end of the tube into a rubber gasket fitted into the glass panel and pumped the green goo into the narrow space between the copper and titanium coated plates, infusing the glass with a subtle green glow.

Lisbet tightened a final bolt. "Wings are ready to deploy! Let's not waste any more daylight!"

"Stations!" Val called.

His crew scattered.

Dýri shot her a smirk, but kept his mouth shut as he hurried past. Hildur climbed stairs to the bridge while her wife headed downward into the hull, presumably to the engine room.

Which left her alone on deck with her husband.

He waved her to his side, where he stood beside a speaking tube.

"Should I be holding onto something?" she asked.

"You'll be fine. Experimental, yes, but we've done this many times. Most of the kinks have been worked out." His infectious grin was somehow not reassuring. Nor were his next words. He pointed. "But if the loftskip catches fire, head for that escape dirigible." He lifted the tube's mouthpiece. "Cut engines."

A shudder rippled through the mass of wood and iron. The smoke pouring from the overhead stack thinned, then stopped. The rotation of the rudder slowed, leaving the airship silent and adrift.

"Ready for alternate power." Lisbet's voice echoed from the tube. There was a loud clang. "Turbines on standby."

"Connect photovoltaic biocells," he called back.

"Connected."

Val grinned. "Bridge, you are clear to initiate wingspan."

"Initiating," Lauf announced.

Clink. Clack. Snap.

One by one, the triangular panels shifted, locking into place as the *Grænndreki* spread her green-gold wings, a lady's fan unlike any other.

"Wings are deployed," Val informed his crew. "Engage engines."

A low hum, barely noticeable, rippled beneath her feet, then faded away. But slowly, little by little, the tail rudder began to spin. Faster and faster, until its thrust almost—almost—matched their earlier speed.

"Silent." Val slipped an arm under her cloak and around her waist to draw her close. His gaze fell on her lips. "Clean. Renewable."

"Making the voyages of the huldufólk all but untraceable." Would he kiss her again, properly this time? "Very on point."

He laughed. "Limited only by available sunlight."

"And the continued functioning of your equipment."

Hildur joined them. "I hate to interrupt a moment, but my wife requires your assistance in the engine room. Something to do with salinity controls and an excess amount of chlorine."

"Chorine gas?" Alarm raced across his face. Val glanced at her, then pointed at his first mate as he strode away. "Don't cause trouble."

The Valkyrie's mouth pulled into a tight line.

At last. Opportunity.

Ignoring the north wind that plucked and yanked at her cloak, at the cold seeping through the thin fabric of her satin slippers, Angela focused on the tall woman. "What is it he doesn't want me to know about his fiancée?"

The first mate squared her shoulders, rocked back onto her heels. Digging in. "Are there reasons I should share?"

"Oh, I don't know? Married to an airship captain, kidnapped by a troll, privy to experimental technology developed by Icelandic elves." She tapped her chin. "Oh, right, conducted an autopsy upon a woman with glass runes inscribed in her skin." She shot Hildur a look that challenged the Valkyrie to deny her answers. "Katla was his fiancée. Can—will you elaborate?"

"On the topic of Katla?"

"To begin."

A spark of rebellion caught fire and danced in Hildur's eyes. "As you'll be presented to the council tonight as Valtýr Árnason's unbound wife, perhaps you're entitled to a little inside information."

"Unbound?"

With a sigh, the Valkyrie cast her eyes skyward but pulled the hair away from her nape and tipped her head. Behind her ear was a small green tattoo in the shape of a flower. "We call it a sálbundið mark."

Angela's hand lifted to her neck. "Soulbound?"

"A marriage mark of sorts. An old-fashioned marriage tradition, rarely observed these days."

Yet worthy of mention? There was so much she didn't know. "Why—"

"Ask Val." Hildur released her braids. "But I will tell you all about Katla." A conspiratorial smile curved her lips. "If you'll share all the details about the red glass runes."

Freyja, had she mis-stepped? She ought not have assumed Val would have told Hildur of the autopsy results. Though there was little reason to keep them secret from the crew. They would need to be on alert. Angela might as well be the one to deliver the news. And he'd not mentioned anything about a council.

"Over tea?" A hopeful question. Hat, mittens and cloak

were holding up to prolonged exposure to the north wind, but her silk slippers were not. If she stood here much longer, she'd not be able to move. "Such tales should be told beside a warm stove, out of the wind with a cup of wormwood tea in hand."

Hildur led her up a set of winding stairs and opened a door into the small greenhouse nestled atop the airship's roof. Thick iron scrollwork, both decorative and practical, braced the many-paned windows against the biting chill of northern winds. Warm air spilled out as the door swung wide and she stepped into a space alive with rows of hardy herbs and winter vegetables. Tucked among them were a few bright splashes of pink primroses. In one corner, a small iron stove radiated steady heat. A dented copper teapot perched atop it, releasing a soft trickle of steam into the air.

The first mate flapped her hand at a nearby table surrounded by a scatter of wicker chairs and set about measuring out generous spoonfuls of tea laced with Artemisia absinthium into a brown tea pot.

With an almost involuntary groan of relief, Angela dropped onto a chair and slid her frozen feet beneath the stove. "I need a second pair of leather boots. Fur-lined, if possible."

Hildur snorted, pouring hot water into the teapot, set it upon the table and popped an adorable felted wool tea cozy on top. As the tea steeped, the sharp, bitter fragrance of wormwood rose into the air. "What you need is a dash of snowdrop extract with its antifreeze properties." She placed a small brown glass bottle in front of Angela. "Only one drop. Too much is toxic."

"That helps?" She frowned. "Don't all parts of the plant contain poisonous alkaloids?"

"It's not meant for humans as it only works if you're Huldu." The Valkyrie placed a bowl of sugar cubes, tongs and teacups upon the table. "The more tattoos, the better."

Could it be so easy? More tattoos as a cure for the cold? She turned the vial over in her hands, recalling the many unlabeled bottles of potions and tonics scattered across Grandmother's dressing table. The bitter bite of winter never bothered her, no matter her age. A trick she'd not taught her granddaughter. Her heart squeezed. She regretted her dismissive words, her concerns that neighbors would whisper about "witchcraft" and the "crazy old woman who wrote in runes." Worries that drove Angela to approach her studies with scientific vigor.

What good had it done? Rømer had still hunted them down.

"Katla." She dropped the topic into the heavy silence. "You've seen her runes?"

Hildur nodded. "I'm the one who carried her body from the tunnels."

"Tunnels?"

"We found her beneath a notorious London pub, all her green tattoos gone, her skin covered with runic scars. Her only possession a bottle of Tyrian Absinthe."

"Tyrian Absinthe?" She frowned. "My brother and his friends drank an entire bottle the night of the Icelandic ball."

ANNE RENWICK

Her body tensed. "Rømer bribed him. There was no auction. I was bought." Fury simmered beneath her skin.

"Sounds likely. Katla offered us a bottle in exchange for her rescue. We'd have gone anyway, but Val wasn't opposed to the profits he'd make selling it to Jarl Haukr."

"But you were too late." She hesitated, not wanting to sound callous. "The absinthe?"

Hildur sighed. "During our exit, someone shot at us. The bottle broke."

"Someone tried to kill you!" But her shock was short-lived. The Valkyrie merely shrugged, as if such dangers were a common occurrence. And perhaps it was, aboard airships.

"Kill? Stop? No way to know." She held up a hand to forestall more questions. "Enough about smuggled alcohol. Tell me what you found so I can paint a whole picture for you. One lump or two?"

"Two." While Hildur poured, Angela explained bioactive glass, described the biological material that suggested dinoflagellates were involved, that Rømer might be trying to revive the Eldskrift tradition.

"Eldskrift. There's something you don't hear mentioned among huldufólk except in hushed whispers." She fixed Angela with an uncertain stare. "None of the elders will discuss the process except to say such tattoos were for an old warrior class, for the huldufólk who volunteered to defend the mountain as the tunnels, rooms and halls were cut into the rock, and no longer necessary."

Tunnels? So many questions. She sipped her tea and focused. First, she needed to pry free information about

Katla. So instead she nodded, playing along. "What happened between Katla and Val?"

"Don't imagine some gothic love story—that relationship was doomed from the start." Hildur let out a long sigh. "This loftskip doesn't stay in the sky without funds. Val's father dragged his son to some fancy ball, to rub elbows with men who might be interested in sponsoring his photovoltaic biocell research. When a pretty woman caught Val's eye... well, huldufólk also marry for status and money. In a matter of days, there was an arranged marriage." She rolled her eyes. "But it wasn't a good match. Katla would smile but always had somewhere else to be. You could see the strain on Val's face."

They locked eyes.

"I see," Angela said.

"Precisely." Hildur nodded. "When Katla traveled to Reykjavik, trousseau shopping, she met Rømer."

Wide-eyed, Angela straightened in her chair. "He didn't kidnap her?"

"Not at all." The woman shrugged. "He's a handsome man."

She couldn't argue that. "But dangerous. Best viewed from a safe distance."

Hildur snorted. "From the note she left, she fell in love and decided to elope. She disappeared. Was occasionally sighted in Norway, but the next time we heard from her, she was begging Val to rescue her."

He'd not been in love but still put himself in danger on Katla's behalf. Angela pondered the implications and didn't like the paths her mind began to wander down. Was she merely another damsel in distress he'd felt obligated to rescue?

On the other hand, Rømer was a monster who deserved a slow, painful death.

At some point, Katla had been kept from the sun, fed a carnivorous diet. Starved, her body had cannibalized the chloroplast-bearing cells, destroying the tattoo. A tortuous process, according to Angela's grandmother. All to make her a blank canvas for the alchemist to write upon.

And when she'd succumbed to the damage wrought by bioactive glass?

Rømer had needed a new victim for his mad experiments.

Angela's stomach twisted, shoving her heart into her throat. Hers had been a narrow escape from finding herself locked in a windowless room, fed nothing but meat scraps and water while her fern tattoo faded and died.

And she wasn't safe yet.

CHAPTER SIXTEEN

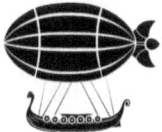

"T HEY'RE NO LONGER TRACKING US?" He leaned over his pilot's shoulder. "You're certain?"

"As the sun rises in the east." Lauf twisted a dial, shifted a lever, adjusting the angle of their approach as they neared Húsafell.

Outside Reykjavík, an airship had begun trailing behind them. As it flew the Norwegian flag of Vestfold, Val was certain Rømer's minions were aboard, even if their leader was not. Which was why he ordered his pilot to detour past Þingvellir, a rift valley where, nearly a century ago, chieftains had gathered to recite laws, settle disputes and lay the foundation of the Icelandic nation. There, beneath the winter sky, a Þorrablót feast was underway, celebrating their Viking heritage in anticipation of the wedding that would win them their independence. Every old tradition was proudly on display.

Thousands attended—from sheep farmers to ranking

politicians—among them was Katla's father, the Icelandic ambassador. The crowd had swelled with international guests and even the Danish princess, Margrit, was rumored to be among them. The snow-covered fields beside the rift valley were dotted with colorful búðir, traditional tentlike shelters used for sleeping, cooking and, most importantly, feasting. Much winter food for the culinary brave was on the menu—fermented shark, sour ram's testicles, boiled sheep's head—along with an overabundance of alcoholic spirits including vast quantities of mead and brennivín.

Given Rømer had lured the ambassador's daughter away only for her to turn up, years later, dead and disfigured under suspicious circumstances, he knew the man would steer his dirigible in another direction. An intoxicated father with political pull might not stop to ask questions in a valley where condemned men once lost their heads for such crimes.

They'd flown overhead, unremarked among a flotilla of other airships and boats, before continuing north.

On their right rose the Okjökull glacier. To their left stretched the western farmlands of the Viking sagas. Soon he and Angela would discreetly disembark—alone—while the airship and his crew continued on. A decoy designed to lead their pursuer astray. Behind the waterfall, inside the mountain, she would be safe from kidnapping attempts, troll or otherwise.

Presenting the granddaughter of Eyrún Guðjónsdóttir to the council was not a task he anticipated with any sort of pleasure. If Angela was indeed related to Sigríður Guðjóns-dóttir, the high-ranking councilwoman would be irritated to learn of any connection to Val by marriage. Given he was contractually engaged to another woman, Sóllilja, he expected Sigríður to challenge the legality of their union.

Such was the entire reason he'd refused to consummate their wedding vows. Oath-breakers were not well-tolerated.

Once he spoke directly with Sóllilja to formally end their understanding, he would be free. She'd known this day might come and would, presumably, have plans she herself must set in motion. Whether or not they included Dýri remained to be seen. Which was why this task was best done without his crew present as witnesses.

Obligation fulfilled, he would confide in Angela. No more secrets. Only honesty. Assuming she would still have him. If she decided to dissolve their marriage, there was little he could do to stop her. Should she choose to do so, his wife might tell the council of her husband's involvement with Rømer, of the dangers the alchemist presented. Such would be her right, given her life and those of other huldufólk were at risk.

Though he very much doubted she would. If she spilled Val's secrets, he might spill hers. And that would end any hope she had of pursuing her research into finding—or creating—a fire fern. For a life lived inside Sigríður's circle of influence meant a political marriage and very little, if any, time spent in a laboratory.

An icy ball formed in his stomach at the thought of watching high-ranking fae court her favors, but the decision was hers. He'd protect her whatever path she chose. If the worst came to pass, he'd bury himself in work.

What if photosynthetic dinoflagellates capable of flashing red light were the solution to the problem of winter flight? Replace the green algae in the photovoltaic solar panels with these crimson critters, organisms more adapted to growing in low light environments, then spread the dragon wings at sunset. Would they be able to fly under cover of dark, sailing the skies on nothing more than moonlight?

Red.

The color of Eldskrift runes. Somehow, Rømer had also concluded red, bioluminescent dinoflagellates lay at the heart of the tradition. But while Angela's grandmother claimed a fire fern was required, the mad alchemist had turned to bioactive glass to support the creatures in fae skin.

Val certainly had his regrets about his role in this mess, but the stories inscribed upon those old vellum pages belonged to the huldufólk. Ignoring the hard work of past generations was wasteful and wrong. Their scientists ought to be studying the pages, applying ancient knowledge to modern problems using scientific principles.

All he wanted was a chance to help his people survive—and thrive—in an era of ever-increasing technology and international travel. The world was shrinking. Complete isolation was not the answer.

First and foremost, the Huldu needed clean energy inside the mountain. His uncle's work in the geothermal sector was of the utmost importance. But his research didn't extend to facilitating travel. Trekking about by horseback was quaint but took too much time. Nor could it move items in large quantities or quantities of large items.

Airships were the future, and the possibilities burned like a banked coal fire in his chest. Yet until the current situation was resolved, the long hours in the laboratory necessary to test this new hypothesis weren't possible. Above all, Rømer needed to be stopped.

"After you drop us off, head to Mývatn." Val's command sounded as if it were a suggestion, but it was an order, nonetheless. He turned to Hildur. "Take Lisbet to the Grjótagjá caves and spend some time soaking in the geothermal springs. Dýri can keep an eye out for trolls."

If they played their cards right, dragging their pursuers to the basaltic lava fields of the north could provide an excellent distraction. They might even celebrate, believing that the troll attack had Val and his crew turning over the wrong rocks.

"So romantic. That's not what he'd be looking at and you know it." Hildur rolled her eyes. "The man's mind is full of smut."

"Hey!" Lauf called. "What about me? Those hot baths unwind the knots in your shoulders like—"

"You'll be at the helm," Val cut him off. "No leaving the airship unmanned."

Lauf sighed but set the coordinates.

Not only was Mývatn far from Húsafell, trolls made their homes in the rough volcanic pillars and black ash that surrounded the base of a volcanic crater. Blanketed in fog and covered with snow, the caves filled with steam and hot blue water were a winter luxury few could access for many reasons. Distance, difficulty and the proximity of trolls discouraged most from ever undertaking the journey.

"We've questions the trolls might be able to answer," Val continued. "Catch some brown trout from the lake first and take it along to the pools. It's a treat they can't resist."

Trolls loved fish. But, built from stone as they were, tended to avoid crossing open water, lest they pitch overboard and sink to the bottom. A fact that made him believe the troll that abducted Angela had been coerced.

"It's January. That means ice fishing first." Horror rippled across Hildur's face. "And dead fish have no place beside a hot spring if one wishes to relax."

"You'd rather approach Grýla empty-handed?"

"The giantess?" His first mate snorted. "You think her sons, the Yule Lads, are involved?"

He shrugged. "Can't hurt to ask." They were in desperate need of clues. "Not only were there runes carved into the troll's back, there was also a single othola rune incised in its chest." He described what Angela had spotted. "Maybe she knows something about the bolt of electricity that dropped Dýri." A new and worrisome feature he couldn't explain. "Tell Grýla about that. Hint that another clan is risking forbidden magic. That might loosen her tongue."

Grýla, the mother of trolls, and perhaps her sons would chase Rømer and his people underground, force them to huddle deep inside a dark sulfurous cave where they could be easily dispatched.

Dýri stuck his head through the door. "Everything's ready."

"You're certain about a parachute drop?" Hildur asked for the millionth time.

Val slid her a glance. "Are you worried for our safety? Or just disappointed that you won't be present for Angela's presentation to the council?"

"Yes," she answered.

His laugh held little light, much like the now dark sky. It wasn't late. Simply a normal winter afternoon at a high northern latitude. He strode out onto the deck and jogged up the few steps to the jump platform. There he shouldered a parachute pack and set about buckling its straps. His wife wore a terrified expression and a sturdy harness atop her wedding finery and beneath a fur cape.

Wife. Would he need to stop thinking of her in such terms? To not notice how the deep purple of her gown set off her golden hair? To shrug off the terror of chasing after her across a junkyard and the relief of finding her unharmed when he stripped her naked in his cabin. To forget how she'd offered up her body, that he'd declined.

Never had he regretted being an honorable man who upheld his promises more.

"You can't be serious." Her mitten-clad hands clutched the steel railing as the wind tried to snatch the hat from her head. At her boot-clad feet rested her satchel, the book of ferns and moss tucked within.

"At some point, the *Grænndreki* needs to refuel," he answered. "Your presence aboard this loftskip risks all our lives, all our work. Better you and I leave to hide you and your grandmother's book someplace safe."

"Understood." Angela stared out at the moonlit landscape that stretched beneath them. "It's the method I'm questioning, for I'm very much over dangling from the end of a rope, wondering if death awaits below."

He flashed her a grin. "Then you'll be relieved to hear your descent will be by way of a parachute."

She groaned. "Not at all. Tell me how jumping out onto a lava field covered in snow and ice improves our situation?"

The piles of jagged black rock protruding above deep drifts of snow that glinted in the moonlight spoke to him of home. But to an outsider, they were intimidating. Wander aimlessly without a compass or proper equipment and you'd not last more than a few hours, if that. At such low temperatures, the wind relentlessly stole away body heat rendering a person increasingly perplexed and confused.

"My crew is off to bargain with trolls in the north." He grimaced. "They'll do their best not to be eaten. You and I, however, are destined for the ground, for warmth and comfort after a brief period of travel."

She tipped her head, frowning. Suspicious. "Comfort? Is that why I'm wearing this impossible corset with damp boots? Why my petticoats and skirts are bunched around my hips to accommodate an unpleasant harness? Not once has a formal gown ever equated comfort. Comfort would involve trousers, but Lisbet insisted first impressions matter. My knees are freezing."

"Approaching drop point." The announcement echoed from the copper speaking tube.

He stepped close, amused by her grousing. "Good thing you wear my wonderfully thick, fur-lined cloak." He bent, threw the strap of her satchel across his chest. "It'll all be over soon." He clipped her harness to his, then pulled the cinch straps tight, an action that crushed the soft mounds of her breasts against him. "Ready?"

She buried her face in his scarf. "No."

A bell clanged.

"That's our signal. Hold tight."

Her arms clamped around him, then he jumped.

Wind whistled past. Clothing flapped. Hair whipped. All while he counted down... Five. Four. Three. Two. One.

He yanked on the rip cord. *Woosh. Yomp.* The chute caught air, jerking them to a stop. Well, to a slow float. He felt Angela's head turn, felt her sudden gasping intake of air. The scenery before them was breathtaking, but it could also be treacherous. He focused on steering, on landing them in the middle of a field where hay grew thick during summer months.

Crunch. Thunk. His boots hit snow, then ground. He let his knees bend while rolling onto his hip—careful to take the impact of the fall as he hauled Angela atop him.

For a moment, they laid there. Silent.

That worried him, the silence. Despite the darkness, the hour was not late. This was a working farm. Animals needed tending. Worse, the smell was wrong. He detected the usual smell of manure, hay and sour milk. But there was no overlaying scent of smoke, no hint of a fire burning to cook the family's dinner.

Angela pushed against his chest to stare down at him. "This is becoming a bad habit."

He tried for an easy grin. "Third time's the charm?" He reached between them and unclipped their harnesses, then quickly bundled the parachute away. No traces of their whereabouts were to be left. Especially not with the fine hairs on the back of his neck standing at wary attention.

She staggered to her feet and turned slowly, taking in the vast and seemingly barren landscape. "Where are we?" The wind snatched the words from her mouth, lending them a waiflike quality.

"Húsafell." He caught her arm, supporting her as they walked to the nearby building, as she tripped and stumbled over uneven stones and clumps of dead grass. A faint light flickered in a tiny window. Somewhat reassuring. "Farmland in West Iceland."

"Farmland?" She sounded unconvinced.

Something about the shadows was wrong. Had that pile of rocks always rested so close to the house? Nothing shifted. Not that it counted for much. Some of the deadliest things in Iceland held perfectly still until *Hel* erupted.

"Hard to imagine in the dead of winter." He kept the conversation casual, hoping his instincts were off. "The dairy farms in the area produce the most amazing skyr, a thick, rich yogurt. This is all a vast expanse of green in summer, when the cows are free to graze. Snug in winter, with the barn built right next to the house, half buried in the ground, wrapped with a wide layer of stone and topped with a turf roof."

"But the smell..."

"True." Horses. Cows. Pigs. Goats. Chickens. Unwashed humans. Olfactory nerves suffered. "But survival trumps all." He sniffed the air. "The farmer keeps a few Icelandic horses for us. I'll saddle a pair and we'll—"

"What accounts for the tang scent?" Angela wrinkled her nose. "Are they butchering—"

His hand shot out, halting her in her tracks. "Stay here." Words spoken under his breath, only loud enough to reach her ears. A few cautious steps closer and the smell of blood grew overwhelming. A farmer might sacrifice an animal now and again to feed his family, but not so many at once. He pushed at the barn door, which moved beneath his hand far too freely.

And opened upon a horrific scene. Slaughtered animals everywhere. Blood soaked the floor. Entrails were heaped in a corner. Feathers, heads, hooves, anything inedible, tossed aside. Only a few wild-eyed horses and a single goat had been spared. But that was not the worst of it.

The farmer lay in the middle of the floor, the flesh of his leg torn and shredded beneath his trousers, his hands gripping a knife driven deeply into his stomach. Nearby lay his family. A woman missing fingers and two small children whose features were clawed beyond all recognition. Yet midst the tattered remnants of their clothing, he could see deep runic gashes cut into their arms and shoulders.

Someone had attempted to tattoo this human-fae family.

Though it appeared an interruption had arrived in the form of a shadow death cat. Vicious creatures, skuggabaldurs.

Angela gasped. Her fingers dug into his arm. Foolish him, thinking she'd follow orders.

He closed the door, latched it. Feeble protection from anything outside, but he'd take whatever concealment it offered.

"Make no sound," he breathed. The skuggabaldur that had slaughtered the farmer, his family and livestock might still roam nearby. Careful as he crossed the slippery floor, he stopped at one body, then the next. Fingers touched to throats found only cold skin without a pulse. He glanced at Angela, still beside him, and shook his head. No survivors.

She grimaced, then reached inside her satchel and withdrew a small jar and a pair of tweezers. She pointed at one of the runes, indicating she was going to take a sample. His eyebrows drew together, impressed at her fortitude in the face of such horror.

He watched her tug a clear thread from the gash on the man's shoulder as she pulled three more threads, one from the wife and one from each of the children. Then with cotton-tipped swabs, she repeated the process, sealing the bloody samples inside separate corked test tubes.

Samples that, unless his eyes deceived him, flashed a faint red.

"Help." More a whimper than a word, called out by an unseen individual.

They spun, directing their attention to the stall where the remaining horses sidled, wary of the broken heap of a person huddled in the straw at their feet. Could this be the perpetrator, his plea a trap?

Val inched closer. Kept his voice low. "You're hurt?"

"Something's wrong." A groan of pain edged with panic. "Hot. Cold." The man rolled onto his side, reaching. But his fingers fell limp as he collapsed, unconscious.

"Is that a tail?" Angela whispered, her gaze focused upon the man's posterior where a hole had been cut through his trousers. "Is he a huldrekall?"

Val nodded. Then a glint of purple caught his eye. He kicked at the hay and let out a low whistle.

"Tyrian Absinthe." Words she hissed through her teeth.

"Loki laughs," Val muttered. "Hildur told me about your brother's bottle. That's three times we've connected Rømer to this drink."

Since London, nothing had gone right. That was wrong. Since university, when he'd befriended an alchemist. His fault. His problem.

She glanced behind her. "You think this huldrekall was experimenting upon the farmer and his family?"

"I do. And acting under Rømer's orders." He bent, unbuttoned the Hulder's shirt and yanked it from his shoulder, exposing a twining, twisting string of runes. Every cut, every marking, red and swollen.

"That's badly infected," she said. "Friend or foe, we can't leave him here."

Basic human decency agreed, though hauling the huldrekall behind the waterfall would touch a match to dry kindling. He snorted. As if bringing Angela wouldn't. All that before he broke the news about a rune-carved troll. This situation was rapidly spiraling out of control.

She misread his hesitation. "He's only just been tattooed. We might be able to remove bioactive glass threads, stop the mark from integrating with his skin." She hesitated. "Or at least document the process..."

Study him? An excellent plan. And the bottle of Tyrian Absinthe would serve nicely as compensation. Industrial quality borosilicate glass tubes didn't come cheap. "Help me saddle the horses."

CHAPTER SEVENTEEN

THE MUSCLES OF HER THIGHS CRAMPED as she gripped the sides of her small, shaggy horse during their descent into a narrow and deep chasm. One cut into a snow-covered lava field by a rushing river that casually tossed about giant chunks of ice from a distance glacier she'd glimpsed from the deck of the airship. A mountain there might be, but between the icy spray of water, blowing snow and the occasional slip of her horse's feet on slippery stone, the view wasn't the first thing on her mind.

Like a child, she wanted to ask, "How much longer?"

Not that Val would hear the question over the roaring water and howling wind. Everything about the landscape was frozen. Save her, her husband, another fae creature, three horses and the bleating goat they dragged along by a rope tied about its neck. The goat hadn't stopped complaining, not once, about leaving the barn's shelter. At first, she'd thought it ungrateful. Now she rather understood the animal's point of view. After all, icicles clung to its matted fur and—

Could hooves grow numb?

The blood and gore-filled scene of the barn refused to stop clawing at her mind, insisting she contemplate and analyze every detail of the horrible slaughter. From the stench that hung in the air, to the slip of her boots on the floor. Heart in her throat, she could almost taste the panic those poor—and likely coercively tattooed—people must have felt as death approached in the form of a skuggabaldur, a not-so-mythical creature from her grandmother's stories. Half fox and half cat, the animal was known for menacing livestock, if only occasionally attacking humans.

She was left wondering what other creatures lurked about, waiting to leap from the shadows. Growing up in England placed her at a decided disadvantage.

With numb fingers beneath woolen mittens, she clutched her fur cloak tighter. A persistent thought nibbled at her brain, like a black plague rat. According to Val, the farmer was human, his wife huldufólk, and the children both. Was this an experiment to see if the bioactive glass and dinoflagellates would take in offspring of mixed heritage? And how did he know to test the runic tattoos upon *this* family? Did Rømer suspect the Huldu Mountain was nearby? Had he purposefully sent the huldrekall to that farm?

Had the tailed Hulder cut the tattoos himself? Or had someone else been present, abandoning the family and the sick huldrekall to make an escape?

The surviving fae had an entire string of runes wrapped around his arm, recently cut and therefore raw and inflamed. There was a chance he could be saved. If she plucked the bioactive glass tubules from his arm soon and disinfected the cuts, he might heal without repercussions. But for that, they needed a safe shelter, away from dangers such as blood-thirsty shadow cats and Loki knew what else. This barren—to her eyes—landscape that might as well be the surface of some distant planet. She'd seen no evidence of life save the few creatures inside a sod-covered barn, survivors of a brutal culling.

Yet Val insisted there was an entire city nearby.

She desperately hoped they reached it soon, before frost-bite started claiming fingers and toes. Already ice crystals flowed through her veins as the marrow in her bones solidi-fied. Her muscles shook, an endless shiver to maintain func-tion as they adjusted for the horse's strange gait. Not at all the homecoming she'd wished, dressed as she was in a ruin of her wedding finery, laced into a cursed corset and bound by yards of soiled silk and thick-soled, damp leather boots.

Of course, she was much better off than the half-dead huldrekall draped face down over the back of the middle horse, unconscious. Lashed in place and covered with wool blankets, his fever was high enough to melt the snow that fell, leaving him encased in a shell of ice.

The deafening roar of water cascading over a basalt outcropping far overhead kept her from questioning Val's sanity aloud as he led the three horses along a narrow rocky ledge and behind a waterfall. How could this be a destination? There was nothing but black rock and frothing white water.

Not that she wished herself still at the dairy farm.

Val slid from the back of his horse. He tugged off his mittens and reached with bare hands to manipulate the rocks before him. Not magic, as one might expect of an elven creature, but instead pushing and pulling large chunks of granite in a manner that reminded her of dialing in the combination to unlock a safe. He moved a final stone, then stepped away.

More rock shifted, then more. Clicking and grinding and scraping until an opening formed. Not a warm and welcoming entrance, but rather one that was brooding and ominous. He reached for his horse's reins and stepped into the abyss. The goat objected with a bleat but, one by one, the horses followed and the mountain swallowed them whole.

From some dark alcove, Val pulled a long staff, one he shook until a globe mounted atop its end began to glow a brilliant blue-white. Light that reflected off the polished black stone of the walls. Enough illumination to guide their way.

The rock door closed behind them as they walked into the chasm, down a narrow passageway that bent left and right at random and strange angles. At times, Angela could swear the stone shifted and moved but, when she fixed a direct gaze upon the granite, all was still.

The horses clomped along for what felt like a small eternity before a soft glow brightened the hallway. Then the rough and jagged walls flared, and they stepped into a vestibule.

"Welcome home, Valtýr Árnason." A stable boy wearing

the oddest of fashions took the reins of Val's horse. He touched the boy's shoulder, speaking softly, before the child hurried away with the horse.

A second boy, similarly dressed, approached, frowning at the body draped over the back of the second horse. "Should I take him to the infirmary?"

"Soon." Val untied the many knots, then eased the fae man to the ground. "He's huldrekall and must be presented. We'll need a stretcher to carry him."

"Presented?" That snapped her out of her trance. She frowned. "An official presentation? Now?" Her voice squeaked. "Looking like *this*?" All sense of place was lost. All she knew was icy snow, rushing water, and towering rock. Where exactly were they? How could there possibly be a fae court here? From the moment she'd climbed aboard the *Grænndreki*, her world had turned upside down.

"Now. Protocol must be followed." Val gripped her waist and lifted her down. *Thunk*, she landed on unsteady feet. "We need to alert the council of the outside threat and inform them of your return."

She pulled off mittens and hat and began combing her damp hair with fingers, doing her best to untangle wind-blown knots while he handed all their belongings—including her bag—to one of the boys for safekeeping. "There's no chance of visiting your quarters first? Miracles can be accomplished in mere minutes with hot water, a comb and a mirror."

Though Lisbet had insisted Angela wear her finest, with her gown ruined by their gruesome discovery in the barn,

Angela had assumed the event would be postponed. She shook out her skirts, smacked at them with what bordered on violence. But there was no hope for the wrinkles. As if such a thing mattered when the hem was darkened by grit, water and blood.

"I'm afraid not." His expression was pinched. "Follow me."

He grabbed the luminous staff and beckoned her toward a door cut into black granite into another hallway. With as deep a breath as her tight-laced corset allowed, she followed. Her footsteps crunched on the black gravel pathway beneath her boots and, little by little, the air grew warmer. The sounds of distant voices caught her ears along with the sound of trickling water. A moment later, they stepped into an enormous cavern, a courtyard straight from a fairy tale.

A gentle light suffused the evening landscape. Moss dotted the ground. Ferns grew in nooks and crannies, on ledges that protruded from stone walls. There were even a few trees. All of them a vibrant green. In the dead of winter. Tucked here and there were small turf-capped houses with brightly painted doors. Lanterns were scattered about the town, strategically positioned to cast light upon the twists and turns of pathways that wound through a field of soft moss. A gentle stream flowed through the cavern, one of hot water, judging from the steam that rose from it into the air, warm and humidifying.

Elves truly had carved out a hidden city inside a mountain.

"Angela?"

She blinked, realizing she'd stopped walking to stare in awe. "How is this real?"

"Someone will be happy to recount a history. Later." He cupped her elbow with a steady hand and tipped his head. "At the moment, you need to make your curtseys before the council."

All about them, people—huldufólk—paused to gawk. A few gathered in groups, exchanging wide-eyed whispers. Was it her strange clothing? The blood on her skirts? The unconscious huldrekall the stable boys carried on a litter?

The women wore brightly embroidered black vests and skirts. Belts of filigree silver looped around their waists. Men wore knee breeches and double-breasted coats. Unfamiliar fashions that, to her eyes, seemed decades out of date. As if here, hidden from the modern world, time had stopped.

At the center of the cavern stood a single carved rune-stone. Beside it waited three people. A gray-haired woman with leafy tattoos twisting across every inch of visible skin, including her forehead and the backs of her hands. A younger, blonde woman with a sword belted to her waist had only a small tattoo peaking above the collar at her neck. The third person was a middle-aged man with tattoos upon his fingers.

Members of the council, she presumed. Would they welcome or judge her?

She swallowed, straightened her back and followed Val along the path and, the moment Val drew to a halt, she curt-sied deeply in a gesture of respect.

"Uncle Aron." Val nodded to the man. "Sigríður

Guðjónsdóttir." He greeted the older woman, bowing from the waist. "It is my great honor to present my wife, Angela Eyrúnsdóttir, your sister's granddaughter."

"Wife?" The young woman's eyebrows rose. "You broke our vows?" Her expression suggested she might toss Val into the cauldron of an active volcano. A goodbye and good riddance with little sacrifice involved.

"Valtýr," the man growled, shaking his head.

Vows?

"Will someone please explain?" Angela glared at her husband. Anger bubbled and seethed. Her hands balled into fists. Was this why he'd refused to bed her? "You already have a wife?" Words that emerged half-choked.

"Fiancée," the woman corrected, crossing her arms.

"Excuse me?" Angela spat. The *humiliation*. Her face grew hot. She would murder him in his sleep. Twice.

"It was necessary, Sóllilja." Val's words were far too calm. "The only way to free her, to bring a descendent of the sólættir to her rightful home." His eyes narrowed. "Our agreed upon terms accounted for such a situation."

The infuriating man spoke as if both women ought to be grateful for his actions, as if he'd done them immense favors by acting without their knowledge or informed consent.

But Sóllilja nodded. The woman looked away, avoiding Angela's outraged gaze. What were they not saying that mattered so very much?

Instead, she directed a question at her great aunt. "Sólættir?"

Disapproval stiffened the councilwoman's spine. "The

highest of ranks among the huldufólk. Though my sister ought to have taught you about your ancestors, I find myself unsurprised at your ignorance. We will speak more of such things at length."

She was a member of the fae nobility? Angela glared at Val. Had he married her for her status? Was she nothing more than a project? A prized possession hauled to Iceland, presented for accolades and advancement? To think she'd trusted him, even started to fall for him. Her arm twitched. If she moved with surprise and speed, she might land a solid punch. It would serve him right to spend his first days home with his eye swollen shut.

On the other hand, her husband had gone to heroic lengths to marry her, to rescue her from a troll, to jump from a perfectly good airship. All to keep her out of Rømer's clutches. And he'd spoken with her as his equal. Such husbands were remarkably difficult to find.

A deep steadying breath and a slow exhale later, she resolved to hear him out, to provide him with the opportunity to offer an explanation. A whirlpool of emotion spun in her mind. Married, but not quite. Part human, given her father, yet welcomed as a lost citizen of a fairy-tale world. The fern, the living tattoo picked into the crook of her elbow, the only proof she needed to belong.

Her great-aunt stepped forward and cupped Angela's face in her palms, turning her head from side to side in silent examination. Tipping her head to the side to look behind her ear. Was she looking for a marriage tattoo? Possibly. But her face revealed nothing.

Finally, Sigríður nodded. "You have the look of her." Her next words were whispered. "Did she find it, the fire fern?"

Find? A question Angela could answer without hesitation. "No."

Grandmother had never mentioned a sister. She'd left this mountain home for a reason and kept her secrets close. Until Angela understood why, she would not be divulging any information about their research. If directly asked, she would disclose the details of Rømer's work, not her own. Not unless Val forced her to tip her hand.

Even then, he'd find it hard. She'd wedged the vials of pyrocysts behind her bodice, grateful—for once—of a tight-laced corset.

"All that fuss and nothing to show for it." Her great aunt pinched her lips together and turned to Val. "You have proof of her lineage?"

"You know that's unnecessary." Val's uncle frowned. "We've been watching all these years."

Watching. If not closely enough to intervene after her grandmother's death. Angela felt like a failed experiment, a disappointment.

From inside a coat pocket, Val pulled a handful of folded papers. "I do." Insult churned deep in her gut as he produced both their marriage license and another official government document with an unbroken wax seal. "Her birth certificate, still sealed, as provided by a British government official."

Sigríður snatched them away. After a quick glance at their license, she slid a fingernail beneath the wax to confirm

Angela's legitimacy. "I'll hold on to these until the entire council has a chance to examine them."

A pensive smile touched the corners of her great aunt's mouth. A smile of the variety that had often graced Angela's mother's lips moments before she made a pronouncement her daughter would hate. What machinations ran through the mind of this high-ranking elder huldufólk?

"On to the problem you've dragged in." Val's uncle gestured at the huldrekall's infected arm, making no move to touch. "There are runes carved into his skin. Runes which appear infected." His eyes threw daggers in Val's direction. "Why have you brought his kind here?"

"It's a long story." Val drew a deep breath and informed them of Katla Dagsdóttir's death, the official autopsy results and the subsequent troll attack, including the bolt of electricity it had thrown. He then went on to speak of the reason for their precipitous arrival at the Huldu mountain, of Rømer's likely involvement, British concerns about the imminent royal wedding, ending with finding the huldrekall at the farm in the wake of a skuggabaldur attack.

Val had the rapt attention of the council members from the moment he mentioned the discovery of the ambassador's daughter. Notably, her husband left out his connection with the alchemist by way of university and made no mention of his wife's work with ferns or bioluminescent dinoflagellates.

Perhaps, once she heard the facts, he might be forgiven for failing to disclose a secret fiancée.

"This must be stopped." Sigríður's eyes narrowed. "Not only do our interests align with the rest of the island's, our existence needs to remain hidden. This Norwegian cannot be allowed to disrupt the royal wedding plans."

"Which is why we thought it best to bring the huldrekall with us," Angela volunteered. "As the runes appear to be in the early stages of the implantation process, we might learn much. This is a tattooing method vastly different from our own, one reliant upon an inorganic material to fuse living tissue with fae flesh."

"You're a physician?" Aron asked.

"A research scientist," she clarified. "With interests and knowledge in the field of botanical dermatology. The cleansing of his wounds will require special attention that I am capable of providing. I assisted with the autopsy aboard the *Grænndreki*." If such a statement was a slight exaggeration, so be it. She refused to let them cut her out of this investigation. "Rømer has attacked our kind and now a close cousin, I wish to know why."

"I'll take a team to the farm, see what we can find." Sóllilja rested her hand on the hilt of her sword and addressed Val. "Did you speak with the house nissi?"

"I caught a glimpse of his pointed red hat in the rafters when I searched the building." He glanced at Angela, his lips pressed together, a silent apology for the few minutes he'd left her alone. "But he refused to answer. I didn't dare linger."

Nissi were real? Why not? She mentally added a new fae creature to her list. So much to learn and no chance to ask.

Aron cursed. "Shall I see the huldrekall kept under guard while under my niece's temporary care?"

Sóllilja nodded, but Angela's great aunt narrowed her eyes. "That huldrekall remains here only as long as is absolutely necessary, Aron. He's not our guest and, in fact, might be an active threat. See that he is secured."

"Follow me, Angela. Now is your chance to prove your expertise." Aron turned on his heel, following a stone pathway that led to one of the quaint turf houses. He paused to issue orders to the boys holding the stretcher with the huldrekall, then glared at his nephew. "No, Valtýr, you stay. You and the councilwomen have much to discuss. Once you've made amends, come find your *wife* in my laboratory."

CHAPTER EIGHTEEN

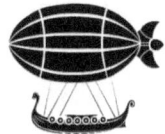

"WE HAD AN ARRANGEMENT!" Alone, Sóllilja's outward calm fell away. But her agitation wasn't one of romantic betrayal. Only that the Pied Piper had presented a notice of payment due. "A contract."

"No one appreciates an oath-breaker, Valtýr." Sigríður glowered. "Bound by such promises to *two* women is an unacceptable state."

Now *three* women wished to strangle him. Not that he was in the wrong, but Odin help him if any of them managed to conspire. He pressed his hand to the runestone. "Upon this standing stone, I swear I am no oath-breaker. She is unmarked and still a maiden."

"Then you have done our people a great service, fetching her home." Sigríður's eyes burned with visions of how this new-found relative might best serve her purposes. "I will see this remedied. Angela deserves better than an airship captain."

There it was, right on cue. Classism. Val tamped down his anger. For first he and Sóllilja needed to speak privately, to formally sever their agreement.

His fiancée snorted. "Did you not see how he looked at her?"

"I'm old, not blind," the council member snapped. "But he is here, hand on a runestone, swearing he has not betrayed his promise. It is, however, understandable if you wish to call off your engagement." She drew up straight, poised to act. "Arrangements for travel to Þingvellir are easily made. A number of men worthy of your hand attend the Midwinter Þorrablót Feast this year. An excellent chance to find you a husband of rank and possibly attend the wedding of the century."

Sóllilja blanched. Only their engagement protected her from such political machinations. Her father would snatch at an opportunity to place his daughter among future Icelandic royalty. She'd be effectively exiled from the mountain. Forced to surrender her sword. To drape herself in silks and furs and silence. Condemned to feign subservience that she might inveigle her way into the Queen's court, where her only function would be to eavesdrop.

A fate he'd promised to help her avoid.

Neither, however, did he wish a similar fate to befall Angela. Much as he wanted to protect both women, Sóllilja had known for years she needed to make alternative plans. His wife had only known about her high-ranking status among the huldufólk for a few minutes. Sóllilja was a good friend, but Angela was his priority. Their marriage came first. His wife had questions, and he'd see them all answered. Then she would decide. "It would be a mistake to rush anything." He pushed a note of warning into his voice as he addressed Sigríður. "My wife is new to her heritage."

"Stop calling her that." The conniving old woman pointed a vine-wrapped finger at Val. "If it's funding for your airship you're after, I'll see you kept aloft if Sóllilja's father withdraws his financial support. That is, provided you cooperate."

His lips flattened. The bottle of Tyrian Absinthe could be sold. The check handed to him by a spy cashed. As it was not an official dowry, he could argue the money was a gift and therefore his to keep in the event of a dissolution. Yet covering costs by such methods would negatively reflect upon his honor. He was no airship pirate. Nor, however, did he want to discontinue research that would benefit all of Iceland, fae and human alike.

The councilwoman took his silence for agreement. "I'll see to the paperwork, then guide her future choices. Rest assured they will be good ones. You're not to interfere further."

Val kept his mouth shut. He'd promise nothing, as he intended to obstruct the councilwoman's goals at every turn. He'd not sign any documents dissolving their union unless Angela begged for release. A wave of heat coursed through him. He'd like nothing better than to have her beneath him, begging for exactly that. Tonight, if possible. He cleared his throat. "Angela's expertise on the matter of the huldrekall's skin-carved runes is required. I'll need to consult—"

"The prisoner is mine to question, mine to evaluate," Sóllilja interrupted. As head of mountain security, she possessed that right. "After we search the farm and speak with the house nissi, I'll decide what security risks this outsider presents."

"Don't think to cut me out of your investigation." Val leaned forward. "The attempt to imitate traditional Eldskrift markings is of concern. Have there been increased troll attacks?"

"There are always more trolls about during the dark winter months." Sóllilja frowned. "Though usually not so many in the south. Your story of a troll throwing off bolts of electricity worries me, but it's the first I've heard of such a thing. I've argued in favor of resurrecting the ancient runic tradition, if only on a small scale to defend our borders, but the mountain council collectively voted against re-establishing the Fire Script Guardians."

"Because modern times call for modern solutions." Sigríður's mouth set in a tight-lipped smile as she fixed her gaze upon his former fiancée's sword. "Better to handle relations with diplomacy. Such as the kind strategic political marriages accomplish."

"On that we disagree," his fiancée rejoined. "Some creatures cannot be reasoned with, such as a skuggabaldur. Trolls respect a show of strength. If the elders would allow us to search the library for—"

"Stop." The councilwoman held up her hand. "This

Norwegian you label an alchemist is nothing but a mad scientist dabbling in that which he does not understand. He has no chance of success. My sister devoted her entire life to the same goal. She failed. This discussion serves no purpose." Her eyebrows lifted. "Unless you have something to share, Valtýr?"

He thought of the dead fern decomposing in his cabin. Of the book filled with runic scribblings. Of the dinoflagellates his wife cultivated. Secrets, all of them. Ones that, if shared, would end his marriage. "I do not."

"Then I'll leave you two to discuss your future." The councilwoman turned on her heel and departed.

Alone, his friend spoke freely. "Where is the rest of your crew?"

He blew out a frustrated puff of air. "Our arrangement was intended to buy you time, not keep us chained to each other for decades. We agreed that when one of us decided to marry, our engagement would end."

"To end *before* we married," she spat back. "Even if your bride agrees to dissolve your union, this situation reflects poorly upon me. There will be rumors. Fix this."

"What if I don't wish to?" Only their long-standing friendship kept his feet rooted to the ground. "Enough time to establish your career before you broke with tradition. That was the agreement. Now you're head of security. It's time to speak with Dýri."

She narrowed her eyes. "And where is he?"

"In the north with the airship. He and Hildur are attempting to speak with the trolls of Mývatn. Modern solutions. Possibly backed by sharp pointy objects and explosives."

Sóllilja jabbed him in the chest. "You sent them to speak with Grýla without alerting me?"

"We were being pursued." He threw his hands in the air. "You want to work with Dýri, at his side? You know where he sleeps. If you can't speak to him, try seducing him." Val thought of Angela's half-dressed form warming his bed. Of the overwhelming temptation of her arms wrapped about him, soft lips trailing down the side of his neck. "If he finds you there, waiting when he returns—"

"Listen to you, full of romantic advice." Her face flushed red. "I need more time. Until after the royal wedding. Whatever you're feeling for this woman, you'll get over it. Find someone else. It's not worth risking the *Grænndreki*, is it?"

It was, but he'd not be sharing such heartfelt thoughts with anyone but Angela. He settled with a simple fact, emphasizing his seriousness. "I'll not be the one who ends our marriage." He softened his tone. "He's interested, Sóllilja. Let him know he has more than half a chance..."

"And if he turns me away?"

He lifted a shoulder. "Dozens of men would happily bind themselves to you. Chose another."

"Is this an ultimatum?" Face contorted in a mixture of angry panic, she yanked her hands away. "What is it about Angela Eyrúnsdóttir that made you speak vows so readily?"

"Fate?" A simple word to describe the tangle of emotions that wound through him, binding his heart to another woman. "But enough of that. We've a more pressing situation. Rømer is hunting fae creatures, experimenting upon them. He's grown careless—or desperate—enough that the British have taken notice. We need to stop him."

"We?" Sóllilja crossed her arms, still angry. "You think I have any interest in working with you—or your wife—at all?"

When word reached the mountain that Katla had called off the wedding and run away with a Norwegian, it hadn't taken Val long to suss out exactly what had happened.

Betrayal. On two fronts.

Infuriated, he'd sworn retaliation.

Sensing opportunity, Sóllilja had approached him with a unique proposal: a fake engagement.

Per the terms of their contract, her wealthy father would fund his research and she would be free to pursue a career on the council as head of mountain security. Should one of them wish to marry in the future, they need only inform the other to nullify their agreement.

"I've shielded you from your family's matrimonial hopes for years," Val countered. "This isn't simply an inconvenience. Our people are at risk. Rømer's insane experiments killed Katla. He recruited a troll, possibly gave it dangerous new electrical powers. And now a huldrekall. Perhaps he simply likes glowing tattoos. Or he might want to attack our mountain and steal our secrets. Maybe he'd also like to disrupt the royal marriage that makes Iceland an independent kingdom. To stop him, you need our help—and we need yours."

"Fine." Sóllilja huffed. "You're free. Our engagement has ended. We'll work together. But only if you tell me everything that's going on. No hiding important details. For example, what is it you don't want the council to know?"

Much. His shoulders relaxed. Having the head of security, an old friend, on his side was no trivial thing. "I think Rømer is the one behind Tyrian Absinthe. And I'm beginning to wonder if there's more to it than an effective money-making scheme." He explained how Katla and the huldrekall had been found with bottles, how Angela's brother had obtained one. "It's being sold to those of royal heritage yet denied to Jarl Haukr."

"A man who is not yet a king," she finished. "I've heard he's mad to acquire a bottle, to toast his bride after their wedding. You think Rømer is taunting him?"

"I do. Soon Iceland will finally be free from Danish rule. Rømer, along with others, has rallied for Norwegian sovereignty, for freedom from Sweden, yet their cries have been largely ignored. He's bitter and spiteful and inclined to cause trouble."

She tipped her head and narrowed her eyes. "You forget that we've known each other for decades. I can tell when you're not telling me something. What is it you're leaving out?"

Angela's tiny glowing pyrocysts. How Rømer had known to hunt for them in the first place. "Not here," he answered. "And there's more information to gather. We should all meet later to share, to discuss how to proceed."

"One more thing," Sóllilja began. "You promised me a position aboard your loftskip. Take me with you when you leave."

She'd wanted to travel with him for ages, but he'd refused. "You know the conditions," he said. "Only if you speak to Dýri first." It was the only way he'd permit her aboard the airship.

Eyes locked, they stared at each other.

"Fine," she snapped. "Have it your way." She strode away, stopping and turning when he failed to follow. "Let's go."

"Go where?" He rolled his eyes. "To Mývatn? I don't think so. They'll be back soon. Your declaration of unwavering infatuation can wait."

"The farm," she growled, stalking back to him and jabbing him in the chest. "And that conversation is over. We'll not speak of this again. The only *creature* I want to speak with is the house nissi. He'll have answers."

Val glanced at the tunnel leading to his uncle's laboratory. The fire blazing in his wife's eyes had threatened to burn everything to the ground. She had every reason for her fury. Much as he wished to follow, to explain, he needed to speak with his mother first. She deserved to learn of his marriage without delay. More, if he handed her these new life threads, would she be able to weave something that might predict the future? She'd foreseen he would not marry Katla, but instead a foreigner, and he could use whatever direction she might provide.

Sóllilja snapped her fingers at him. "Come or stay."

The answer came easily. "Stay."

With a huff, she stomped away.

With one last uncertain glance at the tunnel that led to Angela's side, Val chose another path.

"AND YOU MARRIED HER?" Smiling, his mother pressed a hand against her heart. "Just as the Norns predicted." She hurried across the room to a trunk and pulled out his baby blanket, the one she'd woven the day before his birth while in a deep trance. She returned, held it out with great expectation.

He sighed. His mother was a völva, a Norse witch, who placed great significance in the rituals of seiðr. Val refused to take it from her. "You know I cannot read the threads."

His mother nodded. Unfolding the blanket, she pointed to the strand of dark wool that ran through the pattern overlapping a thread of gold. A story he'd heard before, one endlessly recounted. A prophecy his mother was certain would come to pass. "Gold for marriage. But a black strand..."

The black could mean many things. A certain alchemist's interference, for example. Death and destruction. Not of him, for the weave continued years past that moment. But he didn't wish harm to his wife, Sóllilja, or any member of his crew.

He dropped into a chair and fell forward, elbows to knees. He ran his fingers through his hair. "Sigríður Guðjónsdóttir is drawing up papers of dissolution. She does not want me married to her sister's granddaughter."

"It's not her choice. That belongs to you and your wife."

"Knowing the councilwoman, she'll find a way to separate us." His voice was full of exasperation.

But laughter danced in his mother's voice. "You've angered many, marrying in haste, leaving the bedding for later. All to hang onto a thin, fraying thread of an oath you made to Sóllilja. Now you wish to repair the situation with your wife but aren't sure words will be enough. Love does that to a man."

Love? Rational thought insisted it was too soon for that. Instinct only insisted he fulfill a deep-seated craving. Was that love? Lust, certainly. But he couldn't shake the feeling that their fates were entwined. He needed Angela, needed her as his wife. He lifted his head. "My father will object." His parents had never married. His father had offered, grudgingly, but his mother preferred a life alone with her craft. "I need your help."

"You certainly do." Folding the blanket, she shook her head in disappointment. "Two nights without you in her bed, she'll have doubts. Don't worry about your father." She waved a hand. "I will compose a *galdr* charm to persuade him to your point of view. As for your wife..." His mother pulled a thin pattern book from the shelf and shoved it into his hands. "Would you offer her this?"

"A *sálbundið*?" Marriage tattoos were rare these days. Given the long lives his people lived and how the marks were believed to entwine the souls, they'd fallen out of fashion. In the event a relationship soured, couples might separate, find new partners, and neither wished for a permanent mark on their skin to recall how they'd once pledged themselves to another. "I would, but we've known each other only a few days." A sálbundið was an intimate act, one of choosing. "She's not likely to know the significance."

Such a tattoo would hinder—if not stop—Sigríður's plans to end their marriage, to use Angela as a political pawn. Among the upper echelon, huldufólk men preferred a woman without prior romantic entanglements. Not to mention, after her brother's attempt to auction her off, she would refuse to cooperate. The situation would be, at best, uncomfortable.

But Angela might even now be having second thoughts about their marriage. He needed—wanted—time alone with her, but under current circumstances, such time was likely to be a rare commodity.

"Then tell her. Explain. She should be certain." His mother lifted tube after tube from a rack, checking the viability of her purified chloroplast collection. As a völva, many turned to her for help when selecting a new tattoo, choosing particular plants to mark specific occasions. "Not the best time of year for variety," she complained. "Mountain avens, stone bramble berry, angelica..."

All flowering plants.

"Do you have anything from a simpler plant?" Primal and primitive suited his state of mind. "A moss or liverwort or fern?"

Her hand stilled. "Is there a particular reason you do not wish for flowers? They're traditional."

"Angela is a botanist and might enjoy using one of the simpler plants which are the focus of her studies."

"A botanist? Ferns?" A slow smile stole across her face. "Eyrún never gave up. How Aron has stewed all these long years. His own bride-to-be abandoning him to pursue her quest, certain she could somehow puzzle out the mystery of the fire fern that we might once again win the protection of the Eldskrift."

"Why am I only now hearing about this fire fern?" Val sank deeper into the chair. "First from my wife, now from you."

"Because no one wishes to offer their first born in sacrifice."

A thunderbolt shot through him. He'd been right to seek his mother's advice. Might she make sense of the runic scribblings in Angela's book? "That's a cryptic answer in need of an explanation."

"I'll tell you everything but, if you're to do this, you need to exchange your tattoos tonight." Her hand tightened around his wrist. "Before Sigríður manages to sink her claws into her niece."

"Niece? Not grandniece?" His eyebrows flew upward. "Start talking, Mother."

CHAPTER NINETEEN

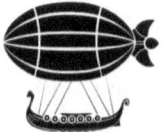

NGELA SLOWLY PIVOTED, TAKING IN THE cobweb-covered space. A laboratory? More like an alchemist's workshop. Had she traveled back in time to the last century? Glass-doored cabinets held grimy bottles with handwritten labels. Dried herbs. Powdered substances. Liquids of unknown concentrations. A workbench displayed a collection of tools fit for an herbalist. A black cauldron hung from a hook inside an enormous fireplace. Upon a desk shoved in a corner rested a fountain pen and a dusty journal with yellowed pages.

"You expect me to work here?" She ought to turn, frown at Val's uncle. But found herself entranced by an array of stone crystals. "Sulfur?" Impulsively, she blew at the dust covering a yellow rock and ended in a sneezing fit.

"Sulfur," Aron confirmed. An unimpressed expression twisted his lips. "Antifungal. Antibacterial. Possessed of keratolytic activity." An eyebrow lifted. "I thought you claimed to be a dermatologist?"

The young men who'd carried the unconscious huldrekall transferred him onto a narrow canvas cot.

"Used to treat rosacea, seborrheic dermatitis, dandruff, scabies, warts." A snap answer for a snap judgment. She knew skin.

Of all the various rocks and minerals arrayed upon the shelves, it was the only one with much medical use. The place seemed designed for witchcraft, not research. Which, given recent experiences, probably shouldn't come as such a shock. Just what kinds of "experiments" had been conducted in this subterranean chamber?

Val's uncle clamped a shackle about the Huldrekall's ankle and secured him to a nearby pipe.

She frowned. "Is there no medical ward?"

"After what you discovered in that barn?" Aron asked, incredulous. "Skuggabaldur aside, he's a threat. That makes him a prisoner, not a guest. Besides, with so many marks, there's little chance of his survival. Unless you manage to eliminate the infection, he won't be released, not when humans believe glowing red tattoos are a mark of sorcery and the devil."

She had to admit he made valid points. "Still, he's a patient with open wounds. This is a poor environment for recovery." She swept her hand in an arc, gesturing at the room as a whole. "At the bare minimum, I require clean water and bandages. And that's before we address the lack of a microscope, let alone the deficiency of modern laboratory equipment."

"Much as we don't house potential criminals in our infirmary, most surprise guests aren't afforded the luxury of their own research space, but you indicated a need for the immediate study of his wounds." He tipped his head, studying her face. "As this once belonged to Eyrún Guðjónsdóttir, I thought you might make use of it."

Her eyes widened, reevaluating the windowless room carved into the mountain. The only hint that plants might have been cultivated was a single Wardian case placed beneath a strange glass prism inserted into the ceiling. A source of light for plants? Impossible to determine until the sun rose.

"Here?" She blinked. "Did you know each other?"

"Rather well." His lips pressed together. "Once." A word that struggled to leave his mouth as he turned away and headed for the exit. "My laboratory is next door, should you wish to avail yourself of my aetheric microscope and other assorted *modern* supplies."

She threw a concerned glance at the fae creature upon the cot as he stirred, letting out a faint moan. Feverish, the man managed to be both pale and flushed at the same time. He needed attention. Much as she intended to probe his wounds, to tease the bioactive glass fibers from the runes carved into his skin, to collect fluid samples for microscopic study, it was beyond cruel to leave such cuts unbandaged, to offer him no pain relief.

Concern roiled her stomach. Why was everyone so dismissive and uncaring of the huldrekall's health? What if he wasn't guilty, but a victim much like the farmer and his family? There *was* an infirmary. One with physicians, nurses, or healers—whatever they called them here.

"Shouldn't medical staff at least pay a visit?"

With a sigh, Aron crossed the room to a wooden cabinet and yanked open a drawer. "Ethyl alcohol. Linen bandages." He waved at a sink. "Hot and cold running water. Be careful with the hot water, it's pumped directly from the ground near the hot spring, Selgil, and is quite hot." He turned and walked away. "As to the rest, you're a physician. You'll manage." A challenge thrown over his shoulder.

"Researcher," she reminded him, following on his heels. "In the field of botanical dermatology. Any and all medical knowledge I possess was acquired by way of book learning."

Her brother Jack had been the only one to attend medical school. Not for lack of trying on her part. Every year she'd applied. Every year she'd been denied. Instead, she'd buried herself in the country estate's greenhouses, churning out monographs detailing the antioxidant and antimutagenic properties of chlorophyll. She'd turned that knowledge into a cosmetics line, developed with her grandmother's guidance, to offset Marcus's extreme expenditures. Some of the coins she sewed into the hems of her gowns, reinvesting the rest of the profits into acquiring new and unusual liverworts and ferns from distant lands.

For all the good that had done.

"Unsurprising. Given you're a fae female."

"I'm sorry?" She jerked her shoulders back, offended. Val's uncle's remark cut to the bone. "Women are perfectly capable—"

"Please." He shook his head. "Stow your tirade. Equal rights for women or not, Eyrún would never have let any true-breeding progeny of hers anywhere near one of Britain's medical schools. We're not in the habit of drawing attention to ourselves."

True-breeding?

She'd not expected to be treated like a science experiment among her own people. Stuffing down her objections, she focused on her immediate goal. "About that microscope..."

"Follow me." He crossed the hall and threw open a door, one that opened into a gloriously modern laboratory suffused with a strange purple glow.

Across the room, a diligent assistant worked, noting down measurements and readings from a number of dials, barely looking up from the clipboard in his hands to acknowledge their arrival with a brief nod.

Glass tubes stretched from floor to ceiling. Each cylinder was connected to the next via a U-shaped pipe, one after the other, to form an array. Undulating through the water-filled vertical network was what looked like algae? Her nose wrinkled. Whatever he grew produced the most *awful* smell. Like spoiled fish rotting in a swamp beneath the sun. Ugh, she could even taste the fug on her tongue, thick and pungent.

Fighting the urge to gag, she touched fingertips to the nearest tube. Comfortably warm. Also a product of the nearby hot spring? Likely. Slowly, she turned, overwhelmed with awe.

A pump circulated warm water through the glass pipes, keeping the contents—spirulina blue-green algae, if she wasn't mistaken—in a state of constant motion. But there was precious little noise. No coal, no gas burned to heat the water or fuel an engine. Instead, a small motor hummed, nearly silent. Was it possible? Could it run on geothermal electric power?

Iceland *was* known for its fumaroles, geysers, thermal pools and volcanic eruptions. But she'd only read monographs that read like fantastical science fiction, predicting that heat drawn from the earth's molten core might someday be captured and used to replace wood and coal. Hypotheses dismissed by most gentlemen scholars as the rantings and ravings of mad scientists.

But why not? Had she not stood this morning upon the deck of the *Grænndreki* and witnessed something similar where blue-green algae harnessed the sun's rays to fly them home, allowing them to travel during daylight hours without burning so much as a single lump of coal? Here, generating energy would be even simpler, harnessing volcanic heat from beneath the ground. Her eyebrows slammed together. If the huldufólk had electrical power...

Aron snapped his fingers in her face. "Focus."

She glared. "Are you always so rude?"

"To those who cannot keep up? Yes." Val's uncle crossed his arms. "I know the sight before you is fascinating but save your questions. We were speaking of Eyrún. Did she tell you nothing of why she left Iceland?"

"To marry my grandfather?" She hated the note of doubt that crept into her question. Her Grandmother had possessed her own laboratory. Yet she'd abandoned it all to marry an English lord?

"Hardly." Aron barked a laugh. "She ran away to avoid marrying *me*."

"You?" That drew her up short. "But..."

This man was Val's uncle. Her stomach turned queasy. Was Aron about to inform her that he was her father? No. Impossible. Grandmother had married her grandfather and lived in England for many years before Angela had been born. Which dropped another fact into place with a loud clunk. The passage of time.

"You're thinking I'm too young?" He smiled. "Or that Eyrún was too old?" He snorted. "The hidden folk of Iceland live to a ripe old age, a gift bestowed upon us by our living tattoos. Did you never wonder how a woman her age managed to look so youthful?" His grin widened. "Oh, by the way, she's not your grandmother. She's your *mother*."

"Mother? Impossible. I've two older brothers—"

"Those are your nephews." A diabolical light suffused his eyes. "Born to the son of your father's first wife."

"What?" She pulled a face.

"Do you think we didn't know where she was? We trace our lineages closely, even when someone leaves our community. Especially those who are high-ranking elves."

"All this time you knew of me." She was weary of all the half-truths and lies by omission. "And did... nothing?"

"She's the one who chose to sever all connections." Aron sighed. "Did Eyrún tell you nothing? You really haven't a clue?"

Angela crossed her arms and narrowed her eyes, mimicking his posture. "Anything she taught me was presented in the form of fairy tales."

He rolled his eyes. "Then let me begin with your father, the man you believed to be your grandfather. He was a known huldrekall changeling placed in the cradle of an English lord."

"I'm sorry." She gaped. It never rained but it poured. *Changeling?* "You're telling me I'm only *half* huldufólk?" This entire conversation was a confusion of impossibilities, all of them chasing the others while nipping at heels.

"Yes. Human subspecies are everywhere, much like other cryptids. Most don't stand out much from standard humans. Unlike, for example, selkies."

Selkies were real?

But her mouth failed to form the questions before he continued. "Your father grew up without knowledge of his origin, married a human and produced an heir. Unfortunately, this first wife died in childbirth. Years pass and that heir, who was *not* your father, married a woman—*not* your mother—and fathered the two men you think of as your brothers. Meanwhile, *their* grandfather married again. A young bride who, quite embarrassingly, was unable to produce any spares—or any children at all—until the lord was elderly. Only a daughter he named after the angels, heaven sent as she was."

Angela.

Could it be? Angela sucked in a sharp breath. One she instantly regretted. The horrid algal experiments Aron conducted were none of her concern. But her heritage, that should concern her, should it not? Else why closely guard such a family secret? Was societal shame enough?

Perhaps.

Who else had known? Not Jack. He would have told her. But the woman she called mother and her eldest son, Marcus, were horrid individuals lifted straight from fairy tales like *Cinderella.* Fitting, she supposed, if what Val's uncle said was true. And painful, given the control that evil woman had exerted over her life. Though the worst of her not-brother and not-mother's plans hadn't been enacted until her not-grandmother had died.

After which they'd been quick to capitalize on her existence by selling her hand in marriage to a man more interested in her living tattoo than her. To a man who had sent a troll to kidnap her when he was denied possession. To a man whose research worried Val enough that he leapt from a perfectly good airship to drag her behind a waterfall where Rømer couldn't follow. All so she could...

What?

Help him stop a monster from carving toxic glowing tattoos into all manner of fae creatures?

But she was getting ahead of herself. Understanding her

past might be key to understanding what was happening in the present.

"You're carefully considering my words and finding truth, aren't you?" Aron tipped his head. "Let me guess. Your 'mother' always favored your 'brothers', treating you as an abomination, leaving her 'daughter' in 'grandmother's' care. In the countryside. Where Eyrún tucked herself away as a social recluse to avoid societal scrutiny."

"Impossible." But Angela's lips pressed into a flat line. Much as she hated to admit it, his assessment of her familial structure rang true. It wasn't unheard of for older women to bear offspring at an advanced age. It was, however, rare for them to survive childbirth, to outlive a husband by so many, many years.

She cast her mind back. Now that she thought of it, Grandfather had always been spry, even in his last years, zipping about with a vitality that caused many to remark upon his youthful vigor. Until a horrible accident stole his life. Grandmother herself had always appeared young, a trait she attributed to her plant-based diet. On the other hand, she hid in the countryside. And had a habit of "brightening" her hair using bleach, stripping away all color leaving it fine, wispy and white.

He rolled his eyes. "Were you taught nothing about fae? We live longer... and produce far fewer offspring."

She recalled the bedtime fairy tales read to her as a small child. A nugget of truth? "Due to low fertility?"

"Call it what you will." He waved a dismissive hand. "You are the product of your father's second wife, Eyrún

246

Guðjónsdóttir and a Nordic huldrekall of dubious lineage. One hundred percent undiluted fae." His eyes narrowed. "An unsanctioned breeding experiment that, judging from your tattoo, worked." He tipped his head. "Any chance you've a tail?"

That drew her up short. "Rude."

He shrugged. "Just curious."

"Yet if I'd failed to assimilate plant cells on a cellular level?" The tattoo she'd given Jack hadn't lasted more than a few days, possibly because he was only a quarter Hulder and not at all Huldu. "What about my father did she find promising?"

"An excellent question, most huldrekall are incapable of hosting plant cells." Aron's smile didn't reach his eyes and the bitterness of a jilted groom colored his words. "A risk on her part, given the huldrekall are distant relatives, but better than choosing to breed with a human, no matter his wealth or social status." He rolled his shoulders, more a dismissal of the topic than a shrug. "Save your patient and perhaps he might have answers for you."

The floor rumbled and shook under her feet. Her eyes popped wide open. "Is that an earthquake?"

"What else would it be?" he barked, turning away to call to his assistant. "Status?"

Ding. Ding ding ding. The clapper on a copper alarm bell sounded. A green mass was snagged on something inside the glass tube. At the pipe joint beneath it, a fine spray of water emerged with a loud hiss. A pool of water rapidly formed on the tiled floor, filling the air with the smell of sulfur.

"The vibration caused an entanglement," the assistant replied calmly. "I'm reducing flow rate now..."

The floor heaved. A crack appeared at her feet. Books tumbled from a nearby shelf. Metal groaned and a metal band securing a glass tube pulled away from its rivet with a loud *crack* leaving behind a fracture along the length of the tube.

"We have a rupture!" The assistant flipped a lever. "Shutting down now."

"Not again." Cursing in Icelandic, something nonsensical about horses, fish eyes and his angry spleen, Aron pushed a cart at her and pointed to the center of the enormous space that was fitted up with a wet lab, all bright lights and polished stainless steel. "The pipes might shatter. Load the aetheric microscope on the cart first. Take as many supplies as you can manage, haul it back to your laboratory. Work fast. If there's another aftershock like the last, this room might become a disaster zone."

As he jogged to his assistant, calling out numbers and values and issuing orders, she seized the cart and ran to the bench top.

Wrapping her arms about the enormous microscope, she dragged the device across the counter, ignoring the horrible ear-piercing screech of its rubber and metal feet. Microscopes of this size weren't meant to be lifted and heaved by a single person. Still, she was about to try. A shower of water, algae and glass would ruin an aetheroscope.

She took a deep breath, braced her legs, and lifted. Managing an entire inch. Just enough clearance to twist about and drop the aetheric microscope on the cart.

A glance in Aron's direction wasn't reassuring. Soaked from head to toe by foul-scented water, he and his assistant fought to turn a huge bolt with an equally enormous wrench. The hands of various dials fluctuated wildly, a few moving into red-painted zones, and several more of the glass tubes had developed hairline fractures.

She threw open the cabinet's glass doors and started grabbing boxes and racks. Aetheric cartridges. Slides. Cover-slips. Test tubes. Tweezers. She needed many things.

But supplies weren't the only items of value. On a wooden desk was an open book. A diary of sorts. Mostly hand-scribbled equations possessed of as many Greek letters as numbers. Engineering math? She was about to turn her back when something scratched in the margins caught her eye. A string of mixed fuþark runes and bindrunes. The same odd combination her grandmother had used. She snatched up the book and flipped pages. All of them were inked with runes. And bindrunes. Sometimes the strange writing system filled entire pages.

A single word caught her attention: *Eldskrift.*

Were these the pages Val had "borrowed" and shown to Rømer? No. They were new. Written upon modern paper and not hers to take. But if she left the book here, it might well be destroyed. And she wanted to study the scribbles. Closely.

The floor heaved beneath her feet. The fissure in the

rock opened wider. More glass cracked and water began to flood the ground, a miniature waterfall inside a rock cavern pouring into the earth's depths.

"Go!" Aron yelled. "We can't shut the system down. Catastrophic failure is imminent. Run!"

He'd thank her later. She tossed the book among the supplies she'd gathered. She heaved the overburdened cart at top speed through a spray of water toward the door, hoping her grandmother's—mother's?—laboratory would prove a safe haven.

CHAPTER TWENTY

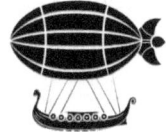

THE OLD LABORATORY HAD SUSTAINED no significant damage from the earthquake beyond a few hairline fractures in the floor. Nothing new, she gathered, given several older fissures had been filled in with black gravel.

That's what came of building one's home inside a mountain. The cabinet doors holding the multitudes of bottles made more sense now. How else to keep from dying from a random chemical reaction when all of your reagents fell from shelving to smash on a stone floor where they could mix at will?

She held her breath as the floor shuddered. Gently. As if settling in and finding the new arrangement suited. Something she needed to do herself. To move past half-truths and outright lies told to her by people she ought to have been able to trust. She was done accepting things at face value. Done letting others determine her fate.

And that included being told what to wear. Her hated fancy court gown was thoroughly ruined. Blood. Sulfuric water. Grit and grime. But the cursed garment was bound tightly about her torso by lacing and hooks and ties.

There was a patient who required care. Toxic skin carvings to investigate. Ancient papers to study. But first she needed dry clothing. She could call for help, kick up a fuss. Demand someone deliver her clean clothes. But in the chaos following the earthquake, she'd been forgotten. Left to her own devices.

And she intended to use every precious minute of that freedom.

This was what she'd wanted, wasn't it? To break free. To visit Iceland. To meet the other branch of her family. Never in a million years would she have guessed they lived deep inside a mountain harnessing geothermal powers to hide their purportedly long-lived existence. All anomalies that generated far more questions than answers. But that was neither here nor there. She'd begin as she intended to continue. Every journey began with a single step and other such platitudes.

Marching across the room to a tall wooden cabinet, she gripped the handles, bowed her head and offered up a silent prayer to the gods. A lab coat. A cloak. Even a rough woolen blanket would suffice.

She threw the doors open and laughed. Even better. A Skautbúningur—traditional Icelandic garb. A black woolen skirt, its hem embroidered with a floral design. A jacket with long, close-fitting sleeves. A traditional headdress. Stockings and shoes. All of it roughly her size. Wearing this, she would no longer stand out among the other huldufólk.

Her mother's? Likely. If what Aron said could be believed. Regardless, warm and clean clothing, no matter a slight mustiness, represented progress. Now to rid herself of British attire. A glance at her patient confirmed he remained senseless.

She yanked open drawers, one after the other, hunting until she located a dangerously sharp knife with a wicked curve. Perfect. She hooked the blade behind her waistband and pulled. Ruined silk skirts and petticoats fell at her feet. The bodice followed, leaving only her corset and combinations, stockings and boots.

Tempting as it was to free herself from the tight-laced corset, it held and hid the vials of pyrocysts that her *mother* insisted were the key. She left the hated undergarment in place and pulled on the old skirt and jacket, hooking them closed and reveling in the dry warmth that enveloped her.

Ought she light a fire? A basket of kindling and a bucket of coal waited upon the hearth. But when was the fireplace last used? This laboratory was a museum to times long past. Would the chimney pull a draft?

She snagged a blank sheet of paper from the countertop and rolled it lengthwise. Tilting a lantern, she touched the tip to the flame, then held the paper inside the fireplace. The smoke drafted upward—and not back into the room. Worth the risk. A fire would take away the chill and, from the looks of him, the huldrekall needed the heat. She laid a fire. Crumpled paper. Kindling. Coal. Then touched a match to the paper. Slowly, heat built. Though it might take hours before this rock-hewn chamber was truly warm. Tugging off her still-damp boots, she set them before the fire.

Necessities attended to, she turned her attention to her tailed patient. Bloody and dirty, his cuts ought not be ignored or infection might set in and kill the fae.

Hot water poured from the tap, as advertised, into a basin. Clean clothes waited in a drawer alongside the bottle of ethyl alcohol and bandages. Piece by piece, she assembled her equipment onto an enameled tray. Tweezers, swabs, tubes and a loupe completed her tools. With that, she knelt on the wool carpet beside her patient and gently cleaned the blood and filth from his arm.

The huldrekall barely stirred.

What looked to be an entire sentence had been incised, starting at the shoulder winding around his upper arm to end at the inner elbow. Though she marveled at the faint flashes of red light emanating from the wounds, the cuts were angry. Puffy, hot and inflamed. Infected.

Were the dinoflagellates responsible? After all, they ought not thrive in human—or fae—skin. Or was it bacterial, acquired as he lay in the hay and manure of a horse's stall? Both?

She wrinkled her nose at the foul odor that rose from the dirty water. Regardless, his wounds needed to be sterilized. A process that would also kill the dinoflagellates inserted alongside the bioactive glass filaments. Which meant she needed to collect all her samples first.

Placing the loupe against her eye, she turned up the

lamp's flame and bent close. Tweezers in hand, she worked quickly, her stomach twisting at the thought that he might wake at any minute and howl in pain. Better for both of them that he remained unconscious. For now.

When he woke, would he be able to answer any of the questions that spun and flipped through her mind? She hoped so. For her sake. For others. Rømer's experiments were cruel and inhumane. Had this fae been captured, drugged, held down against his will? Was he a new recruit, a willing participant who worked with the alchemist to locate and tattoo other potential fae? Both possibilities seemed likely, though if it was the latter, he would be furious upon awakening.

She teased out filament after filament of bioactive glass, collecting them in a Petri dish. The prodding and poking of pointed metal roused the fae, but only just. A few groans. A flinch when she removed a deeply embedded strand. After working her way around his arm, she wiped away the blood that oozed from his many wounds and squinted. Had she missed any filaments? Not that she could tell.

That task done, she returned to the laboratory bench and set up an entire rack of test tubes. This was the experimental portion of this gruesome examination. Determining which species of dinoflagellate had been implanted inside the many cuts alongside the bioactive glass. Had Rømer pinpointed the same bioluminescent creature as her mother?

Standing before her mother's workbench, she threw open the cabinet doors, hunting down various salt solutions. Sodium chloride. Potassium chloride. Magnesium sulfate.

Grabbing paper and pen, she calculated a variety of ratios and dilutions and proportions, exhausting all reasonable possibilities for dinoflagellates, each formula designed to support different species from different habitats. From saltwater to freshwater to soil-dwelling.

Overkill?

Probably. Red bioluminescent species were rare. But neither did she wish to risk killing whatever dinoflagellate the alchemist's tattoo artist, for lack of a better phrase, had implanted alongside the bioactive glass.

With a grease pen, she labeled each tube. Then set about pipetting liquids, placing a measured amount of each solution into its corresponding tube.

Back at the huldrekall's side with a jar full of cotton-tipped swabs, she collected samples—rune by rune—until she had completed the entire sentence and filled every tube.

By the time she was done, the fire had chased the chill and damp from the room. Snatching up a sheet of paper and a pencil, she recorded the runes carved into the fae's arm, then set aside the page.

Now for the hard part. Sterilizing the man's wounds. And just in time, given her light touch to his hot forehead informed her he was extremely ill.

Jaw set, she poured a generous amount of concentrated ethyl alcohol over his shoulder, catching the runoff on a clean rag.

With a howl, the fae sat up and glared down at the rag in her hand, screeching in horror. "What are you doing?"

"The cuts are infected," she informed him. This time she

directed a splash of the clear liquid at the crook of his elbow. She sat back. "The germs causing your fever need to be killed."

"Kill?" His voice climbed another octave. He snatched away his arm and held it close. "No! Stop!"

Well, then. She had her answer. A willing test subject.

"Where am I?" His head lolled as it swiveled about. Wide eyes took in the shackle about his ankle and he yanked, knee to chest. "Let me go!"

"I'm sorry, but I don't have the key." She waved the alcohol-soaked rag. "Hold still, please. I need to finish cleaning and bandaging your arm."

"No!" He scooted away to the edge of the cot, pressing his back to the stone wall. He raised a foot, ready to kick her if she came any closer. "You're ruining everything."

"I'm trying to help!" she yelled, all attempts at bedside manner gone. She wasn't a physician, why play one for an ungrateful lout. "Did you see what happened in that barn?"

He glared at her.

"That could have been you. Dead." She huffed. "Instead, we brought you here."

A calculating look entered his eyes. "Where is here?"

Her gaze slid to the length of chain. Should she tell him? Probably not. And questioning this strange fae was best left for Val. Or Sóllilja. A thought which brought on a fresh wave of anger. What was she to think of a man promised to another? Yet speaking vows meant to bind Angela to him for life? "My laboratory." Let him wonder. "Where I have much work to do." She set down the ethyl alcohol beside the bandages and took three giant steps back. His choice. He could let the infection rage or daub the wounds himself. Cultivating an air of indifference, she turned away and began unloading the boxes of supplies and papers that surrounded the aetheroscope.

"Where is my absinthe?" he demanded, fuming. His tail smacked against the floor again and again. "Tell me you did not leave that behind."

Aron had stated their distant cousins were incapable of sustaining living tattoos.

"What use has a huldrekall for *La fée verte?*" she asked.

The green fairy was officially known as absinthe verte—green absinthe, colored as it was by the flowers and leaves of *Artemisia absinthium* and other herbs. Every afternoon as far back as Angela could remember, her grandmother—mother—had served a simple wormwood tea along with cucumber sandwiches. This herbal tea, she'd been taught, contained a ratio of phytochemicals that nourished and sustained their living tattoos and was to be imbibed regularly. Preferably while basking in a square of sunlight cast across the tea table by a nearby window.

Occasionally, late in the evening and with great ritual, her *mother* would indulge in absinthe in its alcoholic spirit form. After pouring a small measure of the spirit into a special glass, she would rest a perforated spoon on the rim, placing a single sugar cube on top. Ice cold water poured slowly over the sugar dissolved the sweetener and turned the green liquor a milky white.

Angela had begged for a sip, but only once her skirts

dropped to her ankles had she been permitted to partake, to enjoy the heady rush the indulgence produced.

"Not the horrid green fairy," he snapped back. "*Eitr.* The Tyrian Absinthe. I am to be a prince among men."

She rolled her eyes. Smelling of cow droppings had done nothing to damage his pride.

A year ago, she'd have thought him suffering from delusions of grandeur. But might the prisoner have a more immediate use—*need*—for the drink? All this fuss over a variety of the drink known as Tyrian Absinthe. Was it more than a purple variety of the spirits? The links to Rømer were many. Her brother. Katla. And now this fae. She lifted the flap of her satchel and tugged out the bottle of the purple spirits found in his possession. "This?"

"Hand it over." Quite the imperious prisoner, this fae. Especially given his outstretched arm shook with need.

A few questions couldn't hurt. "Your name?"

"Sigge."

"Why purple and not green absinthe, Sigge?" She turned her back on him. Standing at the workbench, she used her knife to pry the cork free. She sniffed. "Wormwood. Anise. Fennel." All the usual plant derivatives along with something that reminded her of the ocean. "Seaweed?" She glanced over her shoulder. "Care to tell me about the extra ingredient?"

"No."

With a shrug, she reached for a beaker, wiped away the dust, then splashed a generous amount of the drink into the vessel. Holding it to the light, she swirled the liquid, studying its purple color.

"Stop! It's mine." Sigge looked panicked. "I need it."

"Why?" She fixed him with a look. "Give me a reason."

He pursed his lips. Then relented. "It stops the fever of transformation."

She lifted her eyebrows.

"Fine." Glowering, he spat out words. "It stops the crystals from spreading. I *need* to drink it."

"Stops your muscles from hardening?" Holding out the beaker, she took two steps toward him, stopping just beyond his reach. An expensive and hard-to-access cure for an ongoing problem seemed ill-advised. Not that there was any evidence that Rømer cared about the destruction that followed in his wake.

"No. Yes." He growled through clenched teeth. "Keeps them out of the gut. Slows it elsewhere. Works better if you're part fae."

"Like trolls?"

He snorted. "As if we'd waste it on them."

"We?" She tipped her head. "Are you working with Rømer?" Was he more than a test subject? Instead an outright accomplice?

Caught out, his eyes narrowed. "You're the half-breed. The woman he's to marry."

This creature knew more about her fae heritage than she had. A new wave of annoyance washed over her. *Mother* had shared so much, yet so little. "Why does it matter who my parents were?" What was so very important about being half Hulder and half Hulda?

The annoying huldrekall shrugged. "He's obsessed with mingling the blood of old and new fae. Something about a transformative intersection that enables fusion."

Brow furrowed, she puzzled at the confusion of his words.

"Please." Sigge held out a grasping hand. "It's all I know."

She doubted that. But keeping him alive was a priority.

The moment she surrendered the beaker, he guzzled the undiluted contents. With a sigh, he fell back upon the cot to stare at the ceiling.

"Your wounds," she prodded.

"Leave them," the fae hissed, baring slightly pointed teeth. His tail twitched. "Leave me."

"Fine." She'd seek answers on her own, then ask better questions when he demanded another drink.

Absinthe, up to seventy-five percent alcohol by volume, was enough to kill infectious dinoflagellates outright. If she wished to determine any specific effect of the mysterious purple ingredient, she needed to evaporate away the alcohol first. Boiling was not an option, for that would risk damaging the chlorophyll and other constituents.

Instead, she poured small amounts of the purple absinthe into wide-necked vessels, then nestled them together in a basin filled with warm water to encourage evaporation. An excellent beginning, if in need of a control.

Rummaging through dusty bottles in various cabinets,

she'd almost given up hope. Until, grinning, she hauled out an old bottle of absinthe verte. Still sealed, the high alcohol content ought to have preserved the relevant ingredients. Popping the cork, she repeated the same procedure with the aged absinthe.

Then poured herself a measure, diluted it with glacial melt water, and drank it down without benefit of sweetener.

It was going to be a long night.

CHAPTER TWENTY-ONE

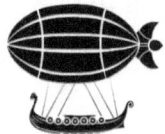

THE GROUND RUMBLED BENEATH HIS feet. New cracks appeared in the walls. Impossible to live near geothermal springs without accepting a certain amount of risk. Earthquakes weren't uncommon but rarely did any significant damage to the mountain city.

They did, however, tend to crack the glass tubes in his uncle's laboratory. An expensive problem that all too often set their work back by weeks and months. Which was why Val now insisted that every time one was replaced, they install a rubber base isolator and a flexible utility connection to dampen the vibrations.

And while he might be accustomed to such geologic events, Angela was not.

He hurried his steps.

His uncle was not a nurturing man and she would be forgotten if the network of glass tubes was threatened.

Married. Kidnapped. Tossed off an airship into bloody chaos and hauled inside a mountain. She'd endured enough and, as there would be more, the least he could do was to stand beside her and help bear the burden.

His mother was right. They needed a respite, uninterrupted time alone as husband and wife. A brief hint of a honeymoon. Tonight, with the privacy of the mountain hut and the geothermal pool reserved for them where they could make their union official.

If she still wished to do so.

The ground beneath his feet shook again. Violently.

The bioluminescent lights affixed to the tunnel walls vibrated and the agitation set off an enzymatic cascade, brightening the lights and urging everyone to hasten their steps. He broke into a run, turned the corner and threw open the door to his uncle's laboratory. Water splashed beneath his feet, and he slowed his pace so as not to slip on the strands of filamentous algae that streaked the floor and hung from shattered tubing in long, sad tangles.

She wasn't here.

"Where's Angela?"

His uncle turned with a frown. "That's what you want to know? When we've cracked tubes, a flooded facility and months of data collection ruined?" Uncle Aron grabbed a sodden rag and walked to the geothermal piping, turning the shutoff handle. "No point in heating the space. We'll mop up. Bleach everything. Start again."

"Angela?" he repeated. "Is she in the infirmary with the huldrekall?"

His uncle's experiments were not Val's current priority. There would be no "we" during the salvage stage. Repairs? Yes, he would assist. But until his dirigible returned, until it could tether, until the glassworks shipment could be unloaded and hauled on hooves into the mountain, his wife came first.

"In her laboratory." His uncle waved a hand. "With my aetheroscope."

"Alone? With the huldrekall?" He turned, ready to abandon his uncle to the mess, but realized he had no idea where he was headed. "*Her* laboratory?"

His uncle heaved a sigh. "Across the hall, two doors down."

Without another word, lest he speak in anger, Val exited. He barged into the room without a knock and skid to a halt, wondering how far back in time he'd stepped when he'd crossed the threshold. A coal fire complete with a cauldron suspended from a chain. Bottles stashed on shelves behind soot-darkened glass doors. Woolen rugs strewn about. Oil lamps and candles that barely dispelled the gloom. The space was both a chemical and fire hazard tucked in a rock-walled room. "Angela?"

She stood in stocking feet, her hair a wild, tangled mess. Her soiled gown shredded and discarded in a heap before the fire in favor of faded ill-fitting fashion from another generation. Enterprising and resourceful, such was his wife.

Thank Odin, she was safe.

The most modern items in the laboratory sat atop a cart. An aetheroscope—his uncle's—surrounded by piles of supplies, as yet untouched. Instead his wife bent over a note-book, pencil in hand, copying runic phrases onto yellowed paper.

His chest tightened. "Is that," he squinted, "my uncle's writing?"

"I was only supposed to take the microscope." She straightened, lifting her pencil. "But when I caught a glimpse of mixed runes and bindrunes..." Her lips pressed together. "Well, I couldn't leave the notebook behind where it might be destroyed by the flood." Despite her justification, guilt was etched on every feature. She waved a hand at a work-bench. "The samples need time to incubate, so I thought I'd see if anything your uncle was researching overlapped with my own work. I can't quite make sense of the archaic language, but I think Aron knows something about the red runes."

"Yes, I suspect you're right." She asked not a single question about his ex-fiancée. A bad sign. He cringed when his gaze fell upon an uncorked bottle. The spirit's value was now reduced to zero, no matter the currency applied. "You opened the Tyrian Absinthe?" He'd planned to save that bottle. To offer up for analysis the vial of purple fluid he and Hildur had squeezed from the fabric of her bag. He rolled his shoulders, trying to shrug off the loss, but with the ever-present concern of covering airship costs, it was hard to let go.

"I did. Sigge insisted he needed to drink it, that his survival depended upon the purple liquid."

"Sigge?"

"The huldrekall's name." In pinched and tight words, she recounted the events of their time apart. "A dead Huldu. An electric troll. An infected huldrekall. At least three different kinds of fae. All incised with runes. Two of them via the same methods. Will such rune ultimately kill a troll? Unknown. But they killed Katla. And our prisoner is feverish. His outcome is uncertain as I cannot determine if the bioactive glass crystals have entered his bloodstream yet in sufficient quantities. Perhaps he will survive long enough for your fiancée to question him."

"Ex-fiancée," he corrected. "I know you're upset. You have every right."

She tossed down the pencil and stared at him with barely suppressed ire. "You might have explained yet said nothing."

"I could not. A miserable attempt to honor the vow I made, to not become an oath-breaker. As a point of pride, huldufólk do *not* break their vows."

"So you said before council members." An angry heat bloomed in her cheeks. "A sacrifice in service of your people, rescuing a poor, if high-ranking, inconveniently lusty, lost daughter of the huldufólk."

He closed his eyes. "My engagement to Sóllilja protected her from an unwanted political marriage and granted me, a low-ranking fae, access to research funds. We never intended to actually marry. Per the terms of our agreement, however, she had to be informed before I took an official wife."

"Accomplished by means of refusing to bed your bride?" Her words snapped, cutting as sharply as a razor. "Congratulations on availing yourself of a convenient loophole."

"Self-righteousness does not become you," he growled back. "Not when our marriage was arranged by a pair of British spies." He tipped his head. "Tell me, what did *you* agree to on behalf of the British?"

Her face flushed. "Nothing."

"Now who's lying?" he scoffed. "Will you tell them about the hidden folk? About my dragon's wings? About the glowing runic tattoos?" His eyebrows lifted. "That's called spying. Your loyalties are divided."

"They are not!" She stomped a foot. "They requested I observe and report back about anything unusual. I spoke no words of agreement."

His laugh held an edge. "Now who's the devious fae, carefully parsing words?"

"Whose fault is that?" She planted fists on her hips. "All I ever wanted was to return to my mother's people, to continue her botanical work."

"By trapping a husband."

"True," she conceded. "Artifice and trickery applied by both sides." Her laugh was bittersweet. "A marriage of mutual connivence. My mistake, thinking there was also a spark between us. I spoke no lies when I bound my fate to yours." Tears welled in her eyes and his thumb ached to brush them away. But it was time to speak plainly.

"Nor did I." He stepped closer. "I married you, first and

foremost, because I wanted *you*. Everything else is secondary." He held out a hand. "Come with me. Let me take you someplace private where we might spend time together alone, where I can answer your every question without fear of interruption."

Angela snorted. "As if my aunt would let that happen."

Aunt.

"You know?" He glanced over his shoulder. "That your grandmother—?"

"Is actually my mother? Yes. Your uncle, bitter all these years, followed her life—and mine—best as he was able from such distance." She threw the sleeping fae a glance and lowered her voice. "By his account, I'm the daughter of a huldufólk and a huldrekall changeling. A half-breed. Which may or may not explain Rømer's intense interest."

"Interesting." A fact *his* mother had not known. Or had not thought to mention.

"That will lower my status here, will it not?"

They'd promised each other no lies. "It will."

"Is such my fate?" Suspicion pursed her lips. "Sigríður Guðjónsdóttir has the look of a politician. She'll want to use me to her advantage, to offer my hand in marriage to some ranking gentleman."

"She might try," he admitted, stroking his knuckles down the side of her face. "If you weren't already married."

He dipped his head for a kiss, but she stepped back. "Almost married," she reminded him.

"Almost," he agreed. He was done splitting hairs.

"Regardless, you must choose. There will be no more toiling inside laboratories or greenhouses or traveling about on dirigibles for you, *ástin mín*, unless we consummate our union. Tonight."

"Tonight?" She squeaked. "It's late and I'm a mess." She swept hands over the old musty clothing she wore.

"You are." He grinned. "Nothing that can't be set right. I've reserved the bath house and hot spring for private use. Ours and ours alone..." He placed his mother's pattern book and tattoo kit on the edge of the table, wondering if this tradition was among those Angela had been taught. He took a deep breath. "I would offer you a *sálbundið*, proof of my honorable intentions."

Her eyebrows drew together, uncertain. "A soulbound marriage tattoo?" With fingertips, she touched the soft spot behind her ear and he knew a moment's relief. She *did* know. "Aren't they irrevocably binding?"

"Not exactly, but they can make divorce and remarriage more challenging."

"For us both?"

He nodded. Equal risk. But she didn't reach for the items or meet his gaze. "Unless you've changed your mind about being married to an airship captain?"

"Tonight," she repeated. "I'd hoped for more time."

And that was the crux of the problem, wasn't it? How much longer could they hope to be left alone? The more time her aunt had to think about her windfall, the more she would pressure Angela into a dissolution. And Rømer's antics could not be ignored.

His was a life spent on the move. Unstable. Unpredictable. What could he offer to entice her? Save for a small greenhouse laboratory aboard a dirigible where she would be free to conduct the research she wished?

Perhaps whatever spark had ignited between them wasn't meant to be. Were the gods destined to deny him happiness? Heart in his throat, he continued. "I'll not force you. Nor do we need to be married for me to swear I'll see you protected from Rømer. But I've no plans to stay in the mountain for very long."

She swallowed. "Will you return?"

He sighed. "Eventually. But I'll either leave married, or I'll sign papers of dissolution, swearing you remain untouched and unmarked."

A shadow darkened her expression. Did she really want him? Or was he simply the lesser of two evils? Not that he cared why she chose him, so long as she belonged to him—and he to her—before her aunt and the entirety of the council interfered. Still she hesitated. "Loyalty to each other first? You'll answer all my questions and I'll not reveal the hidden folk to the British, nor discuss your technology without permission?"

A negotiation of terms? "Agreed." Then he added a stipulation of his own. "The alchemist's work must also be kept a secret, given its direct ties to our people."

"About that." She set the old diary aside, neither agreeing nor disagreeing with his last condition. "We cannot leave this room without analyzing the samples I took from the huldrekall's rune markings. Or the effects of the Tyrian Absinthe upon the materials Rømer embedded."

"Then you'll come away with me?" He refused to discuss the tattoos further until she answered. "To the hot spring? If nothing else, there's a warm bed where we might sleep, undisturbed."

"Fine. We'll go." Her verbal agreement lacked certainty and excitement, but an enticing blush colored her cheeks. "But, for now, I'm not promising more than a conversation involving many questions."

He nodded. Some would call him a fool for not taking advantage of her wedding night enthusiasm, for insisting upon old-fashioned traditions. Breaking an agreement properly. But he did not wish to build a future on shaky foundations. First his scientist deserved an explanation—and a complete picture of her place among the hidden folk. He'd pushed enough. Perhaps lab work would help her sort through her emotions. "What do you need me to do?"

She exhaled in relief. "Dinoflagellates that flash red are rare. In fact, save for my own, the red color has only been reported by those who've dared dive deeper in the ocean than is technically safe. Even then, their colleagues argue the color was nothing but a hallucination brought on by oxygen deprivation. I'd like to confirm the color microscopically to determine if Rømer is using the same species my mother discovered." She waved at the cart. "If you could carry the aetheroscope to the table?"

He did so. Muscle he could provide.

She set racks of tubes beside the microscope and used

bulbed pipettes to place a single drop of liquid atop each slide before labeling it with a number.

"Why so many slides?" he asked.

"Each tube holds a different kind of saline solution designed to mimic conditions found in freshwater, ocean water, human interstitial fluids and variations therein." She waved at a screw-capped jar. "I removed the strands of bioactive glass from his wounds, perhaps sparing Sigge the tissue-hardening effects, but glass is inorganic and incapable of bioluminescence. The living creature implanted on top of the glass is the key." With a twist, she affixed an aether cartridge to the machine. "Unfortunately, the vacuum chamber of the scope will soon kill whatever we insert by depriving it of oxygen. We'll need to work fast."

She placed the first slide on the microscope's stage, closed the viewing chamber door and punched a button. A soft hiss sounded as breathable air within the chamber was replaced with aetheric gas, creating an environment that would allow a high level of resolution that a light microscope couldn't hope to achieve.

Engineering might have been his focus of study, but one didn't work with photosynthetic energy without learning a measure of botany and zoology.

"Sample one." She scratched a number on a sheet of paper, then bent to stare through the lens, twisting various dials. "Disintegrated. As expected." She marked an X beside the first number. "Seawater is too hypertonic." More slides entered, then exited. "Freshwater pond and river are close but—" Her words cut off with a sharp intake of breath.

"What is it?" he asked.

"I've never seen such bright scintillations!" She sat back, eyes wide, hand pressed to her heart. "It was an afterthought, filling a test tube with a sample of water from the sink, water your uncle claims is pumped directly from the hot spring?"

He sniffed the tube, catching a whiff of sulfur. "It is."

She flicked off the light and stepped aside, waving at the eyepiece with excitement. "Look fast before the chemical reaction fades."

He peered into the aetheroscope. "I see tiny flecks of light flickered and flashed, glinting and glittering like tiny red stars in a night sky. Bioluminescence? This little creature is responsible for the glowing runic tattoos?"

"It is. Dinoflagellates are sometimes called pyrrhophyta, meaning 'fire plants'. The light is produced inside organelles called scintillons. Tiny but dense vesicles that, when exposed to shear stress, shaking of any kind, release chemicals that react with oxygen to flash light. Red light is unique to the ocean-dwelling varieties."

"And the lack of oxygen inside an aetheroscope is why the light is fading before my very eyes? They're dim now. Bleached of color."

"Yes." When he looked up, she was grinning. "But I can confirm that this dinoflagellate is the same species that I've been studying all these years." She spoke with a scientist's caution, even though her voice vibrated with excitement. "Keep in mind these are the only live samples collected. The living material from Katla's runic tattoos was degraded and I've yet to microscopically examine the troll's tattoo. And that's before we address the strange bolt of electricity that arced from its body into Dýri."

"That might yet be a possibility. My crew is, even now, attempting to speak with Grýla and her troll sons to see if they know anything about the electric troll we encountered."

Her jaw dropped. "They're real? The Yule Lads are real?"

CHAPTER TWENTY-TWO

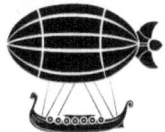

T HE VERY EXISTENCE OF TROLLS STILL rattled her. As did the idea that they could speak, especially as personal experience indicated otherwise.

Yet Val had sent his crew to *question* them, to find out what they might have heard about the runic carvings in the back of an electric troll. The bedtime stories told tales of wandering humans entering and winning a contest of wits against generally rather slow and dense trolls. But human storytellers were inherently biased. Perhaps the troll who had grabbed her aboard the airship was coerced and in pain. Conversation, witty or otherwise, was not at the forefront of its mind.

"Quite real," Val answered. "All thirteen of them. Early December, Icelanders start warning their children to behave, lest they be kidnapped by Stekkjarstaur, Giljagaur, Stúfur— or any of the rest. They'll also make certain everyone has a new sweater, to allay any worries about Jólakötturinn eating them."

She added to her list the reality of a giant black cat wandering the frozen landscape, terrorizing anyone so unfortunate as to not possess new clothes.

So much had happened in so little time. It was a lot to process. Including the knowledge that her marriage was far from stable and secure. Frustrating, those few moments after she spoke her wedding vows, believing that, after a simple autopsy, she could focus on her research, free from further concerns.

For now, she forced her mind back to the strangeness that the skin biopsy of a troll might present.

"Trolls wear their battle scars with pride," Val said. "I've never heard of any with deliberate patterned engravings."

She shrugged, knowing only what she'd seen. "There's more than one troll involved, if perhaps unwillingly. The huldrekall admitted as much when he told me they don't share the *eitr*, the Tyrian Absinthe, with the trolls."

"Eitr?" Val stiffened. "The mythical poison that can kill as easily as it can create?"

"Why not?" She threw her hands up. Going forward, all Icelandic and Nordic myths would be taken at face value until proven otherwise. "Sigge sneered at *La fée verte* and demanded Tyrian Absinthe, claiming it would stop the 'fever of transformation'. I pressed, and he admitted that fae who drank the purple absinthe stood a *chance* of slowing the spread of the glass crystals."

Dismay pulled at Val's features. "I rue the day I ever

discussed huldufólk with Rømer, making us a target of his fascination with biological transformation."

Silent, she pressed a hand to his shoulder. "You acted in good faith. He did not."

Everything he'd done had been in service to his people and no one had been harmed. The same could not be said of the alchemist, even if he believed he acted for the good of Norway.

Why else would she consider a sálbundið? One did not lightly make such promises. Divorce among the huldufólk was, it seemed, in line with old Nordic traditions, making it much easier to obtain than among the British. Unless their souls were—however hypothetically—bound.

"None of that changes the fact that I am responsible for telling an outsider about the ancient tradition of Eldskrift." Rather than self-blame, his tone suggested a steely determination to set things right.

"Yes, about that." Easier to study the pyros than the emotions lodged in her heart. Botanist that she was, it was hard not to let the entirety of her research define her. But it mattered deeply. To her. To the huldufólk. To Val. She slid another sample into the microscope's field of view and adjusted the focus. This time, she did not activate the aetheric chamber, leaving the tiny creature alive. Time to share with him the finer details. "Look again. If it's a plant, what's missing?"

"There don't appear to be any chloroplasts at all."

"Correct. This species is an osmotroph."

His eyebrows drew together. "Meaning?"

"That these particular dinoflagellates are parasitic. They absorb nutrients from their surrounding environment. In this case, the huldrekall's body."

"That sounds unpleasant." He grimaced. "Especially as they look to be wearing platelike armor and possess two whip-like structures—flagella—that allow them to zip about at high speed." He looked up at her. "They move fast and are hard to kill?"

"If placed in the correct environment, yes."

"Which Rømer has found in the skin of fae?"

"It appears so. A situation which serves to underscore the fire fern requirement." She tapped a finger on his wrist, where the leaves of his tattoo sprang from a tangle of vines. "Huldufólk living tattoos are green because our fae cells incorporate the chloroplasts of living plants through a process known as endosymbiosis. A process that is staid and quiet and... plantlike. The tattoo remains sessile—more or less immobile."

"These dinoflagellates are anything but." His eyebrows drew together. "You never mentioned where your mother found them?"

"After they married, my... father took my mother on a fern-collecting honeymoon. They traveled extensively through eastern Europe, listening to locals tell tales of the 'red fern flower', then hiring guides to help her hunt the countryside for the plant. Everyone thought them mad, given the mythological bloom is said to only appear on Midsummer's night. She persisted, collecting samples of any and all ferns. But none flashed red."

A teasing light entered his eyes. "Look to legends and find the core truth."

"Precisely. In the Tatra Mountains, locals pointed them to a supposed witch who lived in the woods beside a thermal pool. None would accompany my mother, but they did tie a red ribbon about her wrist and point her in the direction of the spring. She found the old woman living a solitary life in a hut and managed to pry out a story of a glowing red fern that had once grown at the water's edge. After a rain, the woman claimed, flashes of light could still be seen in the hot water. They remained in that village for weeks as my mother collected samples in and around the spring."

"The dinoflagellates."

She nodded. "Which she took to calling pyros, given their red light flashes. But without a host plant, we thought they couldn't be used to tattoo huldufólk."

"Hence the glass threads?"

Tossing him a smile, she reached for her collection vial. "Let's experiment and find out." With fine-tipped tweezers, she pulled free a strand of the glass and placed it on a slide. To that, she added a single drop of spring water that held the brightest of the pyros. "Care to be the first to look?" she asked, setting the sample beneath the microscope.

Val let out a low whistle, then stepped back. "It's *eating* the glass."

She peered through the eyepiece. The creatures had swarmed the filament, sticking tightly to its surface. Not so much eating as absorbing minerals. "Rømer solved one problem and created another. The pyros will only be happy until their food source is consumed."

"A process resulting in death, slowed only by imbibing Tyrian Absinthe," Val said.

"So he claims." She sighed. "We—" She stumbled over the pronoun. Her research was solitary now. "*I* have been trying to induce endosymbiosis."

He rubbed his chin. "You'll need to explain that."

"It's when one organism engulfs another at the cellular level, then the two together become something entirely new." She smiled at the confusion that lingered on his face. "We inoculate—introduce the dinoflagellates—by mixing them into water and pouring them over the plant's roots."

"So when the fern pulls water from the soil, the pyros travel along with the liquid?"

"Exactly. A plant will defend itself with chemicals, attempting to kill the invader. The dinoflagellates respond in kind. The hypothesis is that, when the right fern is found, chemical warfare ends and the fern's cells incorporate part, but not all, of the pyros into its cells."

"Let me guess, keeping the fun red sparkles all for itself." He grinned. "At least until a determined huldufólk harvests its fronds, collects its cells and uses them to tattoo fae skin."

She laughed. "No one has quite phrased it in such a manner, but yes."

"But there's a dark side to Eldskrift," he reminded her. "The reason the council abolished the tradition of offering second born sons for the ritual tattoo. Many did not survive initiation."

"But some did." A weak counter argument. "I would postulate that not a single one of Rømer's victims lives for long." She paused, then revised. "Possibly the trolls do better?"

"Because they've liquid glass running through their veins?" His smile faded. "Which brings us back to Rømer's slowly failing experiments. This silicate-based bioactive glass would appear to be a scaffold, designed to anchor dinoflagellates in the skin. Except, the glass isn't staying put. It travels through the body. Crystalizing in skeletal and cardiac muscle, impairing movement and hardening the heart."

"Hence the need for eitr—a poison?" Using an eyedropper, she dripped a tiny amount of the evaporated purple absinthe—now alcohol free—onto the slide. "Keep a close eye on the pyros. Tell me what happens."

Val sucked in a deep breath. "Their tails are slowing."

She took a turn at the microscope. "Impaired movement. And a few have fallen off the glass strand."

"That explains the Tyrian Absinthe." He pursed his lips. "Is it a cure?"

"If Rømer is attempting to recreate Eldskrift, to build an army of his very own fire guardians, the pyros need to survive in the skin. That's a problem if the drug—whatever provides the purple color—is absorbed into the bloodstream. It would course through the blood stream, leaving no part of the body untouched, and kill all the pyros."

Val lifted a finger. "Dose makes the poison," he countered. "At seventy percent alcohol, a fae would succumb to

---

alcohol poisoning first. But at low doses, might the eitr slow the spread of infection?"

She shrugged. "So the huldrekall claims."

"For how long?" he asked. "None but the richest can afford the spirit. And that's before we address how hard it is to locate a bottle. Rømer is interested in biological transformation. What if he grants each lab rat a bottle or two? If—when—they fail to sustain the glowing runic tattoos, he dismisses them as inferior?"

"And chooses a new test subject?"

"Victim," he corrected.

She cast her gaze to the huldrekall. His breaths were shallow and sweat beaded on his face. Was Sigge aware he was considered disposable? "Worse," she added, "dead *or* alive, this dinoflagellate releases toxins. Neurotoxins. Symptoms can include joint pain, pupil constriction and behavioral changes. Mucous membranes might turn blue. And if a large enough population of the pyros entered the blood stream at once..." She rushed to the huldrekall's cot, dropped onto her knees and pried the man's mouth open. "Oh my gods."

"What's wrong?"

"Sigge's tongue is blue."

"That indicates?" He knelt beside her.

"Heart failure."

His eyes grew wide. "Which we treat how?"

"By transporting him to a modern medical facility with trained cardiologists. This situation is far beyond my expertise."

"We're not without resources, though the infirmary falls short of your description." Val cast about the ancient rock-carved room, searching. Then yanked on a dusty braided pull cord. Gears ground, stiff with rust and disuse. "We can't be sure anyone will answer."

The fae moaned.

Angela grabbed the bottle of eitr and poured more into the beaker, ready to dose their patient.

"Wake up," Val ordered, patting the man's cheek with an edge of anger. "Or keep sleeping and die."

"Harsh."

He shrugged a shoulder. "Not only did he willingly submit to Rømer, but we also found him at the scene of a massacre." He lifted the fae's shoulders, holding him as she tippled a little of the purple drink into the fae's mouth. Val clamped the huldrekall's jaw shut with one hand and squeezed the man's neck with his other, quickly releasing his grip when the man broke into a coughing fit.

"Are you trying to kill me?" Sigge wrenched away from Val's grip, sputtering and spraying a fine purple mist from between his teeth.

"Quite the opposite." She swirled the purple fluid in the beaker, held it out. "You ought to have let me disinfect your wounds. The infection has spread."

The fae's eyes grew round. He snatched the glass and guzzled the liquid. "More."

With a sigh, Val passed him the bottle.

The door to the laboratory slammed open. "Are you questioning my prisoner?" Sóllilja demanded, then her nose wrinkled. "Is that a coal fire? And what are you wearing? Have we fallen through some kind of time portal?"

"We're trying to save his sorry life so that you have time to question him," Angela rejoined. "But he needs proper medical attention."

"What did you find at the farm?" Val asked. "Anything?"

"The farm?" All the blood drained from Sigge's face. "There's a huge catlike creature on a killing spree."

"No worries," the head mountain guard addressed the fae, eyes narrowed. "You'll be staying with us. We found the house nissi hiding in the rafters half-mad with fright, his red hat missing and his long beard twisted into knots. A warm cup of milk brought him back to his senses, after which he had much to say."

"Lies!" the huldrekall cried.

"We found these at the scene." She reached into her pocket and pulled out a handful of rough purple rocks. She tossed one at the huldrekall's feet. "I hate all trolls, especially the ones who summon a skuggabaldur to clear the way. Still, you and I will be discussing such creatures at length. You have much to answer for." She held up a hand at Val's indrawn breath, forestalling his question. "A raven arrived with news. Hildur and Dýri arranged for a meeting with Grýla tonight. They expect to return tomorrow."

Val tensed.

Sóllilja nodded. "Which leaves the two of you with a limited window." She addressed Angela. "Val's nothing but trouble, but he's a good man. Be sure you want him, because it's time to decide."

The cold hard knot inside her stomach loosened. Though decidedly grumpy at the moment, his ex-fiancée appeared to harbor them no ill will. From the beginning, he'd told her the truth, even if he'd not revealed everything.

How was it this adventure was but days old? That Valtýr Árnason—and his world—meant so much to her already? An escalating avalanche of an adventure from the moment of their first bungled kiss. What were the odds she'd find another brilliant man who would treat her with such consideration? One who would champion her expertise and grant her laboratory space aboard his airship? One so strong and capable, with such raw primitive appeal that his mere presence set her every nerve ending on fire?

She'd expected to marry out of duty. To smile and nod in her husband's company, then slip away to her greenhouse and lose herself in her research. Instead, she'd trapped a man already intent on rescuing her—*because he wanted her*—and discovered that marriage could be more than a stilted societal arrangement.

Was she in love? Perhaps. Lust, certainly. Val was the first man to make her believe that romance was more than a fairy tale story. *Freyja*, they *were* fae. Huldu. But their vows weren't binding until...

Her face flamed. "I do."

"Then your lives are about to become very difficult if you don't hurry. Sigríður is on her way here now, dissolution papers in hand. She's called an emergency council meeting to ratify them."

"Already?" Val grumbled. "Not once did she ask if we might *wish* to remain married."

"You think she cares? Word is that an army of seamstresses was summoned to Sigríður's rooms." Sóllilja fixed Angela with a look. "To prepare a trousseau. So if you'd rather an airship captain," she tipped her head sideways at Val, "than a politician, you'd best wrap things up and tie it with a bow."

Angela's heart pounded. Had Val lied by omission? Yes. But only to honor prior vows. And now the "other woman" championed him as the better option.

"The choice is yours." Val's voice was flat as he met her gaze. "Politics or science. Time to choose." No emotion registered on his face. Her stoic Viking. A dead giveaway that he felt too much. "Or should you wish, I'll smuggle you to Reykjavik that you might return—"

The bottom dropped out of her stomach at the thought of leaving him. "It's not home," she interrupted. "Home is here. Your airship. Wherever your heart beats."

He caught her hand. Tugged her close. And pressed her palm to his chest. "You have my heart."

"Aw. So sweet my teeth hurt." Sóllilja rolled her eyes. "Enough. You'll have time for that later. Time to move." She swung the shaggy wool blanket cape from her shoulders and wrapped it around Angela. "Grab your boots. My guards in the hallway will escort the huldrekall to the infirmary. He'll be treated with all due fairness."

Val snatched up the bottle of Tyrian Absinthe, jammed a

rubber stopper into its neck, and handed it to Sóllilja. "The huldrekall needs to dose himself to keep an infection at bay."

"Tell your physicians that he's infected with dinoflagellates." Angela stuffed her stocking feet into still-damp, if now warm, leather boots.

"See that a sample of the drink is sent to the laboratory," Val added as he threw her cloak about her shoulders, shrugged into one himself. Which was when she noticed his clothes, the sword slung upon his hips. "Ask them to confirm if the purple color is a product of the sea snail Murex. If not... well, let the chemists figure out what it is."

Sea snails? She'd ask later.

Angela shoved his uncle's notebook into her satchel alongside her mother's book, then tossed the bag across her shoulders. The encroachment of huldrekall and trolls upon the Hulda mountain entrance meant the alchemist knew too much. This might be her official wedding night, but they still needed to figure out how to stop Rømer and put an end to his madness.

Noises echoed up the long stone hallway. Strident voices demanding the guards allow them to pass.

"*Frigg and Hel.*" Sóllilja swore. "Time's up. Run while the path's still clear. You remember the way to the back door, Val?"

CHAPTER TWENTY-THREE

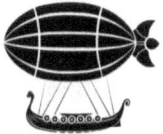

V AL GRABBED ANGELA'S HAND AND pulled.
They tore down the hall, took a sharp right, then
ran up a flight of stairs. More turns. More stairs. As
they passed, Huldufólk cried out and jumped aside, flat-
tening themselves against the rock walls, their eyes wide.

"Please," she gasped, staggering to a halt, pressing a hand
to her chest. Cursed as it was, the corset kept the pyrocyst
vial secure, if jammed against her sternum. "Laced. Too.
Tight."

He slowed. But only long enough to turn and bend. To
catch her behind her knees, to toss her over his shoulder.
"They'll guess where we're headed, and we need to pass
through that doorway before they catch us. Sóllilja will
refuse them the code."

More stairs, more twisting tunnels. All passed in a blur
of blue-white light. Then it grew so dim, so dark that Val

slowed to run his hand along the rough stone walls, navigating the final turns by touch.

When he finally set her down, they stood before an unassuming door of cast iron.

Her every rib ached. She swatted him, though secretly impressed at how he'd swept her off her feet. "Never again, Viking."

"Viking?"

Her face grew hot. "Hauling me away to make me your bride."

He huffed a laugh. "Tell me you didn't enjoy it."

They'd only known each other a few days. They shared a common goal: stopping Rømer. But what came after that? Travel and research? A family? Or were there other secrets lurking in his past, waiting to destroy their future?

She crossed her arms. "Fine. There's a certain appeal. But—"

"But you have questions," he finished. "I'll answer them all while we soak. After that," his grin shot lightning through her, waking unnamed desires, "we'll be too busy to speak." He pulled a small Lucifer light from his pocket and gave the globe a shake. "Hold this so I can see the numbers?"

"Where are we?"

"At the back of the mountain's peak. This is a sealed exit, reserved for emergencies, with codes known only to security staff. Long ago, we used to steal Sóllilja's father's code, then sneak out. Anything to escape the expectations of our elders."

"Sneak out to do what?" She hated the note of jealousy that crept into her voice.

With two hands he cranked an iron wheel left, then right. A full spin back again to the left stopping at the number nine. Loud bolts clanged, groaning and scraping as they withdrew from steel-lined rock.

"Soak in the hot spring, what else? But we were never alone, *ástin mín*." He snorted. "Hildur gazed longingly at Sóllilja while she, in turn, snuck glances at Dýri. Lauf and I rolled our eyes and dreamed of flying."

"Sóllilja and Dýri?" Not a pair she'd have predicted, but she could see how that might work. "Yet you proposed and she accepted?"

"A temporary measure to buy her time to declare herself. I'll explain later."

"Did you ever encounter trolls, befriend any?"

"Socialize with a troll? Never. And it's been ages since any dared approach the mountain." He glanced at her. "Why?"

"Lauf seemed to know the one who attacked me. I could swear he called him Bjarki."

"Did he? How strange." His eyebrows drew together. "But it must wait. We need to go."

Thunk.

The heavy door cracked open and a blade of icy air sliced into the hallway. She was so done with being cold.

"How much of Niflheim must we cross?"

He barked a laugh. "Half the realm of cold and ice, but not the frozen river." With a shove the door opened wider and they stumbled out into a driving snowstorm. "I promise the hot spring is worth the journey." He squeezed her hand. "Follow me."

The door closed behind them with a decisive clang, a sound nearly swallowed by the howling wind.

The path before them, if one could call it such, looked to have been carved by sheep. But Val strode forward with confidence. Wind whipped at her cloak and snow snuck inside the tops of her boots as she trudged onward, stepping into the footprints he left.

Crossing a land of ice to reach the land of fire.

THE GROUND RUMBLED beneath his feet, shaking snow from the overhead birch tree branches as they trekked down into the hidden valley to the hot spring. Realizing his wife was struggling with the rapidly deepening snow, he'd scooped her off her feet.

"Almost there." They were so close now he could see steam rising from the pool beside the small turf house. "My mother sent a raven, so the house nissi should have everything ready for us."

She shivered in his arms, nodded her head beneath his chin and pulled her cloak closer.

Moonlight illuminated the snowy landscape with a soft glow, lulling the inexperienced into a sense of security. But earthquakes shook free rocks and pebbles, sending them tumbling down the mountainside before burying them deep with winter snow. Disaster awaited any who stepped into the wrong snow drift. No huldufólk unfamiliar with the path would follow.

The ground trembled again.

"How often?"

"The earthquakes? Hundreds a week. Mostly minor. You grow used to them. Still, my uncle's tubes crack every few months. It's a problem we're working to solve."

"Your research and his? You work together?"

"We did. Once." He rounded the curve of the path, happy to see the welcoming yellow square of light of a tiny window. "And his work inspired mine."

The nit-picky oversight of a bitter uncle was the reason he'd left to study abroad, to earn a formal engineering degree, to arrange for a project that Val alone designed, tested and implemented. At university, he'd been so cocky and sure of himself that he'd been drawn to Rømer's intensity, so eager for outside collaboration that he'd shared huldufólk secrets without once considering the danger.

Ever since, he'd held back from connections, from trust. Waiting for ulterior motives to present themselves.

Thank Freyja he'd trusted his instincts about Angela, giving in to the overwhelming desire to claim her as his wife. Even so, his suspicions about her motivation had taken time to melt away. She was brave, courageous and loyal. More, she was committed to him, to their people. Even if her closest friend did live in a house full of British spies. Quite simply, he'd lost his heart to her. And tonight he would share his every last secret, willingly and without reservation.

Angela's teeth chattered as she shivered in his arms. Given his toes grew numb, he'd be lying if he claimed to be unaffected. Even the short distance from the mountain door was too much without proper winter clothing. Thank Odin they were almost there.

He lifted his chin. "Look ahead."

Black and white, a vast stark landscape rarely relieved by color in winter. Making the rare glow of light that promised warmth and safety all that much more precious.

"Oh!" Words that emerged on an amazed gasp. "And it's all ours?"

He saw the turf house again through her eyes, as if for the first time. Its wooden façade with the door and peaked roof. The small window. The broad stone shoulders that spread to the sides. All of it covered with turf, living insulation against the cold. Grasses that were dormant now beneath a thick blanket of snow.

A path led from the bathhouse to the hot spring at its side. There, the warm water melted away the snow, forming a shimmering circle edged with black stone. Shallow steps invited a descent into its warmth.

"For the night." A temporary retreat from the world. "The house nissi is nearby, should we need anything. Otherwise, he prefers his tiny abode, halfway up the mountain, and a life of solitude."

He set her on her feet, captivated. He didn't care much for poetry, preferring the sagas, but the sight of her standing on their ancestral lands with snow clinging to her hair moved him deeply. Not enough women received their due in the sagas. Perhaps one day he'd set pen to paper and record their own tale of romance.

First, however, several more chapters needed to be lived.

He pushed open the wooden door and drew her inside, pulled her to stand before the small peat stove, and set aside their satchels. "Strip." He shrugged off his cloak and tugged off his boots, ignoring the cold pain that burned his hands and feet. "There's no better place to warm up than a hot spring."

She held her hands above the stove. "My fingers are too cold and stiff for laces."

"That I can fix." He flicked open the clasp of her cloak, lifted the garment from her shoulders, helped her out of the old, musty jacket she'd found in the laboratory. When she stood in her corset and skirts, he drew a knife from his belt. Not for the first time he wondered at the reason women chose to bind themselves in such instruments of torture. Baffling. Yet also alluring, emphasizing the concave and convex. Soft curves he wanted molded against his hard planes. "Don't move." He sliced through the tightly knotted lacings at her waist. Both her skirts and corset fell loose.

"Val!" she cried, hand pressed to her chest as her skirts fell to the floor. "Stop."

He didn't. Vikings wouldn't. And he was tired of hearing her mutter about the garment. Sliding the curve of his knife down beside the arc of her spine, he ripped through the remaining strings with a single sweep. "My mother instructed the nissi to leave you a change of clothing. Traditional huldufólk bodices will suit you better."

"Careful!" She spun to face him. One hand pressed the corset to her chest, while her half-numb fingers fussed at something tucked between the garment's inner and outer layer.

He plucked it free, turning the corked vial this way and that, eyeballing a loose brownish sediment. "What is this?" His eyebrows lifted. "Pyrocysts? You've tight-laced your corset all this time to hold this in place?"

"Yes." She tossed the garment away and held out her hand. "Be careful, it's my only vial."

He returned the test tube. "And likely one of the items Rømer wants."

"There is that." She propped it in an earthenware mug, then sat down on the edge of the bed and tugged at her boot laces. "But I think he also wants me as his personal laboratory rat, to force his runic tattoos on someone with both Huldu and Hulder blood."

"And as his wife." Val rather thought the man might hope to mingle their heritage in the form of a child. An unacceptable outcome he could barely stand to contemplate. He placed the tattoo kit in the middle of a simple wooden table. "A sálbundið is a free choice. But with or without the mark, I want our marriage to stand."

She tossed aside one boot, then the other. "You don't want my answer now?"

"Later." His wife made for a distracting sight, wearing nothing but a simple shift. "After." He glanced at the bed piled with soft furs and tried to focus. "One commitment at a time." He wished to be chosen for himself. "First the hot spring. We'll share any remaining secrets, leave nothing between us. Then decide."

She stood and tugged at his chin, rising up on tiptoes to press a kiss to his lips. "I like that plan. But you're wearing far too much."

A situation quickly remedied.

Naked they ran on bare feet to the hot spring's edge, descending into the warm water and, with bone-deep sighs, sank onto the submerged ledge. Water lapped at stone, gently sloshing with their movement, from the upwelling of heat that filled the pool from some deep, distant crack in the earth below. Steam rose from its surface, softening the edges of the surrounding cliffs. He tipped her chin to face the skies where ribbons of light danced overhead.

He pointed upward. "Look!"

"The aurora borealis!"

Flakes of snow melted on their faces as they watched the shimmer of green, purple, and red. "You've not seen northern lights before?"

She shook her head, speechless.

"Rare, the color purple." Much like his wife.

They needed this time together after the exhaustion of their journey. Alone, cut off from the outside world. To regroup and recover. To join as one, then seal their vows with an ancient tradition.

As the last of the chill melted away, he drew his wife onto his lap, admiring the view of her unbound breasts. Gently, he cupped her skull and drew her mouth to his. A kiss that rapidly grew needy. On a soft moan, her lips parted, inviting him inward. Tongues tangled. Pushed. Pulled. Anticipating primitive movements with entirely too much greed.

He needed to slow things down.

They broke apart. Her chest rose and fell. An enticing flush suffused her pale skin and the damp strands of honey blonde hair that had escaped her braids to cling to her neck and shoulder were alluring beyond words.

He'd promised her words, but all he wanted to do was to bury himself inside her, hard and fast while screaming her name.

She cupped his jaw, as if to draw him back. "Why me?"

Two simple words that snapped him to his senses. A simple question easily asked, if not easily answered. "There have been women before." He stroked the soft unmarked skin of her damp shoulder as he spoke. "No one special. But from the moment I saw you across a ballroom, my heart began to sing. I knew I needed to make you mine."

"Please." She swatted the surface of the spring, splashing him. "Viking plunder, that's all I was. Admit it, you were too busy planning a kidnapping to notice the weak knees of every unmarried—and married—woman in the room."

What woman did not wish to be told she was irresistible? He barked a laugh. "True." A man on a mission, determined to save her from whatever Rømer had planned. And he'd be lying if he denied the appeal of praise and glory and riches. "Your beauty drew me close, but your words captivated me. Then you sealed your fate with a kiss."

In that winter garden, he'd found a rare bloom. Intelligent. Beautiful. Fae. And, yes, dead set on marrying as a means of escape. Anything to travel to Iceland.

Best luck he'd had in ages.

Save her closest friends were British spies. Not that a person could be faulted for defending their own. But such was why alliances needed to be carefully chosen.

He leaned back. He'd promised to tell her everything. "Romantic dalliances are not forbidden among the huldufólk, but as there are risks, most prefer that vows are first spoken. When a child is born, an irrevocable bond forms. My parents never married. Despite my father's grudging offer, my mother declined. He is a member of the upper class and my mother is a völva."

"A witch?" Water swirled and her hip brushed against his hard cock as she shifted, threading her fingers into the damp hair at his nape. "A lower status?"

A problem? She professed to wish to avoid the royal courts, those of high rank. Yet wealth provided luxury and comfort, something a scientist or an airship captain could rarely promise.

He took his own liberties, nipping at the soft flesh of her neck where, soon, a tiny tattoo would—if he had his way—mark her as forever his. "Yes. Much." Cupping her breast, he ran a thumb over her peaked nipple and grinned as her back arched on a soft exhalation. The sooner discussions of his family concluded, the better. "Social expectations would have made a marriage between them miserable. Not that it stopped my father from trying to arrange *my* marriage to a ranking woman."

"Katla." She kissed the corner of his mouth, then nipped. Jealous enough to add an edge of pain.

He liked that. "I ought to have refused," he admitted, struggling to focus as she placed a fingertip to the side of his ribcage to trace the downward path of a vine that disappeared beneath the water's surface. Submerged, her palm changed course at the crest of his hip, angling tantalizingly close to his aching cock. It was all he could do not to take her hand and wrap those nimble fingers about his hard length. "I would have been relieved when she ran off, had it not been with Rømer."

"So you threw yourself into another engagement?" Water swirled as she drew back, frowning, concerned only with the history of his romantic entanglements and what it might predict about their future.

He did not wish her to think him capricious with his attentions. "Sóllilja found herself facing a similar trap. Dýri was—is—so far beneath her that even an affair would cause scandal."

Her lips curved. "Dýri doesn't strike me as the romantic type."

"Nor is she. They're perfectly suited, if only they'd admit to their attraction." He shrugged. Wanting society to leave him alone, he'd agreed to a strategic engagement. "She wished for a career defending our mountain, but her parents pressured her to marry a diplomat based in Reykjavik. Our agreement put an end to such rumblings, gave her time to establish herself as a council member, and an advance on her dowry funds my research."

She twisted, brow furrowed. "Your airship is at risk?"

"No." He needed to confess. He stilled his hand on her hip. "Your Mr. Black handed me a bank draft, a dowry of sorts. It'll keep us aloft for some time."

"And indebted." She frowned, shook her head. "No. It's a gift. When we married, I became a citizen of Iceland. I owe no other country allegiance. Besides, I promised Mr. Black nothing. If we share anything with the British, it'll be by mutual agreement."

He nodded, satisfied. "For the safety of both countries."

"What will become of Sóllilja now that we're married?"

"She'll sort out her own future—or not—with Dýri." He ran a hand over the curve of her hip, caught her at the waist and hauled her tight against his insistent erection. "Enough of other people. What of us?"

"You're not hiding anything that might make me regret binding myself to you?"

"You know the worst." He tugged at the damp tangle of honey-colored hair that clung to her bare back, tipping her face to the stars, pulling hard enough that her breasts rose from the water. Cooler air rushed across their wet rosy tips and they hardened. He pressed open-mouthed kisses against her chin, neck, chest. Slowly making his way toward his goal. Would she scream when he nipped their peaks? "You've married down."

"I disagree." She whimpered. The sharp bite of her nails in the skin of his shoulders shot a bolt of lightning down his spine, sparking a gathering need at its base. His hips flexed in response. "With a huldrekall changeling for a father, my rank is questionable. Besides, as long as I'm allowed to set up a small laboratory in the corner of the greenhouse, to travel and work alongside you, I'm content."

"Then we're agreed?" He growled the question. His capacity for clear thought and speech was fast eroding beneath her touch. "Husband and wife?"

CHAPTER TWENTY-FOUR

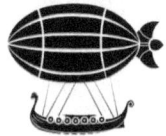

HIS MOUTH CLOSED OVER THE TIP of her breast, and teeth gently toyed with her nipple. Sparks flared and she gasped.

"Answer me." A growled demand that set her skin on fire.

"A thousand times, yes." A heavy and needy heat had settled low in her pelvis. "Never did I believe it would be so hard to convince my Viking to ravish me." Angela wrapped her hands about his neck, hoping to hold him there, to encourage more. More biting, more sucking. All while the rough hairs of his beard scraped bare flesh to the delight of her every nerve ending.

"Ravish?" He laughed darkly against her skin, then nipped the underside of her breast. "Such can be arranged, if you're certain it's what you want. There's a soft bed—" He shifted as if to climb from the hot spring.

But she caught his arm. "No. Now. Here in the pool."

"Here?" Uncertainty overtook his expression. "If it's your first time—"

"It is. But I've read books. Seen pictures. I want this."

Excitement flared in his eyes, but he shook his head. "Easier for you on a bed of furs—"

"No. Here." Slow explorations of each other's bodies could wait. What better beginning could there be? A primitive joining beneath the stars while immersed in waters that flowed from unknown depths.

His hips flexed, and he groaned. "I've less control here. This will be fast. Raw." Words that emerged from his throat with a rough edge.

"Good." She curved her lips with heat and intention. "I did ask to be ravished." He'd already stolen her heart. If he asked again, her answer would still be yes.

Yes, to being his wife. But a soulbound partner? Not something she should agree to lightly, even if it meant no one could ever barter her away in marriage again. That she'd have a firm hand in controlling her own fate.

He grew still, predatory. "If you change your mind, tell me to stop."

Her heart hammered. Gods, she wanted this with every fiber of her being. "I won't."

But rather than resuming his efforts, his fingers dug into her hips, lifted and turned her away to face the center of the pool. Cool air rushed over wet skin as her arms lost their mooring, as her legs floated out into the swirl and flow of the upwelling hot water. Adrift. Deprived of any control. A sensation she did not enjoy.

"Not what I had in—" He hauled her back against his pelvis. "Oh!"

That was new. Rather than at the curve of her lower back, the solid rod of his cock was buried between the soft flesh of her thighs.

"Hold on." He pulled her hands to his hips, anchoring her. "As tight as you want. Vikings don't mind a little pain."

Strong arms wrapped around her, broad hands cupped her breasts. Thumbs again found their tips, circling, scraping nails over sensitive nerve endings.

Yes, this was what she wanted.

Her head fell backward, damp and wet, atop his shoulder. With the slight turn of her head, she nibbled at his earlobe. "Nor do their wives."

His laugh rumbled darkly a moment before thumbs and forefingers clamped down and rolled.

"Gods!" Her hips bucked at the sweet electrifying ache his roughness brought. "Don't stop." He'd all but stolen conscious thought and reason with his first move. Instinct suggested she deliver the same. Releasing a hand, she reached between her thighs.

His turn to groan now as she slid her hand over his rigid length. Lower and lower until she located the other paired treasure men so greatly prized. She rolled them in her palm. Squeezed.

He bit down upon her neck. Teeth scraped over her skin as his hands left her breasts and landed on her knees. Without finesse, he spread them wide. A heartbeat later, an arm banded about her waist, clamping her against his chest. His free hand skimmed across her soft inner thigh. A rough movement slowed by water, one that gentled when his fingers found her folds. Teasing, he drew circles around the tight bundle of pleasure at her core, exploring every inch.

Her hands lifted, wrapped about his neck, then buried her fingers in his damp hair. Holding on as her hips bucked. "More." She issued a demanding word.

"Impatient, are we?" Words accompanied by a plunging hand. Thick fingers nudged at her opening. One slid into her swollen depths. In and out. "So tight." A second finger joined the first. In and out. At her back, she felt his breaths grow uneven. "Yet so very ready."

A most gratifying stretch, one worth the slight discomfort. The stretch faded, only to be replaced by a growing ache. One growing with each stroke. "Val." His name spoken as a choked plea.

His hand left her. His arm loosened. "Turn around."

For a moment, she floated. Then found herself pulled close once more. Straddling him this time. Chest to chest. Hip to hip. Groin to groin. A delightful new array of sensation. The tips of her breasts shifting against rough hairs. Her soft inner thighs gripping his hard ones. Her aching emptiness pressing against his stiff cock.

A harsh sound escaped his throat. "Last chance. Bed?"

She managed a rough shake of her head. Her knees found the stone ledge beneath him and she rose up. Reaching for his cock, nudging its broad tip against her opening. "No."

Blunt-tipped fingers dug into the soft flesh of her hips. "Hold on."

Her hands clamped down on his shoulders as his hips thrust upward. Seated deeply, fully within. He hesitated. "Angela?"

The burn faded, leaving behind an indescribable, demanding ache. "I didn't know it could feel so good."

"But only with me." Possessive words edged with a promise. He nipped her throat. "You're mine."

"Only yours." She kissed the strong column of his neck where his pulse throbbed. "Do that again. And, this time, don't you dare stop."

He moved against her. Pulling away, pushing inside. Over and over.

Sensations lifted her to new heights, but she couldn't quite reach the peak. Gravity and buoyancy and the heaviness of water worked against them.

With a frustrated growl, he buried himself deep and stood, hauling them from the pool as one.

She gasped as warm stone, soft moss, and a thin crust of icy snow met her backside. Hands landed on either side of her, he drew back. Then he was surging into her, over and over. A new angle, new sensations and renewed urgency. She clung to him, relishing his heavy weight, then cried out as his arm curled around her waist to yank her even closer as he drove into her. Feet planted on the pool's edge she met each thrust with a hard flex of her hips as the ache tightened its grip, demanding— "Val!" Blood roared in her ears and something broke free. An explosion that tipped her world askew and swept shuddering waves of pleasure through her body.

His breath came fast as he shoved into her. Once. Twice. And she watched, bewitched as his face contorted, as he called her name while his climax hauled him over the edge.

Shattered. Collapsed. Both of them left gasping for air. Propped on elbows above her, he gazed down at her in wonder. Skin to skin, joined as one, they'd broken. Melted. And would now form something entirely new.

His weight was warm and welcome, but the outside world returned with insistence. A cold chill about the edges. The moon slid behind a cloud as cold wind blew a gust of snow across their bare, wet skin.

Val caught her lips in a slow kiss, then pulled free. With a few fast movements, they dropped back into the hot water of the spring. There, wrapped in each other's arms, she breathed in the wonder of finally—at last—truly becoming husband and wife on a physical level. More than content, she sagged against him.

Finally. A chance to look—really look—at her husband. With damp-dark gold hair, a satisfied smile tugging at his talented lips, and a muscular arm stretched across the rough-cut stone of the hot spring, he was the very vision of a Viking explorer, secure with the knowledge that this new territory was all his. From the snow-covered mountainside to the woman shoulder-deep in the water beside him.

Much as he was all hers.

"That was... amazing." She pressed a kiss to a spray of

leaves that trailed across his collar bone and smiled. "So many designs to examine."

He brushed his thumb over the tattoo embedded in the crook of her elbow. "This is your only one?"

"As of the moment." She tipped her head at the hesitancy of his words. "That surprises you."

"At your age, most Huldu have far more tattoos."

A true statement, judging from the leafy twists of green her eyes feasted upon. "If hidden ones." She dropped a fingertip onto a twist of tendrils that wrapped about his biceps. "My mother judged it unwise, given a British husband would disdain even a single one." No one had ever asked if she wished to marry the gentleman whose property adjoined theirs, they'd simply assumed. "Why so many?"

"Your mother never told you?"

With narrowed eyes, she pursed her lips and reminded him, "She hid much."

Frowning, he answered his own question. "Perhaps to forestall your wish for more. The living plants inside our cells extend our lives. Your mother lived more than a full century before she had you."

"More than a century?" She gaped, her exploration stalled by this revelation. Was that why her mother had hidden herself away in the countryside more and more as time marched forward? To forestall uncomfortable questions?

"With enough tattoos, huldufólk live a few hundred years. The greener a fae's skin, the older they tend to be— and the more hidden from humans."

She assessed the number of his tattoos. "How old are you?"

"Thirty-eight."

She blinked. Not too much older, though the number still caught her off guard when she'd thought him only a few years older than herself. "I want more." She'd not be left behind, aging faster than her handsome spouse.

"Not too many too quickly" He laughed. "Each needs time and care and sunlight to integrate. The process is harder in winter. Why else would my uncle be trying to farm algae?"

"Using geothermal electrical power?"

"Figured that out, did you?" His grin was proud. "We've had electricity for as long as Britain, save our mountain burns not one lump of coal to produce it. Instead, we use the steam from hot water reservoirs deep in the ground. Bit of work, drilling that far. But worth the effort."

"Greens to support the tattoos?"

He nodded. "The green powder from all that algae is a touch bitter but packed with vitamins and minerals. Enough so to keep an entire population of mountain-dwelling huldufólk from developing photosynthetic anemia during the winter. That is, if he can manage to scale up production."

"The earthquakes?"

"Those and a variety of other technological problems. But enough of my uncle's plans." His eyes heated as he bent his head to press a kiss to the side of her neck, sending a new rush of desire through her. "There is one special mark I'd like to place in your skin. But I won't pressure you."

"A sálbundið?" A mark that upswept hair would reveal to the world. "Yes," she breathed. "I want my choice made clear. Tonight?"

"Yes." He pulled her close, pressed a kiss behind her ear. "I thought the cells of a tiny fern might serve as our ink. Perhaps we choose a frond from one of the plants growing here beside the hot spring to mark our union." He lifted his chin, pointing at the small rivulet of water that trickled down the mountainside, winding between rocks to reach their pool. Its edges were lined with tiny patches of green. "When I mentioned your interest in ferns," he tugged them off their ledge, deeper into the pool, "my mother reminded me of a new fern that began growing at the edge of the spring last summer."

"New? Could it be—" Possibilities exploded in her mind, tying her tongue in knots.

"A host for your pyros?" He shrugged. "We can try." He kissed her nose. "After we wear marriage tattoos."

"After."

They swam to the far side of the pool, where tufts of moss and ferns and other plants thrived in the warm mist. A tiny, miniature world in various shades of brown and green. Sprinkled throughout? Small elfin ferns with fronds no more than three inches long.

Her feet found purchase on a tumble of underwater rocks. Val joined her, steadying her as she reached out. "Lance-shaped, hanging leaves with a slight curve." She pondered its features as she turned over the frond, wondering as to its species. "It's the wrong season for spores." She glanced at Val and smiled at his raised eyebrows. "Which is to say I can't quite identify it, but it looks to be family Blechnaceae."

He rolled his eyes. "Just admit you've never seen one before and that we will be cultivating it aboard the *Grænndreki* because it fascinates you more than me."

"More than you?" Laughing, she pinched him underwater. "That is such a stereotype. Scientists can be equally interested in several things."

"Oh, now I'm a thing." His voice held a teasing note.

"You matter far more than any fern." She stared down at the frond. "But yes. What if this is *the* fern?"

"Quietly growing, minding its own business, not knowing the glory of scintillating pyros?"

"Precisely that." She eyeballed the various tiny clumps that looked as if they might happily call a teacup home. "A could-be fire fern. Beside a hot spring, exactly as my mother predicted. What if our people simply over-harvested the fern? Perhaps more of its kind were safely tucked inside rocky crevices alongside hidden springs in the mountainside?"

"About that." He turned her face to his. "When I named you Angela Eyrúnsdóttir, my mother told quite the story."

"She knew my mother?" She sank deeper into the water, listening.

"They were friends. They met in the library where both of them were mining the archives, chasing after the truth of the same legend among old manuscripts, parchment scraps, looking for anything that made mention of fire script. Your mother's interest was primarily scientific, botanical. Mine was focused on the powers conferred by the bindrunes."

"Powers?" she scoffed. "Not all aspects of a legend need be truth."

He tapped her lips. "Don't pull a face. Who wouldn't enjoy being swift to heal, able to see in the dark and walk through a snowstorm without suffering from frostbite? Not that it matters as the process of 'inscription' came to an end during the reign of Haakon the fourth—"

"That was over six hundred years ago!"

"Precisely why no one living had ever seen a huldufólk with glowing bindrunes. When my mother learned you still searched for a fire fern, she wanted me to warn you that the practice had grown so dangerous. Every year, more and more initiates died from the fever following 'inscription'."

Angela nodded. "Quite likely a result of a dinoflagellate infection."

"Despite the long lives of huldufólk, we rarely have more than two or three children over the decades. Every life lost was a heavy blow." He frowned. "Which was why, once Iceland recognized a king, grieving parents objected, claiming there was no longer a need to employ such primitive methods to protect our mountain. The ferns were ripped from the ground. Written instructions were burned."

"Such a loss."

"The last year half of those initiated died, Angela. *Half.*"

She recoiled. "So many?"

"The risk from 'inscription' became higher than the risk of encountering wandering trolls. So, yes."

Myth. She reminded herself not to discount it, but to lean into the myth. "The idea that a glowing tattoo might produce such powers is fascinating." She swallowed. "If not the risk of dying. But ours was a scientific pursuit," she admitted. "I doubt my mother thought much past recreating the fern, studying the process by which two separate organisms become one."

He shook his head. "My mother disagrees. They believed the tradition needed to be revived. The world was—is—shrinking. Ships, dirigibles, trains. All of them bringing people closer and closer together, forcing those of us who aren't quite human to hide our traits, our talents. It's why we conceal our living tattoos and the reason we hesitate to share our technology with strangers. Our mothers planned to revive the tradition, to figure out why it was so dangerous, to fix the problem. They wanted to send a handful of Fire Script Guardians to live outside the mountain, unnoticed. Guardians who could wait and watch and sound the alarm should outsiders arrive with the intent to do harm."

"And when my mother couldn't find a fire fern here in Iceland, she left to scour the countryside for a suitable fern?" That fit. Her mother must have been so hopeful early on in the process, then disappointed, and—finally—frantic. It would explain the mad scribbling of runes in her book of ferns.

"About that," Val interrupted her thoughts. "Those papers you stole from my uncle's laboratory? We need to take a closer look—at his writings as well as hers. My mother insisted that they were working on solving the problem *together.* Until an argument broke out between them, one that ended when your mother snuck away in the dead of night."

A lover's spat. But over what? The fire fern? Treading water, she turned back toward the tiny fern. Couched in a patch of green illuminated by the moon's soft glow. What if?

"Fire fern candidate or not, it's perfect." His voice had softened, allowing her time and space to contemplate his revelations. "Shall we use it for our sálbundið ritual before you inoculate its roots with pyros?"

How well he knew her. A certain peace settled over her. Was this love? "I'd like nothing more."

CHAPTER TWENTY-FIVE

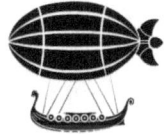

S O BEAUTIFUL, HIS WIFE.

Kneeling atop a pile of woolen blankets before the warmth of the cast iron stove, she pulled back her damp hair and tipped her head, exposing the tender skin behind her ear.

"In this life and the next," he whispered, then dipped the hollow copper needle into the macerated fern preparation that would serve as living ink. Flickering lamplight guided his work.

She barely winced as he pressed the tip into the delicate skin. They'd settled upon a simple bindrune, one created by placing Icelandic runes, one atop the other, to spell out the word *hjarta*. Heart. A symbol of love and courage. A symbol of their hopes for their future.

He'd known theirs would be a story for the ages from the moment she'd taken his arm, offering him her trust in that winter garden. Much between them had been rushed.

Which made him grateful for these quiet moments beside a fire inside a small turf building wrapped in a thick blanket of silent snow.

The skin behind his own ear throbbed, but he welcomed the pain as first to be bound, an offer of trust. Her technique unpracticed, her hands shook as she worked. But the resulting sálbundið was flawless, art he now endeavored to match.

Each time the needle pierced skin, capillary action embedded individual fern cells into her skin. There they would fuse with flesh, marking her as they marked him.

Long minutes later, it was done. He wiped away the excess greenery, smoothed a thin ointment over his work, and spoke the final words of the ceremony.

"That's it?" she asked. "It's done?"

"It's done." He took her hand, pulled her to her feet and cupped her head, drawing her into a deep kiss.

As she wrapped her arms about his waist and stepped close, her hair tumbled down. Soft and silky, a golden curtain feathering over their bare skin. For that was a requirement, nakedness. Nothing between a couple as they marked their commitment in each other's skin.

"Mmm." Her fingertips explored the rise of his arse.

The tips of her breasts brushed over the crisp hairs of his chest, a soft tease. Half erect through the entirety of the ceremony, his cock rose to full attention, nudging at the soft curls at the apex of her thighs, aching to slide deep inside her tight channel yet again.

He drew her toward the bed. "Come, we need sleep." He could wait.

"Sleep?" She drew back, tossing him a sly, incredulous glance. "Not until I've had a chance to map your tattoos." Her hand rose between them. Planted itself upon his chest and shoved.

Caught unawares, he fell backward onto the pile of furs. The tip of her tongue darted out, moistening her lips. Following her gaze, he said, "That's not a tattoo."

"Is that an objection?"

"Not even close," he laughed. "Aren't you sore?"

She shrugged, then crawled onto the bed. "Not enough to waste a perfect opportunity." Dipping her head, she pressed a kiss to the jut of his hipbone where a leafy tattoo sprouted. Slowly, leaf by leaf, she kissed her way across his lower abdomen, lifting her face to toss him a naughty grin before her hot wet mouth wrapped itself around the tip of his cock.

"Angela." A hoarse groan, for she'd stolen the oxygen from his lungs. Fingers curled around his thick root a moment before she sucked and pulled. His back arched at the rush of pleasure as she drew him deeper, as her tongue played along his length. His hands fisted in the damp silk of her hair. He was awash in sensation, every nerve ending wholly awake. A few moments more and he would spend.

Not that he was ready for this to end.

He caught her arms, dragging her from his cock with a soft wet pop. "Your turn."

She kissed her way up the vine atop his ribs, dragging

ANNE RENWICK

tight nipples across his chest until her mouth arrived at the rough edge of his beard. "Mine?"

Sinking fingers into the round flesh of her rear, he urged her upward. "Over me."

"Over?" Her breath caught as he drew a thigh above his shoulder and rose to sweep his tongue over her deep pink folds. "Oh." She fell onto her hands as his lips closed over the tight bud at their apex. "Oh! Val!" With tongue and lips and the gentle scrape of his teeth, he mounted a most rewarding exploration, not yielding until her cries and moans turned into desperate pleading. "Val. I need—"

He rose above her, growling. "What is it you want?"

"You. Thick." Her arm stretched toward his groin. "Inside and pushing."

As if he'd argue. "Then straddle me." He pushed at her hips. "Take what you want."

Sexy, hot and flushed, she moved over him. Golden locks spilled over his chest as her fingers wrapped around his cock and guided him inside her tight channel. So tight that he fought the flex of his hips, waiting for her to stretch, for muscles to relax their grip ever so slightly, for her to move. Slowly at first and then faster.

His pelvis flexed upward as she dropped. Sweet, sweet friction. He would never get enough.

"Yes. That," she ordered, her voice made raspy by desire. "More."

He followed orders. Over and again, driving her to ever-increasing heights, ones he also quickly climbed. So close, he was so damn close. His heart raced as need coiled at the base of his spine. "Angela, *ástin mín*, hurry."

A moment later, she threw her head back and cried out her release. Sinking his fingers into her buttocks, he drove into her. Once. Twice. Then his world exploded. Stars streaked across his vision as he yelled her name.

She bent over him, kissing him as she collapsed onto his chest, as he wrapped his arms around her, both of them breathing hard, still joined as one.

He was a lucky man. Instincts were not to be ignored. He harbored no regrets about the methods required to acquire his smart and sexy wife. In the pool, on the furs and their marriage just begun. He looked forward to at least a hundred years with her by his side. Children, perhaps, in time. He'd spend a lifetime proving himself worthy of this woman, of this blessing granted to him by the gods.

She rested her head upon his biceps. Her breath feathered, warm and gently over his chest. "A few more minutes," she whispered, eyes closed. "Then we can try to untangle my mother's scribbles."

He laughed, kissed her forehead. "Not yet. We've barely slept these past few days. Better to rest, to sleep so that we approach things with clear minds." In a few hours, the sun would creep up over the horizon. Light would pour in through the tiny window and the house nissi would arrive with breakfast. And when they returned to the mountain, for they must, trouble would be brewing. "The papers can wait and, you said so yourself, the pyrocysts need time to wake, to realize what lucky creatures they are."

"Let's hope." She huffed a laugh, but didn't move away. Instead, she snuggled closer, throwing her leg across his thigh before drifting into a deep slumber.

His gaze caught upon the tiny fern she'd planted in a floral teacup and set on the table. A task quickly seen to the moment the door closed behind them in the bath house. There, she'd sprinkled the soil above its roots with a few pinches of tiny, granular pyrocysts. A trickle of water to settle the roots and wake the dinoflagellates from their desiccated slumber. With luck, the small creatures would colonize the plant.

No need to fight the droop of his eyelids. Cocooned here with his soulbound wife, any disasters momentarily at bay, he could rest. The room blurred at the edges as he fell asleep, smiling at the pinpricks of pain at the base of his skull, satisfied with his current fate.

ANGELA BOLTED UPRIGHT, clutching the blanket to her chest. A swirl of cold air moved through the room. Someone had opened the door. She blinked at the sight of a small man wearing a peaked red cap. The house nissi waggled his eyebrows and winked. Then he set down a tray, turned on his heel and disappeared. The door shut, and they were alone once again. This time with the promise of hot tea and warm buttered bread, creamy skyr, and a plate of sliced meat and cheese.

"Mmm." Val's arm caught her about her shoulder and

pulled her back down. "Steamed rye bread." His stomach rumbled. When was the last time they'd eaten? "Not that I'm inclined to leave our bed."

He rolled, landing his heavy and—his hips flexed—interested weight atop her.

"Nor am I." She ran fingertips over the rough hairs of his short beard, remembering the wonder of it scraping across her inner thighs. "But—"

"We're agreed then." His talented mouth found her throat and began trailing kisses over her skin that left her breathless and unable to fathom why she would possibly object to such intimate morning attentions.

Sometime later, he hooked an arm beneath her knee and slid inside her, groaning her name and praising the gods. Thick and hard, over and again. Shoving them ever higher until they both fell over the edge.

Reason and logic crept back. Unwelcome. For it meant they needed to leave this bed of furs. For the first time, she wasn't keen to crack open a book or examine experimental results.

She ran splayed fingers over angles and planes of his hard chest, more than pleased with the husband fate had thrown into her life. If the emotions twined about her heart were any indication, she might well be falling in love with him.

Whatever these feelings were, it was too soon to speak of them aloud. Instead, she forced her mind to the tasks before them. "The sun is up and the day here is short. How long can we hide away before someone comes looking for us?"

He groaned. But her husband—*hers*—slid from the bed. She admired his firm backside, a perspective she'd only glimpsed beneath the moonlight as they ran to the hot spring, and again, now, while he splashed water into a shallow basin and washed.

As he dried himself with a towel, he threw her a knowing look underscored with a satisfied grin. "Don't lay there when you've a fern to tend to and runes to read."

Laughing, she joined him.

Fairy house that this small mountain building was, the clean, folded pile of clothing that awaited was exactly her size. Petticoats, blouse, stockings and shoes. A heavy skirt with beautiful floral motifs embroidered above the hem. A vest with matching velvet panels, one laced together by means of silver filigree loops and a silver chain. A striped apron to tie about her waist. A tasseled cap.

Less fuss and fancy was applied to Val's double-breasted vest and coat, or to the trousers cut close about his shapely calves, but there were shiny buttons in abundance, not all of them functional. She flicked a few, commenting thus, and was told she was welcome to inspect the ones at his waistband.

Laughing, she declined. "For now. Not for lack of interest."

A comment that had him sweeping her off her feet for a kiss that ended with him depositing her upon a chair. "Eat."

She did. A simple and satisfying, if now cold, breakfast. The bread, steamed in a pot buried beside the hot spring, was thick and heavy. The skyr—a kind of yogurt—sweet and filling. All of it food of the fae. As she *was* one, no worries about finding herself trapped among them. She'd made her choice. Before long, there was nothing left but a few crumbs.

The fern, still green, but also quite hale and hearty, served as their centerpiece. Hard not to hope that this time, at last, she'd found the right species.

She lifted the teacup, holding it beneath the bright light slanting in the window, examining each and every leaf. "So far, so good." Excitement shivered in her belly. Could it be? "This is, by far, the longest any fern has lasted without exhibiting any negative effects."

"Excellent news." Val set his uncle's diary before him and held out her mother's book. "I expect you'd be the best person to interpret Eyrún's handwriting?"

While Angela had been peering at fern fronds, Val had been scratching out runes on paper. Elder Fuþark, Younger Fuþark, Icelandic Fuþark and their corresponding sounds. A necessary cheat sheet, if she was to make progress with any speed. Casting runes had only provided her with the most rudimentary familiarity and her literacy with Icelandic as written using a Latin-script alphabet was elementary.

"I'll need help." She sighed, sweeping her hair away from her neck, twisting it into a knot before stabbing it into place with a pencil. "Especially with the bindrunes." Made as they were from stacking multiple runic letters atop one another, there was little hope she could untangle them on her own.

"Of course." He squeezed her hand, kissed her fingers. "Given that my uncle's diary seems to be written in the same amalgamation of runic alphabets and bindrunes, working together will make the task faster and easier."

Shoulder to shoulder they set to work transcribing everything into modern Icelandic. Her literacy improved by the minute.

Low on the horizon, the sun shifted in a manner that made tracking time difficult. For her at least, this being the first of her arctic winters.

Exhausted by the effort of working with runes in textual patterns that read like a secret code, she fell back against the rungs of her chair, scanning the notes she'd made. "Save rambling hypotheses about how a fern-dinoflagellate endosymbiont might form, there's little new to add. She did note the exact geographic location of the hot spring in the Tatra mountains and the precise mineral levels of its waters. And far, far more details about the formation of dinoflagellate pyrocysts than anyone—save a primary researcher— might wish to know."

Val looked up. "Like Rømer?"

Her heart sank. The alchemist sought exactly this kind of information. "She died to protect her knowledge. As it stands, Rømer does not appear to know anything about the requirement of a fern."

"About that." He frowned. "My uncle's notes confirm my mother's suspicions."

She sat up straight. "That my mother found a fire fern, here at the spring?"

He nodded. "According to his scribbles, Eyrún not only located the bioluminescent plant, but she was also working to propagate it, collecting spores. He wrote that she had plans to carry them into the mountains when the snow began to melt, seeding various hot springs in hopes of restoring their dwindling ecological footprint."

"I sense a conflict?"

"They argued," he said. "Eyrún wanted to trial the fern using her own skin as host. He objected. Told her the," he leaned over his notes, "stabilizing organobromide he'd chemically synthesized in his laboratory only reduced the spread of the cultured fern cells in a Petri dish by fifty percent."

"Lowering the chance of death by tattoo to only twenty-five percent?"

"That." He nodded. "She believed that to be an acceptable risk." Val waved his hand over the fanned pages of his uncle's diary. "Asserting that the huldufólk immune system would lower the danger even more."

"She was correct."

"He disagreed. Their quarrel resumed, escalating to an all-out fight wherein—" he cleared his throat, "spiteful words were exchanged."

"Of the kind you'd rather not repeat?"

"Those. Feelings ran hot to the point that he snuck in and poisoned her plants."

Angela shot to her feet as a thundercloud of emotions descended. "He eradicated the only remaining specimens of an entire species!"

"If his confession is taken to confirm the story my mother reported, yes." Val flipped the pages and pointed to a run of angry runes, ink slashed onto the page with the sharp point

ANNE RENWICK

of a fountain pen. "His last words are written in Icelandic. *Það er búið. Hún er farin.*"

"It is done. She is gone," Angela translated. She met Val's gaze. "She packed up and left him. I'd have done the same. What kind of marriage is there when one would sabotage the other's life work?"

He cocked an eyebrow. "Is that a warning?"

"Yes." She glanced at his uncle's notebook. "Does it say what organobromide?"

Loud thuds sounded at the door. Val slammed the notebook closed and stowed it, along with her fern book, in her satchel. Only then did he cross to a small window to see who knocked. He threw the door open. "Dýri?"

"Come quickly." The guardsman slid a look at Angela and fixed upon the small tattoo behind her ear. His lips quirked, the tiniest hint of a smile. "Legally, Sóllilja can't imprison your uncle, but she has him—temporarily—under lock and key. We're hoping you might know why he tried to destroy the entire crate of Tyrian Absinthe gifted to us by Grýla."

"An entire crate?" Val's voice was laced with incredulity.

Dýri nodded. "Worth thousands."

Val looked at her. "Tyrian purple is an organobromide."

"Don't tell me you're not slightly tempted." She tossed his words back at him. "Who wouldn't enjoy being swift to heal, able to see in the dark and walk through a snowstorm without suffering from frostbite?"

Still. A twenty-five percent chance of death.

"Did you discover something about the corrupted Eldskrift?" Dýri asked.

"Much," Angela said. A motion beyond the doorframe caught her eye. She squinted. "Why is there an enormous black cat with you?"

"Him?" Dýri grinned. "Jólakötturinn is on loan. Resentful, as he'd rather be napping in a warm cave, but as the creature is most excellent at sniffing out trolls and two of the Yule Lads never returned home after their holiday frolics, Grýla ordered him along." Dýri's smile somehow grew suggestive. "No worries. Yule is long past and, even so, you're both wearing new clothing. But I'd stay away from his claws."

Angela gaped at the Yule Cat. She was here in the flesh —er—fur.

"Enough staring." Dýri rolled his eyes. "We've much to discuss. Gather your things. The sun is setting and you'll be safer inside the mountain."

CHAPTER TWENTY-SIX

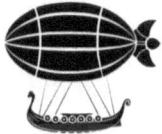

J ÓLAKÖTTURINN DRAGGED HER TAIL through the snow, clearing them a path back to the mountain. Dýri followed, Angela was next, and Val brought up the rear. When they reached the door, his guardsman walked past the giant cat and punched in the code, waving the troll's pet inside.

"I gather we're going with 'ask for forgiveness'?" Val quipped. The council would not react well if they learned the cat had been allowed inside the huldufólk stronghold.

Dýri glowered. "Sóllilja told me everything. I thought you and I were friends."

"We are." He'd been thinking more along the lines of the council's reaction to receiving aid from trolls, not of Val's false and broken engagement. "But she's also my friend—and I was sworn to secrecy."

He grunted and wrapped his fist around the cat's collar, leading them on a winding return though dusty old passage-

333

ways. The only fae they passed were Sóllilja's guards, men and women who said nothing as the enormous cat sauntered past. Any alarm or surprise was noted only in a stiffening of their posture.

Dýri opened the laboratory door, announcing, "We've returned."

The cat ducked inside, heading straight to a pile of blankets arranged hearthside where he curled into a ball. Disinterested yet suspicious, the cat did not slip into slumber but instead watched them with slitted eyes.

"What have you done?" his uncle roared. "You know we do not associate with trolls."

"He's not a troll," Dýri replied. "The whiskers and the tail are dead giveaways."

"The enemy of my enemy and all that," Val quipped. "None of us like trolls, but the situation required we open a conversation with Grýla."

Without glancing at his uncle or speaking a single word, Angela carried the basket protecting the teacup fern to a corner of the laboratory. Not only had the man betrayed her mother, he'd destroyed rare and precious ferns with the intent of driving a species to extinction. An unforgivable act. To maintain civility, she busied herself nestling the potential fire fern inside a small glass Wardian case beside a steaming cup of mineral water drawn directly from the hot tap. Heat and humidity. Safe until they could find the plant a bit of sunlight.

Sóllilja dismissed the guards, sending them to wait in the hallway while Val hung his cloak on a waiting peg. He made no move to divest himself of his weapons. The cat appeared inclined to behave, but cats were fickle creatures, and this one lived year round with trolls.

Much as he wished to hear Dýri's report about his meeting with Grýla, he didn't dare broach the topic in front of his uncle.

"I demand you release me this very minute." His uncle glared from his seat upon the cot the huldrekall had so recently occupied.

"Are the shackles necessary, Sóllilja?" he inquired.

"They are," she replied. "Unless you want him running to the other council members carrying tales." His former fiancée's gaze shifted to Val's sálbundið tattoo. "Many congratulations." She offered him a broad smile before returning to the unpleasant topic of his uncle. "Much as it pains me to restrain him, Aron has indicated he intends to destroy the remaining Tyrian Absinthe despite knowing its value and of his future king's desire to toast his coronation with the purple drink. I thought you two might settle the matter, fae to fae."

"You're defending this oath-breaker?" His uncle barked the question at Sóllilja.

"We never intended to marry," she snapped back at him. "Only to fund your joint research, you ungrateful old man."

Val relaxed. Only one bottle was missing from the crate. Sóllilja had acted quickly. As he stared at the purple bottles, a thorny possibility occurred to him. "You were there in Reykjavik," he began. "When Katya Dagsdóttir ran off with Eirik Rømer."

"What of it?" His uncle crossed his arms. "It was a normal supply run. I had nothing to do with her."

"No?" Val raised his eyebrows. "So you were not the one who told Rømer about the effects of a certain organobromide, one you worked so hard to synthesize on behalf of the huldufólk?"

His uncle paled. Glanced away. Then looked back. "A scientist doesn't hold back information that might benefit another. We met, yes, but only briefly. He complained of an infestation plaguing dulse, *Rhodymenia palmate*, a seaweed he was cultivating as a nutritional food source. As the infection was of pyrrhophyte origin, I offered my educated opinion as to how he might eradicate the tiny creatures."

"Red flashing dinoflagellates." Val kept his voice flat. Odin help him, his uncle had also been taken in by the alchemist's earnest charm. "Not, to my memory, a problem we've encountered in your laboratory. How would you know about such creatures? Care to explain?"

His uncle's expression slammed shut. "No."

The ice encasing Val's heart thawed. He wasn't the only one who'd unwittingly shared fae secrets with a foreigner and failed to admit as much. Was there a difference between them?

Yes. One of them had acted to destroy a piece of huldufólk culture, the other to preserve that same tradition.

Val pulled the diary from the bag slung over his shoulder and tossed it at the man's feet. "Try again."

His uncle yanked on the chain that bound him. "I had no idea Rømer would kidnap your bride-to-be. All I offered him was an honest solution to a problem he'd encountered farming algae. I said nothing of the fire fern, of Eldskrift to an outsider. Can you say the same?"

Sóllilja stiffened but held her tongue. Dýri sent him dark glance.

"No." It was a direct punch to his gut. "But I am working to set things right." Val turned to Sóllilja. "The huldrekall?"

"Still alive, thanks to Angela's swift treatment," she said. "For now. He's receiving supportive care, but it's too soon to assess the damage caused by the dinoflagellate toxins."

In the corner of the room, well within hearing distance, his wife moved about. Collecting various flasks and tubes. Filling them with liquids and powders. Setting them atop wire mesh stands and lighting alcohol burners to heat the contents. Connecting nozzles to coils of glass tubing using rubber hoses. Laboratory behavior he'd not thought to associate with botany. Curious though he was, he'd not ask in front of his uncle.

He stared at his uncle with narrowed eyes. "Knowing of the Eldskrift tradition, you saw those glowing runic markings upon the huldrekall and pretended ignorance." Anger boiled in his chest, a slow, creeping heat that threatened to erupt. "With a possible cure close at hand, you turned your back and left him in Angela's unpracticed and uninformed care."

His uncle's lips flattened.

"Would this purple absinthe work?" Val pressed. "To manage the side effects of a traditional huldufólk fire script tattoo?"

Uncle Aron's head snapped up. "Did she find one? Eyrún? A fire fern grown in a distant land?"

"No." Val shook his head. Not a lie.

In the corner Angela shifted, listening.

His uncle slumped in relief. "I'll tell you what I told her. Organobromides will only prevent the symbionts from parting company—from separating back into fern and dinoflagellates—as they embed into our skin. But Tyrian purple will do nothing to counter the release of dinoflagellate neurotoxins. There was no way to know who might react to the toxins beforehand." He lifted his head and fixed Val with a glare. "The Eldskrift tradition ended for a reason. It should remain buried in our archives, not dragged into the sunlight."

From Uncle Aron's suggestions, Rømer had developed the Tyrian Absinthe for his experiments upon elves. But without first combining the red flashing dinoflagellates with a fern, the tiny creatures embedded in the skin never fused with their flesh. Instead, the pyros had multiplied and spread via the blood stream, carrying bits of bioactive glass crystals throughout the body and depositing them in muscles like little grains of sand.

All while releasing their neurotoxins.

At best, regular consumption of Tyrian purple would keep their numbers in check. But the victim's life—their very existence—would become painful. Gritty skin. Aching muscle. Stomach pains. Difficulty breathing as the heart slowly crystalized. If the tiny creatures were not eradicated completely, there was ultimately no escaping death.

Dýri growled. "Am I hearing that there was a plan to re-establish the fire script guardians?"

"He was studying the process alongside Angela's mother," Val answered. "Exploring the possibility."

"Eyrún, impatient as always, wished to experiment upon her own flesh," his uncle said. "It was too risky. We argued."

"He destroyed the last of the Icelandic fire ferns," Val finished.

"And your fiancée left you." Sóllilja nodded. "Wise of her."

"You don't understand!"

"Oh, I think we do," she replied. "You violated her trust."

Val looked to Sóllilja. "He's done much that's unethical, if not illegal."

Angela gave a sharp jerk of her chin, agreeing. Then turned her back on them all, focused on her work.

"What! No." His uncle leapt to his feet. "I've done nothing wrong!" Suspicious, he glared at Val. "What did you find at the hot spring?"

A life partner. Love. A future Val hadn't known he wanted. "Nothing that need concern you." Anyone willing to sabotage a life partner could not be trusted. He slid a glance at Sóllilja. "I believe we all have more to share, if not in my uncle's presence?"

She nodded, summoned two guards into the laboratory and issued orders. "Confine the councilman to quarters. No visitors, no matter their rank."

The guards unlocked his uncle and dragged him away, protesting.

Before the door swung closed, Hildur and Lisbet slid in. Nearly everyone he trusted in one room.

"What did we miss?" his first mate asked.

Dýri filled them in. "Sóllilja already told us everything else."

The shake of her head was almost imperceptible. She clarified, "About your onetime friendship with Rømer."

So not *everything*. She'd yet to declare her undying love for Val's guardsman. Her choice.

He nodded only in response to her words. "It's true. This entire situation is one of my making."

"Rømer chose this path," Angela objected, joining them. "Not you. He might have worked with you to understand Eldskrift, discussed how any findings might be applied fairly and ethically. Instead, he chose a dark path, experimenting upon uninformed men and women knowing full well they'd likely die in service to his goals."

Katla. An electric troll. The huldrekall in the infirmary. The farmer and his family spared a slow death, but dead, nonetheless. There would be others, victims of the alchemist's early—and likely flawed—experiments. Individuals unlikely to ever be counted.

"What are his goals?" Sóllilja raised her eyebrows, interrupting his thoughts. "What purpose do electric trolls and inscribed fae serve?"

That he could answer. "Rømer is an alchemist who believes he can accelerate biological transformation to create new and better species."

Sóllilja frowned. "Ones in possession of unique abilities by way of Eldskrift?"

"Heal quickly. See in the dark. Immune to the cold." Val listed off the traditional powers granted to fire script guardians. "Perhaps trolls with the ability to release bolts of electricity were a happy accident?"

Dýri cleared his throat. "This is why you were right to send us to speak with Grýla. Basalt trolls have gone missing. A few here, a few there. Young ones prone to wander the volcanic lava fields. No one thought much of their absence until the numbers began to rise. Put simply, he's building an army."

His friend waited.

"An army." Val turned the idea over in his mind.

"To ruin the royal wedding by storming the floating castle?" Hildur considered aloud. "Though it seems unwise. Basalt trolls are heavy. Difficult to transport and likely to sink." The corner of her mouth twitched. "Like a rock."

"Rømer is also a Norwegian nationalist," Val added. "One of many angered by Iceland's forthcoming independence."

All the ostentatious posturing, the pomp and circumstance, the construction of an entire floating castle—a feat of modern engineering—to celebrate a wedding that would create a new kingdom upon a small frozen island while Norway remained under Sweden's thumb angered many.

"It's one of the reasons we met at a ball for the Icelandic delegation," Angela pointed out. "The Jarl's presence in

London was to shore up support for the upcoming wedding when he'll be crowned King of Iceland."

"No," Sóllilja said. "Not at the wedding. Jarl Haukr is to be crowned King of Iceland at Þingvellir in three days' time."

"At the Midwinter Þorrablót Feast?" Val stared at her, then blinked. That explained the unusual size of the gathering. "When did plans change?"

"Do you not pay any attention to royal news?" Sóllilja rolled her eyes.

"As little as possible," Val shot back. "The Jarl has been hounding me—and every other Icelandic trading vessel—to provide him with a bottle of Tyrian Absinthe. Free of charge. Without consideration to the costs of keeping an airship afloat, let alone contributing to research expenses."

"Fair enough," Sóllilja said. "While you were out solarizing your dragon wings, Jarl Haukr lodged a complaint. It was a matter of Icelandic pride, he argued, that he be crowned first. Princess Margrit, he maintained, ought to become queen when she married a king—the traditional manner in which a woman gains her title."

"Rather than him becoming a king because he married a Danish princess." Men wishing to be cast in the light of powerful Vikings. Strong. Virile. Subject to no woman.

"Precisely. At first the Danes balked at such a plan, wishing to maintain the upper hand until the wedding ceremony, but even the British queen backed the jarl, pointing out that Iceland deserved to crown one of its own first to avoid stirring further nationalist tension. With the wedding only three months away, Denmark bowed to political pressure, not wishing to endanger political or trade alliances."

"It's good that Grýla insisted Jólakötturinn travel with us," Dýri said. "The cat will be useful sniffing out trolls."

"You believe Rømer plans to launch a troll attack at Þingvellir, to ruin our chance at independence out of spite?"

Dýri shrugged. "Is that not how you win at chess? Capture the king?"

"Or perhaps he means to hold a princess hostage?" Sóllilja suggested. "The Danish Princess Margit is to attend the investiture ceremony. To present her affianced with his regalia—a crown, scepter and sword."

"Why not both?" Angela asked.

"Stop the wedding, take a hostage or two, negotiate with Scandinavian countries for Norway's independence?" He hated the shape this scenario was taking.

But could it be? They'd been so focused on Eldskrift and elves, both Huldu and Hulder, that they'd not given proper thought to the possibility of a massive troll attack. Trolls weren't known for cooperating on such a large scale, but if the runes carved into their skin and embedded with flashing pyros threatened their lives, would they do Rømer's bidding if he claimed to possess the cure?

They might.

Val's mind whirled, imagining an army of electric trolls swarming over the black granite cliffs that formed the rift valley of Þingvellir, a location enshrined in Icelandic history as the birthplace of their nation.

"What do you know of the ceremonial plans?" he asked
Sóllilja.

"Very little," she replied. "Only that there's to be a
twilight procession along the path between the cliffs to
Lögberg, where he'll be crowned King."

"Lögberg?" Angela inquired.

"Law Rock," Hildur replied. "Where a lawspeaker traditionally stood to preside over the Alþingi, Iceland's original
judicial assembly. Though the last such meeting was held
over six hundred years ago in 1262. That's why they've
chosen the location for his investiture—it's deeply symbolic."

"A time period after which," Sóllilja reminded them,
"Iceland fell under *Norwegian* rule."

"All the more reason for Rømer to disrupt proceedings,"
Dýri said.

"A bottle of Tyrian Absinthe would gain us an audience
with the Jarl," Val said. "But I don't think he would heed a
warning. He's human. To him, the huldufólk and trolls are
nothing but myths. We will be laughed from his búð—or
whatever temporary dwelling a future king occupies at
Þingvellir."

"Then the huldufólk must rise to the occasion. We're
well-equipped to fight trolls." Sóllilja flashed a bloodthirsty
grin at Dýri as she dropped her hand onto the hilt of her
sword. There was nothing she liked more than fighting trolls.

"Not electric ones." Dýri frowned, no doubt recalling
how one had dropped him to the deck with one jolt.

"Then we avoid hand-to-hand combat," she countered.

"We'll rely upon arrows and spears with long wooden handles."

"The council would never approve such a measure," Hildur pointed out. "Fighting an unknown number of basalt trolls at night who might, with a single touch, electrocute fae?" She shook her head. "Especially when we've no evidence and no time for reconnaissance, let alone the vaguest hint of a plan for a counterattack."

"Would it make a difference," Angela asked, "if the guards were able to see in the dark, heal swiftly and not worry about frostbite?"

"What? Am I to understand that you found a fire fern at the hot springs?" Sóllilja's voice buzzed with excitement. She nearly bounced on her toes at the possibility of leading a contingent of fire script guardians into battle on behalf of Icelandic independence. "That we might fight trolls who are as black as soot and operate entirely during the dark hours? You need to ask?"

"Found?" Angela repeated. "Not exactly. But we seem to have made one."

CHAPTER TWENTY-SEVEN

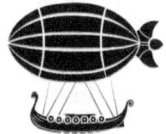

V AL'S GAZE CAUGHT HERS, INCREDULOUS. "It
worked?"

"It worked." She grinned back. "Come see." In
the dark recesses of the rock hewn laboratory, the formerly
green teacup fern had turned reddish brown. "Watch." She
lifted the glass lid of the terrarium and gently tapped a
fingertip against a fern frond.

Tiny pinpoints of red light sparked, then faded.

The wide eyes of three warriors and a mechanic stared
back at her. Sóllilja, Dýri, Hildur and Lisbet momentarily at
a loss for words.

Angela gave them the briefest of overviews. From her
mother's exile to her travels in the Tatra mountains, to the
trials of multiple ferns and, finally, Rømer's own methods, a
tale describing how his obsession ended in untold numbers
of deaths, including that of her own mother.

"My mother's notes," she did not wish to call them mad

ravings, "indicate that she intended to return to Iceland—if she could restore a fire fern to its natural habitat. If only she'd come sooner..."

"I'm so sorry." Sóllilja reached out and placed a hand on her arm. "But Aron is a bitter—if brilliant—man. He would have resurrected old grudges. Between the high death rates involved with Eldskrift and the human perception that glowing red tattoos are a mark of sorcery and the devil, the council would not have let her research continue. Likely, these tiny infectious pyrocysts of yours would have been confiscated and destroyed."

"The past is now irrelevant." Dýri's voice was gruff. "More importantly, is the fire fern the same as the original? Can the plant be used to produce a living tattoo? And do we have enough Tyrian Absinthe to guarantee survival and transformation?"

Terrifying how quickly they'd zeroed in on all her concerns.

"Is it the same fire fern?" Angela repeated. "No. Which means I can guarantee exactly nothing. Will the purple absinthe work to contain the tattoo? No one's ever tested it in precisely this situation. Whoever trials Eldskrift will be little more than a laboratory rat."

Sóllilja frowned. "We can't afford to have our best guards ill, let alone risk their deaths."

"Agreed." She lifted a fluid-filled vial and a sharp-tipped lancet. "Fortunately, there is now a quick and harmless—if not painless—skin test, one not available to our ancestors. I've concentrated the toxins produced by the pyros. I'll scratch a little toxin into the skin of your forearm and then we wait. If blisters form, you cannot tolerate the fire fern's presence and, therefore, cannot be initiated into the Eldvörður."

"Is that what you've been working on over here, a screening test?" Val moved to her side, examining the network of flasks and tubes, filters and vials she'd assembled upon the workbench.

"Precisely that. Would you like to be first?"

"Yes." He unbuttoned his cuff and rolled it back, exposing twisting roots and vines wrapped about corded muscle. A magnificent, enticing display of manhood that—

Hildur snorted, breaking Angela's reverie. She jerked her head up.

Behind him, Sóllilja rolled her eyes, grinning. "It's not a small laboratory," she quipped. "But if the newlyweds require privacy, the rest of us could go first, then make ourselves scarce?"

Everyone, including Lisbet, had bared their forearms.

"Not necessary." Angela's cheeks heated. "This only takes a moment." With an eyedropper, she dripped a measure of the concentrated neurotoxin atop a bare, untattooed patch of Val's skin. Then, holding his wrist steady, she used the lancet to prick his skin several times. "A reaction should occur in minutes."

He drew his hand away, but not before his fingers closed gently around hers for a moment. "Brilliant work, saving lives with such a simple test."

Warmth spread through her chest. She sterilized the

lancet by dipping it into alcohol and waved it through a flame. "Who's next?"

Those most suited to wage battle went first. Sóllilja. Dýri. Hildur.

But Val's skin reddened, then began to blister angrily as tiny pustules formed. So too did Sóllilja's. Then Dýri's and Hildur's.

Her heart sank to her knees. All that work, all that hope. Was the pyro from the Tatra mountains compatible with the fern, but not with the Icelandic huldufólk?

With a shrug, Lisbet held out her arm. "You might as well try mine. I'm half Danish Hulder, but my mother is Huldu."

All hands on deck? Why not? "And I learned yesterday that I'm half Huldu, half Hulder."

Angela dripped the toxin onto their forearms, then repeated the procedure. Her own skin reacted not at all. Nor did Lisbet's. She frowned. "How strange." The two least suited to the role of Fire Script Guardians were the best biological match. She met Lisbet's gaze. "Odd that mixed blood passes the test."

"Is it?" Dýri asked. "Perhaps the rest of us are simply too inbred. Maybe both of you are what this mountain needs. New blood—or rather—old. After all, the first fae arrived here alongside the Vikings. And it might explain why the initiation ceremony became more deadly over the centuries."

Sóllilja tapped her lips. "An interesting possibility. There are a few among my guards born to traveling merchants. We could ask if any of their parents are Hulder.

Test the willing." She frowned. "But your test, it only predicts who is unlikely to die from the toxins these tiny creatures release. That means they could still break free from the plant cells and become free-living parasites?"

"They could." Angela's stomach clenched. "It's inevitable that a few of the cells will enter the blood stream. Which means initiates might grow ill from a generalized infection. We think that's why Val's uncle was working to synthesize an organic compound that would kill any pyros exiting a fern cell."

"He quit when her mother left," Val elaborated. "But inadvertently tipped off Rømer."

"Who then brewed this Tyrian Absinthe for his own experiments?" Sóllilja glanced at the case of Tyrian Absinthe. "How many guards do we think we could recruit to our cause? One per bottle?"

Were they really going to do this? Angela's heart pounded. "There's no way to know. The purple absinthe should work, but we've no idea of the dose required. Whatever the amount, they should be able to stop once the living tattoo is fully integrated into skin. We could run some tests—"

"We don't have time for tests," Sóllilja interrupted. "The huldrekall was provided with a single bottle—"

"Meaningless," Val spoke up. "Katla's tattoos were fully healed and still she carried a bottle on her person."

"But her tattoos were formed with glass strands and free-living pyros," Hildur pointed out. "Without the fern cells, no permanent tattoo could form."

"This is morally problematic." Sóllilja crossed her arms. "And, practically, I need my guards fit and healthy."

"Which is why we must prove this will work." Angela took Lisbet's hand and offered her an uncertain smile. "Shall the two of us attempt to reestablish the Eldvörður?"

"Yes," the engineer replied without hesitation. "I'd like nothing better."

"You're not trained guards," Sóllilja objected.

"Angela is not." Hildur grinned. "Though my wife is deadly with a knife in close quarters and quite competent with a cross bow." She stared at her captain and raised an eyebrow in challenge. "But some spies do no more than observe and report. If we insert them among the Icelandic and Danish courts at Þingvellir, no one will suspect a thing. They could carry messages of warning to the Jarl and the princess. At least their guards would not be taken unaware."

Her blood ran cold. So much for avoiding politics. She straightened her back. She could do this. For Iceland, for the huldufólk, for international peace.

"Spies?" Val's entire body was stiff with objection. "Leave them on the ground in Þingvellir when we suspect an army of electric trolls might attack?" He shook his head. "Lisbet's skills are critical—she keeps our airship flying—and Angela needs to monitor the health of any volunteers who agree to a fire tattoo."

"We look a bit alike, Princess Margrit and I." Lisbet patted her hair, piled atop her head in artful twists of braids. "What's more, I speak Danish. With the right clothes, I could slip inside and hand deliver a message. Perhaps, if she's amenable, she might let me take her place for the ceremony where, if my new abilities include enhanced night vision, I could keep an eye on the surrounding cliffs for trolls during the coronation ceremony."

Hildur jumped to her wife's defense. "But if my wife is to serve as decoy, I insist upon accompanying her as a lady-in-waiting. A personal guard, armed and dangerous, ready to fight."

"I'm not a physician." Angela stepped into the argument, her voice tight. "And even if someone else warns Jarl Haukr, we need more than one person to trial the fire tattoos. Two isn't much better, but it's something." Narrowing her eyes, she added another thought. "We could always learn from a negative control. Would any of the rest of you care to test the premise, see if you manage to stay out of the infirmary and morgue?"

Silence.

"I didn't think so." She locked eyes with Val. "If this works, we could have guards on the ground with enhanced night vision, high tolerance to cold, and rapid healing. If we wait, the council will stop us. Better to ask for forgiveness."

His jaw flexed, but he couldn't argue her point.

Angela looked to Dýri. "If this is successful, we'll need more ferns to inoculate."

Dýri nodded. "I'll head back to the hot spring and gather more."

There was no way of knowing how many of the teacup ferns existed in the wild, and her heart jumped at the thought of accidentally removing too many ferns for the population to survive. She gave specific instructions. "Be careful. Bring back no more than twenty percent of the ferns you find. Conservation is important."

He nodded. Swinging a heavy cape over his shoulders and snatching up the basket Angela held out, he called to the Jólakötturinn and headed back to the hot spring with the enormous black cat slinking behind him.

Sóllilja's gaze filled with longing as she followed his exit. Angela bit her tongue to stop herself from commenting. She barely knew Val's friends.

Frigg, at moments like this, she wondered how well she even knew her soulbound husband. Her entire life she'd worked with her mother to reestablish a fire fern that its cells might be used as a tattoo. That he would stand in her way from receiving the Eldvörður mark?

Back stiff, she hissed under her breath. "Recall that my mother died to protect her research, to keep it from Rømer's hands. I will do whatever is required to stop him."

"Does your wish to trial the tattoo worry me?" He bit the words out. "Yes. But I'd trial it myself, save for your test. It's the spying that worries me. You've no combat training. None."

"Then escort me. We've both high-ranking parents. Could your father arrange for us to attend the ceremony?"

"Possibly." He rubbed his hand over his jaw. "It's not a bad idea, but if we're right—"

"An army of trolls." She nodded. "Not ideal, but neither do I wish to hide away."

When the door closed behind Dýri, Sóllilja turned all

business. "We have everything we need. If we're to initiate guards, we'll need to do so soon." She stared down at the single case of Tyrian Absinthe. "Angela is correct. We can't inform the council we believe a mad alchemist gathered an army of trolls with plans to attack the Jarl or the princess. Or both. There's no chance I'd be allowed to lead fae troops to Þingvellir."

Val cleared his throat. "So we ask for volunteers. They all know how to handle tröllabanar, potassium weaponry, but we'll need to work out a method to discharge their electricity from a distance. If this fire fern functions as intended, they can work in groups stationed in different locations about the site, each with a designated Eldvörður spotter."

"Excellent." Sóllilja brightened. "Lisbet and Hildur infiltrate the Danish contingent with a warning of the nefarious plans a villain might have in store for her, and an offer to take her place during the royal procession." She paced as she planned. "Angela and Val make their way to the Jarl's side with a similar warning. Flanking the future King and Queen of Iceland during the investiture ceremony, you'll be perfectly positioned to send up a flare, a warning if—or when —a threat is detected."

Val squeezed her hand. "You're certain the fern is ready for a trial?"

"Let me run a few tests," she hedged as the enormity of all that had been proposed washed over her. "It's only been a few hours since we applied the pyros to the plant's roots."

"We have three days." The guardswoman fixed her with a stare. "To initiate fire script guardians, to plan, to mobilize."

"Understood." People always wished to rush biology. "But plants grow as fast as they grow. The pyros integrate when they integrate. It's a positive sign that the leaves already grow, but I'll examine the interior workings of its cells beneath the microscope's lens. Only then can we know."

"Unless there are objections," Val began, "the inscribing of the first fire guard in centuries ought to be marked with the proper ritual. Who better to conduct the ceremony than a völva who has studied the ancient tradition and refuses to conform to society's expectations?"

These past few days had been a whirlwind. From expecting to manage her own household in the English countryside to conspiring with a witch to prevent a villain from meddling in international politics. And finally—*finally*—a chance to test the fire fern within her own skin.

She gave Val a bright smile. "I look forward to meeting your mother."

CHAPTER TWENTY-EIGHT

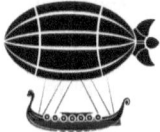

EQUALLY DELIGHTED TO MEET HER son's wife, incite rebellion, and conduct a forbidden ancient fae ceremony, his mother's footsteps flew down the stone passageways. "When Eyrún ran, I thought to follow." Her voice was breathless. "But you'd barely begun to crawl. The risks were too great."

She left many words unspoken. With no husband, no funds and no prospects, she'd set aside adventure in favor of safety and security. Val found himself glad of her choice even as he regretted the sacrifice she'd felt necessary. Had she chosen otherwise, he wouldn't be the man he was today.

On the other hand, he wouldn't have stolen his uncle's manuscript and shared it with an enemy of his people. Was he personally responsible for their situation? He certainly felt at fault. Worse, he couldn't even offer himself up to the initiation ceremony. If Angela's skin test was correct, his body would—at best—reject the fire fern, leaving him incapacitated and ill when he needed to be in top form to stop Rømer.

He held up a hand to glance around a corner, found the corridor empty, then waved them onward. "Had you chosen otherwise, we wouldn't be here now, positioned to bring back the fire fern."

"If only Eyrún herself had returned." His mother sighed. "Brave and determined of her to travel so far. I can't help but wonder if the spring she discovered in the Polish mountainside was once home to a *rusalka* or a *vila*..."

Val gathered such creatures were fae of some sort, but he had little patience for abstract theory at the moment, not unless it applied directly to that of Eldskrift. He glanced at the old vellum book in his mother's arms. Little more than a collection of yellowed pages, the thin book looked to be held together less by its binding and more by the strands of wool yarn wrapped about its cover. "You're certain of the ceremony?"

"A certain as twenty years of study in the archives can make me." She glanced at the door to her brother's laboratory as they passed. "Back then, I always believed Aron would be part of this. He never would tell me what they fought about, and now I learn my own brother erased one of our most sacred traditions in a fit of protective selfishness? Serves him right that Eyrún left."

They reached the laboratory where their small band of rebels gathered.

Dýri had returned and was busy in the far corner where he and Lisbet worked to tuck tiny ferns into teacups—after carefully drilling a hole for drainage—and settling them inside the glass case. Heads bent together, Hildur and Sóllilja had scratched out a rough map of Þingvellir and covered it with Xs, Os and sweeping arrows as they plotted how trolls might swarm down the black rock of the fissure to attack Lögberg.

Upon the hearth, the Jólakötturinn lounged, barely cracking an eyelid to note his return.

"Goodness," his mother whispered, staring at the over-sized cat. "I never thought to lay eyes on the creature."

Angela abandoned the aetheroscope and her notes, rising to greet them. If his mother's extensive tattoos or the long twists of her braided hair intertwined with small charms of carved bone beads and metal rune rings surprised her, she gave no indication.

"Mother, meet my wife Angela Eyrúnsdóttir. Angela, this is my mother, Katrín Geirsdóttir."

His mother shoved all she carried into Val's arms, took Angela's hands and smiled. "Beautiful, intelligent and a force to be reckoned with, much like your mother before you. I'm so pleased to learn you and my son have tied your lives together. If I may?" She lifted a hand.

Angela nodded and his mother swept his wife's hair aside to examine the bindrune.

"Healing nicely. Under normal circumstances, I'd like a tattoo to be fully bonded before inscribing a new one, but I understand the Eldskrift ceremony must take priority?"

"I'm afraid so." Angela threw him an apologetic glance. He hated that he'd given her reason to doubt him. "Two of the least likely candidates, Lisbet and myself, have passed the test." His wife briefly explained how she'd tested the pyro toxins in their skin, how only those who were half huldufólk showed no reaction. "Dýri believes it is because we carry fae blood from the old countries." She took a deep breath. "I will be the first to step onto the ice."

His mother's eyes widened at hearing the phrase, one they'd found among Eyrún's runic scribbles. "And take inside the light of the fire." She nodded. "Your mother wondered the same thing about the fading ability of our people to host a fire script tattoo. It's why she sailed east, to the old countries, in her hunt for the ancestral fire fern. Much as I wish to hear everything about her efforts, we need to focus on the present. Three days is a narrow window. Is the fern ready?"

"I believe so. Their cell membranes have fused. There are a multitude of sparking scintillons and I cannot find any flagella—the tail used by free-living pyros to move about. In short, they seem quite cozy together."

"And this drink," his mother tapped a bottle. "You believe the purple color will keep the two organisms from parting ways?"

"That is the hope," Angela answered.

"6-6'-dibromoindigo." Val named the dye his uncle had worked to chemically synthesize, before abandoning that work, turning instead to indoor—in mountain—algae farming. "Tyrian purple as collected from Phoenician sea snails."

His mother's lips pursed. "All the purple splotches that used to stain my brother's clothing. Groans would echo through the halls when his laundry arrived—they charged him double." She tipped her head. "But why would he seek to stop their spread?"

"What do you mean?" Angela asked. "Our understanding is that initiates died when the tattoo failed to bond, when the pyros broke free to wander."

"No. No, no, no. The wandering is necessary, else how would you acquire any powers from something so small as a single bindrune?"

Angela caught his gaze. "Could that be why—"

"Rømer carved entire sentences into his victims?" Val continued.

His mother clapped her hands together, demanding their attention. "You've pieced much of the process together, but you've missed an important element. The light—pyros as you call them—must escape the tattoo from time to time. They must wander. They must also *die*." She paused, allowing them to absorb the import of this new information. "The initiates who did not survive were slowly overcome when their bodies failed to limit the proliferation of the light. Night by night the blaze spread until they were incandescent, consumed with light and heat to the point of self-immolation."

"They caught fire and burned?" His wife stared, open-mouthed.

His mother nodded.

"But successful initiates?"

"Lights would occasionally spark. If their skin was touched, a brief glimmer. An onlooker would blink and wonder if the flash was their imagination. Nothing dramatic." She snorted a laugh. "It's not as if anyone wanders the countryside here in the nude."

His wife blushed. Was she thinking of their dash to the hot spring? Of how he'd laid her out upon stone and moss to—

No. He could not allow himself to replay the experience. Not in mixed company.

"Still," his mother tapped her chin, "a single glass of this purple drink, if it does as you claim, might accelerate the integration of fern and fae. As speed is of the essence, we'll incorporate the Tyrian Absinthe into the ceremony. But only a single glass." She crooked her fingers, beckoning his wife close. "I must officially ask. You attempt this under no duress?"

"None." Her voice was confident, even if a glimmer of fear haunted her eyes.

His mother nodded, then tugged at her sleeve. "You'll need to partly disrobe. The bindrunes belong in the skin above your heart." She turned away to toss a bundle of dried herbs on the fire and the air filled with a sweet, heady scent. More items emerged from her lambskin bag. Two long, thin birch sticks. Pots of salve and ointment. A mortar and pestle into which she sprinkled calcite crystals of Icelandic spar.

"Viking sunstone?" Val frowned, unhappy that something even remotely resembling glass was required.

In the past, sunstone was valued by their ancestors as it polarized light in a manner that allowed them to navigate the seas by locating the sun on overcast days. Today, the calcite crystal was prized for manufacturing optical lenses. Such as those in the aetheroscope.

An enigmatic smile touched his mother's face as her *seiðr* personality slipped into place. Loops of colorful glass beads circling her neck rattled softly. "Wait and see."

Angela slid him a questioning glance.

"Sunstone introduces an unpredictable element." Worry swirled in his gut. "Calcite isn't glass. It's calcium carbonate as opposed to the silicon dioxide of bioactive glass. Different. Not necessarily safe."

She blew out a slow breath. Inhaled. "Yet traditional?"

"Very much so." His mother's hand slowed as she ground the spar into a fine powder. "If you wish, I can attempt the ceremony without it, but—"

"No." Angela stopped her. "We've enough new variables already. Shall I prepare the plant cells?"

"Please do." His mother glanced at him. "Go. Gather the others as witnesses."

Soon, they all stood beside the hearth.

Sóllilja arrived with a tray holding two absinthe glasses, two perforated spoons and two sugar cubes. She placed the tray upon a low table beside a carafe of cold glacier melt-water and a bottle of Tyrian Absinthe.

She and Dýri looked mildly vexed, Hildur pained and her wife anticipatory. Val found himself conflicted. Anxious yet also proud. If this worked, his wife would restore an age-old practice. Some would celebrate her as a heroine, others would paint her as a villainess. Not that such bothered him. His only concern was for her health.

Angela presented his mother with a small vial. Inside its clear glass walls, red sparks glinted and flashed, swirling through the green. The macerated frond of a fire fern, reduced to the smallest units of life.

She and Lisbet knelt before the fire on a wool carpet, their upper chests bare before the völva.

With reverence, his mother accepted the vial, placing it beside a gleaming, sharp-tipped hollow copper needle. Flames jumped as she pulled a long, thin birch stick from the fire and held it aloft. Tendrils of smoke curled through the air carrying with them the fragrance of soot and ash.

His mother spoke. "Angela, three bindrunes were chosen by the ancients: *hjarta, þokki,* and *ást.* The first is a mark of 'heart' and stands for bravery and courage. The second is the mark of 'grace' for you will often be under duress. The final bindrune is 'love' as you devote yourself in a selfless manner to protecting your people. Combined into a single stave, fire script mark tells all that you are favored by the gods, an Eldvörður working outside the mountain to preserve the lives within."

As the flickering flames threw shadows and light across her skin, his mother transformed into a völva, old and young at once, timeless. The tattoos that spiraled about her arms and hands seemed to writhe and twist before dripping from her fingers.

"Living a life apart requires that you endure ice and fire with courage, grace and devotion. To aid you in your tasks, the fire fern grants the ability to see through the darkest of nights, to resist the freezing cold, to heal wounds with speed. Do you accept these duties without condition?"

"I do."

Using the tip of the charred stick, the völva traced the bindrune stave in charcoal upon his wife's breast.

"Dark and light. Cold and warm. Ice and fire." Vial in one hand, hollow copper needle in the other, she pierced the smooth skin above Angela's heart, over and again. Blood and ash mixed with flashes of red as Angela knelt, still and stoic. As flashing cells of the fire fern were embedded within her skin.

When Val might have expected his mother to wipe away the blood, soot and fern, to seal the mark with a salve, instead she lifted a small obsidian knife and made a series of tiny cuts into the freshly inked tattoo.

More blood trickled down his wife's chest. Though she barely flinched, pain danced at the corners of her eyes, in the press of her lips, in the tightness of her shoulders.

The völva scooped fingers through the ground sunstone in the bowl and dabbed them onto the bindrune stave tattoo, gently but firmly rubbing the calcite crystals into the cuts. All while she chanted. "Kristalsís binst og bognar er eldur vaknar upp og glóðir loga. Kuldinn mun ei lengur bíta, né nóttin fela skugga sína - sár munu dofna og styrkur eflast."

Crystal ice binds and bends as fire awakens and embers burn. No longer will the cold bite, nor the night hide its shadows—wounds will fade, and strength will rise.

Angela began to shiver. He clenched his teeth so as not to sweep forward with a woolen blanket. Finally—*finally!*—

his mother wiped the bloody mess from her chest and applied an herb-laced balm to seal the bindrune tattoo.

Offering her no further comfort, the völva beckoned Lisbet closer to repeat the ceremony.

Long minutes later, the two fire guard initiates shivered violently, as if dropped into glacier melt water.

How much longer could he and Hildur stand by without acting? Not long, judging from the tooth enamel she also ground from her molars in an effort to hold still, to serve as witness.

"Thus bound," the völva concluded, "your journey of transformation begins." She blinked, as if returning to the mortal plane. "The absinthe."

Placing sugar cubes atop the perforated spoons that balanced on goblets that held purple and green spirits, she lifted the water pitcher. Slowly, she trickled water over the sugar, dissolving it into the absinthe. Water mixed with wormwood oil, swirling into a milky-white cloud.

A moment of uncertainty transformed the völva back into his mother. Sharp clarity entered her eyes. The tremors that had overtaken Angela and Lisbet rendered them incapable of lifting anything. Forget tipping a glass to their lips.

"If spouses will assist?"

They sprang into action. Arms about their wives, Val and Hildur each lifted a goblet of a drink resembling a night sky's purple aurora borealis.

"To living ink!" his mother toasted.

"And strong bonds!" the witnesses replied as one.

"Drink, Angela." Words whispered as he pressed the

crystal glass to her lips, gently tipping it upward in hopes the diluted drink would pass over her chattering teeth.

She managed a tiny sip. Then another. And another. Slowly, the level dropped, with only some escaping the corners of her mouth.

All while Val wondered at the cause of her tremors. They'd used the same fern for their sálbundið, applying their tattoos without any negative effects. And it was too soon for the new tattoo to become infected. And the shivers had not begun until the crystals were applied. His mind pondered potential chemical reactions between sunstone and dinoflagellate toxins, but he could think of no reason for her fever.

When she finished, he set down the glass and wrapped a blanket about her shoulders and gathered her close. "Talk to me." Soft words, but an order, nonetheless. "I need to know if you're all right."

"I'm fine." A tight, forced word. "Cold is radiating from the bindrunes like cracks spreading across thin ice." She dropped her head to his shoulder. "The blending of flesh and fern?"

"I hope."

Sóllilja placed a bucket of cold water on the hearth between the two initiates. "I'm told the next step is—"

Lisbet gasped. Tossing away her blanket, she yanked at the neckline of her blouse, pulling sticky cloth away from her bindrunes. "What's happening?"

A moment later, Angela stiffened. "The bindrunes. It feels as though a hot steel wire is tracing the marks." She too pulled at her blouse.

All eyes turned in the direction of the initiates. Across the pinpricks of their marks, tiny lights sparked, flickered, then faded. Then again. Every time, a single flash that set off a chain reaction. Tiny red glimmers atop a base of green. Bioluminescent light reflected and scattered, made brilliant by the embedded sunstone crystals.

"Ice and fire awaken," his mother intoned, tossing another bundle of pungent dried herbs in the fire. "The magic of the elders."

An ancient wonder given new life in his wife's skin. The first Fire Script Guardian in hundreds of years.

"Hot," she moaned. "So hot."

Entranced by the pyrotechnic display in miniature, he'd not noticed the heated flush that had enveloped her. She clawed at her skirts, dragging hems above her knees to yank at garters, to shove at woolen stockings.

Val dunked a cloth into the cold water, wringing it out to drape across her forehead. Hildur did the same for Lisbet.

As the women stripped off clothing, Dýri watched with interest and raised eyebrows until Sóllilja swatted him hard across the chest. With a shrug and an eye roll, he poured himself a glass of green absinthe and retreated into the far corner of the room, sinking onto the stone floor to lean against the giant cat.

"How long until the tattoo implants?" he asked his mother.

"An hour?" She lifted upturned hands. Her eyes grew distant, unseeing. "A day? Such is an answer lost to time."

CHAPTER TWENTY-NINE

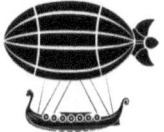

NINE. THE ANSWER WAS NINE HOURS. Nine miserable cycles of cold and ice followed by ones of heat and fire.

Her memories of the time were sketchy. She remembered Val's careful attention. Of Sóllilja bringing guards to the laboratory, of toxins tested upon their skin, of the handful found worthy. In the middle of the chaos, she and Lisbet were carried elsewhere to rest and recover.

As the fever and chills of transformation faded into a dull fatigue, Angela's eyes peeled open, finally free of the burning grit of coal embers and frozen shards of saltwater that had plagued her disjointed sleep.

Where was she?

A solarium of sorts. Slanted winter sunlight poured through panes of glass that surrounded her on three sides. Snow drifts covered the lower planes, but inside baskets of plants hung from hooks, perched on shelves and rose from stone planters. Tucked among the foliage was the Wardian case where fire ferns grew in teacup planters.

Whenever ill, her mother had always insisted recuperation was best done in the greenhouse, propped on a bench covered in blankets and pillows that were nestled into a sunny corner. Her mother would always check on her by rolling up Angela's sleeve to inspect the green color of her fern tattoo. Recharging, she'd called it. Photosynthesizing, as Angela now knew it.

She rocked her head to the side. Beside her was a narrow cot, empty but for a neat stack of folded woolen blankets. Soft voices murmured nearby. The initiation of the ancients ought to have left her as limp and as wrung out as a dirty dishrag. Instead, she felt clear-headed, her body loose and limber. Lifting her head from a downy pillow, she braced herself upon her elbows.

The sun-drenched space was attached to a rock-hewn room. A bedchamber, judging from the furniture. Haphazardly tossed atop an enormous bed were all manner of luxurious garments, richly embroidered and edged with woven trim and fur.

Lisbet and Hildur held up each in turn for inspection, softly discussion fashion, nodding or shaking a head only to snatch up another equally splendid tunic or gown. All while Val frowned at rough sketches, scratching notations in the margins.

Plans to infiltrate the royal courts looked to be well underway.

Hildur glanced in her direction, then nudged her wife

and whispered in her ear. Without another word they slid from the room, closing a door so softly behind them that Val missed their exit.

Their lack of concern and animated preparation promised good news.

Angela's hand landed atop her chest, atop the mark that made her a Fire Script Guardian. Though to call her such felt like a stretch, given her top knife skills included the ability to make paper-thin cuts of plant tissue before mounting them upon a glass slide for microscopic inspection. She threw back her blanket and swung bare feet to the floor.

A moment later, Val was at her side. He cupped her face with his hands and poured a mix of emotions—relief, worry and pride—into a soft kiss. "How do you feel?"

"Surprisingly well." Though the bindrunes inscribed upon her chest felt raw and tender. She pulled at the gathered neckline of the sleeveless cotton shift she wore, glancing down. "It worked? I gather I am expected to live?"

"It did. You are. As hoped, the Tyrian Absinthe sped up the bonding of the tattoo. For you and everyone else."

"Sigge?"

Val shook his head. "Not for him. Our physicians managed to eliminate the dinoflagellates, but the huldrekall was pretty sick when he escaped."

"Escaped?" Her voice rose with alarm.

"Shh," he soothed. "No worries. Sóllilja let him slip free. One of her guards follows, hoping that Sigge will lead us to Rømer, or to where his men and trolls were hiding. If he finds them, the guard will send back a message."

An excellent plan, stopping the battle before it could begin.

She relaxed.

He handed her a mirror, angling it so that she could better examine the tattoo. "Tap it gently as it's not quite healed. A single fingertip."

Her light touch to the dark green mark sent pinpricks of cold fire radiating outward. More, a tiny electric shock. A thin whisper of an ache, any discomfort dwarfed by the heady breathlessness of watching red sparks flicker and jump along the lines of the bindrunes.

"Have the pyros spread?"

"They did." He brushed aside a lank of her hair and cool air rushed over her sálbundið. "A few engineered a significant relocation."

Her pulse jumped. Her soulbound tattoo also glittered. But only faintly. Which meant that when the pyros wandered, a few had found her still-healing marriage tattoo and taken up residence inside the fern cells. "Anywhere else?" She lifted the mirror and tapped her cheek. Nothing.

Val plucked the mirror from her hand. "Let's see if we can find them. Scientific inquiry and all that." He tugged her to her feet. The cotton fabric of her shift whispered past skin in one smooth motion as he stripped her bare.

"What—" But her protest died on her lips when he shed his shirt, pulling it over his head and tossing it to the floor.

Oh, that kind of inspection.

Her heart sped up as she stared at his bare torso, at a loss for words as heat gathered between her legs. Neither the flickering flames of fire nor the shimmering overhead northern lights had done his body justice. Only full sunlight displayed his many charms to perfection.

Her husband was a glorious Viking.

Not that she was provided with sufficient time to fully study and catalog the hard planes and chiseled valleys of his chest. A few seconds weren't adequate to admire how the muscles of his arms and shoulders shifted and flexed beneath skin. Nor did the half-second she stole to appreciate how the sun-kissed golden hair swept back from his forehead, all but a single stray lock.

For his fingers stabbed into the tangle of her hair and hauled her lips against his, a kiss that was anything but tender. Strong hands framed her face as his mouth plundered hers, demanding a counterattack.

Soft and pliant, she fell against his solid form, wrapped her arms about his waist and dug fingertips into the dense bands of muscle that ran beside his spine. His pelvis rocked against her lower stomach, his hard length informing her exactly how his investigation would end.

Abruptly, he pulled her away, staring down at her. Thumbs brushed over her cheekbones, swept across her forehead, her chin. "Found one." He bent to nibble the corner of her mouth.

"Only one?" She dropped her gaze to her own chest where the rosy tips of her breasts pebbled, desperate for his attention. Arched her back to emphasize her suggestion. "Seems to me there's a great amount of territory to explore."

A devious grin curled the corners of his mouth. "Some of it with great depth."

Her belly tightened at his words and she squeezed her thighs together. "And force?"

"How else could we call ourselves scientists?" His hands dropped to her shoulders, slid down her arms to her hands. "No flashes. But perhaps it's the shadows we need."

Without warning, he lifted her arms overhead, securing both her wrists in one hand. With his other, he pushed, walking her backward into a dark corner as he studied her jutting breasts with mischief dancing in his eyes. Her bare back met cold, rough stone. Fingers brushed across her collar bone, then lower, sweeping tantalizing paths over the skin of her upper chest, skirting the bindrunes. "Unresponsive."

"Why does that feel like a criticism?" She twisted against his grip, but his hands tightened.

"Stand still."

He curled his fingers, skimming their backs downward over the slope of her breasts, stopping short of her pebbled nipples. His palm slipped over her ribs, shaping itself to the indentation of her waist, the flare of her hips. Then slid upward to cup her breast. A rough thumb pad swept across its peaked tip.

"That's hardly enough force to activate anything."

"Oh?" He pinched one nipple. Hard enough that a cry tore from her throat. "Like that?"

"More."

He rolled the tip with unforgiving pressure. Arrows of desire shot downward, settling between her legs. "Still nothing." He clasped her other nipple between forefinger and thumb and squeezed. "Ah, found one."

She glanced down. Tiny sparks flickered.

He increased the pressure and her body responded. Brighter sparks, ones that ignited and tore along her nerves, every sensation shooting straight to her core.

"Val." His name emerged on a sharp indrawn breath. Her hips flexed.

"Entirely irresistible." A whispered comment. Then his mouth replaced his fingers, his teeth clamped down and he sucked. He drew back studying the faint flashes of red light glistening on the wet tip of her nipple. He blew air across it and laughed, a low husky sound. "Beautiful. Does your skin feel any different?"

"No." She twisted against his restraint. Wanting to plunge her fingers into his hair and pull him back, hold him there. "More."

"Perhaps later, once we find a few more," he teased. "But only if you cooperate." He released her wrists, dropped to his knees and pushed her feet apart. "This might take a while."

She groaned. His fingertips resumed their explorations. Gentle pinches. A soft scrape of nails or teeth. From time to time, he called out a discovery, pressing a rough kiss to each. One at the protuberance of an ankle. Another upon the inside of a knee. His hands were everywhere and nowhere—until they reached the delicate flesh of her inner thighs.

A slow, deliberate torture, this ignoring of nerve bundles. Her fingers fisted in his hair, tugging. "Val."

But he was not to be hurried.

His hands stilled, holding her thighs apart, pushing her to the stone wall when her knees grew weak and her body sagged. His teeth nipped, his lips soothed, and the rough hairs of his beard scraped and teased. Closer and closer to her core. Thumbs found her folds first, pressing, stroking, parting. Then his mouth closed around her. His tongue lashed and his mouth sucked.

She cried out. Then gasped.

He pulled away. "Found another."

"Enough!"

He laughed against her quivering skin, enjoying her outrage. "Not nearly. I've only examined your front half." Lifting his face, he stared into her eyes and pressed the width of his hand against her twisting hips, pinning her to the wall. Then drove two fingers deep into her tight channel. Then a third. Stretching her. He pressed, hunting for that spot that had made her—

Her nails dug into his scalp as she screamed.

Perfect.

Pumping, he kept up the teasing sweep of his thumb across her nub. A glimmer of red flashed each time he circled, each time he pressed. A fascinating effect, true, yet it was her wanton, visceral reaction to his touch that drove his efforts. She was a vision that would fuel erotic dreams—but only his.

Her knees trembled. "Please."

Was she begging for release? She was so close. So very close. But he wasn't nearly done torturing her, no matter how desperate her cries. No release until he'd sunk his cock deep into that tight wet heat.

"Please, what?" He nipped at the flare of her hip. His hand kept up its tortures, unceasing. But lighter now. He'd drive her over that cliff. Soon. But he wanted to seat himself deep and fall with her.

"I need you." She hauled in a ragged breath. "Inside me."

He shoved deeper and her knees nearly collapsed. Sweet agony. "I *am* inside you."

She flushed. "You want me to beg?"

"Yes. Be specific. Scientists are."

She cursed. "Not your fingers. Your cock."

His fingers plunged, the base of his hand ground upward. One last time. "But I've not finished my inspection."

Her body bucked. "Freyja!"

Enough. The torture was too much. He stood, flicking open the closure of his waistband, shucking his trousers, freeing his hard-as-stone cock. She stared, licked her lips, reached for him. He almost let her, almost pushed her to her knees and let her take him in her mouth. But he wouldn't last and he had other plans.

Sweeping her off her feet, he carried her to a stool. One that rested before his dressing table. Upon which rested a mirror. He dropped her on her knees, grabbed her hands and planted them on the table before her. Then thrust his cock between her soft thighs, biting back a groan.

"Watch." He pinched her nipple, rolled it as she gasped,

ANNE RENWICK

both at the pleasure, at the flash of light, at the push of his heavy cock as he gripped its base, guiding it along her wet folds to her weeping entrance.

His smart, adventurous wife, little more than an innocent, quickly grasped his intentions. He needed to know more of that instructional book she'd studied for she bent forward, lifting her backside and parting her knees. An invitation he'd not refuse. He shoved, digging his fingers into the bones of her hips and seating himself deep.

Her mewling cry had him withdrawing, ramming in. Hard enough to make her back arch.

He stilled, throbbing, fighting the urge to dive onward. Giving her muscles time to stretch. Last night she'd begged him for hard, for deep. But this was a new angle. "More?"

"Don't you dare stop." She glared at him in the mirror and pushed back against his thighs.

He reached a hand around to find her nub, circling it, until she cried out in frustration. Her face twisted as she cursed at him, as she tried to escape his grip that she might slide along his length under her own power.

Loki laughed. He'd met his match. She was his everything. His fate. His love. The other half of his soul.

A growl built in his throat. Control slipped and primal urges took over. He pulled out, almost leaving her tight wet channel, then thrust inside her. Over and again. Plunging, withdrawing, setting a rhythm that was hard and fast and feral. One she matched, pushing back to meet him.

A tingling gathered at the base of his spine, then spread to his balls. "Come for me, Angela," he growled. He pulled at her hair, bent over her, arching against his chest. Forcing her to stare into the mirror. To watch as their bodies worked together, moving in unison as they climbed higher and higher, racing to the peak that had become the only thing that mattered.

Tiny red sparks flashed across her skin. And then she fell, screaming her climax as he drove into her clenching muscles. Pressure that had him exploding, catapulting over the cliff's edge.

Frigg and Hel. He would never get enough of her.

His cock was still pulsing inside of her when the ground beneath his feet shook. "Another earthquake." He laughed, low and throaty and satisfied against her neck. "This one is our fault."

"Arrogant of you," she panted, her ribs heaving. "And unscientific."

He slid free and, with the last of his strength, scooped her into his arms and carried her to a pile of blankets, draping the weight of her sweet body across his to lie beneath the angled sunlight of the winter solarium. "True. One data point does not denote a trend. We'll need to keep studying the effects."

She nipped his neck. "Now?"

He rolled his eyes and offered an exaggerated sigh. "Give me a few minutes?" He ran his fingers through her golden hair. "Some of us don't have sparkling superpowers."

"Only a few." She lifted her head and met his gaze with a slow, sultry smile. Her palm drifted across his stomach, sliding lower. And lower.

His cock jumped against her hand, half hard at her touch.

"See?" She threw her leg over his hip. "Already you're up for the challenge."

Which, of course, was when the pounding began upon his door.

"Val?" Dýri thumped the solid wood again.

He moved fast, grabbing the edge of a blanket and dragging it over Angela's exposed backside. Not a moment too soon, for his airship guardsman threw open the door and strode in.

A lurid smile leapt onto Dýri's face as he took in their sprawled forms. "Glad to see you two enjoying each other, but we've a problem. An incoming storm. They've moved up the investiture ceremony to tonight. Which means we've no time for tact and diplomacy or a site-wide reconnaissance."

"For Odin's sake, look away," Val ordered, irritated at the man's complete and total lack of shame.

"Oh, I don't think Odin would mind, but for the lady's sake..." He turned his back. Slowly.

Leaving the blanket to his wife, he stood and began to dress. Dýri had seen him naked often enough, if not aroused. The clothes left for him on his bed weren't his usual, but at least they weren't court attire. Those attending the Þorrablót were all wearing traditional Viking clothing as befitted the ancient gatherings at Law Rock. Practical, warm and—for those of rank—trimmed with quiet luxury.

Angela would be happy to leave her corset behind.

"We need to head out," Dýri continued, his voice

amused. "Lauf has the airship ready as Sóllilja wants to kidnap the princess and move her aboard the *Grænndreki*, the most secure location we can offer her."

"Kidnap?" Angela exclaimed.

Val agreed with her distress. "Such an extreme measure seems unwarranted."

Dýri shrugged. "How else are we going to insert Lisbet in her place? There's no time to win a princess's loyalty."

This didn't bode well for Val's plan to approach his father's booth, to politely introduce his bride and hope for an offer to stand among the other ranking council members at the crowning of Jarl Haukr.

"But no worries, your mother sent a raven to your father. His reply all but ordered you—and your bride—to Þingvellir."

"Why would he do that?" Angela asked, suspicious.

"I'll leave you to your explanations. Finish dressing but hurry." Dýri exited, closing the door behind him.

Val sighed and met her gaze. "Above all else, my father loves power and the tales of our glorious past. It's part of why he remains loyal to my mother, though she refuses to marry him. He's also one of the few councilmen who voted in favor of Eyrún's efforts to find a safe path back to restoring the Eldskrift tradition."

Her eyes narrowed. "You think she told him of my transformation."

"I do." Val pinched the bridge of his nose. "She will have also mentioned that we are soulbound. Add to that your rank among the huldufólk and he will be most pleased."

"It matters so much to him?"

"Ambassador Dagur Sveinsson will have appraised him of the events surrounding our marriage, no doubt rubbing his face in the fact that his son has married an ordinary human. Except you're not. They've been at odds ever since Katla broke our marriage contract to run away with Rømer. Had I tried, I could not have chosen a bride that would please him more."

"I've no intention of living a court life." She rose to her feet and dropped the blanket, reaching for the fine linen *serk* he held out. "But we'll have to disabuse him of his hopes another time. For now, if we warn him of an imminent troll attack, will he offer his aid?"

The corner of his mouth kicked up. "To defend a king and become a folk hero?" His wife was brilliant. "He'd sell his soul for the chance."

CHAPTER THIRTY

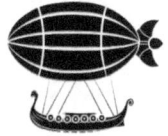

"AMAZING." WITH MITTEN-CLAD HANDS, Hildur gripped the sides of her cloak and drew them close. "Twenty-four hours and already neither of you are cold. It's freezing out here, but you've not so much as ruddy cheeks or pink-tipped noses."

Lisbet laughed. "For the first time since I followed you to this land of ice and snow. It's like standing in the sun on a cool spring day."

"Eldskrift stole the bite of the wind," Angela agreed. She had no need of the mittens she wore, but to pluck them from her hands would garner odd looks once they stepped into the encampment. No matter how the wind whipped, tugging and pulling at the wool cloak draped over her shoulders, she simply was not cold. For once she was able to lean over the airship's side without worrying about frost bite to study the stark countryside below, a winter's scene in black and white.

Easy to see how a basalt troll might blend in, unseen.

Þingvellir valley was a gash torn into the earth, one lined by black cliffs and cut through by the Öxará River. In the distance, a waterfall cascaded over the cliffs, formed a river to rush downhill over volcanic rocks, paused to form a deep pool, then flowed onward at a more sedate speed toward an enormous frozen lake.

Such was the scenery that rose above the temporary dwellings that dotted the snow-covered assembly plains. Drifts piled up against the low walls of turf and stone and weighed down the cloth roofs of these búðir, but the cold did little to dampen the merrymaking. Groups gathered around fires where spitted sheep roasted and cauldrons bubbled, drinking from horn cups. Others wandered about, arm in arm with friends, visiting merchant stalls. All paths led to a larger and grander structure, this one constructed of wood in a manner that resembled an oversized Viking hall from days long past.

One fit for a king.

There Val's father and any number of important Icelandic dignitaries would surround Jarl Haukr in preparation for the procession to Law Rock. Later—if there was a later—there was to be a grand feast.

To the side, a smaller—if no less magnificent—dwelling flew the Danish flag.

Like the other airships, they dropped anchor onto—not into—the nearby enormous frozen lake, Þingvallavatn. A location that allowed the dirigibles of the wealthy and privileged to remain close enough to provide their owners all the comforts of home while remaining at a sufficient distance so as not to spoil the atmosphere. Horse-drawn sleds ferried passengers to and fro, to shore and back again.

The *Grænndreki* would serve as a base of operations, if only because the clockwork ravens were programmed to return to their roost aboard the airship.

Replacing the princess without causing an international kidnapping incident was the first step of their plan that faced a test. To that end, they all wore clothes that befitted their various roles.

For costumes were requisite for the momentous event.

In a show of unity, both Icelandic and Danish nationals wore the traditional garb of their ancestors, clothing that the Vikings landing on the island's shores would have worn in the year 874.

Women wore *serks* beneath *smokkrs* held up with oval broaches with an abundance of amber and colorful glass beads strung between them. Men sported belted tunics and kirtles, trousers wrapped from the knees downward. All of them adorned fingers, arms and necks with as much copper, silver and gold jewelry as they could. There were a variety of colorful hats and mittens, and everyone wore at least one heavy cloak, many of them embroidered or trimmed with fur.

Val's mother and Sóllilja had worked miracles while Angela and Lisbet slept off the effects of the Eldskrift bindrune ceremony. The völva initiated nine other guards, hastening their binding with no more than a few glasses of the purple absinthe. Recruitment complete, the two women had split up, attending to separate preparations to infiltrate the Þorrablót.

Katrín, with her deep knowledge of tradition, had found them costumes while Sóllilja oversaw the careful arming of her rebel band with as many potassium arrows, knives and swords as she could smuggle from the mountain. Her armorer had worked furiously to devise a weapon he called a graphite grenade. The device would explode, launching fibrous strands of graphite above the trolls. When the filaments drifted downward, they would form a kind a net that would trigger an electric discharge and short-circuit the trolls.

The only problem was building enough in the short time allotted. Every Fire Script Guardian had been handed a single graphite grenade.

Now to infiltrate the camp.

An unopened bottle of Tyrian Absinthe had been pressed into Angela's hands as she boarded the dirigible. Harder for Jarl Haukr to exclude a woman from his retinue if she presented him with such a regal gift.

The men and women assembled aboard the *Grænndreki* wore every manner of Viking attire. From that of landed countrymen, to warriors, to jarls with vast land holdings. All in favor of scattering into the crowds, fading from notice while they surveyed the valley, hunting for hidden trolls before taking up positions to defend the jarl during this evening's coronation.

If a few members of their company occasionally sparked a glint of red at the corner of an eye, across the flare of a cheekbone, or along the angle of the jaw, the light was easily dismissed as a trick of the eye beneath the bright winter sun.

Though such a dismissal would grow more difficult once the sun sank beyond the horizon. But by then, the guards would be hidden among the granite cliffs, waiting. Watching. Ready to rise up to defend their homeland.

Only she and Lisbet, as society-facing brides, had made the effort to mask any stray flickering lights by smearing a heavy, tinted cream across their faces.

Pleased that her attire dated to a time and location that had yet to involve whalebone or coiled steel bands to reshape a woman's waistline, Angela reveled in the loose freedom of her gown. A black apron over an underdress of deep blue bordered with tablet weaving in stunning colors. Broaches and beads. A belt with a sheathed knife. Woolen stockings and leather boots. A fur-edged cloak. All of it chosen for fine needlework atop cloth of a luxury weave. But nothing that might flash or glint or otherwise catch the torchlight once the sun sank beneath the horizon.

Even with her hair braided and twisted and swept up under a cap, she'd never been so comfortable or warm on a winter's day.

"What if the maid was wrong?" Lisbet worried, fussing with the embroidered purse that hung at her waist. "What if the princess refused to play along with the Viking theme?"

"Miss a chance to ditch her corset?" Angela teased. "I doubt it. But if so, when you take her place, tip your nose up and announce a change of opinion. No one argues with a princess."

"I'm afraid you'll need to put your advice the test." Val appeared beside her, his face grim. "Lisbet, you're needed in the engine room." He tipped his head to the side. "Immediately."

They all spun to look. White smoke billowed from a hatch in the deck.

"The boiler tubes are leaking. Dýri is down there now. Lauf is shutting down the engine, but if Rømer attempts an escape—"

"We must be able to follow," Lisbet finished. "As if I'd risk a boiler explosion." She grabbed Angela's arm, locking eyes. "The princess has been studying Icelandic. If anyone addresses you in Danish, make them repeat themselves in Icelandic to commemorate this historic day." She turned to her wife, kissing away the objection forming on Hildur's lips. "Don't you dare think of staying. The guardians need you on the ground." Lisbet ran to the hatch and dropped into the belly of the *Grænndreki*.

"I don't like this," Hildur grumbled. "It smacks of sabotage."

"By whom?" Val challenged. "Lauf has not left the dirigible since London and swears no one save our crew has boarded. All risks wait for us below. Perhaps it's better this way, sticking together. Introducing my bride to my father and his multitude of friends would have been a distraction."

"She's right," Sóllilja disagreed. "Something is amiss, though I cannot say what." She snatched the bottle of Tyrian Absinthe from Angela's hands and looked to Val. "I will warn your father, councilwoman to councilman. I've sent another raven to let him know plans have changed. We'll double the guards near Law Rock, protect Jarl Haukr at all costs. You need to focus on removing the Danish from this equation."

Angela bit her lip. *She* was to take the place of a Danish princess? Without knowing more than a handful of words? What choice was there? Rømer could not be allowed into Princess Margrit's presence. There was no telling what the man might do.

"Chin up." Val wrapped his arm around her, escorting her onto the loading platform to stand among a handful of guards, a few finely dressed, a few dressed for a drunken brawl. "You can do this. The hardest part will be carrying a heavy crown on a pillow."

"Until everything goes sideways," she reminded him as they descended. "When the trolls launch their attack."

"They might not."

Hildur snorted.

Aboard the sled they held their tongues. The mission had begun.

On shore, the guards scattered in pairs, disappearing into the crowds only to reconvene outside the Danish búð a short time later. Within minutes, a choreographed commotion erupted in a fistfight mere feet from the royal dwelling. As distracted royal guards dropped hands to sword hilts, Angela, Val and Hildur slipped inside.

Val made it no more than three steps before he was grabbed and held at knifepoint, and she was stopped by an outstretched hand and a warning look. Only Hildur managed to advance—and only until she came to a sudden halt.

"Ingrid?" Surprise rippled across her features.

Another Valkyrie strode forward. Without warning, the woman's fist connected with Hildur's jaw, hard enough to send her staggering. "I warned you to never show your face again."

"*In Denmark*. Did you forget you're in Iceland?" When the other woman's hand fisted again, Hildur lifted both hands, palms out. "We're here to warn you of a threat to your princess, to offer help."

Angela chanced a look in Val's direction. He tipped his head and sent her a rueful smile. There was a story here, one she would dig free another time.

Ingrid advanced until she stood nose to nose with Hildur. Anger flashed in her eyes. "This had better be good."

"Quite." She leaned forward, dropping her voice as she spoke softly into the guardswoman's ear.

"Trolls?" The corners of Ingrid's mouth tugged downward. She stepped back and pointed, snapped her fingers.

A Danish guard hurried over to a blanket-covered heap that lay to the side of the búð. He threw back the covering. At first glance, the troll appeared to be no more than a pile of rocks with a large blade wedged into a crevice. Save it wore a shirt, trousers, and shoes. "Like this one?" The Danish guardswoman crossed her arms and waited.

"If you'd lower the knife," Val prompted, "I'd be happy to explain."

At Ingrid's nod, the guard lowered his arm.

"While you've evidence they do not turn into stone during the day, sunlight hurts their eyes and burns their skin.

Hence their nocturnal behavior." Val waved at their jötunn prisoner. "And the knife in the troll's back? Have you tried removing it?"

The woman snorted. "Why would I do that? The guard who put it there died for his efforts. You're welcome to try to pull it out. But be warned, it's likely to be a shocking experience."

Val glanced at Angela.

"The pyros must still be active," she postulated. "I understand little about neurochemistry, but somehow they appear to energize a troll's nervous system."

"And what would you know of such electrified trolls?" the Danish Valkyrie demanded.

"Almost nothing," she admitted. "Though one precisely like this individual kidnapped me, but not before electro-cuting a man. I was lucky. By the time his rocky arm wrapped around me, the voltage generated had discharged." Let the Valkyrie wonder how Angela had survived. An air of mystery might help their cause. "Are there markings carved into its back or chest?" she asked. "Runes? For such are the source of the troll's unusual power."

"And if there are?" Ingrid challenged.

Val spoke up. "More trolls are on their way. With the ability to send an electric bolt of lightning though anyone they touch. You need our help."

Harshly whispered words broke out among the group. A few nodded.

"Silence!" Ingrid barked. "Explain."

"There is a madman who wishes to destroy relations

between our two countries. We seek to stop him." Val offered a detailed explanation, if one that only told a tale of trolls. No need to detail the various political forces at play. The riots in the streets of Norway had made clear the threats.

Lips pressed into a flat line, the guardswoman nodded. "Fine. Even though I believe you leave out much, I trust Hildur to do what is best for her people." Lips twisted with annoyance and regret, her gaze swept down Hildur's form. "If not herself."

Hildur looked away.

Ingrid pointed at Angela. "You are to stand in for Princess Margrit?"

"I am."

"Then come. You alone."

They stepped through a door that led to a small room hidden behind a wooden partition. There, a beautiful young woman patted her hair and frowned at the mirror.

"What now, Ingrid?" The princess sighed. "Do tell me there's not been a delay. I am quite done pretending to live as my long-dead ancestors."

"I'm afraid we have a situation. Trolls." Princess Margrit shuddered as her guardswoman relayed the news. "In short, we do not know if this madman will attempt to kidnap or kill you. Or what he intends for your betrothed."

"And this woman, she proposes to take my place at the investiture?"

"She does."

"I ought to object," she said. "But I won't. This country is an icebox. No amount of wood, peat or coal dispels the chill.

If you wish to carry the crown, sword and scepter through a dark valley where the icy wind never ceases and electric trolls might steal you away, you are welcome to the task." She looked to Ingrid. "We will, of course, send a contingent of our own to guard the small fortune on that velvet pillow?"

"Yes, Your Royal Highness."

The princess swept her gaze over Angela. For a moment, she thought the princess's lip might curl. But two decades of training won out and her alabaster face revealed nothing. Instead, she plucked the coronet from her head and summoned her maids. "Fix her."

In minutes, Angela had been stripped to her serk. The maids wanted her boots as well, but she refused. "The path is strewn with rocks and ice. There will also be trolls."

They relented. A richly embroidered smokkr replaced her own. Golden broaches were pinned in place to hold strings of polished gemstone beads. Finally, the golden coronet with unfaceted gems was placed on her own head, and a heavy cape lined with fur was thrown over her shoulders.

All while Ingrid enumerated the many steps of the ceremony, making Angela repeat them over and again.

The princess nodded. "You'll do."

Ingrid marched Angela back into the hall. Above the fire, the hole in the roof revealed night had fallen.

"It's time," Hildur said. "Let's move."

"Wait." Val crossed to the fallen troll and wedged a stick under the creature's torso, then shoved a log beneath it, forming a crude fulcrum for a lever. "I have questions."

"Impossible." Ingrid snapped. "It's not moved in hours."

"The groans," a guard breathed. "Not the wind."

Val pulled on the lever. "I'd like to not walk blindly into an ambush."

"Fine," Ingrid huffed. "But hurry. The princess is never late."

It took four people hanging from the lever to roll the creature onto its side.

Val crouched down, nudging its face with a stick. "Give me your name," he ordered the troll, "that Grýla might know of your death."

Rocks shuddered. Golden eyes blinked open. "Gluggagægir."

"A Yule Lad?" Angela gaped. "The window-peeper?"

Hildur smacked her arm. "Hush."

Everyone leapt away as a stoney arm swept outward, tossing a rough sack in their direction. "Take. Bag. Aluminum. Save brother Ketkrókur."

"And where is he?"

"Don't know!" the troll wailed. "Here soon?"

Angela swept up the bag, loosening the drawstring, dumping the contents upon the floor. Vials filled with gray-white tablets tumbled out. She picked up a vial, turning it in the firelight.

"What is it?" Val asked.

"Salt crystal pills?" Frowning, she stuffed the vials back into the drawstring bag and handed it to Val. "It's been ages since I studied chemistry, but aren't aluminum salt compounds highly reactive with water?"

"Frigg and Hel," he muttered. "You're right. Some produce toxic gases. This will need to be kept dry until it can be analyzed."

"Aluminum sulfide!" the troll insisted. "Make brother eat."

"Eat?" Val's eyebrows drew together. "Why?"

"Gas!" the troll yelled. "Cure is aluminum salts!"

"Salts?" Val pressed. "More detail, Gluggagægir."

"Reacts with skin and blood," the Yule Lad said. "Neutralizes."

"Frigg and Hel," he muttered again, dragging his hand over his face. "This will need to be carefully controlled."

"Why?" Angela demanded. "Tell me."

"How to simplify several chemical equations all at once?" He raised his gaze to the tented roof. "The aluminum sulfide pills will react with water and silicon dioxide—"

"Components of basalt troll blood," Angela interjected, clarifying for the onlookers. "Silica crystals."

Val continued, "Neutralizing the troll's infection by producing a miasma of toxic chemicals. Unfortunately, the resulting substances will further combine with each other, forming yet more poisonous compounds." He ticked off a list of nasty gases, including hydrogen sulfide, sulfur dioxide and sulfuric acid.

"Toxic to trolls?" Hildur asked.

Val shook his head. "Not to them. To us." He drew a deep breath. "Worse, the trolls generate electricity. The chemical reaction that occurs is bound to be... explosive."

"Loki laughs." His first mate stared at Val. "And you want to keep these tablets on your person?"

Val shrugged. "Are you willing to risk Grýla's wrath if we leave them behind?"

"After meeting her? No."

"Enough." Ingrid pointed at the door. "Jarl Haukr waits. We need to leave now."

"The troll's mother is quite a powerful influence," Val informed Ingrid, handing her a vial containing several aluminum salt tablets. "It would behoove you to court her favor by healing her son." He tied the bag with the extra vials to his belt. "Find a way to remove the knife."

"Knife!" Gluggagægir yelled.

"Then transport the troll to an open-air environment, have him submerge neck-deep in water, then leave him with those pills." He locked eyes with her. "I'd advise all humans move at least twenty-five feet away before he consumes them. Gas masks would be a reasonable precaution."

"As if we keep them on hand." Ingrid's lips twisted. "Fine, I'll take all this under advisement. But we'll do nothing before daylight." She barked orders.

A maid shoved a velvet pillow into Angela's hands, one that held a golden crown studded with diamonds and rubies. Two finely dressed guards took up positions directly behind her, holding the sword and scepter. For now, all she needed to do was not trip. Until a certain alchemist and his trolls made an appearance.

Ingrid threw open the door, and they stepped into the torch-lit night, where shadows danced across the gathered crowd. A man raised a horn to his lips and blew a deep, reso-nant note. The sound rolled through the air like a summons from the past—haunting, primal and steeped in the island's Viking heritage.

Her fingers dug into the purple velvet. With each step, she scanned the crowd, her breath quickening. Was it only the flickering torchlight that made the shadows shift against the cliffs? Or was her sharpened vision catching something others couldn't—lurking trolls waiting to strike?

CHAPTER THIRTY-ONE

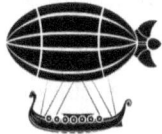

V AL TOSSED THE CLOCKWORK RAVEN into the darkening sky. By now, gods willing, Lisbet would have fixed the engine and would be waiting for the bird's news.

In the last minutes before the eerie sound of the horn cut through the night, he'd scribbled a few extra words onto the scrap of paper the raven carried, informing them of the Yule Lad, his possessions and his words. Despite the troll's claim that the crystals he carried were meant to save his brother, Val was unconvinced. Rømer might well have something far more deadly and disruptive planned. To which end Val instructed Lisbet and Dýri to locate their gas masks, praying to all the gods that the rest of his crew was still aboard and not tucked unseen and waiting to fight amongst Sóllilja's guards.

The dark moonless sky and the flickering torchlight made searching out enemies near to impossible, though they were conditions that ought not impede any Fire Script Guardians. Provided the stories were true. Night had fallen while they were inside the princess's búð, and he'd not been given a chance to ask Angela if she could see in the dark. He could only hope that his wife's placid expression and calm demeanor indicated there was no cause for alarm.

The crowd murmured and shifted as the procession wound its way toward Lögberg. Small gasps of excitement echoed through them as they caught the first public glimpses of the glittering crown meant for Iceland's first king. Impossible not to have wind of the speculation about which gemstones the Danish would gift the jarl. Now they knew.

Diamonds and rubies to symbolize the Land of Fire and Ice.

The path wound upward now, climbing to the peak of Law Rock where two officiants waited—a bishop and a Viking goði. While the first clearly represented the church, the Icelandic man might represent a secular politician from the days of the Alþingi, the original Icelandic parliament, or he might be a pagan priest.

Though Jarl Haukr had indicated no interest in reviving a pagan polytheistic religion once he took the throne, there were those who hoped he might at least permit its return, while others were horrified by the possibility. Were he so inclined to abandon centuries of Christianity, Val suspected the Jarl would wait until he'd cemented the throne. Until well after the wedding and quite likely not until the princess produced an heir or two to secure the succession. Only then might the man begin to relax.

Time would tell.

But first he must be crowned King of Iceland.

The procession drew to a stop. Standing atop Law Rock provided all onlookers with an excellent view. It also raised the elite members of society over the general populace. Here, above the sheltering walls of the valley, the icy wind howled, snapping cloaks and snatching at hoods.

But the Jarl sat, serene, upon a wooden throne built in the Viking style. The posts rising from the back corners of the chair were carved into birds of prey, giving the impression that two gyrfalcons perched upon his shoulders. As the Jarl's "bride-to-be" approached, his expression remained unchanged, save for the pleased glint that sparked in his eyes as his gaze settled on the crown. If he worried the ceremony might be interrupted, he gave no indication.

But behind the future king, Val's father stood with two other huldufólk, frowning. Something was amiss.

Perhaps it was nothing more than his sire resenting the loss of an opportunity to present his son and daughter-in-law to the Jarl's court. Or perhaps the other council members representing the huldufólk clung to their name, the hidden folk, collectively deciding not to inform Jarl Haukr of a possible troll threat.

Or both.

He locked eyes with his father and, tight-lipped, gave an almost imperceptible nod of acknowledgement. In return, his father's eyebrows lifted and his gaze flickered to Angela, followed by the faintest of smiles. An acknowledgment that his only son had finally—*finally*—married well.

As if that mattered.

Val let his stare drift over the surrounding basalt cliffs, but the bright flames of the many torches compromised any hope of night vision. When he returned his focus to the Jarl's entourage, the frown had reappeared on his father's lips and grown more serious. Val caught the man also assessing the guards flanking Jarl Haukr.

Those men appeared alert, though most of their spears were not tipped with potassium. Val counted only three fae in possession of tröllabanar. And none of them carried a graphite grenade at their belts. Not only did the courtiers gathered around the Jarl not count, they would be a detriment if suddenly confronted with menacing creatures they knew only from fairytales.

Worry gnawed at Val's stomach. Their numbers were insufficient to fend off an attack.

Was this the best his people could do? To protect their own way of life, the huldufólk needed to ensure Icelandic sovereignty. Val's message had been clear: if steps were not taken, tonight's proceedings might fall into chaos and, if so, bright blood—human and fae—would be spilled upon fresh snow.

Given the lack of precaution, the odds did not stack in their favor.

The bishop stepped forward, lifted the crown and began in a booming voice, "We are gathered here today upon Lögberg to mark a historic moment!"

But Val had no interest in ceremonial words. His gaze flicked continuously between Angela and the black rocks, scoured of snow by the winds. Waiting. Worrying. When would—

Her arm shot out, pointing. "Troll!" his wife pointed down and to the right. She tossed aside the velvet pillow and unsheathed the knife at her waistband.

The fae among the guards reacted by running to the cliff's edge, following Hildur's lead, and leaping into darkness to enter the fray. Metal clanged against stone while the humans stood frozen, startled and confused.

Val remained, sword drawn, ready to protect those still standing atop Law Rock. A pile of basalt rose from the ground with a roar, but before he could take two steps, a glinting potassium arrow sliced through the night sky, embedding itself into the troll's back. He was glad to know Sóllilja's teams were in place.

Sparks flew. The troll bellowed, but even as more and more arrows arced, studding his back, the creature advanced, cutting down two guards with a single swipe of his battle axe. Bright blood pooled beneath their slain bodies.

Jarl Haukr was on his feet, his own weapon in hand as more trolls swarmed up the side of the hill, their massive shapes emerging from the dark, seemingly from nowhere.

The trolls that followed the first bore no weapons, save their hands. Lightning exploded from their fingertips the moment they laid hands upon the braver members of the Jarl's retinue who attacked in defense of the would-be king. Shuddering and twitching, these guards stiffened and fell to the ground in a kind of frozen rigor. Unconscious or dead, he couldn't tell.

He leapt across those men, slicing at the vulnerable joints of the attacking trolls, lost in the roar of battle. Arrows whistled through the air and piles of rocks tumbled, all while Val fought his way toward his wife.

A troll grabbed Angela, wrapped his stony arm about her neck, and stood unflinching when she plunged her potassium-tipped dagger into his leg, his only reaction to tighten his grip. She thrashed, gasping for air.

Desperate, he redoubled his efforts to reach her. More trolls fell, clutching at the burning wounds the tröllabanar carved into their elbows and knees. Then one knocked the potassium-laced blade from his hand and caught him about his own throat, squeezing. As he struggled to breathe, he fought on. But his blows barely landed, glancing off thick, gritty skin with little effect.

Stars danced on a field of black.

"Stop!" A man bellowed.

The pressure at his throat eased, but as vision returned, the sight before him turned his blood to ice.

Rømer held a knife to the Jarl's throat. "No one moves or lives will be forfeit, beginning with that of Jarl Haukr." The alchemist's gaze swung to Val. "Followed by that of your wife."

Everyone stood still atop Law Rock, including the electric trolls.

"A king *will* be crowned," Rømer announced. "But not this pretender." He shoved the Jarl aside, into the hands of another man who placed his own knife at the Jarl's neck. "Not a word, Haukr, nor the slightest effort to escape, or my man will end you before you witness Iceland's first moments of independence."

Lauf?

Their eyes locked. Razor-sharp betrayal tore through Val's chest, slicing deep. A man he'd called friend, a man he'd swapped tales with over bread and mead, a man to whom he'd handed the helm of a secret and pioneering airship.

His ex-pilot offered a casual half shrug. As if Val ought to have known how his childhood friend spent his free time away from the airship, why he'd been so interested in the inner workings of the photosynthesis wings that powered the *Grænndreki's* engine. Had the lure of riches led Lauf to sell the valuable technology?

Likely.

And it appeared he'd struck a bargain with Rømer.

With access to ravens and their punch cards, Lauf could easily have informed Rømer of their whereabouts. Which meant he'd told the alchemist how and when to send a troll to kidnap Angela. She'd tried to warn him, insisting that his pilot seemed to know the troll's name, but Val had mostly dismissed her concern.

Mostly.

The possibility had wormed itself into his subconsciousness. When Hildur suggested secrecy, Val had agreed they shouldn't reveal that the ancient tradition had been revived. Which meant Lauf had not been informed nor, working on the bridge, had a chance to see the flickering sparks of Eldskrift.

But he'd know what Rømer wanted.

And today, the traitor had sabotaged the airship's engine, purposefully throwing their plans in disarray. The alchemist had known all along of their plans.

Fury scorched Val's veins as his heart pumped hard, planning saga-worthy retribution. But first, he needed to see Angela safe. His blindness to a traitor in their midst had delivered her, once again, into troll hands. The danger to her eclipsed all else, turning him merciless, cold and unforgiving.

Bold and ruthless, Rømer strode to the throne and sat. He ignored the sword and scepter that lay at his feet, dismissing the symbolic weapons. Easy to do with an army of trolls under one's command. His lips curled into a victorious smirk. "Continue, Bishop. Crown me king. It's long past time that the Viking descendants of Norway once again ruled this island."

A murmur rippled through the crowd, uneasy and low. Several stepped forward in protest, only to fall back as Rømer's men raised their swords without a word. A hiss escaped Val's throat. He strained at his bonds, every muscle tensed to strike—but there was little to do save choke on his helplessness.

"You'll not get away with this," the Jarl yelled.

"Silence!" Rømer commanded. "You'll not receive another warning."

Lauf dug his blade deeper into the Jarl's throat. A trickle of blood ran down the man's neck.

The officiant stumbled forward. His hands trembled as he muttered the sacred words, each syllable a betrayal of his religion. Surrounded by electric trolls and traitors with sharp blades, there was little choice save obedience. He lifted the crown and placed it on Rømer's dark head. As soon as it settled, he snatched his hands away and retreated, knowing the act damned him.

Rømer accepted the pagan priest's brief blessings, dismissing him the moment he finished speaking. Then the false king stood, his stolen crown illuminated by the flickering fire, to face the Jarl. "You betray your people, consorting with the Danish. Not even your princess dared attend this ceremony. As to her imposter," Rømer's gaze turned to fall upon Angela, "show me her arms."

Two guards advanced, throwing aside her cloak, yanking her limbs straight, cutting through cloth to expose her arms while another yanked the coronet from her head.

"Is the fern tattoo green?" he asked his men.

"It is."

Lauf twisted his neck, watching the test with interest.

"Tap it," Rømer ordered. "Does it spark red or glow?"

The guard obeyed. "No, Your Majesty."

"How disappointing. So much effort to capture her, only to find there's nothing special about her at all..." Rømer stroked his beard. His gaze crawled over Angela as if she were an insignificant insect. One barely worth crushing beneath his heel. "Still, her crimes cannot be ignored. She eloped with another man while we were betrothed. Such qualifies as 'loose morals', does it not?" His men nodded and murmured assent. "Therefore, we shall revive an old

Þingvellir tradition. Take her to the Drekkingarhylur. Drown her."

The Drowning Pool? Adultery? Incest? She was guilty of neither. Only of spurning the madman's marriage proposal.

"She's my wife! *Farðu til helvítis, drullusokkur!* Angela!" Her name tore from his throat. His muscles strained. Ligaments and tendons popped. But the troll's grip didn't budge. He fought anyway, kicking and thrashing.

"I never agreed to marry you!" Angela cried. "Why would I? You're nothing but a murderous leech masquerading as a genius."

She tried to run the moment the troll pushed her toward Rømer, but her efforts were fruitless. She'd taken no more than two steps before a gunny sack was thrown over her head, a cord was wound about her neck and knotted at her throat before they shoved her to her knees and tied her ankles together.

Val's heartbeat thrashed in his ears and pain shot through his chest as he struggled. But he was unable to free himself from the loathsome troll's grip while she screamed, while her cloak was snatched away, while her arms were wrenched behind her back and her wrists bound with rough rope.

"Lauf will behead all men present as they are guilty of attempting to prevent Norway from reclaiming its rightful lands." Rømer waved a casual hand in his minion's direction. "With a blunt axe, as I hear that is how executions were once carried out here. But first they are to join us, to watch this woman drown."

"But—" Lauf swallowed, his eyes wide. "I don't think, Your Majesty, that—"

"Precisely." Rømer tilted his head, slowly turning his gaze upon his minion. "No thinking. Do as I order, unless you care to join their number."

Lauf froze, managed a tight nod, and kept his knife pressed to the Jarl's throat.

Val's stomach lurched. His eyes darted about, looking for help, but save for that of the traitor, Lauf, he found only unfamiliar faces. Was Hildur aware of the situation? Were Dýri or Sóllilja or anyone else hidden nearby, waiting for the chance to strike?

He could only hope.

CHAPTER THIRTY-TWO

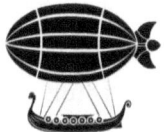

NGELA CRUMPLED TO THE GROUND, dragging air into her seizing lungs. Not that Rømer intended for her to have the use of them much longer. Guards snatched at her clothing, attempting to grab hold of her flailing body, hissing at her to hold still. As if the condemned ought help to speed their own demise.

"Help!" she cried. "I've done nothing!"

Her boots scraped through black gravel and slush as men dragged her downhill. At first, there was only a hushed silence. Then there were whispers. Men, women and children recognizing her clothing, wondering why the Danish princess had been taken prisoner. Boots shuffled, fabric rustled. But the armed men marching behind her kept anyone from stepping forward.

That and the confusion of finding their newly crowned king was not the one they'd expected.

As if in answer to their silent questions, a voice rang out.

"This woman is not the princess, but an imposter! To Drekkingarhylur!"

The Drowning Pool. Death by oxygen deprivation as her lungs filled with water. Or possibly cardiac arrest due to immersion in near freezing water. Even if the Eldskrift might save her from the latter, if she could not breathe, death was certain.

Lauf's betrayal twisted in her gut. Though she barely knew him, Val had believed him a steadfast friend, not the enemy within. She'd told him about how Lauf seemed to know the troll sent to kidnap her, but they'd never returned to the topic. She'd been about to broach it with his crew when the fire fern had glowed a faint red—and all else had been driven from their minds.

A fatal mistake.

Val was restrained by a troll. Hildur missing along with all the other fae guards who'd bravely fought the jötunn swarming the cliffs, Sóllilja with them. Lisbet and Dýri sent to fix an engine and were unaware of their pilot's icy betrayal.

There was little hope that anyone might come to her rescue.

"Let me go!" she cried. "You serve a false king!" Strain as she might to hear anything of her husband—his voice or his fate—the sound of rushing water grew louder and louder until it drowned out all else. Drowned. A lump of panic clogged her throat. There was a knife tucked in her boot, but with her arms bound, reaching it was nearly impossible—her chances of cutting herself free even less so. "Please!" she begged. "Let me explain!"

Without warning, the guards tossed her onto the ground. She landed in a shallow pool with a splash. Sharp rocks scraped her face through the rough fabric of the sack and jabbed into her hips and shoulders. Damp seeped through her clothing.

She tried to sit, but someone shoved her down again and tied a rope about her waist. Before she could wonder why, strong arms lifted her from the ground. With her limbs bound, there was little she could do to resist, save for slamming her head backward in hopes of breaking his nose.

"Thrash all you wish, traitor," her captor growled in her ear. "It'll be all that much more entertaining for the spectators as you're dragged into the middle of the pool."

Dragged?

"Please," she begged. Tremors overtook her body as she fought against the ropes that bound her. "Don't do this."

"Defend you?" His answering laugh was cruel. "Not a chance. I'll be keeping my head attached to my neck in hopes of following the king into your mountain."

"You know of the huldufólk?" She jerked in surprise. The huldrekall's presence at the farm, the tattoos carved into the skin of the farmer and his family. Not at all happenstance, but a deliberate encroachment. Rømer had been looking for a way into the mountain—and she and Val had carried Sigge inside.

Had the huldrekall been found? If he had, it hadn't been in time to stop the attack on Law Rock. But perhaps, after

ANNE RENWICK

her death, she might be avenged. Rømer—and his horrible experiments—might still be stopped.

"Oh, yes, we know about your home, about those who live within. And for my part today, I'll be among the first to be granted my very own fae. The king will rule from within the hollow mountain, the most secure fortress ever known."

He dropped her legs, and her boots splashed into knee-deep water. Rough hands pulled at the broaches pinned to her chest, ripping them away along with the gemstone beads that hung between them. "Stand or collapse, it makes no difference."

"Please!" she screamed.

Hands grabbed at her ankles. The rope loosened, fell away. Then he cut through the bindings at her wrists.

"Are you—?" Hope kindled, then died when he laughed.

"Not a chance." Rock crunched beneath his boots as he stepped back. "By the King's command. He wishes to test the mettle of a fae woman."

Blind, she lashed out, but her fists connected with nothing but air before a sharp whistle pierced her ears. Without further warning, unseen hands yanked on the rope about her waist, pulling her from her feet and into the Öxará.

Turbulent freezing cold water closed over her head, dousing her as it stole all heat from her body with one gasp. A gasp that filled her lungs with icy shards of pain. Agony erupted everywhere, so much so that her skin barely registered the rocks beneath her, or their sudden absence as she was hauled into the depths of the pool.

A quick death.

No. Even now, a flame flicked to life within her chest. She was Eldvörður. And her limbs were unbound. She would not go without a fight.

She surfaced. Coughing and sputtering and dragging in air through wet fabric. A stick struck her shoulder, another her back. A third stick shoved at her chest, tearing cloth as it pushed her under once more.

Beneath the water she reached for the knife in her boot, pulling it free, cutting at the rope tied about her waist. All while kicking for the surface, gasping, only to be pushed under once more. The rope tethered at her, stopping the current from sweeping her away.

Snap! The final fibers at her waist gave way. The rush of water caught hold, yanked her under, tossing her against rocks, stealing her blade as it flung her downstream. Voices called out—cheering for her death or protesting her punishment, she couldn't tell. Rocks cut at her skin, over and again until the current finally slowed and dropped her in a shallow pool.

But she could still hear the cries of the crowd. She wanted more distance between them. Frantic, she shoved herself onto her feet. Forced herself to stumble forward even as she tore at the wet rope about her neck.

"That's far enough." Rømer's voice. "Hold her."

She howled at the injustice. Survival wasn't sufficient. She had to escape this madman's clutches.

Merciless troll hands dug fingers into her arms. Someone cut the twine at her throat and yanked away the gunny sack.

Overhead, long ribbons of green twisted and pulsed

ANNE RENWICK

across the night sky, casting the scene before her in an eerie luminescence. She glowered at the false king who stood before her, backed by his jötunn thralls and a smattering of men whose eyes glittered with greedy hopes of war spoils.

Did Val still live? A question she dared not ask. Nor did she dare to look, to search the crowd for his face.

"You ought to have drowned, the shock of the cold water alone should have..." Rømer tipped his head. "Your skin, there's a spark. How is that possible?" With a blade, he sliced through the sopping fabric of her serk, exposing the skin of her chest. "Well, well, well. What have we here?"

"Leave it be!" As he reached toward her bindrune stave, she twisted and kicked. But wet skirts tangled about her legs and an unyielding troll held her firm.

His fingertip landed on her runic stave and tiny red lights flickered and flashed. Rømer's lips curled into a smirk, eyes gleaming with a dark satisfaction. "Quite the unexpected prize. It seems I was too hasty ordering your death. But fortune favors me still."

She jutted her chin, refusing to give him the gratification of a reply. Better to die than let him discover her secret.

"Oh, you need not answer." Cold amusement curdled his voice. "We will carve the answers from your chest this very night." He snapped his fingers. "We leave for Raufarhólshellir—to the lava tunnels!"

As the troll wrapped arms around her waist and shoulders, clamping her arms to her sides and scooped her off her feet, an arrow whistled, slicing through the air and lodging in the troll's shoulder.

416

Help had arrived. Hope surged, sharp and sudden—then collapsed. There was little chance they were close enough.

The creature roared but didn't drop her. Instead, his grip tightened as he ran, leaping from rock to rock with ease, jolting her with each step, without any care for the careful keeping of his cargo.

Angela screamed. Beat her fists against the stony chest. To no avail.

Nothing mattered to the creature save his orders to transport his prisoner alive. To carry her to some underground lair where Rømer would lock her away in some secret subterranean laboratory, a prize specimen to be poked and prodded and questioned.

She'd be lucky to meet the same fate as Katla.

In the distance, a piercing ululation, a high and wavering sound, split the air and sent shivers down her spine. An ancient war cry meant to terrify opponents. Shadowy figures atop cliffs fired silver-tipped arrows at trolls while yet more warriors appeared on the black rocks of Þingvellir.

Defenders who launched dark spheres at the trolls. *Boom!* An explosion released swaths of fine filaments into the air, ones that formed haphazard nets as they drifted over the trolls, fibers that only became visible when the discharge of electricity flashed through the night.

Drained of power, the trolls were reduced, if only temporarily, to their natural state. After which the warriors moved in, swinging swords that gleamed in the torchlight, to dispatch those loyal to Rømer.

Reinforcements that far outnumbered the men and

women they'd recruited from Sóllilja's small band of warrior fae. Ones that could only indicate a change of heart by the mountain council.

A reversal, cruel in its timing—too late to save her. The knowledge carved a hollow ache into her chest. Yet the thought of Val and the others safe softened its ragged edges.

CHAPTER THIRTY-THREE

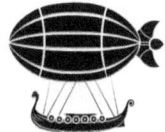

V AL'S MUSCLES BURNED WITH FUTILE effort as he strained against the stony grip of the troll that held him immobile. Every moment stretched into an eternity of guilt, terror, helplessness and soul-crushing anguish. A sick dread punched at his stomach as water closed over her head a second time. His throat was raw from screaming Angela's name, from cursing the gods who ignored his pleas to intercede on his behalf, to alter her fate.

Then the rope that held her in the center of the Drekkingarhylur snapped and the current of the Öxará swept her away from the men tasked with holding her underwater with long poles. Fast and furious, the water tossed her over a spill of rock, flinging her downstream.

Trolls, men loyal to Rømer, and even the false king himself gave chase, running alongside the river. From a distance he watched Angela find her feet, marveled as she stumbled blindly away from her pursuers, all while clawing at the ropes at her throat.

Not dead.

But not free. Not safe. Yet her survival rekindled an ember of hope. Rescue. If he could escape the troll that held him, if he could—

With a knife, Rømer cut through the neckline of Angela's clothing, ripped away linen fabric to expose the bindrune stave embedded in her skin. Even from here, he could see the tiny pyros flash and flicker. *Frigg and Hel.* The wet cloth of the gunny sack must have wiped her skin clear of the thick layer of greasepaint and powder, exposing her Eldskrift secrets.

"No!" The word tore from Val's throat, ragged with desperation, as a troll hefted Angela and bounded away, heading out across the plains. For a few minutes, torchlight caught the gleam of her golden hair—then the dark night swallowed them whole. His chest heaved as his pulse hammered with fury and fear. He didn't know how, but he *would* find her. He *would* bring her back. Or die trying.

Zing!

An arrow lanced through the air, piercing the shoulder joint of the troll that held him. Sparks flew. With a roar, the creature shoved Val away to yank at the shaft.

Without wasting a moment, Val pulled a knife from his boot and spun toward Lauf. What would have been an unthinkable act mere hours ago was now as clear as glass. But before he could lunge at his childhood friend, a second arrow whooshed through the night, skewering Lauf's thigh.

The traitorous pilot dropped his knife, releasing Jarl Haukr as he collapsed, howling and clutching his wound.

The Jarl wasted no time, grabbing the dull axe from his captor's belt and lifting it overhead, ready to execute the traitor.

"Stop!" Hildur cried, arriving at a run. "We need him alive."

Jarl Haukr hesitated, frowning. "Why?"

"For questioning." Words added by none other than his engineer, Lisbet. She yanked the axe from his hand and pressed a gleaming tröllabanar sword into the man's fist instead. "We'll see justice served. You are needed in the battle. But beware. The trolls are electric. Be sure they have discharged their lightning before you attack."

The uncrowned king blinked. "Lightning?"

"The trolls possess the ability to deliver a bolt of electricity, enough to drop a man," Hildur said. "Dagur Sveinsson will explain once the battle is won." A primal war cry tore through the night. She tipped her head toward the dark cliffs. "We arranged for reinforcements. Go, take to the field. Stop the trolls, dispatch the political conspirators. Prove yourself to your people. Then reclaim your kingdom upon the bloodstained Law Rock."

The Jarl glared down at Lauf. "If I ever set eyes upon you again, it will mean your death." He nodded to Hildur and Lisbet. "Seek me out and your valor will be rewarded." Without waiting for an answer, he ran onto the field, sword raised, to engage the enemy.

"The *Grænndreki*?" Did the engineer's presence mean

they could launch a search for Angela from the loftskip? Time was slipping through their fingers.

Lisbet shook her head. "Requires new parts. I've sent back to the mountain for replacements, but for now, she's little more than a fancy balloon."

His hands curled into fists, ready to knock a few teeth loose the minute the pilot no longer needed a working jaw to answer questions.

Battle sounds crashed through the air. Arrows streaked overhead. Huldufólk warriors flung giant nets atop trolls and lights flashed.

"It works." Rather than pride, he felt relief. Much of his time spent at Angela's bedside—when he wasn't laying a cool cloth atop her forehead or a warm blanket over her body —had been sketching out battle plans, passing them to Sóllilja, then Hildur, then adjusting them according to their input.

Graphite grenades were a brilliant solution, but the materials were difficult to source and the construction process complex and time-consuming. If they found themselves facing an army of trolls, a few dozen grenades weren't enough. They'd needed another way to discharge the trolls' electricity.

Now it was his simplest, most basic idea that helped turn the tide: a gun that fired salt-water soaked netting with metal grounding corners. Hurl one over a charged troll and you could discharge its stored lightning, reduce the creature to its natural state. Still a deadly pile of rocks, but no longer invincible.

But they'd needed the huldufólk warriors to operate the weapon—and it appeared they had them.

"Sóllilja?" he asked.

Hildur nodded. "She convinced the mountain council to send reinforcements, to hastily assemble the net guns."

Over and again flashes of electric meshwork lit up the night, a vision followed by a battle cry and the clash of steel upon rock. Wounded basalt trolls wrapped in netting tumbled down the snow-covered cliffs, their bodies shattering into jagged rubble upon the stones below, sounds that echoed off the stones—and drew closer.

"Haul the traitor this way," Hildur ordered, urgency sharpening her voice. "Quickly."

Together with the two women, Val dragged Lauf into the relative shelter of a deep crevice in the black rock.

Lisbet tore a strip of her serk and wrapped the fabric around the pilot's thigh, stemming the worst of the bleeding.

Good enough for a traitor.

"Why?" His first mate glared at the pilot. "Riches? Power? What?"

Lauf scowled back. "For the promise of a homeland where fae might walk freely, not hide themselves away." Words gritted out from a pain-clenched jaw. "One with our technology available only to the Icelandic court. For a kingdom that will be acknowledged as a global authority by other countries."

"He's delusional," Lisbet concluded.

"I am not," the pilot spat back. "Rømer himself is Hulder. Raised in the Norwegian forests of his ancestors.

His people will move here. Intermarry. Strengthen our bloodlines. Restore the old magic. Restore Eldskrift."

Lauf didn't know. Which meant Rømer hadn't known about the fire ferns, that they'd reclaimed the skin-bound magic of huldufólk. Not until he'd dunked Angela in the Drowning Pool.

But their secret was out now.

"Enough," Val interrupted. "I don't care what misguided fantasies turned you against your friends. Angela takes priority. Where has she been taken?" He would beat the answers from the man if necessary.

The pilot clenched his jaw and refused to answer. Instead, he glanced away, as if rescue might arrive. But there was nothing to see beyond the occasional flash of light that threw deep shadows across the ongoing battle.

Hildur dropped a hand on Val's shoulder. "Lisbet knows how to find her."

"Sigge led the guard to Rømer's lair?"

She shook her head. "We've yet to hear from him."

"Lauf abandoned the *Grænndreki* soon after you left," Lisbet said. "Stupid man, to think I'd not recognize such obvious sabotage. When I couldn't locate him on the bridge, I tried his cabin. He didn't answer, so I picked the lock and searched his trunks. I found these, marked with a single rune." She pulled a handful of punch cards from her pocket and held them out to Val as she stared the traitor down. "Othala. Home, inheritance, lineage."

"The same symbol as carved into the electric troll's chest." He glared at Lauf. "Last chance. Where is she?"

"Headed to Rømer's laboratory. Where else?" Lauf locked eyes with Val, defiant. "Where she'd be already, if you hadn't interfered when we tethered in Glasgow. Daughter of a huldufólk and a huldrekall, she's the perfect research subject. And, if she'd cooperated, she might even now be Queen of Iceland." His gaze fell on the sálbundið behind Val's ear and sneered. "Instead, she's bound to the likes of you."

His pilot had sold out his bride. Likely the ship's groundbreaking technology had also been bartered away. He seriously doubted Lauf did so alone for the glory of Iceland. When they raided his rooms inside the mountain, how many trunks would they find filled to overflowing with króna banknotes?

"From what I can tell," Lisbet continued, "he informed Rømer by raven of the *Grænndreki's* approach, warned him of my intent to stand in for the princess, sabotaged the loftskip, then fled." Her mouth pursed. "Next time I lay eyes on him, he's holding a knife to the Jarl's throat." She threw Lauf a wicked grin that spoke of anger and spite. "What he didn't do—couldn't do—was inform Rømer that there were men and women aboard the airship who were newly inducted Fire Script Guardians."

"Else Rømer wouldn't have ordered Angela drowned," Hildur said.

"What!" Lauf cried.

They ignored him.

Thank Odin they'd not told Lauf of the fire script

bindrunes or how his wife, Lisbet and a number of the guards on the loftskip bore the markings.

Someone set a torch to a buð, setting canvas and timber alight. Flames flickered higher and smoke curled upward into the night sky. Several trolls roared, disoriented by the sudden intense light.

Lauf gaped. "She grew a fire fern, your wife? How? Where?"

"Not something you'll ever know." Val stared at the blunt axe they'd taken from the pilot's hands. He wouldn't summarily execute the traitor, no matter the temptation. Yet he wasn't opposed to letting the man quake in his boots thinking his former captain might declare himself judge and jury.

"Val, you can't." Hildur's voice snapped him out of his thoughts.

She was right. He'd heard enough. "Lisbet, how is it you intend for us to figure out where he's taken Angela?"

"Easy," his engineer answered, lifting a bag that hung from her belt. "You'll follow a clockwork raven."

He shook his head. "They fly too fast."

"Which is why I modified a punch card. Insert it in one of our ravens, and the bird will fly in loops, slowing its progress. On the back of Jólakötturinn, you should be able to keep up. We sent Dýri to saddle the cat."

Saddle. A cat?

"You want me to ride on the back of a giant cat?" Val gaped. "One that only listens to Dýri?"

"Not alone, of course." Lisbet's eyes danced with quiet

amusement. "You'll need our help. With trolls serving as the alchemist's army, they'll have an underground lair. Caves of some sort. And I can see in the dark."

"There's more than enough room on the cat's back for three fae," Hildur said. "Dýri will tell the cat what to do and the feline will cooperate. Jólakötturinn was, after all, sent to hunt down lost trolls."

"Sóllilja and Dýri are needed to lead the guards," Lisbet pointed out. "I'm useless on the *Grænndreki* until parts arrive and, even then, the technician arriving with them can manage the repair."

His first mate glared down at Lauf. "Dýri will happily chain this traitor in the loftskip's hold until he can be brought before the mountain council."

"There will be no mountain council," Lauf jeered. "Only a Mountain King. Rømer will—"

Hildur's fist connected with the ex-pilot's jaw and the man's eyes rolled back in his skull. She threw him over her shoulder and jerked her head. "Let's move."

They darted out of the rock crevice and kept low, running downhill, skirting the edges of the ongoing battle where heaps of motionless rock lay scattered across the frozen landscape. Crumpled among the dead trolls lay dead and injured people, some of them likely fae.

Arrows streaked overhead, finding their mark, sparking as they embedded in troll flesh and drawing forth bellowing roars that shook the ground beneath their feet. Figures locked in combat moved in a chaotic whirl over terrain slick with blood and frost. All fought for survival.

Lisbet broke into a sprint, heading toward a massive shadow beside the lake. One with gleaming yellow eyes and a lashing tail. Jólakötturinn.

"You found them." Dýri slid down from his perch atop the enormous cat, holding out the reins connected to thick leather straps crisscrossing the cat's giant back. "Not bad for a grease monkey." He pulled gas masks from a sack, handing one to each of them. "As requested." He held out an extra to Val. "For Angela. Hurry, Jólakötturinn grows restless."

Lisbet took the reins, then placed her foot in his cupped hand for a boost atop the cat.

"Hildur next." Dýri reached out a hand.

But the first mate ignored the offer and leap astride.

The large saddle rested behind the creature's massive shoulders, one big enough to hold a single troll—or three fae. Metal rings pierced the leather. Rings to which stirrups had been lashed. Handholds of braided rope stretched over the top of the saddle. Grips necessary to keep additional riders from being flung off as the beast leapt across the countryside.

This was madness, trusting his engineer's intuitions, her rudimentary re-programming of a clockwork creature, to find Angela. But her life was at stake and there were no better options. He grabbed hold of a giant metal ring and hauled himself onto the back of an enormous cat loyal to Grýla and her sons.

Lisbet pulled the clockwork raven from its sack, flipped up a few feathers and opened the programming slot. Into this she slipped the altered punch card. *Snap*, the compartment closed. She inserted a brass key into its chest and wound the mainspring, ensuring a long, slow unwinding that would power artificial avian flight.

With that done, she held out her arm and tossed the raven aloft. The bird let out a soft squawk then took to the sky, spinning upward into the air before careening off across the lake.

"Hold tight!" she yelled.

Dýri clicked his tongue and called out strange words in Grjótmál—the stone speech of the trolls—then waved them off.

The cat's muscles coiled, then released. Living springs with the fluid motion of a predator.

A wild, exhilarating ride that sent his stomach lurching with each leap, his bones jolting with each landing. He gripped the cat's sides with his thighs and clung to the braided handles as they streaked across the frozen waters of Þingvallavatn, following a black speck of a raven illuminated only by the ribbons of green light that danced overhead in the night sky.

The wind whipped against his face, tore at his hair, stung his eyes, but he barely felt it. Nothing mattered. So long as the spinning, flapping raven led them to his wife.

CHAPTER THIRTY-FOUR

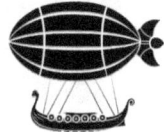

AFTER AN ETERNITY OF GROUND-SHAKING strides, violent leaps and jarring shifts in directions that rattled her teeth, the troll finally stopped before a gaping wound in the earth, one framed by jagged volcanic rock. Moss and ice clung to the stone, glowing a faint green beneath the northern lights that swirled overhead. All of it leant a surreal, dreamlike haze to the world. Reality quickly slipped beyond her reach.

The creature set her down on unstable limbs and pointed into the cavern.

"Walk," Rømer commanded.

Blinking, she looked up at him. "Into the cave?" While he rode in comfort, wrapped in furs and warmed by a brazier, upon a sedan chair built of blackened steel, driftwood and whalebone, carried by two trolls?

"You could also run, though I wouldn't recommend it." Rømer drummed his fingers upon the armrest. There was no force to his words, merely an unspoken promise of unpleasant consequences should she refuse. "We find it best that fae learn how futile an escape attempt would be."

"Walk." The troll jammed a finger into her spine.

Left with little choice, she staggered forward, feeling less like she'd been carried and more like she'd barely survived an avalanche of boulders. A damp, mineral scent rose up to meet her nose as she descended into the earth's maw, slipping and sliding over wet stone, into another world shaped by the lava that flowed thousands of years ago.

Mounds of smooth ice jutted from the cave floor like massive molars, while frozen stalactites dangled from above. The air grew sharper, and the temperature plummeted as they dropped, as the icy teeth closed in, ready to consume her whole.

But though her hair and clothing were wet, she wasn't cold. A blessing and a curse as, mere days before, her fingers and toes would suffer from frostbite. A dead giveaway that she was more than human—and even more than fae.

Her eyes rapidly adjusted to the low light cast by blue glowing orbs scattered about on rock ledges. She stumbled forward over jagged rubble, around the icy teeth, catching herself by pressing a hand to the tunnel's rough walls. Striated bands met her palm, some of the ridges smooth and glasslike, some rough and pitted. Here and there, streaks of stone seemed to drip down the walls. Once hot and liquid, molten rock had streamed over the walls, cooling and hardening as the lava flowed away, leaving the tunnel empty.

Time passed, and in places, the tunnel collapsed. At the

entrance, close to the surface, holes punched through the ceiling to reveal the swirling aurora in the sky above. Below, rockslides revealed colorful stone beneath the volcanic basalt. Red, yellow and a deep blue. Iron, sulfur, copper. Clinging to the intact rock overhead were small white and yellow patches of something alive. Lichens? Non-photosynthetic, if they lived here. Perhaps they consumed meals of chemical energy, oxidizing the iron and sulfur of the stone walls?

A moan echoed through the wide tunnel. There was a faint glimmer of red as a figure shifted in the shadows.

She froze, her eyes fixed on a dark crevice. "What's that?" Bile crept up the back of her throat. Had the wall blinked?

"A few of the early experiments," Rømer answered from above. "We weren't expecting trolls to discharge such large amounts of electricity. Nor to survive so long, fused as they are."

"Fused?"

The troll behind her growled.

"Yes. Fused. Their runes were still freshly carved and oozing. Bleeding, if you will. And lightning strikes applied to silicon dioxide—"

"Will turn it into glass," she finished, horrified. Living creatures, simply abandoned in caves. Stuck to a wall and left to die.

"A bright mind wasted," he sighed, a sound thick with disappointment. "Valtýr possessed no interest in seeing fae openly establish themselves. Instead, he was content to let some distant descendant of the Vikings form an alliance with a Danish princess rather than embracing power that could truly shape the future of the huldufólk."

"So you stepped in. Did what he would not."

"Precisely."

The trolls grumbled something in a language she could not understand.

He sighed but answered them. "First, we deal with this woman, then we'll see about chiseling the Yule Lad free. Icelanders do value their stories and traditions."

The troll shoved her forward. "Move."

The soles of her damp boots gripped the rough stone but did little to save her ankles. Uneven ground caused her stumble as she made her way across and around treacherous and slick fallen blocks of lava. She lost track of how many times she fell, catching herself on hands and knees until her palms were scraped raw and her knees ached.

The tunnel curved. Twice it branched. Each time the troll growled and jabbed a stony finger in her back, urging her forward, down the larger passage. But not before she heard more moans and soft cries that echoed from the smaller tubes.

Again and again, the tunnel twisted. To the left. To the right. Then the cavern widened, and the ceiling rose.

A wooden platform had been constructed and a modern laboratory installed, all of it illuminated by soft blue lights. To the side, a pump connected to a large water tank hummed away, circulating red sparking dinoflagellates through a network of clear glass tubes attached to the wall of the cave. Oxygenating the pyros and combined with the soft blue lighting orbs, bathing the space in a soft purple glow.

Beneath, shelves held bottles of reagents. Drawers hid any number of unknown tools and supplies. Countertops supported strange equipment, unfamiliar machines, save for the aetheric microscope where a single man—no, huldrekall, for a tail peeked out from under his long laboratory coat— worked. In the middle of it all rested a steel table.

The fae straightened and turned, abandoning his micro- scope to cross to a railing, to stare down at her, jaw agape. He rummaged in a drawer, then hurried down the stairs.

Her eyes widened with shock. *Sigge?* To think they'd spared his life, offering medical care and a chance to escape evil's grip. Then set him free. Yet instead of returning to his family, to Norway or Sweden or Denmark, to hide from Rømer, the huldrekall had run straight to the mad alchemist's side.

What had become of the guard assigned to follow him? Had Sigge managed to lose him as he fled the mountain? Her heart thumped. Perhaps even now a clockwork raven winged its way to the huldufólk stronghold, alerting fae guards to Rømer's location.

Not that she held much hope of rescue arriving, not when a battle for the independence of Iceland raged.

Sigge ignored her, bowing before Rømer, enthroned upon his chair of wood and bone. "Success? You are king?"

"I am." Rømer lifted the crown of rubies and diamonds. "Which means my time in the laboratory will, after tonight, be limited." He nodded at the troll that shadowed her. "Show him."

The creature pulled at her torn serk, exposing her glinting bindrune. "This one has mark."

Sigge tipped his head, his eyes sparking with dark anticipation. "A woman with secrets."

"Not for long." Rømer threw off his fur cape and plucked at the embroidered cloth of his tunic. "Prepare her while I attire myself in something more... appropriate." At the snap of his fingers, the trolls carried the false king deeper into the tunnel. Disappearing around another curve to where, presumably, he maintained living quarters.

"Lady Angela." Sigge narrowed his eyes. "I suppose I should thank you."

"Thank me?"

"By the time King Rømer is done with you, we'll have pried your secrets free. Were you hiding those marks all along?" He clicked his tongue. "Never mind. A closer look will reveal all. And then," he swept a hand down his arm, "as you worked so diligently to rid me of my magic, my skin is a clean slate. I welcome the opportunity to try again."

"Why?" She waved at the lab, at the cave surrounding it. Stalling. Her mind raced, searching for an escape that wasn't there.

"You need to ask?" His lips tightened into a thin line. "Norwegian fae are already feared, distrusted, and hunted to the brink of extinction. Like the king, I crave a more meaningful existence, one with a chance to shape the world, not be crushed beneath it."

There had to be something she'd missed. They would have built themselves an escape route. A tunnel. "But—"

"The same can be said of the jötunn. We're done hiding." He clapped his hands together and nodded toward the stairs. "Come. Cooperate and this will go much easier."

Alone. Trapped. With little hope of a miracle. Still, she crossed her arms, defiant. Playing for time. "I don't think so." She turned, as if to leave, when a massive wall of basalt stepped in front of her.

The troll rumbled. Laughter?

"I thought you might object." Sigge crept closer. "But the king is an impatient man and it won't do to keep him waiting." He reached into his pocket and drew out a syringe filled with clear fluid. "One way or another, we'll be taking a close look at that sparkly bindrunes of yours, peeling away their secrets."

From the glint in his eyes, she suspected he intended more than a simple biopsy. As she'd taken his runes, he would steal hers. Would he cut the mark from her skin, stretch it out beneath the microscope?

No.

A cold jolt of fear shot through her. Her pulse pounded in her ears. She couldn't let him get close. Couldn't let that needle break skin.

Before he could move, she bolted—a wild, desperate lunge to the side. She tore down a rough path, deeper into the cave, ignoring the stone that dug into her feet. Her eyes adjusted instantly to the darkness, revealing the jagged surface of the wall and the uneven ground of the tunnel. She had to lose them, to disappear into the shadows, to hide until she—somehow—found a way back to the entrance unseen, unheard and untouched.

"A little help, Glefsugrímur?" Sigge's voice called, distant now.

A foul breeze stirred the air. Rock rumbled. A stone arm reached out from the cave's walls and a rocky fist wrapped around her arm, yanking her feet from under her. A second limb circled her waist, pinning her to the wall.

She screamed, her arm flailing, clawing at stone. How could an electric troll fused to a cave wall be loyal to the likes of Sigge? Her fingers landed atop a loose rock. With ragged fingernails, she worked free a sharp glasslike shard of lava. No sense in jabbing at the creature's fingers. Such would be a futile effort that would do little beyond chip at stone.

But while troll flesh might not bleed, fae flesh would.

She swallowed, adjusted her plans and slid the volcanic shard behind her skirts, then kept her arm still, as if the wall troll held it in his grips. She steadied her breathing, waiting.

Sigge picked his way across the rocks. Slowly. Patiently. His lips stretched into a slow, deliberate smile. He waggled the syringe. A cat toying with a trapped mouse.

"Please," she begged. "Don't."

"You stole my runes, now I'll steal yours."

"I was trying to *save* you."

He lifted a shoulder, unmoved. "And you did. Else I'd not be here today."

Her breath hitched, her pulse drummed in her ears. She couldn't think. Couldn't hesitate. She would have only one chance. Her hand clenched about the sharp volcanic shard, its edges biting into her own palm hard enough to draw blood. Sigge's focus narrowed as he lifted the syringe, fingers steady on the flange and plunger. She struck the instant he stepped close. The shard drove into his side at the same moment the needle stabbed into her arm. Half the syringe's dose—but not all—slipped into her veins, sending a wave of ice rolling across her skin.

Screaming, he released his grip to clutch at his abdomen. Sigge's nostrils flared and a sharp hiss escaped his clenched teeth. "You'll pay for this."

She stared at the blood pouring from between his fingers in pulsing waves. Blood stained his clothes, slicked his hands. Somehow, she'd struck an artery. Not that Sigge realized, spewing vile curses as he bled out.

Reaching across her chest, she yanked the needle from her arm and heaved it into the dark cave—a momentary flash of glass and steel that shattered on a distant rock. An endeavor that took far more work than it ought.

"Rømer will carve you up into sheets of skin and—" His eyes rolled back, and he collapsed on the cave floor.

She tugged against the wall troll's grip, but the resistance was too much. Pins and needles pricked at her nerves, sending a strange buzz through each one. Spots of light danced across her eyes.

"You're quite the spitfire." Rømer stepped into her narrowing field of vision wearing a full-length laboratory coat covered with unspeakable stains. "If only our goals aligned, we might have accomplished great things together."

"What did he...?" The word emerged on a slur, her speech thick and slow. Fear sliced through her mind.

"You're familiar with dinotoxins, or you wouldn't have sent Sigge to the mountain infirmary. That you're still breathing is a testament to the bindrunes that live in your skin." He clucked his tongue, mocking her for asking a question with such an obvious answer. "These dinoflagellates, pyros as you affectionately call them, produce chemicals that, when collected, purified and concentrated, possess impressive anesthetic properties. Makes our work ever so much easier when test subjects don't move."

"What do?" It was a struggle to breathe. "To me?"

"What do I intend to do? Why, what any scientist would." He grinned, all teeth and razor-sharp curiosity. "Unlock the secrets written in your skin." He glanced over her shoulder. "You may release her, Glefsugrímur."

The living wall behind her must have shifted, though she felt nothing. Betrayed by her body's reaction to the chemical, she slid to the cave's floor, landing beside Sigge, limp and numb. A silent scream echoed through her mind as her lungs refused to expand and the edges of her world faded to black.

CHAPTER THIRTY-FIVE

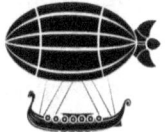

ANGELA WOKE TO A SOFT THUNK, ONE followed by a slow hiss. Her lungs inflated, deflated. Over and again as she stared unblinking at the rocky ceiling of the lava tunnel where a purple light pulsed and shifted.

Thunk. Hiss. Thunk. Hiss.

Memories flooded back. Drowning. Troll. Cave. Needle. Rømer.

Frigg and Hel. She must be in his laboratory. Hauled there unconsciously. Deposited upon the table. Immobile. Attached to some machine that breathed for her. Sharp pricks of pain drilled into her chest, pain where the bindrune had been inscribed.

Did it still remain? Impossible to know, for she couldn't feel her skin.

Rømer's face swam into view. "Angela Eyrúnsdóttir, awake at last. Good." Dangerous curiosity glinted in his eyes.

"Without Sigge to assist, it's rather lonely here in the laboratory. Trolls just don't offer the same level of conversation as other fae. Besides, I'd hate for you to miss this."

A fresh stain marred his laboratory coat. *Sigge. Was he dead?*

"While you slept off the worst of the dinotoxin, I took the liberty of scanning your *mother's* mad scribbles. And here I thought her fern studies to be nothing more than a distraction from her true work with dinoflagellates, while all along it was both." He moved away and the whisper of pages turning met her ears. "Information that Val's manuscript did not include. It took me years to locate the tiny creatures in the Tatra mountains, and only by chance did I happen to hear mention of Eyrún. A local boy who couldn't recall her surname, only that her British husband was wealthy."

So much for her mother hiding in plain sight, believing no one would come after her. A few stray pages of an ancient manuscript placed in the wrong hands and her plan had unraveled.

"But persistence paid off. I now understand all my missteps." The book snapped shut. "Which means it's time to begin. Regretfully, I do not yet possess a fire fern and so your own flesh must serve as its replacement. Lauf informed me you were working on the problem. Sadly, chained to the airship, he was unaware of your success. Did you find one in the wild? Finally, locate a species to host the inoculating dinoflagellates?" He laughed, a sound tinged with madness. "All questions you'll answer later, after I've a chance to personally evaluate your work."

Metal clanked and rattled. A tray of instruments landed beside her atop the table.

Freyja, what was he planning to do?

A scalpel glinted beneath the blue light. Then she felt a faint pressure against her breastbone.

"No worries about pain, my dear. The dinotoxin dulls the sharper senses. I've already made several small cuts and you didn't flinch at all. All healed in a matter of minutes."

He'd been carving into her skin? Marking her? Heat burned in her chest.

"Until then, I have to admit I didn't quite believe Eldskrift would actually enable faster healing, despite watching you navigate the treacherous rock scattered throughout the tunnel with relative ease, considering the low light level. Now, though lying on a metal table in a cave while wearing nothing but a wet chemise, your skin is warm to the touch."

The weight of his hands fell upon her chest, squeezed. "A generous bosom." The heaviness shifted, slid lower. Pressure dug into the flare of her hips. "And a pelvis shaped for childbirth." His face appeared above hers, his lips curling into an unsettling smile.

Enjoying her torment?

"Katla wasn't destined for motherhood, much as we tried." Regret threaded through his sigh. "Every child born died before their first birthday. Nor could her skin host the dinoflagellates without consuming vast quantities of Tyrian Absinthe. It rather rotted her mind. But you, you could do better."

Her stomach churned at the thought.

"Which is why you need not worry about the tube down your throat." His face disappeared. "Once the dinotoxin wears off, if the runes align, we'll discuss your future as my thrall. I'm afraid I can no longer offer marriage, tainted as you are by your association with Valtýr."

No. That wouldn't be happening. Ever. She would not be this madman's whore.

There was a faint tugging at her skin, a vague pinch. The soft clink of a glass slide. The hum of an aetheroscope and an accompanying hiss as an aether cartridge released gas into the specimen chamber. Much as she'd studied biopsies taken from Sigge's runes, Rømer prepared to study hers.

Faint sounds met her ears as the mad alchemist moved about. Wood creaked beneath his feet and the fabric of his laboratory coat swished. Metal rattled atop countertops. Liquids dripped—down cave walls and onto glass vessels. All while the machine breathed for her. *Thunk. Hiss. Thunk. Hiss.*

"Most interesting." His tone held a hint of puzzlement. "There's the expected symbiotic relationship between the dinoflagellates and plant cells, presumably your fire fern. But there's also a glasslike material inclusion." He huffed, annoyed. "An element your mother failed to consider. Then again, her efforts were solely focused upon finding the right fern."

No one, save Val's mother, had recalled that aspect of inscribing fire script into fae skin.

"A transparent, birefringence stone." Rømer hummed.

"Double refraction. Optically active. It can only be calcite crystal, Viking sunstone. Used to navigate the seas beneath cloudy skies." He stood. Machines whirred while drawers opened and closed. Then, again, he towered above her holding a palm-sized piece of a rhomboidal clear crystal.

Sunstone.

"I considered it, of course, but the stone failed to anchor the dinoflagellates in place, forcing me to develop the glass filaments. You're well aware of that deficiency. The hungry little creatures wouldn't stay put, dissolving the silicon dioxide before wandering through the body. Only trolls could tolerate the long-term effects." He turned the crystal over in his hand. "Which begs the question, with a fire fern now available, is the sunstone's calcite a necessary element, or merely present to scatter light for dramatic effect?" His lips pursed. "Either way, I'll include it."

He disappeared for a few long moments, then returned with a tray.

"Frustrating, to gain only a few decades with green tattoos when the incorporation of a handful of tiny glittering single-celled creatures could win one centuries, perhaps millennia."

Tipping her head, angling her face toward him, he forced her to watch as he unbuttoned his laboratory coat and slid it from his shoulders, a move that left his arms and torso bare.

"See that?" He tapped the fading tattoo of a vine that wound about his arm. "My latest. Green tattoos simply do not last in Hulder skin. But with repeated applications, we can benefit from the incorporation of photosynthetic organisms, even if the effects are temporary. Most of my kind shy away from needles, preferring to live more dull human lives. And so the tradition was lost."

Was this the alchemy he sought, a chance to extend his life by decades?

"You think me a fool, perhaps. But if a preparation of ink made from the glittering cells of a fire fern exponentially increased the longevity effects, gaining us a century or more, would my people willingly submit to repeated tattoos?"

The flex and glide of muscle hinted at strength and health, but Rømer's skin was a map of scarred, jagged runes in various stages of healing. Some scarified lines were odd and lumpy, yet silvery and healed. Others were angry and red, hinting at festering infections. Most were stretched and jagged where flesh had rejected whatever he'd embedded in his skin.

Bioactive glass and dinoflagellates?

Most likely.

Nausea swirled in her stomach. Scars that told a story of desperation, of a ruthless quest for the endless life of a god at the expense of... everything else.

"As a scientist, I expect you'd like to watch the transplant."

Transplant?

Upon the tray rested the necessary items for an Eldskrift tattoo. Bits of the sunstone had been chipped away and ground into crystals with a mortar and pestle. A vial of greenish-red cells suspended in a clear fluid sat beside a hollow steel needle. And, to ensure the creatures did not wander, an uncorked bottle of Tyrian Absinthe.

He intended to use the stolen cells of *her* bindrune to implant a tattoo in *his* own arm?

She mentally recoiled, retreating deep into her mind. But she could only watch, helpless, as he picked up the needle and dipped it into the cell suspension.

His gaze crept across her skin like flesh-eating maggots. "Bindrunes appear to be traditional?" Clucking his tongue, he laughed softly. "If only you could answer." He tipped his head, staring into her eyes. "What is fit for the Icelandic King?" With brutal precision, he pierced his skin, inserting the cells. "The third of your bindrunes. An *othala* rune above an *isa*. One rune that stands for homeland. The other for ice, perfect for this frozen land. The end result? A bindrune for courage, one suitable for royalty." With that, he pressed the needle into his skin, punching bits of her own flesh into his. Each puncture was a violation, a forcible binding using her as living ink. As their cells merged, as a flickering, flashing bindrune formed, her skin crawled.

Her mind screamed as a silent fury burned through her paralyzed body. He was a cruel monster, speaking of independence and freedom while enslaving trolls and fae to achieve his goals. A twisted vision of power.

Imprisoned or dead, it mattered not—he needed to be stopped.

CHAPTER THIRTY-SIX

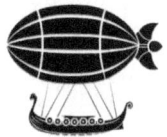

ITHOUT WARNING, THE CLOCKWORK raven flapped a tight spiral and dropped into the ground.

Jólakötturinn leapt into the air, landing on soft cat feet before a gaping black hole edged with jagged rock and ice. The mouth of a lava tube had collapsed, forming a cave-like entrance, daring explorers to take unnecessary risks by exploring its depths.

Given recent events, he expected to find trolls. Ones loyal to—or enslaved by—a mad alchemist who'd taken Val's bride captive.

He released the braided rope that secured him to the cat's back and slid to the ground. There the faint green light of the northern lights revealed trampled snow at the cave's entrance, hinting at an unusual level of traffic—more than could be expected of a family of arctic foxes—passing in and out of the lava tube.

The entrance was tall and wide, some thirty feet high and more than twice that in width, allowing them to enter armed with bows and arrows at the ready. But, over time, such rock formations caved in forming piles of volcanic rubble. Behind them might hide an untold number of deadly electric trolls.

Each beat of his heart pounded against his sternum. She had to be in there. He felt it with a sick, twisting certainty in his gut. He'd failed her once, he'd not fail her again. He would find her. Pull her from this nightmare. End Rømer's life. No matter how many trolls he had to battle. Nothing mattered more than rescuing his wife.

Later there would be time to contemplate the depth of Lauf's cold betrayal, to ensure the man paid for his crimes with his freedom—assuming Jarl Haukr didn't order the traitor hung or beheaded.

He pulled his tröllabanar sword from its sheath and stared into the tunnel's depths. Here and there, as if placed upon stone ledges, glowed the faintest of blue lights. The bare minimum of illumination to allow Rømer and his minions to navigate any obstacles strewn in their path.

Hildur slid to the ground beside him. "We need to move quickly," she said. "Jólakötturinn will stay here, stop any more trolls from returning." She flashed a bloodthirsty grin. "Or exiting."

"Wait." He held up his hand, took two steps to the side of the cave. With the toe of boot, he toppled a loose pile of stones.

"What did you—" Lisbet's question died on her tongue.

"This must be Sóllilja's guard. The one sent to follow behind Sigge."

Solemn, her wife nodded. "At least we know we have the right place."

Crossbow in hand, Lisbet slid an arrow from the quiver on her back. If the cave was wide enough, she would do as much damage as possible from a distance before drawing her own blade. "Most trolls will be at Þingvellir." Words spoken softly. "Thank Odin."

"Find and climb the nearest rock pile that gives you a distant line of sight," Val said. As the only member of their rescue team who was a fire script guardian in possession of enhanced night vision, they needed Lisbet to take the high ground, to cover them with her deadly arrows as he and Hildur advanced. "We'll take turns leaping past each other."

"I'll handle any creatures that dare draw near." Hildur unsheathed her tröllabanar sword. Close quarters combat was her strength.

"Not before detonating a graphite grenade," Lisbet reminded her wife. "Be certain they're electrically discharged first."

She dropped a hand to the device at her waist. "Of course, ástin mín."

But among the three of them, they possessed only one. It needed to be deployed judiciously, draining power from as many trolls as possible.

Val pulled his gas mask from his belt, hauled it into place, then shoved it upward to rest upon his forehead. His crew members followed suit.

The Yule Lad had insisted the vials of aluminum salts would cure his brother and any other electric trolls, but the chemical process would likely release a toxic gas. Between that and the carbon dust that would fill the air when the grenade exploded, they needed to be prepared for the effects of tight quarters.

"Let's move."

Val waved Lisbet ahead of them. Though he intended to be next, Hildur followed her wife, second to step into the cave's gaping maw.

"Go!" A word softly hissed. Small and agile, Lisbet had found a perch in mere seconds.

Hildur ran past to the right, crouching behind a convenient boulder.

Val darted left, scaling a low pile of scree. Not without difficulty, given the volcanic rock was wet and slippery. The air hung still and heavy, hovering only a few degrees above freezing. Water dripped from overhead icicles, forming mounds of glistening ice upon the floor, all of it shimmering with a pale ghostly glow.

For a moment they held their positions, scanning for any glimpse of red light that might spark across troll skin, glinting beneath care-worn clothing.

Nothing.

Lisbet raced past, covering more ground as she delved deeper into the cave. She took up a new position and lifted her crossbow. Hildur followed. Then Val.

Over and again, they leapfrogged each other. The floor of the cave dropped ever so slightly into the earth, but not by much. So far, so good. But while there was no sign of trolls, neither was there any indication of a landing perch for a clockwork raven.

A narrow tunnel branched off to the side but was blocked by rockfall and ice formations. Not that way.

They moved on. The ground beneath their feet began to rise as the cave bent and twisted into a new curve. Onward they crept.

Then the tunnel branched again, and all Hel broke loose.

Lisbet hissed a warning a moment before her arrow zinged through the air, thwacking into the cavern wall where faint red lights glimmered. A low moan echoed back.

The cave shifted. Its eyes opened. And the walls around them grew arms.

A handful of trolls rose from the ground and began to advance.

Frigg and Hel.

They were surrounded.

"Masks!" she called, yanking hers down.

Val and Hildur tugged their own into place, covering eyes and airways, breathing through filter canisters that would keep the black dust from entering their lungs.

Then his first mate pulled the pin from the graphite grenade and threw it into the cave, where dark shadows shifted.

Bang!

Carbon filaments exploded into the air, drifting downward over trolls with yellow eyes and glimmering red runes.

As the fibers draped across them in a haphazard format, a web formed and electricity discharged in blinding flashes. Intense, jagged and erratic lines of crackling light twisted through the dark, throwing strange shadows upon the walls as it hissed and buzzed.

The faint ghostly halo of the electric arc revealed a number of trolls whose backs appeared to be fused to the walls. Still alive, but incapable of moving more than arms, legs, heads. Unable to do more than scream their pain and agony as the fiery ribbons twisted.

His breath caught in his throat. He'd seen fire before, but nothing like this searing, unholy glow. Awful, how they were reduced to such measures. But the trolls created by a madman with his transformative alchemy weren't interested in diplomatic solutions. It was kill or be killed.

A loud snapping sound tore through the air and the lightning died. With the graphite filaments ground into dust, a sharp and acrid scent lingered.

Only a few trolls still stood, but the ones who remained roared as they launched a furious attack armed with nothing more than their fists and teeth.

Lisbet loosed a rain of potassium-tipped arrows overhead. The creatures froze in their tracks, howling as they tore the wooden shafts from their thick hides, screaming at the chemical burns that blackened their skin. Between the electrical arcs and the elemental attack, the bioluminescence of their runes flickered, then faded—evidence their nervous system was in a state of physiological disarray.

Such distraction bought Val and Hildur precious time to

move in close. Side-by-side and back-to-back, they wove through the rubble of trolls that lay in heaps upon the cave floor—Were they dead? Still alive, if barely? If the latter, could they be saved?—all while stabbing tröllabanar sword-tips into knee and elbow joints, slicing hamstrings and Achilles tendons, delivering death blows to collapsing trolls.

Around them immobile trolls fused to the cave's walls howled.

The battle was a blur of violence and pain. Blood, but none of it human, spattered the ground—a slick of treacherous silicone. At last, the final troll fell, and they swayed on their feet. Bruised. Battered. But alive.

Val shoved his mask upward. "Onward?"

Hildur dragged her own mask free. "Hear that roar behind us? There's no going back."

"The light is stronger ahead." Lisbet hooked her mask onto her belt, then drew another arrow. "We must be close." She ran forward, scaling a rockfall where she crouched, crossbow raised, prepared to cover their next advance.

They ran past, swords at the ready.

Around the next bend of the lava tunnel, a section of the tube that was wider and taller and, thankfully, devoid of free-moving trolls, the darkness thinned, replaced by an eerie, purple glow.

Tucked into the curve of the stone wall was a laboratory built upon a wooden platform. Rømer's workshop of runic horrors. Tubes coiled like veins along the walls, bubbling with sparks of red light, a madman growing pyros underground. Countertops held a clutter of instruments—scales, mortars and pestles, microscopes, tweezers, scalpels—and an array of glasslike, crystalline stones ranging from clear to opaque.

Then his heart slammed against his ribs. At its center, Angela lay upon a metal worktable large enough to support trolls. A tube sprouted from her mouth while a machine worked a pair of bellows, breathing on her behalf. Needle in hand, Rømer bent beside her, furiously piercing the skin of his forearm over and over, aware of their approach, but unwilling to cease his mad quest for the eternal life of a god.

Whatever the alchemist had done to her, Rømer would reverse. Else the rest of his life would not be spent in a mountain prison. Instead, his remaining time would be counted in heartbeats, not years.

"Stay here," he ordered Lisbet and Hildur. Rage settled inside his chest, cold and sharp. "Guard my back." Val stalked forward, every muscle coiled with purpose.

CHAPTER THIRTY-SEVEN

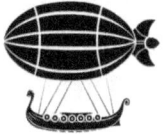

S OUNDS OF A BATTLE ECHOED THROUGH the cave, one that grew steadily closer. A clockwork raven alighted upon the carved wooden perch.

Rømer ignored it all, redoubling his efforts, rubbing tiny crystals of the sunstone into his skin, embedding them deep as he stabbed his needle into his skin, over and over, marking himself with the stolen life essence of the fire fern symbionts bound to her flesh.

As the sounds of bellowing trolls, zapping electricity and the clang of metal on stone reached her ears, she realized the paralytic dinotoxin injected into her veins had begun to fade. If this was a rescue attempt, she needed to be ready. With prickling pins and needles, her skin awoke. A moment later, her fingers and toes twitched of their own accord. Her eyelids blinked and her lungs rebelled against the steady rhythm of the mechanical ventilator.

Thunk. Hiss.

ANNE RENWICK

Too invested in dreams of everlasting life, the mad scientist failed to notice. He pinched powdered sunstone, dusting it across his forearm. Dipped the hollow needle into the cell suspension. Then stabbed it deep into his skin. Every movement relentless and focused.

Thunk. Hiss. Thunk. Hiss.

Her mind raced, thinking of how she could escape Rømer's clutches. Her chest convulsed. Panic surged as her body fought the tube lodged in her throat with a sharp, suffocating rebellion. She closed her eyes, willed herself to accept the intrusion. Failing to do so would alert her captor. Anything to avoid another jab of the needle that brought numb, immobile consciousness. Every breath was half air, half obstruction.

With much effort, she paced her breathing to that of the machine, ignoring the scraping raw pain of the tube shoved down her throat as her chest rose and fell. A forced but necessary physical tranquility so as not to draw Rømer's attention while she tested her movement with the subtle flex of fingers, of her arm.

Relief washed over her as muscles again obeyed the instructions of nerves. Even as he sought fire script powers, he'd forgotten his prisoner already possessed them. Her system was clearing the toxins faster than his calculations predicted.

Overconfident, the alchemist had left the larger piece of sunstone on the steel table beside her, thinking it no more than a crystal with a dull shimmer, if one that might support the life of fire fern cells within his skin. Wrapping her hand around its mass, she stroked a thumb over a sharp, crystalline edge, pleased at the cutting pain that registered.

Val's voice cut through the gloom. "You've lost your mind, Rømer."

"Is that so?" The huldrekall straightened, sneering as he turned toward her husband. "I rather think I've found the answer." He displayed the bindrunes he'd inscribed. "Her flesh is now my flesh." He lifted the bottle of Tyrian Absinthe and drank deeply.

Rage sank its claws in her mind. She gripped the sunstone, rose from the cold steel table and raised her arm, sweeping down with all the force she could manage, driving a sharp edge into her captor's side, somehow managing to cut through skin and muscle to wedge an angle of the sunstone into the very bone of his ribs.

Rømer dropped the absinthe bottle and staggered away, screaming, twisting as he reached for the crystal.

A moment she couldn't afford to waste.

Inhaling with the machine to take as deep a breath as she could manage, Angela wrapped her fingers around the rubber tubing and pulled on the exhale. Fire raced along her windpipe and her throat convulsed at the raw, burning pain. But there was no stopping—she yanked until the tube tore free on a final choking gasp. She rolled onto her side, coughing. Every breath was jagged torture, but it was *hers*.

Forcing her body into motion, she reached with wide eyes for the scalpel the madman left unattended on the metal tray. But succeeded only in knocking the tray and its contents onto the floor. She tumbled off the table after it, her legs tangling in the wet cloth of her clothing, landing hard upon her hip. She shifted onto her hands and knees, crawled across the wooden platform, determined. The scalpel blade had landed only a few inches away. But she was still weak from the effects of the dinotoxin.

She wasn't fast enough.

A booted foot slammed down atop the sharp tool. "I don't think so."

Fingers stabbed into the damp tangle of her hair and hauled with a force that threatened to rip her scalp from her skull. Rømer yanked her onto her feet, dragged her backward over the platform, unmoved by her screams. He released her hair only to band his arm across her chest, pinning her own arms in place. He pressed a sharp edge of the bloody sunstone against her throat, directly above her carotid artery. "One wrong move," he snarled, "and I'll shove this rock so deep it'll sever your windpipe."

Fear surged, but fury followed, hotter and sharper. She'd had enough of being dragged about.

"Let her go." Chest heaving, her husband stood in all his Viking glory at the far end of the platform, sword in hand.

"When she knows where the fire ferns grow? When her offspring might prove to be powerful men and women, infused with bindrunes of fire script?" Rømer hauled her down a flight of steps, onto the uneven floor of the cave. Winding his way through stacks of storage crates, dragging her deeper into the tunnel. "I think not. Not a chance, Valtýr. She lives only so long as she serves her king."

"Eirik, see reason." Val lowered his weapon, took a step

closer. "Your position is untenable. Why not work with the huldufólk instead of against?" He lifted his chin. "Do you think a fiery tattoo is our only bit of biotechnology? You've heard of our mountain..."

"That trees grow within?" The madman dragged her further away.

As he moved, she felt his skin shift against her back through the fabric of her clothing. Granular. As if sand lay trapped beneath and within his epidermis. He wished to be immortal, but given the number of scars that marred his torso, was that possible? Even with a fire fern bindrune? She doubted it. Too many glass crystals riddled his system, hardening essential organs, like his heart, into stone. How much longer until his muscles stiffened, until his runes glazed over, glasslike? Before his life ended, much like Katla's?

The sand that measured out his existence was slipping quickly through the hourglass.

"More than trees." Val followed, scooping up the diamond and ruby crown. "Entire crops. All using geothermal power harnessed from the center of the earth."

"And it will be mine."

"Will it?" Val asked, crossing the platform, descending the steps. "When your trolls lie upon the plains of Þingvellir, nothing more than a scattered field of rubble destined to burn when the sun rises? When the few fae to survive your runic glass tattoos crumble like a child's sandcastle?" He tossed the golden Icelandic crown aside. "The tide already turned and washed away your kingdom."

Rømer kicked at a pile of rocks. "Wake up, Ketkrókur," he ordered. "I've brought you dinner."

The stones shifted, rising, assembling themselves into the form of a troll. In its hand, a meat hook with a wickedly sharp curve at its end. Sparking red runes danced across his gray-black skin. Ketkrókur's yellow eyes gleamed as he advanced.

All around her, the walls awoke and groaned their pain and hunger.

"The vials," she whispered.

"Silence." Rømer dug the crystal's edge into her flesh. Blood trickled, warm and wet, across her skin. "Ketkrókur, kill the huldufólk trespasser."

"Your brother Gluggagægir looks for you," Val unhooked the bag at his waist, held it out to his side. Jiggled it like a lure. A risk, given the highly reactive contents. "He found a cure. You must submerge in a hot spring, consume the tablets beneath the open air."

"What!" Rømer cried. "You work for me. There is no treatment. Besides, no self-respecting troll would give up his powers of lightning!"

"Hurts," the troll said. "Where Gluggagægir?"

"Safe. With the princess."

"Need more." Ketkrókur took a grinding step forward, waved his meat hook about. "For wall trolls."

"First you'd need to," Val glanced behind her, "chisel them free?"

"No!" a gritty voice yelled as rock-hard hands yanked her off her feet. Once again, an electric troll fused to the cave's walls held her in his grasp. This time, however, Rømer was also captive, and he'd lost his grip on his only weapon. The sunstone a shattered pile of crystal at his feet. "Give!" the wall troll demanded, squeezing her arm so hard she thought it might snap in two. "Or I kill them."

The Yule Lad rushed forward, snatching the bag from Val's hand, tugging at its drawstring. "Pills?"

"Give!" the wall troll repeated.

"Yes." Val kept his words simple and clear and loud. "Take one, then wait. Repeat until the runes fade. But they *must* be swallowed outside. There *will* be fumes."

"Ignore him!" Rømer struggled against the stoney hands that gripped him. "There is no cure!"

But the prospect of a cure deafened the trolls to his instructions. Electricity crackled in the air as the walls came alive with dozens of eyes. Heads turned. Arms reached. All of them groaning, howling for relief.

Ketkrókur squinted. Drew a single aluminum sulfide tablet from the bag and shoved it into the gaping mouth of a wall troll.

"Frigg and Hel." Val rushed forward, yanking a gas mask from his belt and hauling it over Angela's head moments after the smell of rotten eggs met her nose. The troll's blood was reacting with the aluminum sulfide to form hydrogen sulfide, a toxic flammable gas capable of spontaneous ignition.

In a cavern filled with electric trolls.

With a bag full of such tablets, if Ketkrókur fed enough

trolls the pills, all it would take was one single spark to ignite the gas, to turn the air into an inferno.

Val turned and yelled, "Masks!" into the dark cave before pulling his own over his face.

As Ketkrókur shoved a tablet into the mouth of the troll that held her, Val brought the edge of his tröllabanar sword down upon the creature's knuckles. Angry and growling, the wall troll lashed out at Val, missing by inches, but releasing her.

Angela staggered forward into his arms.

"There's no time," he said, his voice muffled by the gas mask. "Can you walk?"

She nodded.

Dodging fallen rock, they hurried over the damp scree that littered the cavern's floor, skirting the larger rockfalls. Not quite a run—an impossibility on such an uneven surface —but as fast as their feet could safely carry them away from the many trolls opening their mouths, greedy and impatient for the cure.

Electricity raced over the wet stone of the cavern walls with a crackling hiss as tendrils of raw energy leapt from one troll to the next, forming a system of jagged branching arcs. Bolts of lightning shot beneath the network of glass tubes filled with circulating dinoflagellates and, with a sharp ringing pop, the glass shattered and water hissed as it burst into steam.

Then the wooden platform of the laboratory caught fire.

"Drop!" Val grabbed her, pulling her behind a pile of

rocks and onto the cave's floor, cushioning her fall with his own body.

Whoosh! Blue flames billowed over them and heat licked at her back.

But the danger hadn't passed, only its chemical formula. Hydrogen sulfide, ignited, would unleash a choking fog of toxic gas, adding sulfur dioxide and sulfuric acid to the mix.

They needed to move. *Now.*

Leaping back onto their feet, they hurried toward the cave's entrance. But not before she glanced back.

Rømer, still in the wall troll's clutches, jerked violently as bolts of electricity ran through him. Every muscle seizing at once. His back arched. Blistered, raw welts marred his flesh. But the strangest thing wasn't the burns. A fine white powder crystalized over his burned flesh, forming jagged uneven patches.

Every grain of silica, every single last fragment of the bioactive glass he'd embedded in his skin, rose to the surface, shimmering in the heat. Then it began to melt. She tugged at Val's arm, pointed. The electricity cut off with a crack. In the sudden silence, the molten glass solidified, sealing the alchemist inside a glistening tomb of glass.

Still. Silent. Trapped.

No time to investigate. The air hummed with renewed energy as lightning arced between trolls once more.

They ran.

EPILOGUE

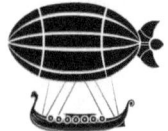

T HEY'D EMERGED, BATTERED AND BRUISED, to find the *Grænndreki* floating overhead and Jólakötturinn pacing back and forth, hissing and spitting. From all reports, the giant black cat had howled her displeasure at the noise echoing from the lava tube, refusing all entry. Given the size of her teeth and the sharp curve of her claws, Val understood.

Sóllilja slid down a long rope, landing hard upon the ground before rushing to them as they ripped off their gas masks and dragged in deep breaths of fresh night air. She'd sized up the cat's antics, concluded that the stench emanating from the cave indicated a chemical hazard and had returned to the ship to hunt for more gas masks before making a rescue attempt.

"Wise decision." Val ignored her demands for an explanation, sweeping Angela into his arms and carrying her to the loading platform that slowly descended from the loftskip.

Lisbet and Hildur came together without a word, wrapping their arms about each other with the ease of instinct—the quiet gravity of love anchoring them, steadying them in the aftermath.

"What happened?" Sóllilja demanded.

"Soon," Val waved off her question. "Water first."

They'd boarded the airship and headed to the bridge where Lisbet took over the helm, setting course for the huldufólk mountain.

All four of them collapsed onto the floorboards, hair stuck to their foreheads, damp with sweat. Clothes torn and streaked with lava dust. Exhausted—but alive. Angela spoke in a hoarse whisper as she sipped from a flask of green absinthe, recounting Rømer's words and actions.

"He cut into your bindrunes?" Val growled. "The man wasn't worthy of a swift death. Electrocution was too easy. Better he'd rotted in a deep mountain prison beside Lauf for all eternity."

"No." Angela shook her head. "The lifespan of a god was his goal. He imagined ruling Iceland for centuries, a tyrant with an iron fist, his proclamations devoid of morals or ethics as he bent humans and fae to his will. Far better that death silenced him and spared us his ravings. Odin help us if he ever broke free."

Val took up the tale, sparing her voice to recount the story of their escape. Of the crackling electricity and the toxic fog. Of finding Hildur and Lisbet bravely beating back electric trolls. Of how he'd paused to bellow at the creatures that Ketkrókur possessed the cure within, informing them they needed to hurry before the medicine ran out.

"And what of the Þorrablót?" Val looked to Sóllilja. "Did the arrival of fae reinforcements turn the tide?"

"It did." She nodded, her grin weary but proud. "But the hidden folk will take no credit. King Haukr won the Battle of Þingvellir."

At midnight, with the trolls defeated and on the run, the Jarl had swooped into the princess's búð, triumphant. Intent upon marking the victory by proclaiming Iceland a sovereign state, they'd marched, hand in hand, to Lögberg. There, the bishop and the pagan priest finished the ceremony—properly —declaring Jarl Haukr Sigurðsson the rightful King of Iceland, placing upon his head a hastily constructed crown of sunstone and lava shard held together by twists of wire.

The night the trolls attacked was a tale that would be recounted by their people for ages.

ONCE THE TOXIC fumes cleared the Raufarhólshellir tunnels, fae geologists had joined a cadre of trolls deep inside the lava tunnel, helping to free the fused trolls from its walls. They'd also found what remained of the mad alchemist. Bone. Burnt flesh. And melted glass.

"Fitting that he was mineralized," she said. "If a bit gruesome, the decision to lock his remains in a mountain cell beside Lauf."

The corners of Val's mouth pulled downward, weighted

by the betrayal of his friend. "With the full knowledge that you were to be kidnapped and hauled to a madman's laboratory, he allowed an electric troll onto my airship, where the creature might have destroyed everything—my life's work—with one bolt of lightning. I don't know that I can ever forgive him."

"Perhaps we simply acknowledge our victory. The Battle of Þingvellir united Iceland—human, fae, and troll—in a manner that would otherwise have never happened. Lauf's betrayal ultimately only served to strengthen that which he tried to destroy."

"A better way to remember him," Val admitted. "For every great tale requires a defeated villain or two."

"So they do."

Her recovery had been swift, thanks to the bindrune's gentle glow—and Val's determined insistence that she rest. In his bed. A slow smile curved her lips as she recalled just how she'd proven she was on the mend.

A raven, flying under the guidance of the punch card provided by Mr. Black, had been dispatched to Reykjavik with news that all threats to the royal wedding had been neutralized. Days later, a beleaguered skeet pigeon arrived—its wingtips frayed, its beak dented—delivered to her by way of the Eldvörður stationed at the waterfall entrance. The message it carried was brief, but clear: gratitude for a mission accomplished, a formal release from service, and a curt but sincere wish for happiness in her marriage.

Strangely, the note included no message from Olivia.

Angela hoped that meant her friend was off on her own adventure.

"That's enough for now." Val drew her into his arms as music began. "After an elopement of a wedding and a scramble of a honeymoon, all I wish is to hold my bride close and dance with her inside our mountain home."

Overhead, black basalt polished to high gloss gleamed in the torchlight from below while crystalline veins of minerals embedded in its surface glimmered and flashed, mimicking a starlit sky.

Val whirled her across a soft moss floor, spinning her through the dizzying patterns of a fae dance that only superficially resembled a waltz. Thank Frejya for her husband's steady arms—he kept her from colliding with other dancers, falling into the trickling stream, and crashing into the runestone that stood at the heart of the mountain.

A celebratory ball held for all the hidden folk, one for which she'd been dressed in full huldufólk splendor.

Val's mother had provided her with a beautiful skautbúningur. The deep blue gown possessed a velvet bodice, richly embroidered with silver thread and adorned with delicate filigree: clasps, broaches and rings of heirloom silver. Atop her head rested a spöng, a metal circlet that anchored an elaborate lace headdress.

She felt every inch a fae princess.

If only for a night.

For tomorrow, the *Grænndreki* took to the sky, a fully funded research vessel in reward for their service. Val would continue his work on the dragon's wings while she spent her time in the newly constructed solarium, studying—among other plants—the secrets of the fire fern.

She and Val, along with his entire crew, had endured a command appearance before the mountain council, where their actions were ruthlessly questioned and analyzed. In the end, the decision was made to overlook the illegality of their revival of the Eldskrift tradition.

Rather than sanction them, the council chose to establish a new protective force: Order of the Fire Fern Guardians. This unit was tasked with quietly safeguarding the mountain's inhabitants and, at the king's invitation, integrating with the Icelandic court to ensure any foreign threats could be detected early.

The huldufólk might remain officially hidden, but King Haukr and his bride-to-be wanted the fae by their sides at all times.

When the music slowed, Angela ran a hand down the side of his face, catching at the collar of his formal waistcoat and pulling him close. For a moment, they stared into each other's eyes, sharing the same breath, recalling the wild adventure that had brought them together.

Then his lips found hers and the world blurred—a distant hum of voices and soft light—until nothing existed save their love.

ABOUT THE AUTHOR

Though ANNE RENWICK holds a Ph.D. in biology and greatly enjoyed tormenting the overburdened undergraduates who were her students, fiction has always been her first love. Today, she writes steampunk romance, placing a new kind of biotech in the hands of mad scientists, proper young ladies and determined villains.

Anne brings an unusual perspective to steampunk. A number of years spent locked inside the bowels of a biological research facility left her permanently altered. In her steampunk world, the Victorian fascination with all things anatomical led to a number of alarming biotechnological advances. Ones that the enemies of Britain would dearly love to possess.

www.AnneRenwick.com

www.ingramcontent.com/pod-product-compliance
Lightning Source LLC
Chambersburg PA
CBHW061536190726
48289CB00004B/1067